An Everyday

Andrew John Bell

Copyright and Disclaimers

Trigger Warnings: This book contains scenes which involve anxiety, depression, suicide, racism, sexual abuse, self-harming, substance abuse, instances where regional dialects are used, and language that some readers may find upsetting/offensive. Due to the subject nature of this novel, it may not be suitable for readers under the age of 18 and/or those presently held in a vulnerable state of mind.

Dedication

In loving memory of Liam and Rob.

This book is also dedicated to my wife and our children, my family and friends, Mandy, Lauren, Steve, Archie, to anyone else who has been affected by mental health ailments, and to those who help others get through life's darkest moments.

Author's Note

Anxiety and depression have been a part of my life since the age of ten years old. I've sat through numerous counselling sessions and tried various medications to combat them — some have been effective, others not so. Nevertheless, my mental health issues adapted to life just as I was trying to. No matter how hard I fought to control them, it felt like I was losing each battle. I alienated myself from family and friends, avoiding any social interaction whenever possible. It was the easiest option, after all, to not talk about my problems or share my feelings with others. The last thing I wanted was to be a burden. But doing so only made matters worse, and it took some poignant life events to make me see things differently — to make me realise the stark truth of how dangerous anxiety and depression are.

I've lost two friends to suicide, and neither one showed any warning signs as to how desperate they had become. At the age of twenty-eight, I had a TIA/mini stroke because of increasing stress levels. My six-year-old daughter and I were playing with some of her dolls when a burning current suddenly shot down the left side of my face, my speech slurred, and I felt like I was going to pass out. I'll never forget the fearful expression on my daughter's face as she watched me succumb to the TIA's debilitating effects. Because of constantly worrying, I'd almost suffered a serious stroke. That was a huge wake-up call. Changes had to be made. I began to identify what the triggers were to my panic attacks/low periods and became even more determined to put an end to them. I found my light in the darkness and what coping mechanisms worked best, but it's still a daily struggle.

I'm not a clinical expert, by any means. I have merely used my own experiences to write this novel, compelled by a strong and personal desire to help raise mental health awareness.

Andrew John Bell

Novels by Andrew John Bell

Contemporary Fiction

One Day of Lucidity

An Everyday Anxiety

Horror

The Skipton Haunting: Tale of The Red Ribbon Witch

The Skipton Haunting: Curse of The Red Ribbon Witch

Fantasy/Debut Novel

Cerebrante: The Sacred Balance

Chapters

Burning Bridges

The Daily Grind

It can't be that time? My alarm clock is saying otherwise, though. But I've barely slept a wink, maybe three hours at most…not like that's anything new, of course. I wonder which alarm it is — the third, the fourth? Either way, and regardless of how many annoying alarms I've set, I'm not ready to wake up. Not yet. Ten more minutes. Just ten more minutes, so I that can pull myself together in some way. Who am I trying to kid? Those extra minutes will only feel like seconds. They always do.

It's no use. If I don't get up now, I never will. I've got classes to teach, bills to pay, a family to feed, a career to build, and a somewhat respectable reputation to maintain. I need that regular paycheque for less honourable things, too, like my growing addiction to alcohol that's equally as important (if not more so). Come on, Thomas Grey. Come on — shift your arse, mate. It's time to wake up and face the daily grind.

Despite the fact it's my last day at work before the summer holidays, when I'll have six weeks of blissful peace away from all those unruly pupils and backstabbing colleagues of mine, I just can't force my body to move or eyelids to open. It's the same old, everyday routine i.e. wake up, get dressed, force a mug of black coffee down my throat, go to work, eat some instant noodles for lunch, fight off some heartburn, trudge back home, drink some beer, eat supper, drink some more beer, watch mind-numbing tv shows for an hour or two, and then eventually — after two or three hours of trying — fall asleep, only to do it all again the next day. That's how it goes for me. Although, it does vary slightly on weekends, which is when I can drink myself into a state where I forget about the previous five days of mental torture. That's my glorious life. Isn't it wonderful? All those hopes and dreams I developed in childhood, of what I would achieve by this tender age, all appear to be gone — dead and buried — just like my ability to look on the brighter side of life. There must be more to living than this, surely?

'You'll be late for work,' says Alice, my wife of eight years, as she pulls our bedsheet further over herself. 'At least it's your last one. You've got six weeks off to look forward to now, haven't you?'

'Yeah,' I say in a cheerful tone, trying to hide my true pessimism. I've got six weeks to arrange the holiday I should have booked several months ago, more like. Money is tight in our humble household, and I doubt Alice will let me get away with organising another camping trip again, given that the last one was a complete disaster. How was I meant to know about the torrential downpours and floods that would follow? I've never seen her overreact so bad. 'I'm gonna go check on Rosie…see if she's still asleep.'

'If you don't mind?' Alice murmurs, turning away from me. 'I'll have another five minutes or so and then get up myself.'

'It's alright for some, isn't it?' I humour, with some slight jealousy evident. 'You get your beauty sleep—not that you need any, mind.'

'You're digging yourself a bigger hole, Tom,' she groans. 'You can always have a lie in tomorrow, can't you? Think of it that way.'

'Maybe? I've forgotten what it feels like to have a decent night's sleep, and it depends on whether Rosie will let us or not.'

'You wanted kids…'

Rose—or Rosie, as I call her—is our two-year-old daughter. She was a surprise addition to our little family, so to say, but I couldn't live without her now. Rosie keeps me going. She and Alice are what compels me to wade on through the shit-stream of existing within this broken world of ours. I love seeing her smile first thing on a morning, and only wish I could do the same. God, it's been so long.

'Can you make me a coffee when you're finished in the shower?' Alice asks me.

'What did your last slave die of?' I joke, but it barely raises a smirk on her face. 'Fine, I'll make you one. At least I'd be making myself useful for once.'

I'm thirty years old but my body speaks otherwise. My legs and arms feel as heavy as lead on moving them away from the warm bedsheets, stiffened by my recurring anxiety tremors. I need my tablets. I need the drugs that constrain these daily and debilitating tremors of mine. Anxiety, my unwanted mistress. Anxiety, the threat that dangles over my head like the Sword of Damocles every-single-day. Taking my medication will just have to wait, however. I smell like I haven't bathed in a week, which isn't too far off the mark, and my breath is just as foul. A shower's what I need. A cold rinse to wash away the dirt, to finally wake me up.

'Keep an eye on the time,' says Alice in an ominous tone. 'I don't want you being late for work again.'

'That was a one-off,' I say, stroking a hand along the side of her body. I can't help it. Alice is so beautiful; she's barely aged since turning eighteen. I'm clueless as to what she sees in me—me—an overweight mess with chronic anxiety and depression. I wouldn't ever dream of admitting that to her, seeing as my luck's bad enough as it is. 'Don't you fret. I won't be late. I promise.'

'You're not the best at keeping promises, though, are you?' she adds, pulling the bedsheet over her face now.

Rosie's fast asleep, granting me some additional time to get bathed and think over what trials lie in wait this morning. I spent two hours last night mulling over and preparing the lesson plans for today, and God knows how they'll turn out. I just can't think straight. I can never think straight. Maybe it's the mild sedative effect from my medication? Or it could be from my excessive alcohol consumption? Or maybe it's from the mini stroke I had last year? The possibilities are endless, and I'd rather not think about them.

One of the worst side-effects from my anxiety is struggling to concentrate. My memory is on par with a goldfish's after having a two-litre bottle of vodka poured into its bowl— seriously. The mini stroke was certainly a contributing factor, but I don't like to reminisce about that fateful night. Rosie and I were playing with some of her dolls, when — Bam! — a hot, electrical current suddenly swept down the left side of my face, and then my speech went all funny. I can remember the paramedic turning up and a little about spending the night at Durham hospital, where I had a few scans and bloods taken — the usual precautions. That was some wake-up call. There I go again, thinking about it. Flashbacks: another unpleasant feature in my life I need to contend with.

After a brisk shower I turn to my bathroom's mirror for a much-needed shave, then stare at the reflection in it with judgemental eyes. I've really let myself go. Alice was right in saying that I could do with holding back on the weekly pizzas and binge-drinking.

'Just look at you, Tom-boy. What a state,' I say to myself while studying the sleep-deprived, chubby, and mournful-looking man in the mirror. 'What happened to you? You've gotten fat, spotty, and reek of cheap lager and tobacco. You're a father. You're a husband. You're a teacher on his way up to a life-changing promotion, for God's sake. You're an absolute, fucking mess.'

The golden sunrays streaming through the bathroom window do little to alleviate this miserable vision; they highlight each roll of fat on my torso and sting my hungover eyes. One can of lager is what I promised myself last night, but it soon turned into four or five. What was I thinking? But that's how I cope, and I can't see me changing these bad habits of mine anytime soon. No way. Sod that for a laugh.

'What are you doing in there, Tom?' says Alice, tearing herself away from the comfort of our bed. 'It's almost eight o'clock. You-are-going-to-be-late.'

'I'm all sorted now,' I say, knowing too well that she's not far off being correct. 'I won't be late. I can't afford to be...'

I reluctantly glance at my reflection again, for all it's worth, and all I see is a man who's being cruelly worn down by modern society; a creature overridden by depressive thoughts; an increasingly resentful and sordid being. I hate feeling like this. I used to be the life and soul of a party, once over, but you wouldn't think that by looking at me now.

Nevertheless, I know these depressive thoughts won't last long, seeing as I've arranged to meet up with some friends of mine at the local pub after work. The tender notion of numbing my relentless tremors with alcohol already helps to alleviate them, even if it is in a self-destructive sense. Why should I care? It's my body. I'm an adult. I can do what I want with it, can't I? Life's too short to think so far ahead.

'Should I make you some sandwiches for lunch?' Alice suggests, still half-awake and immersed in a dream-like state. 'You don't eat properly, and you can't live on instant noodles and Pop-Tarts.'

'Why not? Besides, I do eat healthy at work,' I state, somewhat hiding the truth from Alice that I barely consume a single morsel during work hours. I've developed irritable bowel syndrome among other things this year, adding another layer of salt to my wounds. I don't like to eat because doing so creates too many embarrassing gas-related scenarios, which I'd understandably prefer to avoid when dealing with a bunch of teenagers that are always out to get me. 'I'll take a cereal bar for lunch. I don't want anything too heavy.'

'Aren't you having any breakfast before you go?' she asks, showing some genuine concern in her expression. 'I fancy some porridge. It wouldn't take me long to make you some.'

'Thanks, but I'll just have a cigarette on my way to work.'

'Honestly,' she simpers, rolling her eyes to me. 'I'm making you some porridge, whether you like it or not. Smoking a cigarette is hardly a decent substitute for breakfast.'

'I'm not hungry. I'll be fine,' I plead. 'Give it a rest, yeah?'

Alice walks right up to me now, her expression stern and riddled with disappointment. Rosie awakens at this precise moment, thus saving me from one of Alice's guilt-inducing lectures. Don't get me wrong, I mean, I love my wife more than anything, but she can't half be intimidating when she wants to be.

'Daddy's coming, Rosie!' I shout to her in assurance, stealthily manoeuvring myself around Alice. 'Who's a good girl? Daddy's coming, sweetheart!'

I find Rosie sat on the edge of her bed, rocking back and forth, fleeting her tearful eyes around the room in search of my familiar voice. A wonderful smile and faint burst of laughter instantly emerge from her on seeing me, and I smile and laugh back in return. It's a scene that plays out each day in our household, and it's one I'll never grow tired of.

'She's slept all night,' Alice comments with a proud smirk, as she enters our daughter's bedroom. 'She's growing up too fast, isn't she?'

'Yeah,' I say glumly. 'They don't stay babies for long.' I don't want Rosie to grow up. I want her to stay innocent and happy forever. The last thing I want is for her to become miserable and lonely…like me. 'We'd best get a move on. It's breakfast time, Rosie. We need to get you dressed and fed, don't we?'

I'm holding off the innate urge to eat, but Alice's cooking skills are something that can't be ignored. She's only making porridge, but Alice adds a specific amount of honey and cinnamon to the oats and milk that makes this offer utterly irresistible. I'm going to suffer for this in an hour or so, there's no doubting that, though I keep telling myself that it'll be worth the inevitable bloating pains. I can always blame any embarrassing smells on one of the students, half of which stink of various body odours anyway. I love dropping the odd IBS fart next to the class clowns, the ones that make my seminars a living hell, and then watch as their fellow classmates turn against them. It's comedy gold — karma even — but not exactly professional. Still, it's the small pleasures that make life worth living, isn't it?

'Would you like some more honey on your porridge?' says Alice, holding the jar a few inches away from me.

'I'm sweet enough,' I reply, gently pushing the jar back to her. 'I can barely manage what's in front of me. I'm stuffed.'

Alice chuckles, but I can't help noticing how tired and down she also seems — despite the happiness she's feigning. It's my fault, I reckon. One thing I've always loved about Alice is her ability to stay positive, regardless of what nightmare situations are thrown at her. My best friend, Darren, is the same. Alice has been so quiet and reserved in recent months, especially around me. It's got to be my fault.

'I bet Rose would like some more yummy honey,' says Alice, squinting her nose to our beloved toddler. 'Daddy should set a good example and eat all of his breakfast up, shouldn't he? Daddy's such a naughty boy.'

Rosie's downing her porridge like it's the first meal she's had in ages, whereas I'm toying a spoon through mine like it's the final slice of a sixteen-inch pizza that I've eaten all to myself. I honestly feel full. I couldn't eat another bite, not even a single oat. However, setting off my IBS isn't the greatest of concerns right now. It's nowhere close. My anxiety's really starting to kick in. I need my pills. I need my Mirtazapine.

I make my way into the kitchen and towards the refrigerator, where I keep my medication out of reach from Rosie's wandering hands upon it, only to find the box is no longer there. Panic sweeps in. It's as if time itself has stopped. What a start to the day.

'Where are my tablets?' I ask Alice frantically. 'Where've they gone? Have you moved them?'

'I haven't touched them,' she says with a look of dread. Alice, too, understands the necessity of my medication and dire consequences of me missing a dose. 'You were meant to pick your meds up from the pharmacy two days ago.' She gives me a cold and knowing stare. 'Don't say you forgot.'

I mutter back, 'Erm…yeah.'

Alice rushes over to me, her mouth agape with disbelief. 'Will you have time to pick them up before you start work?'

'No. I'll have to get them after I finish at three.'

'You're joking, right?'

'Nope. I'll be okay, though. No worries.'

As much as I rely on any other sustenance in life, I require my Mirtazapine to function — to keep me normal. I've been on them ever since the mini stroke. Once I've taken my medication—after about half an hour or so—I start to feel all relaxed and carefree, subdued enough to keep me sane. For such a small tablet, it packs a mighty punch. It's the one thing that seemingly keeps these depressive thoughts of mine at bay, or so I've convinced myself. I can't cope without them. What am I going to do? It's too early in the day to turn to alcohol, my alternative cure.

'I can pick your meds up during my lunch break, if you want me to?' says Alice, nodding at me imploringly.

'That'd mean driving back and forth between Newton Aycliffe and Darlington, though. You'd not make it back to your own workplace in time.'

'My boss will understand. You can't go without your meds, Tom.'

Alice falls silent, in stark contrast to Rosie's joyful giggles. I've got to stop being so negative around them. She is right: I simply can't function without my meds. Anyway, it's time for work. I've got to shift myself into gear and put on a brave face—a false mask of contentment. It's time to leave my daughter and wife for eight hours, when all I want to do is stay here with them.

'Are you setting off? But—'

'Yeah.' I then gasp, being that I almost forgot something else important. 'I've put the money for Rosie's childminder in an envelope, which is in the cutlery draw. Can you make sure she gets it?'

'Mum's looking after Rose today,' says Alice, lulling her head. 'She's going to help us care for Rose more often, seeing as we're struggling to pay the childminder bills.'

'I can always ask my mum to help as well. It wouldn't be fair to put all the onus on yours.'

Alice shakes her head back at me slowly, and — without even asking — I know why.

'We can't do that. Your mum has got enough going on with caring for Catherine,' she says, glancing across to a photograph of my sister and nephew nearby. 'It'd be too much for her. Please don't put any pressure on your mum to babysit — it wouldn't be fair.'

'Mum loves spending time with our Rosie, and it'll do them both some good to see more of each other.'

'No,' Alice states more firmly. 'Catherine's health is getting worse.' Then she whispers under her breath, 'You need to be more supportive. I'm only saying —'

'I know, but Cath is…complicated.'

I do want to be more supportive. I honestly do. I want to help Catherine, my little sister, the mother of my boisterous and loving nephew, Harry. I want to spend more time with them both, but it's not as simple it sounds. The thing is, Catherine and I were very close growing up — inseparable. But when she got with Harry's dad — the charmer who preferred to squander their rent and food money on gambling and cannabis — well, our relationship sadly drifted apart. To top it all off, Catherine developed mental health problems of her own a few months back that completely outweigh mine in how severe they are, which is muddling matters further. I want to help improve their lives, but I'm no role model. I'm the last person they need around them.

'You're gonna be late,' Alice bleats. 'Please take care, and don't work too hard.'

'I'll be fine,' I say with my well-rehearsed, happy-go-lucky smile. 'See you tonight, yeah? Love you.'

I kiss Rosie and then go to do the same with Alice, but she moves away from me as if I'm some irritating fly. She doesn't even grant me a parting "Love you" as she normally would. Never mind. I've got my housekey and cigarettes – I'm ready. It's time to go. It's time to face the day. It's time to face reality.

The school where I teach religious studies at is a twenty-minute walk away, allowing just enough time to dwell on what screwups I might commit over the next eight, gruelling hours. The sad fact is, I didn't want to teach religious studies. The job was forced on me after the previous teacher suffered a nervous breakdown, which I'm not far off experiencing myself. I wanted to teach English History, something I'm actually interested in. It's funny how things go, they say. Things always happen for a reason.

Halfway into my journey, I come across a homeless chap called Karam and his Alsatian, Charlie, who have setup a makeshift camp alongside the small stream near my school. Despite his tattered clothes, pungent body odour and grisly appearance, I've grown fond of the guy. You should never judge a book by its cover, should you?

Karam's a Syrian refugee and, like me, enjoys the odd cigarette or two. The poor bloke has fled from a war-torn country to Britain amid our Brexit crisis. He must have been desperate. I always offer Karam a cigarette along this journey to work, given there's not much else I can do for him.

'Morning, Karam!' I say, while offering a cigarette and my lighter to him. 'Have one on me, mate.'

'Good morning, Tom, and thank you,' he says amid a wheezy bout of coughing. 'You are a good man. You are very kind.' Karam coughs heavily again as he collects the cigarette. I can't help but notice how thin his tent is, and in some way feel guilty for adding to his respiratory issues. 'It is only a small cough. It will go in time.'

'Do you not have any extra clothes?' I ask, eyeing up the humble contents of his tent: a sleeping bag, a food bowl for Charlie, and a half-eaten sandwich. Karam's wearing a waterproof coat and some jeans, but they can't be enough to protect him from the cold northern winds. 'I've got a spare coat at home you can have.'

'No, my friend. Charlie keeps me warm at night.' Karam wraps his free arm around the Alsatian, hugging into it with all his might. 'Charlie never leaves me. I am his master, and he is my best friend. Charlie will take good care of me.'

'Hello, Charlie.' I make the stupid mistake of attempting to stroke the docile-looking dog. Charlie is anything but docile — his aggressive snarls and razor-sharp teeth go to prove that. Charlie goes to rip off my approaching hand, proving that a dog's bark is just as worse as its bite. 'Woah! Charlie's a great guard dog as well, isn't he? I say, trying to hide the fact I'm on the verge of soiling myself. 'Bloody hell, Karam. You should have him on a lead.'

'No one would ever dare mess with my Charlie,' he laughs, now thankfully moving the growling mutt away from me. I breathe a sigh of relief and then turn to carry on with my journey. 'Thank you again for the cigarette, Tom. I hope your day is blessed.'

'Same to you, pal.'

I look down at my watch and instantly go back into panic mode. I am going to be late. Shit. But why should I care? It's the last day of term. There are just eight hours to go until I'm free. Just eight hours out of twenty-four. Now, that is staying positive.

The school's headmistress is waiting at the gates with her arms crossed and feet tapping, her face as red as a baboon's backside. Sharon a.k.a. Mrs. Rhodes, a woman who can instil fear into anyone who dares set their eyes upon her i.e. my ill-tempered boss.

'And what time do you call this, Mr. Grey?' she asks in a piercing, high-pitched voice. 'This is wholly unacceptable.'

'I'm sorry, Sharon. My alarm didn't go off,' I say, biting at my lower lip. I'm already missing the sedating effects from my Mirtazapine, and the nicotine hit from my last cigarette is also wearing off. 'It won't happen again. I promise.'

'First off: in front of the pupils, I'd prefer for you to address me Mrs. Rhodes,' she says, glaring at the students walking by us. 'Secondly: if you want to get that promotion, to become Deputy Head, then you'll need to ensure you're here on time. Perfect punctuality is a key skill in our school, is it not?'

'Yes, it is. Understood,' I say ashamedly. 'I am really sorry for being late.'

'I expect you to set a good example to our pupils. Do not disappointment me again, Mr. Grey.'

I enter my classroom and savour in the momentary emptiness within it for as long as possible. I've got a few minutes before the first class arrives, so reach into a drawer nearby to retrieve two sticks of mentholated gum — my sole weapon against the rancid smell of alcohol and tobacco presently wafting from my mouth. Suddenly, there's an unexpected knock at the door. It's another teacher called

Amar, who also happens to be a good friend of mine outside of work.

'I hear Sharon told you off – again,' he says, winking at me playfully. 'Word soon spreads, Tom-boy. Are you still up for a session down the Tin Donkey tonight with me and the other lads?'

'The pub? Too right. I could do with a stiff drink now, if being honest.'

'Whatever,' he sniggers. 'Don't you be late, though, like you have been for work today. You know the rule: last one in has to buy a round of drinks.'

'I won't be late. Anyhow, Sikhs can't drink booze. I don't get why you're so excited.'

'Not everyone needs alcohol to have a good time,' he says, tapping a finger against his left temple. 'Some might say that you drink too much, mate. Ever thought of going sober?'

'Yeah, but where's the fun in that? I don't drink that much, anyway.'

If I was to be honest with Amar, which I should be by all rights, I'd explain how I don't like drinking; how I only use alcohol to numb my senses; how I use alcohol to forget all the emotional turmoil I've been through. It's too early to be depressed, and Amar's right – I do drink too much. I'm not letting him know that, though. I'd never hear the end of it.

'Your poor liver, man. It's a miracle you haven't pickled it.'

'Don't you worry about my liver. I can handle my drink.'

'Yeah, right.' He looks up at the clock behind me. 'Class is starting soon. We've only got another eight hours to get through.'

'Yep. It won't be long until we're free of this festering dump. Roll on 7pm, I say.'

'It's not that bad, Tom-boy. Keep your chin up.'

As Amar leaves the first influx of students come into my classroom. I examine each of their faces, noting how some appear eager to learn while others seem to be in the same, lowly boat as me. The lesson that I'm about to cover entails the story of Moses parting the Red Sea. It's a tale filled with hope and suffering, much like life is in general. I do my best to be optimistic and engaging, but my pupils soon lose interest.

'What have we learned from our lesson today?' I ask to a sea of vacant expressions. 'Would anyone like to comment? Have any of you been paying attention?'

'I don't get it,' says Reece, the self-professed class clown. 'Why did all those people follow Moses? They just ended up walking through a desert for years. It sounds like a pretty crap deal to me.'

'Moses gave them hope,' I explain. 'He led them from slavery to live out their lives in freedom. The moral of the story is that you should never lose hope.'

'I still don't get it.' Reece shuffles in his chair, and I'm sure that he slips me the middle finger. 'It's dumb. This lesson's dumb.'

I don't get it, to be honest. Here's me spouting off about holding onto hope when I can't even do that myself. No wonder the students look bored and confused — I'm bored and confused, and I should have been the last person to hold this class. Never mind. Seven more hours to go. Seven more hours of having to explain ancient metaphors to a bunch of kids who are only interested in updating their Instagram and Twitter pages. Roll on 7pm. Roll on freedom. That first pint of ale can't come soon enough.

Flashback: September 9th, 1995

It's my first day of junior school. I'm sitting alone on one of the playground benches, minding my own business, trying hard to keep a low profile, eating an American cheese and mayonnaise sandwich like there's no tomorrow. That's when the "big boys" line themselves up before me, each pointing and laughing. The leader is a kid called Harold who is two years older and two feet taller than me. He's got curly, ginger hair, and his face is covered in freckles — goodness knows how he shot up the bully hierarchy. Harold makes it crystal clear from the onset that he wants to humiliate me. I hate confrontations, therefore, I'm an easy target.

Harold slaps the sandwich out of my hand and then wraps his greasy fingers around my throat. I want to fight back, like Mum always tells me to, but I can't. Harold is way too big for me to tackle, and he's got his lackies to back him up. I've got no one in my corner. My hands are tremoring like mad — I've got no chance in fighting back successfully.

I'm so small and weak, and the adrenaline flowing through my veins is paralysing me to the spot. I close my eyes, dreading what will happen next, and pray for some miraculous intervention to occur.

'Give us your money!' Harold snarls, tightening his grip around my throat, his friends laughing like hyenas in the background. 'Come on, give us your money!' Turning to his comrades, Harold then says, 'I bet he's skint. Look at his manky sandwich and clothes. Pauper! Pauper!!'

A sweet, feminine voice then cries out from a few yards away, a voice that I imagine to be my guardian angel. 'Leave him alone! Get off him!'

'Go away!' Harold says to her, slowly removing his fingers from me. 'Do you want some of this? I don't mind hitting a girl!'

Without saying a word, she walks up to Harold and then kicks him square in the crown jewels with a precise and merciless strike, forcing him into a tearful retreat. Harold's friends soon follow suit, skulking off like the vermin they are. It reminds me of what Uncle Steven often says about bullies: *take out the leader first and then the sheep will soon follow. Hit them hard and fast.*

'Thank you,' I say to the girl in a meek voice, not daring to look at her. 'Thanks for helping me.'

'You're welcome. My name's Alice. What's yours?' she asks, and my hormones instantly surge. 'Can you not talk? Are you shy?'

'I'm Tom...'

'Hi, Tom. Don't listen to those nasty bullies. Not everyone is horrible at this school, like those boys are.'

Alice sits down beside me and offers up a packet of cheese and onions crisps to calm my shaken nerves, which I eagerly accept. Hands down, Alice is the prettiest girl I've ever seen in my eight years of existence. I can barely talk. I can barely move. My entire body feels like butter melting in a hot pan.

'You have a pretty name,' I say, stuttering over my words. 'And you were very brave for standing up to those bullies. I'm not that brave.'

'You're cute,' she says, giggling to herself. 'Would you like to be my friend?'

'I'd love to be your friend — yes.' However, I quickly fall back into my usual, withdrawn shell. 'I haven't made any new friends yet. Nobody wants to play with me.'

'It's okay,' she implores, resting a hand upon mine. 'I'll look after you. I'll be your bestest friend in the whole-wide world, Tom.'

Home Truths

Alice has come to understand how Tom feels over recent weeks: the perpetual helplessness, fear, self-doubt, and low mood. She was once proud to be his wife, though not anymore. Tom isn't the man he used to be. He's not the funny, carefree soul Alice fell in love with. To her, he has morphed into a living mannequin — a human-like manifestation devoid of any emotion, that is, other than sorrow. She simply cannot tolerate the turmoil anymore. She must think of Rose's best interests also. She has reached a tipping point.

Reluctantly, Alice does the unthinkable and phones in sick at work, something she'll possibly regret further down the line, being that she is on her final warning. She and Tom are struggling with money as it is, but Alice just can't face dealing with customers in the bank where she is employed — people who will no doubt be handing over their dispersible income for holidays and savings, money of which Tom and Alice could use to pay off their amounting debts. It's so unfair, she contemplates. Even though both work so tirelessly, they are still counting the pennies come payday.

Alice's mother, Courtney, is due to pick up Rose soon, to babysit her. Alice checks her phone for any missed calls or text messages, seeing as her mum is usually early, but there's nothing. Meanwhile, Rose is watching TV, blissfully unaware of the crisis taking place around her. That's one good thing, Alice surmises: Rose is too young to understand. Tom's parents divorced when he was ten years old, meaning he could absorb all the angst and uncertainty from them as they argued over and split apart the stable life he had come to cherish. Alice would never wish that on Rose, though she herself has come to the similar crossroad Tom's mother faced.

'Should we see Aunty Hannah and the girls at their baby group this morning, Rose?' says Alice, despite knowing fine well that she won't get a meaningful response from the toddler. It doesn't matter if Rose can't talk back yet because she's a good listener, and that's what Alice needs now more than anything. Hannah isn't really Rose's aunt, just a very close friend, and has also been through some difficult times with her husband. Alice reasons that Hannah is the ideal person to discuss marriage problems with, albeit in hesitation to accept her marriage is failing. 'You'll start nursery soon,' Alice adds, stroking a hand over Rose's pigtails. 'We'll need to make the most of Hannah's baby group before you're too old to go. I'm gonna miss taking you—'

A knock at the front door snaps Alice back into reality. She can just hear her mum's voice calling her name and goes to inspect. Nevertheless, Tom had forgotten to lock the front door, so Courtney wastes no time in letting herself in.

'Alice? It's only me, sweetheart.'

'Hi, Mum.'

'Why aren't you dressed for work?' says Courtney, flouncing her arms around to highlight her frustration. 'Why aren't you ready, Alice, my girl? You'll be late for work. Honestly, what's gotten into you?'

'I've phoned in sick, Mum. I'm not going in today.'

'You look dreadful — ghastly.' Courtney wraps her arms around Alice and squeezes in tight. Alice has so far managed to keep her concerns about Tom and their splintering relationship a secret from others, but it's obviously starting to show. 'What's wrong, darling? Tell me. Talk to Mummy.'

'It doesn't matter. I'm fine, Mum.' However, Alice knows this false pretence won't last long; Courtney is too stubborn to give in, especially when she can sense something bad is afoot. 'I feel a little queasy, that's all. Sorry I didn't let you know. And you've come all this way —'

'Don't be daft. I'm glad I came over.' Courtney eyes Alice up from head to toe, examining every fine detail as a doctor would. 'Whatever's on your mind, tell me. You've not been yourself for a few weeks now. Even your dad — who's clueless about these things — has noticed that you're not your usual, quirky self.'

'I don't want to talk about it, Mum. I'm taking Rose to her baby group, so we can spend some time with Hannah and the other girls. I'm going to talk things over with them.'

'I am your mother, Alice. I'm the first person you should be talking to when you're upset about anything. What is it? Has Tom hurt you?'

'No! Why would you even think that?' Alice asks defensively. 'Tom would never hurt me, at least, not physically. We're having some money troubles, and I'm a bit stressed about work. It's no big deal.'

'Your wellbeing is a big deal to me, young lady. You're still my baby girl, even if you're in your late twenties.' Courtney steps back with her arms folded, staring to Alice with a look of concern. This is the last thing Alice wanted, for her mother to get chewed up like this. 'I'm very aware that you and Tom have both been going through a rough patch lately, despite your attempts to throw me off. It's normal, having the occasional fallout, and nothing to worry over. Your father and I have had plenty of arguments over the years. Marriage has its ups and downs…'

'It's different, Mum. You wouldn't understand. You and Dad argue over stupid things, like what shows to watch on TV and whose turn it is to hoover. Tom's got his mental health issues—'

'Yes, but he has no right to wear you down with them,' Courtney adds, flaring her eyes. 'He's too bloody soft, is Tom. He needs to man-up and take some responsibility for his life. He should be putting you and Rose first—never mind his anxiety issues.'

'He does, Mum. I knew you wouldn't understand,' Alice sighs.

The way she sees it, her mother and father are from a different generation, an era where—if you had an illness such as depression—you'd be locked up in some godforsaken institution, fed sedating medications with horrific side-effects, and shunned by the rest of society, all because of your mental health ailments. Courtney does have

33

a valid point, though Alice hates to admit it. Tom has his problems but shouldn't be taking them out on her and Rose, which he is.

'If you're swanning off to the baby group, I may as well go home,' says Courtney under her breath. This is one of the reasons why Alice feels she can't be open and honest with her mother; Courtney's so rigid and set in her ways, particularly when it comes to discussing one's mental health. The problem is that you can't stick a bandage over anxiety and depression — they're invisible and far more difficult to treat. 'You know where I am if you need me, Alice. Do send my love to Tom. Oh, and give our Rose a big, sloppy kiss from me.'

'I will, Mum. I'll catch up with you later.'

'There's a good girl. I'll speak to you soon, sweetheart.'

Courtney leaves as dramatically as she entered, allowing Alice the peace and solitude she so greatly desires. Alice can't wait to have a good catchup with Hannah. For the most part, Hannah is far more understanding and willing to listen than Alice's parents are, than Tom is. With that in mind, Alice gets herself and Rose ready then sets off for the baby group, which itself takes place in a church a few streets away.

'Hello, stranger,' Hannah says to Alice, her expression lighting up as she ushers both mother and child into the church hall. 'It's so great to see you again. Rose hasn't half shot up.'

'Hiya, Han. It's great to see you too.'

'Come in — come in! The other girls will be over the moon that you've turned up.'

Alice makes out a few familiar faces, such as her friends Rebecca and Gosha, but there are a lot of new ones as well.

'Has it been that long since I last visited?' she asks herself. To Alice, in all fairness, every day and week seem to be turning into one big blur now. Hours have become days, and days have become weeks. It could have been months since her last visit. 'I'm sorry it's been a while. How are you doing, Han?'

'I'm fine, thanks. When *was* the last time you visited?'

'A couple of months ago, I think. I love what you've done with your hair,' says Alice, desperate to change the subject. 'It really suits you.'

'I fancied a change. The hubby's not too impressed, though. John's still getting used to it,' says Hannah, inspecting Alice's own change in appearance, which isn't anywhere near as positive: her dishevelled hair, the black bags under her eyes, the sheer look of fatigue. 'Is Rose still keeping you up at night?'

'How are John and your little girls doing?' Alice asks, even more desperate to move the conversation away from her fractured family. 'Is he still writing books?'

'Yeah. John's just the same, hun. He'll never change,' she sniggers. 'Lucy's almost eight now. Sophia's playing over there with Rebecca's little girl, Melanie. I can't believe how much your Rose has grown. She'll be turning three soon, won't she?'

'Yeah, come October. She's growing up too fast.' Alice hands Rose over to Hannah. The child immediately giggles on recognising her mother's closest friend, somewhat giving Alice the impression that her downbeat mood must be wearing off on her too. 'Can we go somewhere more private, Han? I want to talk to you about a few things.'

'Sure. How are things going with you and Tom, if you don't mind me asking?'

'That's what I want to talk to you about.'

'Oh...'

Hannah takes Alice into the church's chapel room. It's small, secluded, and ideally away from prying eyes. She then moves aside a chair for Alice to sit on and stands herself directly opposite, ensuring to never remove her line of sight from her.

'I've been thinking, Han—'

'What about?'

'I'm thinking that Tom and I should maybe have a break from one another, you know, to think our relationship through and to clear the air a bit. Living with him is becoming unbearable.'

'Have things really gotten that bad between you both? It's a drastic move, don't you think? You and Tom have been together for, like, forever.'

'I know. We've been a couple since we were teenagers,' Alice laments. 'It's just, Tom's drinking and smoking more now, and he won't talk to me about his problems like he used to. It's as if he's completely shut himself off from the world, from his family, from me. It's like being shackled to a total stranger, and the sex is non-existent.'

'That bad, is it?' Hannah glances to Rose, forming half a smile. 'You've been through a lot together. Good times. Bad times. All relationships go through rocky patches.'

'Yeah, but—'

'I know breaking up with Tom would be a last resort for you, though it might be the wake-up call he needs,' Hannah suggests. 'I've thought about doing the same with John plenty of times before, but we've been lucky enough to get through our rough patches. You'll be okay, hun. Everything will turn out alright in the end.'

'It's not like I haven't tried,' Alice states pleadingly. 'I just don't feel like there's any other option. He's not the man I fell in love with.'

'People change, as do relationships. Take one step at a time.'

Their friend, Rebecca, suddenly bursts in with a tray of cakes and coffee mugs.

'Oh, aye. What's going on in here?' Rebecca asks. 'Am I interrupting something, girls?'

'No,' says Alice, finding it harder now to hold back her tears. 'We're only talking about men, Bex.'

'Nothing new there.' Rebecca takes it upon herself to sit down and join in the conversation. However, Alice is glad she's joined in. The more people she can open up to about this situation, the better. 'Which men are you gossiping about? Anyone I'd fancy?'

Hannah replies in a disenchanted mutter, 'Our husbands, so don't get your hopes up.'

'Can we not talk about Tom Hardy or Chris Hemsworth instead? I could chat about them all day,' says Rebecca, laughing.

Desperate to release the pent-up tensions inside, Alice gives into her reservations and says, 'I'm contemplating a break between me and Tom — nothing permanent, just so we can work out our differences. I'm after a second opinion.'

'I knew there was something up with you,' says Rebecca. She gives a cake to Rose and then gently strokes at Alice's hands. It's the reassurance Alice has been longing for; the physical comfort Tom hasn't shown her in months. 'What's happened, babes? You can talk to me and Hannah. You can tell us anything.'

'Tom's a nightmare at the minute,' says Alice. 'I think it's to do with him stressing over the promotion he's being offered, or the fact his depression is getting worse. I can't put my finger on the actual reason. He won't say a word to me about how he really feels.'

'That's men for you,' Rebecca scoffs.

'You're not helping, Bex. Look, whatever's on your mind, Alice, tell us,' Hannah insists. 'It'll do you some good to get it off your shoulders. Whatever you say in these four walls, stays in these four walls. You know we're not into gossiping.'

'We're behind you one-hundred percent,' Rebecca adds. 'I threw my man out years ago and have never looked back. Men are nothing but a pain in the arse.'

'Thanks, girls.' Alice momentarily reflects on what she's revealed. Everyone tends to look at her and Tom as being a perfect couple; they never argue publicly. This is a monumental step for Alice, a step that she thought she was ready for but evidently not. 'Your ex-partner was violent and cheated on you, Bex. Tom hasn't done anything like that to me. It's different.'

'Mental wounds hurt just as much as the physical ones do,' says Rebecca, her light tone now shifting into bitterness. 'Yeah, Scott left me with a few cuts and bruises, but it was the lasting fear and painful memories that hurt most. The physical injuries have all gone, but the mental scars haven't. Looking back now, I wish I'd acted sooner in kicking his arse to the curb.' After taking a few sips from her coffee mug, Rebecca then looks to Alice with a puzzled smirk. 'Tom has depression—really? He's never come across to me as being that way.'

'Tom's an expert at hiding it,' says Alice. 'He's under the impression that men shouldn't talk about their emotions.'

'Fellas don't like to show any weaknesses, do they?' says Rebecca. 'Has he thought about seeing a doctor? My sister got some counselling for her postnatal depression and it worked absolute wonders for her.'

'Tom saw a doctor and had some counselling after his mini stroke,' Alice explains, albeit with some disdain. She'd begged for him to see a doctor long before his mini stroke, but he point-blank refused. Tom was apprehensive about what the outcome could be. He didn't want to rely on drugs to cure his ailments, though was also quite happy for alcohol to satiate them. 'He's been on various anti-depressant tablets since then. The medication has helped Tom, but it's like he's just given up on everything recently—including me.'

'There's no easy solution,' says Hannah, nodding her head sympathetically. 'How do you think Tom will react if you go ahead with this break?'

'That's what is worrying me the most. I'd hate to think he'd do something stupid—'

'Like what?' Rebecca interjects, fleeting her eyes between Alice and Rose. 'You don't think for one second he'd, you know—' She runs a finger across her throat. 'He wouldn't, would he?'

'I don't want to think about it. I've got no choice, though, have I? Tom won't talk to me and won't go back to the doctors, no matter how much I nag him to. What else am I meant to do? I can't live like this, always miserable and dreading what's coming next.' Alice finally breaks down and cries, which she's never done in front of Hannah and Rebecca before. 'What am I going to do, girls?'

'You've got to put yourself first,' Hannah states. 'The Tom I know would do anything to keep you and Rose happy. Taking a break might make him realise what he's missing out on, and what matters most.'

'That's what I'm hoping for. I'm going to see how things go for another week, then — if nothing does change — I'll give him the bad news,' says Alice, trembling with dread. 'I don't know how to tell him, though. It's going to break his heart.'

Despite being in the reassuring presences of her friends, it's like the whole world has come to an end for Alice — along with her vision of a perfect marriage. She can't stop thinking about how separating from Tom might also affect Rose. She doesn't want their daughter to be torn between them, like Tom was with his parents for several years after their divorce. Alice convinces herself to give him another chance, but she's given him so many opportunities to change, which he failed at, and there's still a part of her that believes this awful situation can be miraculously resolved.

'You've got us and your family behind you, Alice. You're not alone,' Hannah implores, and Rebecca nods in agreement. 'At the end of the day, you've got to put yours and Rose's needs before anything else. Have you tried explaining to Tom how down you are?'

'Yes, but he just changes the subject. I can't get through to him anymore.'

'You'll be okay,' says adds, leaning over to offer Alice a much-needed hug. It's amazing how wonderful such a small gesture can be. Alice immediately feels the tension in her muscles ease from Rebecca's gentle touch. If only Tom would do the same. 'You've been through worse, babes. You do whatever you think is right. I know things will work out for you. You don't deserve this shit.'

'I don't know what to do,' Alice whispers, struggling to form her words. 'I can't believe it's come to this. It's not fair. It's not what I want.'

'Tom's isn't such a bad guy,' says Hannah, somewhat reluctantly. 'He'll come to his senses. And if he doesn't, he'll have us to deal with. Tom's not that stupid.'

Education, Education, Education

This is going to be a long-arsed day, I just know it. Within twenty minutes of starting the second class, I had to contend with: two boys fighting, a kid with a nosebleed, a student's mobile phone going off, and being handed a memo from the headteacher's secretary that stated some Ofsted inspectors have turned up out of the blue. Great. Absolutely marvellous. Top all those things off with a raging hangover and it's a recipe for disaster. No wonder I drink so much.

I've made it to morning break with my sanity, in the most part. left intact. But I'm starting to feel the early withdrawal symptoms from not taking my medication. It's like I'm being submerged into a bath of icy water with an electrical current flowing through it. I'm burning up. The sweat's pouring from me. My body won't stop shaking. It's too soon to be feeling this bad, surely? These strange reactions are all in my head—they must be. Now my fingers are going into cramp, too, and there's little I can do about it. I just hope no one else notices them. They're not easy to hide, though, which is the worst part. It's so humiliating, is living like this.

I've secluded myself in the staff room, well away from my insufferable colleagues. They're so two-faced, though I'm hardly one to talk—my nickname should be Janus, not Tomboy. Anyway, I'm waiting on Amar to show up so that he can lift my spirits with his corny jokes, but he's still nowhere to be seen. Roll on 7pm. Roll on filling my body with the only substance that can put an end to these degrading symptoms of mine: alcohol. It's funny how people accept me using medically recognised drugs to combat this depression of mine, but not the odd beer or two or three or four.

Amar appears at the doorway. Thank God. Before I have a chance to react, however, he throws a toilet roll straight into my lap and sniggers.

'Y'alright, Tom?' he says. 'You're early for once. Are they handing out free cakes again or something?'

'No. And what's this in aid of?' I ask, inspecting Amar's peculiar gift. I know our school has budget issues, but there's no justification whatsoever in them buying this bloody sandpaper. 'What's the bog roll about?'

'You got the memo from Sandra, didn't you?' he says. 'I thought some toilet paper might come in handy, y'know, seeing as you must be shitting yourself.'

'Ha-ha, very funny.' I hand the roll back to Amar, but only after crushing it beyond any use. 'Aren't you nervous? You know how nit-picky the inspectors can be.'

'No,' he says, smirking. 'Tom, it's the last day of term. Do you honestly think a bunch of Ofsted inspectors would turn up? It was a joke! Sandra and I were pulling your leg, mate. Relax.'

'Cheers for that.' I feel like a complete tool now, is what I want to add. Nothing new there. 'Who needs enemies when there's friends like you to rely on? Anyway, how's your morning been?'

'It's been… eventful.' Amar suddenly loses his jovial demeanour. 'One of the pupils attacked me; it was pretty bad.'

'No way, man.' I notice how some of our colleagues are looking over to Amar now, each scowling at him. How he can smile and make jokes after going through something like that is beyond me. It must be just his way of coping, I guess. 'That's shocking, Amar. Who attacked you?'

'Isaac Hunt decided to call me the "N" word and then kicked me square in the stomach. I fought back,' he explains with an uncomfortable look on his face. 'All I did was pin him to the ground until he calmed down—nothing too overboard. I've been summoned to Sharon's office, to explain myself. Do you reckon she'll phone the police?'

'If she does, it'll only be her ticking some boxes—red tape, mate. I'd have done the same thing in your shoes,' I say as calmly as possible, although I'm raging inside. 'Sharon will understand. She should be backing your corner, not some little racist's.'

'But I've not been taught how to restrain. I could be done for assault,' says Amar, his breaths steadily turning more rapid. 'I could lose my job. This could end my career in teaching.'

I hate seeing Amar so down. The guy's a joker, a man who'd do anything for anyone. He doesn't deserve this. Why is it always the decent people in life who get shat on the most?

'It was a racist attack. You're the victim, Amar, not Isaac Hunt,' I say, keeping an eye on the watchful serpents nearby. 'You acted in self-defence. You've got nothing to hide.'

'Yeah, but the red tape might see otherwise.'

'Sod the red tape. If Sharon has any ounce of common decency, she'll understand that you were just protecting yourself. Mind you —'

'Exactly,' he says, rolling his eyes. 'We're talking about Sharon. Still, I'm not guilty until proven otherwise, and I'm looking forward to our session down the Tin Donkey later — the thought of that is cheering me up. Are you definitely going?'

'Yeah, I wouldn't miss it for the world.' I smile back as to hide the boiling frustration, which is swiftly making itself known. Poor Amar. He's the real victim here. I've got no right to feel anxious or down in comparison to him. 'We'll have a good laugh, like we always do. I think you deserve a night on the town, especially after the morning you've had.'

'Yeah.' Amar laughs again, but he can't fool me. I'm well versed in the symptoms of anxiety, of wearing a mask to hide them. 'I wish Sikhs could drink,' he humours. 'I could really do with a stiff vodka.'

I'm getting angrier by the second. It's another side-effect of my adrenaline-fueled anxiety, where my turbulent emotions can morph from fear into a debilitating and uncontrollable anger in seconds. My muscles are getting tenser, and my thoughts are blurring into one. I despise anything unfair, even more so when it involves those closest to me, and especially when there's nothing I can do about it. I've got to

45

reign in this rage, however, given that my colleagues have now turned their judgemental eyes on me.

I take in a deep breath through my nostrils for four seconds and then exhale for the same length of time, repeating this until my ears start ringing. It's a technique I taught myself after my parents divorced to help calm me down. It works most of the time, but not always. The success of this technique wholly depends on the severity of the situation I'm in, and this is a whole-new situation.

'If you want me to come with you, to back your corner, I'm more than happy to help,' I say to him.

'Darren text me this morning,' says Amar, clearly wishing to change the subject. 'There's an Open Mic Night competition on at the pub this evening, and you can guarantee John will be get up with his guitar.'

'God help us,' I say, managing to make Amar chuckle slightly. 'We'll be fine, so long as he doesn't play any Oasis songs. How he didn't get bottled the last time we went to an Open Mic night—'

'John's not that bad,' says Amar, unconvincingly. 'Just do what I do: go to the toilet when he comes on stage. John's feelings aren't hurt as much that way, you see.'

'Some "mates" we are,' I scoff. 'To be fair, John isn't really that bad. He could do with varying his repertoire a little more often though.'

Sharon, our headmistress, now makes her grand entrance. And like Moses parting the Red Sea, my fellow colleagues move aside to give her path, though she's anything but benevolent. I want to confront her, to put her straight on how wrong it is for Amar to be vilified over his actions. He was acting in self-defence. He wouldn't hurt a fly. She's nothing but a bloody jobsworth, and there's plenty of them in this place. I've got to remain civil with her, though, as much as it pains me, which starts to eat away at my conscience. But I want and need that promotion, and the extra income that comes with it. So, I push all those volatile emotions deep down inside and prepare myself to do some major brown-nosing. Some "mate" I am.

'Can I see you in my office for a few minutes, Mr. Kohli?' she asks Amar in a monotonous, staccato-like voice. 'Now please, if you don't mind?'

'Shit.' Amar stares at me fearfully, but then smiles as if nothing is wrong. 'Catch you later, Tom-boy. Don't wait up for me.'

If I can't muster the will needed to confront Sharon about this injustice, then I can certainly make my feelings known to those who've done nothing but glare at us for the last ten minutes, thus utilising this adrenaline rush of mine to its full extent.

I approach Malcolm Whittle—the Advanced Maths teacher/biggest, narcissistic arsehole in the school—first. After taking in another deep breath, I make my move.

'Why were you and your pals here staring at Amar?' I ask him. 'What's the crack?'

'You honestly don't know?' says Malcolm in his usual, condescending tone. 'The whole school is talking about what he did, teachers and pupils alike.'

'I know that Amar was attacked by a pupil. And, in my humble opinion, he did the right thing by protecting himself. Wouldn't you have done the same?'

'There's a fine line between self-defence and what Amarjit did, Tom. He pinned Isaac Hunt—a fifteen-year-old boy—

47

down by the throat,' says Malcolm to a succession of gasps from our colleagues. 'Amarjit had no right to do that, even if he had been assaulted. I hope he gets what he deserves.'

'No,' I say, half-dazed and genuinely in shock. 'Amar wouldn't—'

'It took six pupils to pull them apart, and there's fresh bruising to Isaac's throat. I understand you and Amarjit are close friends outside of work, but you shouldn't let that cloud your judgement, Tom. He reacted in a completely over-the-top manner, unbefitting of a professional in his position. He'll have a lot of explaining to do with Sharon and Isaac's parents. If I were you, I'd keep out of it and well away from him.'

That can't be right? That's not the Amar I know. He wouldn't. But he has mentioned on the odd occasion about his time growing up in London, which was pretty grim, by all accounts. His closest family members—including himself—are Sikhs, and were the only ones living on their street. Amar suffered daily abuse for his religious beliefs and lifestyle. His mum even got beaten up once by a bunch of blokes over the clothes she was wearing. Maybe Isaac's racial slur brought up those painful memories, triggering Amar's brash reaction? I know all about painful flashbacks. Still, I won't believe for one second what Malcolm is saying. He doesn't know Amar; not like I do.

'None of us saw what happened,' I state, just holding back my urge to scream at them all. 'Balls to this. I'm going for a cigarette.'

'Your next class is starting soon,' says Malcolm, tapping at his watch. 'You'll be late for it.'

I want to say more, to wipe the smug grin off Malcolm's face, but I've unwittingly managed to expend my adrenaline rush. The stream of energy that had flowed through my veins like a bolt of lightning has all but dwindled now, leaving me drained and feeling nauseous. This is bad. I'm gonna have my work cut out in trying to hide these tremors and cold sweats of mine for the next four hours. Roll on 7pm. It can't come soon enough.

By the time I make it to the school gates, where smoking teachers and pupils alike amass, it dawns on me that I've only got enough time for one cigarette. It'll have to do, but I'd have preferred two or three tabs before facing my next tedious hour of teaching. As I take in my first draw of tar-laden smoke, I imagine the burning sensation coursing into my lungs to be all the negative energy and thoughts that have so far built up inside today; on slowly exhaling, I envision the smoke leaving my body to be carrying with it all that unwanted negativity. I then watch the smoke rise into the air and disperse, convincing myself that this technique is effective, that my body and soul have been purified. It's mind over matter, albeit at the expense of my health and wellbeing. My cigarette break soon comes to its end. The good times never last.

Thankfully, the pupils arriving into my third class are all final-year students and are much better behaved. I find another note from Sandra the secretary on my desk, which I believe to be genuine this time. The memo is an instruction from Sharon, informing me that I am to do a careers advice session. This'll be fun. I can't even give myself decent advice.

'Right, folks!' I exclaim, reducing my students into an obedient wave of silence…gradually. 'Who here knows what career they want to go into? Have any of you even thought about it yet?'

A few reluctant hands rise before me in response. I choose one pupil at random, a girl named Amanda Goodyear, hoping they don't say anything along the lines of "Politician" or "Instagram Model".

'I want to be a nurse,' she says, brimming with confidence. 'My mum's a nurse. I want to follow in her footsteps and help people.'

'That's a very good choice,' I say. 'It can be a challenging profession, but also very worthwhile. I think you'd make a fantastic nurse, Amanda. Do we have any other volunteers?'

'I want to be an artist,' says Dylan Black to some malicious jeers. 'What's wrong with that? There's plenty of famous artists.'

'I agree with you,' I say, scowling at the unruly pupils in attempt to shut them up. 'Without art, this world would be a boring place. I'm assuming you've chosen this profession so that you can express yourself more in life, and there's no harm in that.'

'Artists get to draw naked people,' he adds, turning my pupils into a set of cackling hyenas. 'I'm just being honest.'

'Swiftly moving on, is there anyone else that would care to comment on which career they'd like?'

A boy sitting at the back of my class called Jason, who is normally shy and never utters a word, speaks up. 'I want to be a mechanic, Sir.'

'There'll always be a need for mechanics. A solid choice, Jason.'

'That's not what Mrs. Rhodes told us in assembly the other day,' he says, his expression one of defeat. 'She said that we should go to college and then university. That way, we'll be smart enough to get good-paying jobs and our parents will be proud of us.'

I need to be careful here. What I want to say is: yeah, go to university, where you can land yourselves in a boatload of student debt, which you'll likely never be able to pay off, and then end up doing a minimum wage job at the end of it all, like most my student friends did. However, that wouldn't be in line with Sharon's ideals — or the government's, for that matter. I'm already in her bad books, and I won't get that promotion if I entice her further displeasure. I'm so conflicted, and my anxiety is reaching its full strength.

I sit down at my desk and look over the sea of disenfranchised faces before me, desperately attempting to control my breaths. I need to think this through. I can't tell my students such a harsh reality, but I also can't let them down by being dishonest. I've got to be diplomatic — another weakness of mine.

'Mrs. Rhodes does have a valid opinion, that is, from a certain point of view. There are many successful people in this world who have all studied at university; it's a privilege and an accepted pathway to further yourself in life. However, I'd also like to add that there are some careers where a degree isn't necessarily required, such as sighing up to an apprenticeship — bricklaying, plumbing and what not. My advice would be to do what feels right to you, and to go with your gut instincts.' I'm stepping too far out the comfort zone here. I need to reign myself in again. I've seen too many of my friends end up miserable through their student debt, though. God, this is difficult. 'It all depends on what career you wish you take. When I left school, my first job was performing in a rock band with my best friend. I didn't exactly need a degree for that.'

'You were in a rock band?' giggles Amanda. 'Seriously?'

'Yes. We played in pubs and holiday parks all over the UK, from Scotland to Cornwall. It was a fantastic experience, but the pay was practically non-existent — not to mention all the boring hours of rehearsing and travelling we had to do. It wasn't all fun and games.'

'What made you want to be a teacher?' Dylan asks. The whole class then falls silent again, each pupil eagerly awaiting my response. 'Did you go to university?'

'Yes, Dylan. I studied to be a teacher at Newcastle University, because — believe it or not — you need a degree to be a teacher. Me wanting to teach didn't happen overnight, though. It just kind of, I don't know — happened. It was my wife who convinced me to do it.'

'Did you like university?' Amanda asks.

'It was difficult at times — torturous, in fact — and I didn't help myself much by spending most of it in the student union bar. There's a lot of writing and researching involved, which is the most tedious part. But — '

'Was it worth the effort?' Dylan asks. This lesson is beginning to feel more like a history seminar, one involving the Spanish Inquisition and it's me sitting in the docks. Plus, my neck is killing me from shooting back and forth between my curious pupils. 'Do you still enjoy teaching?' he adds.

'It can be rewarding, in the most part, but — like anything else in life — it can be very stressful too. There's a lot of responsibility on my shoulders…' I hesitate to divulge, seeing as it will probably trigger some unwanted, depressive thoughts. I don't fancy anymore flashbacks today, thank you kindly. But I've got to give my pupils a decent answer. After all, it'd be the right thing to do. 'I've enjoyed seeing how you've each managed to overcome your own obstacles, particularly over the last few months or so with all the mock exams you've had to sit through. There are parts of teaching I don't enjoy, however, like the mountains of paperwork and endless hours of marking that go with it. To conclude this lesson: whatever career you choose, there'll always be good and bad elements associated with it. You've just got to try and focus on the good parts.'

Why can't I take my own advice? I'm making it sound so simple, to focus only on the good things in life. But it's not; not for me. If I was going to be truthful with my pupils, I'd tell them: yeah, I get by each day by focusing solely on the more pleasant parts, but only because I'm swallowing a tablet every morning, filling my lungs with cancer-causing fumes throughout the day, and drinking myself into a stupor every night. I honestly don't know how Alice puts up with me. I'm so lucky to have her in my life.

Come 3pm, I've not heard from nor seen Amar since he was escorted away by Sharon at lunchtime. I can't stop thinking about the allegations made against him, about him reacting in such a violent, uncharacteristic manner. That's not Amar at all. But everyone has their breaking point, don't they? I know what it feels like to lose control, to succumb to helplessness and fall under the influence of negative emotions. I completely understand, seeing as it's something I live with daily – hence, why I find it so necessary to put on these false masks of mine, my alternative personas.

I make every effort in helping others feel better about themselves because I know how awful it is to feel so low. Since being a kid, I've gradually managed to develop these false masks — these perfected versions of myself — which often portray a man who tries to look on the bright side of life, rarely letting anything get on top of him. How I wish that was true. How I wish that I didn't need to live this way.

The need to infuse my body with more nicotine soon takes precedence again. I cannot deny this urge, this impulse that lies on par with requiring air, food and hydration to survive. I've got to keep myself sane somehow. I've got to. I can't go back home all stressed out and depleted, to allow my melancholy to wear off on Alice and little Rosie. No way. A cigarette will take my angst down a notch or two for sure. I might even manage to smoke a second one before reaching home.

Halfway through my cigarette, I pull out my mobile to see if anyone's bothered contacting me. My best friend, Darren — or Daz, as I call him — has taken the liberty of sending me a text, and in it he's asking if I'm still going out tonight. It must be rhetorical, I assume, given my track record. Besides, I'd never let Daz down. I'd better send him a reply before he starts to worry.

Alright, Daz? I'll meet you and the other lads at the Tin Donkey around 7pm. Been a nightmare day at work. Amar's had some trouble. We'll need to give him a night to remember, I reckon.

Within our small circle of friends, Daz is without question the most laidback and reliable. He played bass guitar for the rock band I was in, which is how we first met. Ever since that fateful first encounter we've been the closest of pals, more akin to brothers than anything else. It doesn't take long for Daz to respond:

Hi, Tom. I've had an eventful day myself. I'll explain later, and don't you be worrying about Amar. We'll help him out. Take care – Daz.

Roll on 7pm. Mind, saying that, I do feel some guilt in leaving Alice and Rosie alone while I go out and get plastered with my pals. Alice doesn't ever seem to have an issue with me going down the pub, though I think it does secretly annoy her. We're struggling with money as it is, and me wasting twenty or thirty quid on drink — which I'll literally piss down the drain — could be put to far better use. But alcohol helps me to forget, to numb my anxious thoughts. I need to forget with all these painful flashbacks and scenarios that keep popping up in my head. God knows, I need to forget.

I take a detour into town first before heading back home. I'm praying with all my might that the pharmacy is still open, and that my online prescription went through. It'll be a disaster if I'll have to go all weekend without my Mirtazapine, the thought of which I daren't even comprehend. I'll be fine. There's nothing to worry about. Deep breaths, Tom-boy. Calm your thoughts. I'll be in and out of the pharmacy, with my wonderful medication duly mine, in no time at all. There's absolutely nothing that can go wrong, so stop thinking that way. But I can't. Being optimistic is something I'll never accomplish.

Two Sides of the Same Penny

It was just my rotten luck that the pharmacy closed early for staff training. Happy days. This means I'll have to abstain from my beloved Mirtazapine's calming influence until Monday — that's two whole days from now. It'll be a miracle if I make it through the next forty-eight hours in one piece, but at least I've got alcohol to help nullify the impending torment. Why does stuff like this always happen to me?

I've smoked twice as many cigarettes on my journey home compared to normal, and the sweat pouring from me is becoming intolerable. I need a drink. I need to lose weight. I need to cut down on how much I'm smoking. I need a few, hard, hangover-inducing beers to settle these wayward nerves of mine more than anything else. Alcohol never lets me down. It never has and never will.

My home may have felt warm when I entered, but the atmosphere inside has quickly turned cold and uninviting. Alice hasn't said a word to me since I stepped foot through the door. I've likely annoyed her somehow, but I daren't look further into this. I'm not good at dealing with confrontations, and simply can't bear upsetting my beautiful wife more than I already have. Alice doesn't give me the silent treatment for no reason. Never mind beer, I could use a few shots of whisky right now. I might have some before setting off. One shot of whisky won't hurt, will it?

On a more positive note, Rosie seems somewhat pleased to see me. My little girl is spread out along the couch, hugging into her "snuggie" blanket, half-asleep and smiling as always. I lie beside her, keeping an eye on the living room clock, listening to Alice's frantic footsteps shifting around above us. What is she doing upstairs? So long as she's not packing her bags, I'll be okay. I'll stay put in my comfort zone for a little while longer. I don't deserve her.

Just as I start to fall into a pleasant daydream, Alice calls out to me. 'Tom? Are you there?'

'Yeah, and I have been for the last half-hour.' I reply. 'What's up?'

'We need to talk.'

This can't be good.

'What's the matter?' I ask apprehensively.

'Come upstairs. I want to show you something.'

With each step taken up the stairwell my heart rate increases, my breaths become thinner and more difficult to control, and a pool of scorching vomit rises into my mouth. I'm overthinking things again, as I always do. It's probably nothing to fret over.

Alice suddenly screeches, 'Tom!'

'I'm coming! Jeez…'

I find Alice sat on the edge of our bed with a large, leather-bound photo album resting within the palms of her hands. I can tell she's been crying, but I'm not sure whether they're tears of joy or sadness. It's getting harder to tell these days. I

57

go to talk but my mouth is bone-dry. My anxiety's making its unwelcome presence known again. I'll just keep on smiling, like everything's okay, and see if that works. It usually does.

'I've been looking back through our family photographs,' she says, straining to control her voice. 'This was our school's prom night. We look so young, don't we?'

'Because we were,' I say, relieved that my worst fears are being put to rest. Alice isn't angry at me. Thank God. Come on, Tom-boy, be positive for once in your life. 'We were only sixteen. Look at the state of my hair.'

'I always thought you looked cute with long hair.' Alice turns a few more pages to land on some of our wedding photographs. 'That was the best day of my life.'

'And mine. It was a great day, apart from when Mikey knocked the wedding cake over.'

Alice gulps as if about to choke. 'Is it really your favourite day, Tom? Wasn't that the day when you got shackled to me for life?'

I'd prepared myself for a scolding but not this monumental bombshell.

'What? Why would you say something like that?' I ask, taken back. 'Of course. I was happy about marrying you then and still are now. What's up with you?'

'It doesn't matter,' she simpers. 'I'm feeling a bit emotional today, that's all.'

'Is it your time of the month? Has Aunt Flo come to visit?'

'No!' she snaps. 'You never take anything seriously, do you? I'm not in the mood for any of your corny jokes, Tom.'

'I'm only trying to cheer you up—'

'Well, you're not.'

Alice flickers through the remaining pages, lost in thought. As she turns onto the photos of Rosie, taken moments after our daughter had been born, I place a firm hand upon hers. I'll never grow weary of seeing any photographs of our perfect princess, especially the earliest ones.

'Actually, now I come to think of it, that was the best day of my life,' I say, whispering softly, hoping in some way to diminish Alice's sombreness. 'We were so scared of becoming parents; we had no idea of what we were getting ourselves into. I don't think we've done such a bad job of it. Rosie's happy and healthy, isn't she?'

'You're a great dad.' Alice strokes her fingertips across the photo of us both holding onto Rosie. 'It was a difficult first year, and you helped me through it the most.'

'I tried my best. And it wasn't your fault Rosie was born premature, which I know is what you're thinking. She's as fit as fiddle — you'd never imagine, looking at her now, how poorly Rosie was back then.' I make a point of looking directly into Alice's eyes, in want of emphasising my next point. 'You're an amazing mum. It wasn't a straightforward first year, by any means, with your postnatal depression and that. But we got through it, didn't we? We got through it together.'

'Yeah...'

Alice suddenly slams the photo album shut, catching me off guard again, thus maximising my anxiety tremors.

'What's gotten into you?' I ask, no longer able to hide my frustration. 'Why are you acting like this?'

'It's nothing. You need to get ready, otherwise you'll be late for the pub. You wouldn't want that, would you?'

'I'm not meeting the lads until 7pm — it's only six o'clock.'

'You're gonna be late,' she states bitterly. Then Alice mutters under her breath, 'You always are, Tom. You're always late. You're always so unreliable.'

Before I can counter her claim, Alice throws the photo album onto our bed and then bolts off into the bathroom, slamming the door behind her. By rights I should be consoling my upset wife, but instead I do as I'm told; I get ready i.e. I put on my best "going out" shirt, spray a copious amount of cheap cologne across my double chin, and then slink off back downstairs to spend some more precious time with Rosie. I want to know what's bothering Alice, but I'm too scared to dig deeper into what's causing her uncharacteristic outburst. I'm such a coward. She could do so much better.

'Are you sure you're okay with me going out tonight?' I ask again, on placing a foot into our garden. 'I can always—'

'You need to set off now or you'll be late,' Alice says, turning away from me. 'Rose and I will be just fine. You go and have fun—and watch your drinks.'

'Okay. I Love you.' There's no answer, just like this morning. 'Love you!' Still no answer. 'I'll be back by midnight. See you later, yeah?'

As much as I'm ashamed to admit it, those feelings of guilt soon lift from me on envisioning the drunken escapades that lie ahead at the Tin Donkey pub. If I set off now, I'll be able to sup a few beers before the other lads arrive, and alcohol is what I'm in desperate need of now. I run back inside to kiss Rosie goodbye and then leave without further word to Alice. I know when my presence isn't wanted. That's how I cope with any confrontation: I pretend it doesn't exist.

The Tin Donkey pub is a fifteen-minute walk away from where Alice and I live. Halfway there, I plug a set of earphones into my android phone so that I can rev myself up with some good-old fashioned trance tunes. The first song I choose is *Toca's Miracle* by Fragma, because it reminds me of when I was in comprehensive school; of when I'd drink in a local farmer's field with my friends on a Friday night; of when I didn't need to worry about paying bills, marking papers, staying on top of my council tax, keeping my wife and child happy, maintaining a roof over my family's head amid an economic crisis, worrying about Brexit, and meeting my family's unrealistic expectations. What I'd give to relive just one hour from those golden days.

My friends are nowhere to be seen on entering the pub, so I nod politely to its landlord, Bazza, and swiftly approach his bar.

'What'll it be, Tom-boy?' he asks me, as I place myself upon a barstool before him. 'The usual?'

'Some super strength ale, please. That'll do me,' I say, licking at my lips. 'It's been a long week, Baz. I need a good session tonight.'

'Has been for me, too, pal.' Bazza starts pouring out my ale, which somehow lulls me into a hypnotic daze. 'That'll be four-fifty, and don't ask me to stick it on your tab. Yours exceeded its limit months ago. I don't do overdrafts, you know.'

Under normal circumstances, Bazza would have thrown a stronger insult at me by now. But he hasn't. If anything, he's being overly pleasant. I take the plunge and delve into his own emotional turmoil.

'What's up, Bazza-lad? You don't seem your usual, cheerful self.'

'The dog's not well,' he says. 'I don't know what's up with Percy, but he's been acting strange for a few days — pissing and shitting everywhere, he is.'

'Nice. You've put me right off having pets now.'

'Percy's not a pet to me; he's family. The poor mutt…'

Percy is Bazza's rottweiler and his most-effective tool in keeping order within the pub. Percy's a bouncer you'd never want to mess with — a slobbering, muscular, flatulent nightmare. You'll often find Percy lying beneath the pool table, and — if you're fortunate enough — he'll usually keep well out of your way, so long as you don't entice Bazza's displeasure, which itself isn't hard to manage.

'What do reckon's up with Percy?' I ask, scouring the pub for the dog's unmistakable presence. 'It's pretty weird not having him sniffing around my legs.'

'He's lying on my bed, upstairs.' Bazza shakes his head despairingly. 'I'd rather not talk about it, Tom. Here's your drink and change.'

I take the hint and collect my prize.

'No worries. Cheers, Bazza.'

I've just about finished my second pint by the time Amar shows up. He waves across to me, and in return I order his usual drink: a boring glass of pure orange juice. Amar adores being a Sikh, just not the part that involves him abstaining from alcohol.

'Hey, Tom,' he says, while sitting himself on a stool beside me. 'How're things going?'

'Not too bad,' I say, showing little evidence of this being a lie. 'Never mind me, Amar. Are you alright?'

'Better than I was this morning,' he sighs. 'I'm ready for a laugh with you and the other lads, put it that way.'

'Here's your drink, mate. Get it down you.'

I slide Amar's glass of orange juice across to him, almost knocking it over. For someone who's in the possible process of being investigated, sacked even, he seems so relaxed and joyful.

'What a day,' he groans and then laughs. 'I'm glad it's over.'

'Like I said before, you were the victim. Let justice take its course and stop stressing about it, mate.'

'Oh, I'm not stressing. Sharon made it perfectly clear that she's got my back. I do feel bad about how I reacted, though. Maybe I did overreact?' He shrugs at me. 'There's nothing I can do about it now, is there? Still, Sharon's in my corner…'

I wouldn't take Sharon's word for it. She always puts her career before personal attachments. And It doesn't matter if you've been a teacher at our school for six years, Amar, she'll soon throw you under the bus to keep her own reputation pure—that's what I want to say.

'The other lads shouldn't be long,' I note, looking back to the pub's entrance. 'Daz is never late, for one thing. He won't let us down.'

'The same can't be said for John, Ryan and Mikey, can it?' Amar chuckles, but I can tell he's still feeling down. 'It's crap how I can't drink booze, man. I could've really done with a few shots of vodka or gin after today's events.'

'I'm not surprised. Can you not just have a one on the sly?'

'No,' he says with a look of horror. 'I could never do that. I couldn't live with myself, mate.'

'I was only asking…'

Amar and I spend the next ten minutes whinging about how torturous our professional lives are, that is, until John and Ryan show up. They walk through the door like two outlaws from a wild west movie, or as if they're both suffering from acute constipation. It's hard to tell.

'Evening, lads!' John bellows, as he and Ryan rush across to the bar. 'The first round is on me!'

'Too late. We've already got a drink in,' I say, glancing down to my almost-empty pint glass. 'Mind, I would appreciate another beer if you're offering. I'll have a pint of super-strength, please. Anything below 7% ABV just tastes of dishwater.'

'I'll get the drinks in,' says Ryan. 'Mikey and Darren should have been here by now. Where are they?'

'They'll be on their way. Chillout,' I implore.

It's at this moment I realise there's been a change to the evening's schedule. Bazza's put up a new poster, stating a pub quiz will be taking place instead of the anticipated Open Mic session. 'Hold on. What's this about, Bazza?' I ask him. 'Why is there a pub quiz on tonight?'

'The PA system's blown up,' he explains, directing my vision across to the empty stage with a nod of his head. 'To be fair, I've had those speakers for twenty years. They were ready to blow. Anyway, I thought you lads enjoyed doing the odd quiz?'

'I hate quizzes,' says Amar. 'We never win, man. It's humiliating.'

'We might do tonight?' I say, looking to Bazza inquisitively. 'So, what's the grand prize? A trip to the Bahamas?'

'Beer tokens. Whoever wins will get five pints of premium beer for free. What's wrong, Tom-boy? Are you nervous that you're too thick to win?'

'Oh, we'll win. I'm good at history; Amar knows his economics; Mikey knows his sports; Darren knows his popular music, and Ryan's shit-hot on politics. John here's got to be good at something.'

'Cheeky bastard,' says John, glaring down at his pint of stout. 'I'm not stupid, and you've got some nerve—'

'We'll just have to wait and see, won't we?' says Bazza, before making off towards his next paying customer. He only tolerates our company for so long, which makes me wonder why I bother putting a quarter of my wages into his tills each month. 'It'll be a cold day in Hell when you boys win anything. If you lads do win, however unlikely that'll be, I'll even throw in a bottle of my finest Scotch. How about that?'

'It's on!' I exclaim. 'We'll show you!'

Just then, as I'm about to go into a rant against Bazza, Daz and Mikey stroll in. Daz could easily compete in a Mr. Universe competition, going off the muscles that are showing through his tight shirt. Mikey, on the other hand, looks like he's been dragged through a hedge backwards during a hailstorm while wearing a pair of ill-fitting speedos.

'Good evening, fellas. I see there's a quiz on tonight,' says Daz, as he and Mikey join our little clan. 'Have you signed us up for it?' he asks me.

'Yeah. We'll show Bazza just how smart we are.'

'Bollocks,' Bazza scoffs in response. 'I'd pay good money to see that happen.'

'That's not very hospitable of you,' says Daz, tutting to our gracious barman. 'We're your most-loyal regulars, aren't we? You should be rooting for us.'

'I would…if you all weren't so daft.'

I've set the bar now, pardon the pun. I've made us out to be perfect candidates for University Challenge, when we're more like the biggest collection of intellectual failures known to man — at least where common knowledge is concerned.

Me and the lads get our priorities right: we debate on what team name we should choose first.

'How about *Darren's Dazzlers*?' Daz suggests, to a unified look of disappointment from myself and our pals. 'Suite yourselves. Can you lads think of anything better?'

'Yeah,' says Amar. 'What about *The Aycliffe Academics*?'

An even stronger look of shared disappointment rises on our faces in response, and Amar lifts his hands up in defeat. 'I don't know. It's not easy to choose a decent name.'

'Ye dozy sods couldn't organise a piss-up in a brewery!' says Mikey in his broad Geordie accent, his interest now keenly held on a gambling machine nearby. 'Let me dee the thinking. Ah'm the smartest one here, by miles.'

Mikey's a sound guy, a gentle giant of sorts, and it is funny watching Amar — a Southerner — try to fathom out what he's saying at times. Nevertheless, Mikey has a serious gambling problem (slot machines being his speciality). The other lads and I have tried to intervene before, countless times, though it's just a wasted effort. As I'm addicted to alcohol, Mikey's addicted to throwing away his hard-earned cash on one-armed bandit machines and horse racing. Personally, I don't see the fascination with gambling. I'd rather spend my money on booze or cigarettes, seeing as they have a longer-lasting effect. I'm in no position to lecture him whatsoever, though, and can recognise a lost cause when I see one.

'Where are you off to?' Daz asks Mikey. 'The quiz is starting soon. We need all the help we can get.'

'Ah'm gonna let Bazza know what we've called oor group. Ah've got the porfect name for us,' he says in some fickle attempt to reassure us — a failed attempt, I might add.

'We've been drinking in this pub for twelve years, Mikey, and you've never once made a single profit from that machine,' says Daz, shaking his head to him in dismay. 'I'd dread to think how much money you've thrown into that thing — into Bazza's pockets.'

'Ah'll win the jackpot,' Mikey boasts, pounding a fist off his chest. 'Just ye watch me.'

Mikey proceeds to plough twenty quid into the bandit machine, and — as expected — sees no financial return from it. Then, like a kid who's just been scolded, he returns to our table and immediately downs what's left of his dry cider.

'Any luck, mate?' Daz asks him optimistically. 'Did you win the jackpot?

'Nah, it's a bloody fix! Ah was so close! One more nudge and ah'd have won fifty quid. It's a total fix, man.'

In a peculiar sense, I do get where Mikey is coming from — regarding the short-lived kick he gets from gambling. I have days where I feel some small element of happiness rise into my life only for it to slip away just as I clasp onto it, like a little kid who's been given a balloon just for it to slip out of their hands after a few minutes of pleasure. All you can do in that situation is watch your little bundle of joy float away, never to be seen again. That pretty much sums up my life.

'Evening, all!' says Bazza through his wireless microphone. 'I've got a special quiz lined up for you folks this evening. We have five teams participating: *Sheila's Angels*; *Brian's Brainy Bash*; *Millie's Marvels*; *The Aycliffe Argonauts*; and — last, but not least — *Team: Shower of Shite*.'

'Here — hold on!' Ryan seethes. 'Mikey, have you called our team the *Shower of Shite*?'

'Aye. Why not? It's an accurate reflection of oor intellect, don't ya think?' says Mikey, sniggering. 'Between us we've already supped fifteen pints, and that's including the fact Amar and Darren durn't drink. We've got nee chance of winning.'

'It's not exactly through choice that Darren and I don't drink, is it?' says Amar. 'Sikhs aren't allowed to touch alcohol, and Darren's got type-one diabetes.'

'Cheers for the reminder, Amar,' Daz interjects. He quickly slips out a small, black machine from one of his pockets — his blood monitoring device — proceeds to stab a small needle into one of his fingertips, then allows for a blood droplet to fall onto a thin piece of plastic attached to the machine. 'I haven't checked my blood sugars for a while. 18.3 m/mols. Shit, they're higher than I thought they'd be.' He retrieves an insulin pen from a separate pocket, attaching a needle to it within a matter of seconds. Unfortunately, all this commotion grabs the unwanted attention of some fellow patrons sitting opposite us. 'I'm not a junkie. Everything's legal here. No worries, yeah?' he says to them while thrusting the injection into his leg, infusing the life-sustaining insulin over five seconds. 'That should do the trick. I knew it was a bad idea drinking coke, but it tastes so good.'

'And ye have the nerve to have a go about me gambling,' says Mikey, pretending to be offended. 'That's all we need, ye gannin' into a diabetic coma during the quiz. John will have to help ye oot, should that happen.'

'Why?' says John, almost choking on his drink. 'What makes me so special?'

'Ye work in a care home,' Mikey points out. 'Ah'm not giving Darren the kiss of life — nee way!'

'Thanks a bunch, lads. I know who my true mates are,' he jokes, then winks across to me. 'Come on, lads. We need to prove Bazza wrong. I've got a good feeling that we'll win this quiz tonight.'

It's fair to say that Daz is the only member of our group who is holding onto any hope of this being a possibility. I, on the other hand, well, I'm just trying to hold off another random panic attack. I'm useless when around strangers. Daz must have clicked on that I'm starting to tremble again, seeing as he's giving me a look of concern, unlike the others.

'Are you alright, Tom?' he asks. 'Are your tremors playing up again?'

'Yeah. I need another drink.' More booze i.e. my quick-fix answer to everything. 'I'll be fine. The quiz will help take my mind off things.'

'Focus on your breaths and slow them down,' he says, also well-versed in my usual coping techniques. 'You'll be okay, mate. Focus on your breaths.'

'The beer's kicking in now, anyway. No worries.'

Three questions into the quiz and we're already scratching at our heads like mindless imbeciles. Each question has so far related to Brexit, a dismal topic my fellow companions and I try to diligently avoid. We've had three years of it, which is enough to make anyone go insane.

'This is bullshit, Bazza!' Ryan shouts at him, to some praise from several other patrons. 'Ask us a question about music or football — anything but Brexit. Jesus Christ…'

'Alright, alright. Don't be getting your knickers in a twist,' Bazza cackles. He then flicks through some more pages in his quiz book, grinning back to us sadistically. 'Here's a good question for you, Ryan: in the Bible, which unfortunate individual gets shot to death with darts after getting their head stuck in the bough of an oak tree? You've got ten seconds to answer.'

'You are having a laugh, aren't you?' Ryan despairs. 'How'd we go from Theresa May dancing, to some random bloke getting murdered in the Bible?'

'It's Absalom,' I whisper to him. 'Absalom's the answer.'

'You don't half know some pointless crap,' He sneers, the embarrassment forcing my anxiety to grow even stronger. John and Mikey also start to laugh, whereas Amar and Daz give me a mutual thumbs up. 'How'd you know that, anyway? You're not religious.'

'I've read the Bible from start to finish,' I say, shrugging unashamedly. 'Just write the answer down.'

'I was gonna go with Jesus,' Ryan adds.

'Jesus was crucified, you tit. I'm a Sikh and even I know that,' says Amar. 'We really do have no hope in winning.'

'Whatever, man.' Ryan throws the pen over to me and points at our answer sheet. 'It's your call, Tom-boy. We'll go with your answer.'

After an hour of contemplating my lack of general knowledge, and downing four more pints of super-strength ale, Bazza's quiz finally reaches its merciful end. It couldn't come soon enough, to be honest. I can barely see straight, let alone form a cohesive sentence.

'It gives me great pleasure to announce the winning team of tonight's quiz,' Bazza announces, ensuring not to make eye contact with me and my friends this time. A gentle hint, perhaps? *The Aycliffe Argonauts* came in with eighteen out of twenty questions. Congratulations, guys!'

'This is a bloody fix, just like his friggin' bandit machine,' says Mikey, scowling across the table towards our host. 'Yer wife is in the winning team, Bazza! Howay!'

'Coming in last, with just one correct answer, is the team we all had shared high expectations for — *Team: Shower of Shite*. Sorry, lads. Better luck next time.'

'Tosser,' Ryan remarks. 'This *is* a bloody fix. Mikey's right.'

'Seeing as I'm a kind-hearted soul, and the fact you fellas obviously tried so hard to win,' Bazza continues, attempting to come across as being sympathetic now, 'I'm going to give you a contingency prize consisting of one bag of high-quality, roasted peanuts. Who says I'm not generous?'

'Oh, yeah. We wouldn't dream of it,' says John in a sarcastic tone, slowly clapping his hands to Bazza. 'Thanks a bunch. A packet of manky, out-of-date peanuts is just what we need. Mikey will eat them all in one mouthful.'

'It was still a good laugh though, wasn't it?' says Daz, ever the optimist. 'I've had a good night, even if we didn't win the quiz. It's the taking part that counts.'

'Aye, it's been alreet,' says Mikey, who is now in the process of enjoying our contingency prize.

John and Ryan stand, both fumbling to retrieve their cigarette packets.

'We're off,' says John, clamping a cigarette between his teeth. 'Same again next week, boys?'

'Of course,' says Daz with a sharp glance to me. 'I'll give you a ride home, Tom. You're in no fit state to walk back alone.'

'I'm not tipsy. My legs are perfectly fine.' They're not, and instantly give way as soon as I try to stand. 'On seconds thoughts, I'd appreciate that offer.' I can always rely on Daz to keep me right, to act as my guardian angel. I better not throw up in his car again, though, like last time. Deep breaths, Tom. Sober up. 'Do me a favour and go easy on the speed bumps, mate. My stomach is a little tender.'

'I will. Your *stomach's a little tender* — I'm not surprised!' he says with a roll of his eyes. Daz isn't wrong, though. I've really gotten myself into a drunken mess. 'Focus on the breathing techniques you use against your anxiety. Who knows, they might even help sober you up?'

During the ride home I stick my head out of Daz's car window, taking in as much of the clear outdoor air as I can, trying to hold back the rising need to vomit. My tremors slowly subside, but I'm still on the verge of a full-scale panic attack. I don't know what's setting it off. Unnerving images of Alice giving me a look of disappointment keep flashing in my mind, which could be what is causing this sudden onset? I don't want her to be angry with me nor dampen Daz's good mood. I hate letting those closest to me down, but I always do. It's time to put on that happy-go-lucky face again, to pretend that everything's hunky-dory. Breathe, Tom-boy, breathe.

'Thanks for a great night,' I say to him. 'It's been a blinder —'

'You'll drink yourself blind. You're supping down the whisky a lot more now than you used to,' he says, clenching his fingers tightly around the steering wheel. 'There are different ways to tackle your problems, other than drinking to the point where you're at now. Honestly, if you want to get anything off your shoulders, please, talk to me.'

'I know fine well that I'm drinking too much, and I'm on the case to sort it out. Having the odd drink helps me to unwind,' I say, amid some acidic belches. 'Besides, I only drink socially.'

'The collection of empty lager cans in your recycling bin says otherwise,' he scoffs. 'I'm not trying to sound like a broken record, but—'

'I'm onto it—okay? Don't you worry about me, Daz. All's well.'

'Whatever you say, mate.' He looks over my slouching body, sighs, and then turns on his media player. 'How about some nice, relaxing music for the drive home? Amy Winehouse or Joy Division?'

'Joy Division.'

I manage to fend off the urge to pass out by focusing on the music, its slow beats and hypnotising chords. Music is a great tool to use against my anxiety and depression, seeing as it me helps to concentrate on more pleasant emotions, that is, depending on the song and association it has to certain people and events. But I can't exactly blare out some heavy metal on returning home, can I? So long as I stay quiet and don't wake up the girls, I'll be fine. I'm in no mood for another lecture from Alice. I'm not even in the mood to sleep. It's a perfect Catch-22. I'm too tired to sleep and too tired to stay awake. What I'd give to be in Daz's positive shoes. I bet he doesn't have the same problems.

'Have you ever considered attending one of those informal mental health groups?' he asks, as we pull up outside my house. 'There's a group that's just started up in town a few weeks ago, which is aimed more for men. I think it would be a good idea.'

'I went to the opening night, mate. But I was sitting beside blokes who had been abused as kids, and others who suffered with PTSD and drug problems. I have nothing to worry about in comparison to them. I've not been back since.'

Daz rives up the handbrake and looks to me in dismay. 'If you broke your arm, you'd go to a hospital to have it looked at—right?'

'Yeah, I wouldn't have a choice.'

'Now, imagine that your sitting beside someone who has also broken their arm. The breaks won't be in the same place, though, will they? And you wouldn't necessarily be able to tell how severe their injury is.'

'No, it'd be a pretty big coincidence—'

'That's beside the point,' he says. 'Because the other person has a broken arm—regardless of how severe in comparison to yours it may be—would you just get up and walk out of the hospital without getting any treatment?'

'No, that'd be daft. I'd be left with a knackered arm, for starters.'

'Right? So, in that case, why should you feel that your mental health issues aren't as important to tackle as anyone else's? If there's help being offered to you, then take it with open arms. I'd give that group another shot, if I were you.'

'I'll have a think about it.'

'Good,' he says, clasping his hands together as if in prayer. 'Don't be ashamed of your anxiety and depression, mate. You've got to fight them — tear down the stigma.'

'I will, Daz. I'll look into it tomorrow.'

An Explosive Development

As Tom willingly poisoned his bloodstream with alcohol,
Alice's became reluctantly swamped with adrenaline—a
cocktail of anxiety, guilt, frustration and resentment. It was
after midnight, and she was still waiting on her husband's
anticipated, albeit intoxicated, arrival. Tom had been late
before but never to this extent. Robbed of all patience now,
Alice checks the time on her phone, dreading what position
Tom will be in. He accidently smashed one of her favourite
ornaments the week prior, due to his drunken state, so what
would it be this time? She's beyond caring anymore. Tom's
drunken shenanigans have become too much of a nuisance
for her, this weekly game of guessing how inebriated he'll
be. Enough is enough.

'Where is he?' she frets, hugging into her bedsheets to seek
some minor comfort. 'I hope nothing bad has happened.
This is getting beyond a joke.'

Alice reminds herself that Darren will ensure Tom's safe
journey home, but the thought of him getting into a fight or

passing out on some street corner — which are the likeliest outcomes — still eat away at her. Paranoia creeps in and only the worst-case scenarios become viable, even to the extent of Tom going home with another woman. He wouldn't do that, though, would he?

Alice screams into her pillow, 'He's so selfish! Why say you'll be back by midnight when you know fine well you won't be? It's 2 am! And it'll be me getting up at the crack of dawn with Rose, as per usual. Tom can sleep on the couch. At least I won't have to put up with his snoring then.'

Just as Alice falls into a pleasant realm of subconsciousness, an almighty bang shakes the entire house. After checking on her daughter's wellbeing, in finding Rose to be safe and still asleep, Alice runs down the stairs and into the kitchen, where she is met with a truly horrifying sight.

'What the hell have you done?' she says to Tom, paralysed with shock. 'What-have-you-done?'

Tom is lain face-down on the kitchen floor, seemingly oblivious to what chaos has taken place. All around him are splashes of crimson that litter the walls and other surfaces, and a strong odour of burnt plastic lingers in the air. Alice notices that their microwave is missing its door, and within it lies the mangled remains of a tomato soup tin. Tom looks like he's been shot; it certainly appears that way from the pools of scarlet substance surrounding him.

'Wake up!' she screams, half-heartedly kicking at his legs. 'Get up!'

Tom can hear Alice's heavy pants and sense her standing over him, waiting for a response, but also knows that he's in for a scolding, so choses to stay still and quiet. He's praying that, like a bad dream, Alice will eventually go away, and that she may hopefully forgive him in the morning—possibly seeing the funny side of his unintentional mishap. Tom is gravely mistaken, however.

'What have you done to our kitchen?' Alice seethes, scouring the scene of devastation. 'It's like a bomb has gone off in here.'

'I was a little peckish,' he replies, talking directly into the laminate flooring. 'I fancied some soup to help sober me up.'

'You nearly blew yourself up! Look at the mess you've made,' she says, sobbing now. 'You're so selfish, Tom. I thought you'd been shot! And it's a bloody miracle Rose hasn't woken up!'

'I'm fine, man. Rosie's fine.' Tom goes to stand but immediately falls back to his knees. 'Hey, what a night I had with the lad's—'

'I couldn't give a toss about what you got up to down the pub, and you're anything but fine.' Alice forces her hands against her face to wipe away the tears, desperate to conceal her despair. There are no questions left in her mind now, only actions. 'This is it. This is it, Tom. I can't take this anymore.'

'What do you mean?' he whispers, lifting his head to face Alice's wrath head-on. 'What's wrong?'

'We need a break,' she says. 'We need some time to think things over. I can't live like this, Tom, and neither can Rose. You've driven me to this…'

Alice's declaration, to Tom especially, feels like she is turning her back on all the years of love and devotion they have shared together—all their hardships and achievements.

But deep down, Tom also knows that Alice has every right to feel this way.

'Are you leaving me?' he gulps, attempting to come across as naïve. 'Am I really that bad?'

'I don't want to leave you, but you've left me with no other choice,' she implores. 'I've put up with your mood swings and drinking for long enough. Rose and I will stay with my parents until you get better. You need help—serious help. You need to see your doctor again. You need to sort out your life, Tom. I've done everything possible to help you, but I just can't cope anymore.'

'You don't mean that. You don't really want to leave me, do you?' he pleads. Tom's thoughts swiftly turn to Rosie, his daughter, his only child, the one thing in his life worth living for. He then thinks back to his own parents and their separation, and all the pain that terrible period caused. He can't let Rosie go through the same, horrific, disorientating experience. He can't be a "Weekend Dad", like his was. 'Please don't take her from me, Alice. I'm begging you. I'll change! Please don't take Rosie from me!'

'It's not all about you, Tom. You've said you'll change a hundred times before, and nothing's ever come from it. I need some time to think things over. Give it a couple of weeks, then see where we're at.'

'No—please! I don't want you to go,' he whimpers.

'I'm sorry, Tom. I really am sorry, but there's no other way.'

Before Tom can muster the strength required to stand himself, Alice makes her way back upstairs, where she hastily packs some essential belongings into two suitcases, grabs little Rose from her bed, solemnly contemplating what unthinkable act it is that she is doing now all the while. Tears of sadness, grief and remorse stream down her face throughout this ordeal, though she keeps telling herself that only one path lies ahead of her now, and it's a path Tom can no longer walk along. Not with her. Not anymore.

'I'll change!' he pleads, emphasising his point by throwing himself before Alice as if she were some divine deity. 'I mean it. Whatever you want me to do, I'll do it. You're all I have.'

Looking down at her husband and his display of desperation, as he grovels pitifully like a begging dog, is anything but a pleasant sight for Alice. Tom appears so vulnerable and pathetic, almost reversing her decision for a moment or two. However, a drastic change needs to be made within their fractured household, she reasons. This break could be the action needed in saving their marriage or could destroy it. In sincere reluctance, Alice accepts the gamble she is making. Afterall, she must think of Rose's wellbeing and future even more so than her own.

'I don't know what else to say, Tom. This is the last thing I want—'

'Tell me what I need to do, to make things right,' he whines. 'I can't bear to lose you.'

'Prove to me that you can change,' she says with some hope in her voice. 'Show me. Otherwise, your words mean nothing. You've broken too many promises, Tom.'

'Tell me what to do!'

'I don't know—I can't think! Things aren't that simple.'

Tom reaches out a hand to hold onto Alice's, but she quickly brushes it aside—out of fear, perhaps, that her mind can somehow be dissuaded. You can't teach an old dog new tricks, she tells herself.

'I'll prove it to you, Alice. I swear it. I'll make things up to you.'

'I'm going, Tom, and I'm taking Rose with me. It's too late,' says Alice, sobbing into her hands. 'I never wanted any of this. I love—' She cuts herself off, unwilling to finish her statement. 'I'm going.'

'You still love me, don't you? Go on—say it. I know you still love me.'

'No. I fell in love with the man who always smiled and made cheesy jokes, not the drunken, selfish idiot who is kneeling in front of me now.'

Alice flings open the kitchen door, places Rose into her coat, collects their suitcases, and then peers out into the cold night's sky, utterly lost in contemplation. During the upheaval, Rose wakes up and becomes frightened over what is taking place. The last image Tom has of his daughter is that of her screaming for him—for her daddy—her outstretched hands directed against his knelt position, her cries utterly harrowing.

'My daddy!' Rose screams with a blood-curdling wail. Alice attempts to console the child by stroking at her hair, but it does little to help alleviate the distress being caused. 'Daddy! My Daddy!'

'Don't go!' Tom screams, now crawling along the floor after his wife and child. Despite being unable to fully control his limbs, he manages to stand himself but falls again onto his knees and then straight into a pool of cold, congealing soup. The humiliation. The stark reality of what is happening. It is just too much for him to take in. Anxiety rears its head again, completely rendering Tom. His body convulses from the sorrow and fear, his thoughts blurring into one, overwhelmed by the primal instinct to not lose his daughter. 'Rosie! Alice, please come back! I'll change! Don't go!'

Rose's screams echo in Tom's thoughts as Alice reverses her car out of the driveway. He'd anticipated the pain of succumbing to a hangover in the morning, but nothing on this scale. He wraps his body into a recovery position, reeling from the electrical surges coursing through his extremities, dwelling on how he has come to lose those closest to him. Tom has reached a monumental low point and there doesn't seem any way of escaping from it.

'I will change,' he says, attempting to convince himself. 'I can't lose them. What have I done?'

Without Alice and Rose the house feels so empty now, lifeless, and devoid of any joy. It rapidly turns into a prison for Tom; a place where he can focus on all his negative emotions and wrongdoings without the positive influence of his family to counteract then. The silence is excruciating. The lack of his wife and daughter's presences tormenting beyond any comprehension.

Tom's first action, once he manages to stand again, is to open a bottle of whisky that Alice bought for his birthday. She told him to keep it for a special occasion, which he deems this evening to be.

'Alcohol got me into this mess,' he contemplates, uncorking the bottle with some level of resentment. 'I want these feelings to go away. God, I hate myself.' Tom thrusts the bottle towards his mouth without hesitation. The whisky scorches at his throat on impact, but the discomfort is nothing compared to the agony and mental anguish he now feels. 'That's better. This'll all go away in the morning. Alice will come back. Alice would never leave me. She needs me, and I need her. We're soulmates. Nothing can tear us apart.'

To Tom's dismay, however, the over-proof whisky does little to alleviate his worsening anxiety tremors and depressive thoughts; his fingertips go into cramp, meaning that he is also at the forefront of another full-blown panic attack. He places the whisky bottle onto a nearby worksurface, concerned that he might drop it and therefore smash this valuable asset at any given moment — this quick-fix cure to his ailments. Along with losing his family, that would be a scenario Tom could simply not allow.

The anxiety cramps in Tom's fingertips soon spread to his forearms and up through his shoulders to the back of his neck. It is like being crushed between two concrete walls, with nowhere to run or hide. In desperation, he seeks out other form of comfort, given that his breathing techniques are proving futile and the additional alcohol in his system has not yet kicked in: the untainted companionship his best friend can offer. Tom fights hard to regain control, to use his mobile phone, and is quickly running out of options.

'Daz — he'll know what to do!' Against the crippling cramps in his hands, Tom manages to activate a call between himself and Darren. 'Answer your phone, Daz. Come on, mate. Pick up!'

'Are you missing me already, Tom?' Darren asks in a humorous tone, apparently unphased by his friend's early-morning phone call. 'You're ruining my beauty sleep, you know.'

'She's —' Tom hesitates to answer, almost breaking down again. 'She's gone, Daz.'

'Who's gone? What are you going on about?'

'Alice is gone, and she's taken Rosie with her. They've left me. They've finally left me.'

Darren's Staffordshire Bullterrier, Tyson, barks in the background, signalling for his wife, Michelle, to respond.

'Are you taking the piss?' she asks Tom, clearly upset. 'It's 3am in the morning! What the hell?'

'Sorry,' Tom says guiltily in response. 'I didn't know who else to turn to.'

'Don't you worry about it,' says Darren. 'It's not the end of the world. Get some sleep — that's what you need right now. I'll come over in the morning to see how you're doing, okay? You're in no fit state to be thinking about things, Tom.'

'What am I going to do?' he asks, sniffling. 'What am I going to do, Daz? I knew this would happen...'

'Get some rest and maybe a glass of water. I'll come over tomorrow to help work things out. Don't you worry.'

Tom ends the call, his painful tremors now taking full precedence. He despises bearing his vulnerability to anyone else but himself, though here he is dragging Darren into this nightmare of his. On taking Darren's advice, Tom throws himself upon the sofa, clenches his eyelids together, then spends the next two hours sobbing into his hands. He eventually falls into a restless sleep, confined to his troubled thoughts and held in the uncertainty of his family's future. Nevertheless, Tom knows that Darren would never desert him, for he bears an innate gift to always see the glass as being half-full, a gift Tom could only ever dream of possessing.

Flashback: March 14th, 2008

There's only ten minutes to go, and my arse is still puckering like a camel's during a sandstorm. I'm sweating buckets. I feel sick. I want to go home. But we've rehearsed non-stop for six months — I've got no reason at all to be this anxious. Maybe it's because Alice couldn't make it? Nevertheless, I'm dreading how this first "official" gig will go down.

Daz is tuning his bass up like he hasn't got a care in the world. God, I wish I could be as laidback. I'm playing lead guitar which means, other than our singer, I'm going to be centre stage — the focus of our audience's judgemental opinions. In greater hindsight, I should have taken the keyboarder's role, because that way I'd be stuck at the back of this stage, out of sight and mind. I'm a focal point of attention, which is a dangerous position to be in if you suffer with anxiety… like I do.

'This is it,' says Carrie, our band's manager and lead singer. 'Tonight's performance will either make or break us. No pressure, chaps.'

'Oh, yeah!' says Daz, completely unphased by the so-called pressure. 'It's only some grubby working men's club in Barnsley. Half of the punters are already drunk, and it's not even 8pm. So long as we play *Summer of 69* and *Don't Stop Believing,* we've got nothing to worry about. Chill out. Relax. Buy yourself a rum and coke or something.'

'There's a representative from our agency watching us tonight,' she tells him. 'This has got to be a killer performance. We can't afford to make any mistakes.'

'Relax,' he iterates, smiling across to me casually. 'We're the best of the best. Stay positive. The audience are going to love us. Trust me, guys.'

I can never understand Daz's optimistic outlook on life, mostly because all I do is dwell on what can go wrong. After all, the possibilities are endless: Carrie might forget the lyrics; the drummer might lose his sticks; the keyboarder might choose a wrong sound; I might play several buff notes or snap a string—I'm dreading that the most. There's so much that could go wrong.

The first forty-five minutes thankfully go ahead without a single hitch. We have the audience eating out of our hands and begging for more, much to the appraisal of Barry, our agent's overpaid and snobbish representative. From first setting eyes on the man I felt an instant disliking to him, and my gut instinct isn't often wrong. It's not looking good, not by any means.

'We're gonna finish off with *I Don't Want to Miss a Thing* by Aerosmith,' says Carrie through the microphone, immersing our audience into a greater state of anticipation. 'Are you up to it, Tom? It's your biggest solo.'

'Yeah, thanks for the reminder.' I know what Carrie is hinting at and why she looks so concerned. This song entails me playing an epic six-minute guitar solo at its end, thus landing the onus on me to impress Barry the most. If we are going to leave our audience and agency's rep wanting more, this is going to be the defining moment. 'Let's do this!' I say, feigning some enthusiasm. 'Let's show them what we're made of!'

The finale proceeds as such: Carrie's vocal performance is outstanding; Darren's bass lines are tight and beautifully constructed; Dom the keyboarder doesn't make a single mistake, and our drummer manages to stay in-time. Ultimately, though, it comes down to me to leave a lasting impression. But just as I begin to perform the first arpeggio in my death-defying solo, the b string on my guitar snaps. The world around me, just like my epic performance, then also collapses. My dreams of being a revered guitarist, such as the likes of Randy Rhodes or Jimi Hendrix, have been cruelly poured down the drain. I try my hardest to recover, but the damage has been done. If looks could kill, Carrie's cold-killer stare would have me slaughtered within an instant.

'What was all that about, Tom?' she snarls at me, as we bow to our baying audience. 'I told you to put new strings on before we started. We're never going to get hired again after this!'

'I'm sorry,' I say, genuinely gutted that my unfortunate mishap may somehow ruin our chances of making it big in the clubland scene. 'It wasn't my fault.'

'No, it wasn't,' says Daz, holding out a hand to grasp onto my guitar. 'I'll sort it for you, mate.' He proceeds to restring my guitar in record time, handing it back to me with a sympathetic and endearing smile. 'Shit happens, Tom-boy. It's not your fault you lost a string. We still sounded amazing, and who cares what the agency rep thinks? The audience loved us, and it's been a great gig. We should be proud of ourselves. You should be proud of yourself.'

'Cheers,' I say, feeling some relief from his words. 'Thanks, Daz.'

If only problems in life could be solved as easily as replacing a broken guitar string. If only I could repair the severed bond between myself and Alice with such ease. I'd give anything for that. I'd sell my soul to the devil, even though I don't believe in one anymore. I've made a habit of letting people down over the years, that's the thing. Alcohol became my go-to remedy, just as it was for my dad. I hated Dad when he got drunk, but I've just become a sordid reflection of him. It's funny how things go, they say. At least I've got Daz to keep me right.

A Friendly Intervention

I can't imagine a world where Tom and Alice aren't together; it just seems so foreign and wrong to me. The greatest issue with Tom, my best mate, is that he tends to look on the bleaker side of things — his glass is always half-empty. In fairness, Tom's been like that for as long as I've known him, and he's actually a sound guy. I miss those carefree days when we were in the band together. But life moves on, whether you like it or not. I can accept that, and only wish that Tom could do the same. He's not a bad guy. He's not.

Michelle's still fuming about being woken up at 3am by my drunken comrade. So, in wake of my wife's current low mood, I make a keen effort to prepare a breakfast in bed for her, hoping to somehow break the ice that's formed between us: two slices of wholemeal toast (slightly buttered) with four poached eggs that are nice and runny — just the way she likes them. I accompany this culinary masterpiece with a strong helping of espresso coffee and make one for myself.

There's no point in going along with Michelle's silent treatment. You've got to face your issues head-on, I say, otherwise things just only worse and harder to resolve. That's how I roll. Life's too short to play such stupid games.

The main issue I'm facing now, other than Michelle's stone-cold reception, is my unpredictable blood sugar levels. I forgot to take my insulin on waking up. It can wait, though. I want to see my wife smiling again—that's medicine itself.

'What's this in aid of?' Michelle asks, looking me up and down with her arms folded. 'It's not like you to go through so much effort.'

'Nonsense. I've made you breakfast in bed, like any other devoted husband would,' I say, wholly determined to put this cold reception to rest. 'I just want to see that gorgeous smile of yours again.'

'You're such a charmer, Darren.' She kisses me on the cheek and wastes no time in drinking some of the coffee I made for her. 'Thanks, babe.'

I turn to my trusty canine, Tyson, who's taking up most of our bed. I imagine him winking back at me, if only to make this cringey effort to satisfy Michelle worthwhile.

'Don't be mad with Tom,' I say to her. 'Something seriously bad must have happened between him and Alice for them to break up.'

'They've broken up?' she gasps, almost dropping her cup of boiling-hot coffee onto me. 'Is that why Tom phoned you last night?'

'Yeah. I'm gonna meet up with him this morning to see what's happened. That is, of course, if he answers the door. There's no point in phoning him.' I look across to my digital clock. 'Shit, it's seven-thirty! I'm meant to be meeting the lads for our fishing trip in Whitby at ten o'clock.' That's when a marvellous idea kicks in, a cunning plan of sorts. 'I might take Tom along today. It'll do him some good to get out of town for a while. He'll only sit in the house drinking and smoking himself to death...'

'I doubt he'll be in a decent state to go on a boat,' she says, tutting. 'Given how drunk Tom usually gets, I can't imagine him making it through the car journey let alone anything else.'

'We'll see. I think it's a good plan, anyway.'

'You know, now I come to think of it, you could be right. While you take Tom on your fishing trip, I can catch up with Alice...find out her version of events.'

'If we can't help them to get over their issues, no one can. I better get ready on that note. The thought of driving through Middlesbrough during rush hour isn't worth thinking of.'

The bedroom door slowly creeps open. Nathan, our ten-year-old son, then pops his head around it. 'Hi, Dad. Hi, Mum.'

'You're up early,' I say, raising an eyebrow to him. 'It's Saturday, Nath. Are you not having a lie-in?'

'I would have, but you and Mum woke me up,' he groans. 'What time are you dropping me off at Gran and Grandpa's house?' he asks Michelle.

'About half-past eight,' I reply. 'I'm taking your Uncle Tom on a fishing trip today.' It's fitting I refer to Tom in this way. He is like a brother to me and is Nathan's godfather, after all. 'I've left a bowl of cereal out for you. Be a good lad and get dressed—no mucking about. And don't forget to brush your teeth.'

'Okay, Dad.' Nathan disappears, leaving but the sound of his footsteps going down the stairs.

'Are you alright, hun?' Michelle asks me, clenching her hands around mine. 'You look dreadful. Have you checked your sugar level yet?'

My insulin! Where did I leave it? Even without testing my sugar levels, I can tell that I'm heading towards a hyper episode.

'No...'

'Where's it at?' Michelle's eyes widen, her expression filling with dread. 'You know how high your levels get first thing on a morning. Why haven't you checked them?'

'I wanted to make you breakfast in bed.' My vision's going blurry now. But I'll get through this. I always do.

'For goodness sake, where's your insulin?' she asks more assertively. 'You're unreal, Darren.'

Our bedroom starts spinning around, and I can feel every cold droplet of sweat trickling down my brow, then an unfamiliar feeling of anger rises from the pit of my stomach. Yep, it's going to be a hyper episode. My sugar levels are definitely high. Where did I leave my rapid-insulin pen?

I manage to whisper to her faintly, 'On top of the fridge, I think. I need the rapid mix.'

Michelle calls out to Nathan for his aid. 'Hurry up, Nathan! Bring your dad's orange insulin pen!'

'Coming, Mum!' he replies, soon flying back up the stairwell with my medication.

Despite my blurred vision, I somehow correctly fit the needle into its rightful place, adjust the dosage settings, and then stab it into my upper-right leg as fast as possible. I then fall back onto my bed, landing beside Michelle who holds onto to me as if I'm in my dying moments. I'll be okay. This has happened countless times before. It doesn't bother me so much, but I hate how my condition worries Michelle and Nathan.

'You daft sod,' she says, stroking at my hair. 'You had me scared there for a moment. How are you feeling now? Do you still feel giddy?'

'I'm okay,' I lie. 'I'm feeling better already. It's good stuff, that rapid-insulin.'

Ten minutes down the line, I begin to feel more my usual self. Time's moving on, and so should I. If this fishing trip's going ahead as planned, I've got to make a move right now.

'I'm going to stay overnight in Aunt Edith's cottage,' I say. 'It'll give me a chance to help Tom get out of shell, having a bit of time alone with him.' I prick my finger and wait for the results to show on my screen. 19.4 m/mols. It's not too bad and could have been a whole lot worse.

'Are you sure?' she asks. 'Your Aunt Edith's a stickler for keeping the place tidy, and Tom...'

'Whatever mess he makes, I'll clean it up.' To clarify, Aunt Edith owns a holiday cottage in Whitby that looks out onto the harbour — her pride and joy — and will be my death sentence, should it become tarnished. She gave me a spare key a few months back because I often go fishing in Whitby, and on the premise that I would help maintain its pristine condition. I could have my hands full where Tom's concerned, though, especially after he's had a skinful. 'Are you alright with that?'

'Yeah,' she says with a passive shrug. 'If it'll help Tom, then I'm all for it.'

I knew Michelle would understand. She has a fiery temper but also a heart of gold. I'm not sure how Tom is going to react when I inform him that he's coming along with me today. I won't give him a choice. Hangover or not, he's coming. We've got to put a stop to his anxiety and depression.

'Take care, and don't forget to take your insulin kit,' says Michelle, keenly aware of my poor short-term memory. 'Please be careful, Darren. And text me, so that I know you're both okay.'

'I will.' I get the slight inkling that Michelle's not entirely pleased about this endeavour Tom and I are about to undertake, but it must be done. 'We'll be on our best behaviour. No worries, yeah.'

'Just…be careful.'

After giving Michelle and Nathan a fond farewell, I'm soon in my battered old car and driving out of our council estate to where Tom lives. He's done well for himself, has Tom. His house is situated right in the centre of town—a four bedroomed, semi-detached palace. I'd never be able to afford such a home, at least not on the wages I receive from working as a cleaner down the local chemicals plant. Still, a job's a job. It's better than being on the dole, which I've had the misfortune of being on before. I make enough money to keep my family out of poverty, which is far luckier than some. I appreciate my humble earnings, and there's no purpose on dwelling over what could and should be. If I did, I'd probably end up in the same predicament Tom's in—constantly miserable.

I pull onto Tom's driveway only to come across a dire vision.

'What the...?' The window centred within his kitchen door is covered in some sort of red substance, which looks disturbingly like blood. 'What has Alice done?!' I immediately sprint from my car towards Tom's home and feel invincible like Jean-Claude as I kick it open. In hindsight, I should have maybe checked to see if it was locked first, seeing as it wasn't. Regardless of the loud disturbance I've made, there doesn't seem to be any sign of life as I enter, just the remnants of what appears to be an exploded can of tomato soup. 'There's never a dull moment with you, is there, Tom-boy?'

With the smell of stale tomato set aside, a strong waft of alcohol hits my senses as I walk into the dining room. There—lying face down in front of the TV set, like a lifeless cadaver—I discover Tom. I assume he continued partying after being dropped off by myself last night, given that there are several empty cans of lager scattered around him. I gently kick at his feet to wake him up, then a little harder after this effort fails.

'Who's there?' he slurs. 'Alice?'

'It's the Bogey Man,' I reply, kicking at his feet again. 'It's Daz, ya pillock. Who else is it going to be?'

'Hello, mate. How'd you get in?' he says, slowly rolling over to face me.

'You forgot to lock the door. I might've just slightly knocked it off its hinges, by the way.'

'Oh,' he laughs. 'What're you doing here?'

'I promised that I'd come over. Remember?'

'No.' Tom's head flops back as he moves himself into a cross-legged seating position, barely able to support himself under the alcohol still flowing through his system. 'Alice left me. I can remember that much.'

'I know,' I say. 'That's why I'm here, mate. What happened?'

Tom looks into my eyes and then swiftly removes them. 'It's all my fault, Daz. I don't blame Alice for leaving me. I mean, who'd want to be married to a failure, an alcoholic, a pain in the arse, like me?'

'Don't be saying things like that. Besides, me and you are going to have a look out together today, and it'll be just the two of us. I'm taking you to Whitby for some fresh air.'

'Why?' he bleats. 'What's so special about Whitby? The seagulls there are vicious, man. I'd rather just stay here, well out of harm's way.'

'I'd already planned to go fishing this weekend. It'll do you some good to come along, to get out of Aycliffe. We can stay at my aunt's cottage tonight as well. Free digs.'

'No offense, but I think I'll pass on that offer,' he grumbles, slumping back onto his side. 'I'll find something meaningful to occupy myself with here.'

'No, you won't. You'll only sit where you are now, mulling over things all weekend, probably getting drunk out of your skull. Me and you are going to have a lads' weekend away, whether you're up for it or not. It's just what the doctor ordered, Tom. Trust me.'

'Don't talk to me about doctors,' he simpers. 'I've seen plenty of those over the years, and just look at where that got me.'

'You've got ten minutes to get ready,' I say. 'Come on — shift! Get yourself sorted, down a couple of paracetamol tablets, and then we'll head off. No ifs or buts, my friend. It's now or never.'

Like a stubborn toddler who's unwilling to move, Tom painstakingly stands and then makes his way to his bathroom. Ten minutes turn into thirty, but I remain patient and positive. He's going through an ordeal I'd dread to contemplate. I'd hate to think what he's going through, both mentally and physically.

On Tom's eventual return, I quickly usher him to my car. We both then sit in silence within the confined space for a few minutes, imagining what the other is thinking, before I make the move to set off on our little venture. God, I hope this plan works.

'Have a look through my CD's, mate. I think there's a Stone Roses compilation in the glove compartment,' I say, guiding a finger to show him where he needs to look. 'Put whatever you like on, just not Michelle's Justin Bieber album.'

'I haven't got a change of clothes,' he says, waving a hand over his beer-soaked shirt. 'I'm still wearing the same top from last night. I stink.'

'Don't you worry about that. There are plenty of shops in Whitby that sell t-shirts. I'll even treat you to one.'

Tom makes a retching noise, hardly a good omen. 'All I can taste is vodka…'

'Ryan bought you a vodka chaser before we set off home.'

'The bastard. He knows I can't handle that stuff. My head's killing…'

'The sea air will soon sort out your headache,' I implore. 'You can't beat the great outdoors; the fresh sea breeze; the excitement of reeling in a fish —'

'I've never been fishing before, though. Knowing my luck, I'll probably fall overboard.'

'Don't be daft. There's no chance whatsoever of that happening.' Tom's looking at me now like a rabbit caught in some headlights. 'You can swim, yeah?'

'Maybe, but—'

'Then relax. It'll be something different for you and might even be fun.' In all the years I've known Tom, I've never seen him look so down and worn-out. His hands are shaking like mad, and his skin's deathly white. Never mind saving his marriage, my sole concern now is to prevent him from meeting an early demise. It's starting to look that way. 'There are some strong mints in the glove compartment. Treat yourself to a few.'

Tom pops two sweets into his mouth and then fondles the dials on my CD player. 'How do you turn this thing on? Christ, it's like sitting in a plane's cockpit.'

'It's that button, there, mate.'

'Which one?'

'That one! I'm pointing straight at it.'

'This one?'

I don't know how he managed it, but Tom's only gone and broken the CD player, leaving us with no other choice but to listen to a popular music station. He's still held in an alcohol-induced daze, making any attempt to converse with him nigh impossible.

'I can't stand this pop crap,' he bleats.

'It's Lewis Capaldi, isn't it?' I ask, discreetly checking on my friend's current wellbeing. 'He's a great singer. I was thinking of taking Michelle to one of his gigs.'

Tom just about manages to respond without retching. 'Is he that Scottish bloke? Alice likes him.'

Now that he's brought Alice into our conversation, perhaps Tom will divulge into what has taken place between them.

'What exactly happened last night?' I ask him. 'Did Alice explain why she's left you?'

'I'm not sure,' he says, rubbing at his sore eyes. 'She didn't give a specific reason for leaving me. I almost set the house on fire trying to heat up some soup — could be that? I'm so stupid, Daz. It's all my fault.'

'Accidents happen. Stop putting yourself down so much, mate.' I know there's more to this than he's letting on. 'You and Alice have been together since school. I don't think she'll leave you for good, and over nothing.'

'She's hinted at doing it before,' he says, cupping his head into his hands. 'Alice means it this time. I've done nothing but disappoint her. I've taken out my depression on those closest to me, when all they were trying to do was help. I don't blame Alice at all for what she's done; it's the fact she took Rosie that hurts the most. I'm so used to seeing her little smile every morning. Today was the first time I woke up without Rosie being there.'

'Alice just needs some time to think things over. I can't imagine how hard it must be for you, in not having Rosie around. This is just a small blip in the road, mate.'

'A *small blip*?' he snaps. 'How's losing my family a small blip?'

'It's not going to be permanent, that's what I mean. You'll see.'

'I hope so.' Tom rests his head against the window, immersed in self-pity. 'I'm actually looking forward to this look out today now. It'll take my mind off what's going on.'

'Then let's get to it. Our boat's setting off at 10am.' I look across, staring into Tom's bloodshot eyes. 'It's up to you if you want to come or not. I can always turn the car around.'

'No,' he says, forming half a smile. 'I'll need to get some cash out, mind. It's only right to give you some petrol money.'

'You don't need to give me any cash,' I say, somewhat perplexing him. 'I'll explain more when we get to Whitby. I was going to tell you last night but thought it unwise to reveal anything around Mikey, given he already owes me two-hundred quid.'

'Have you come into some disposable income?' Tom asks with a look of surprise. 'Have you won the lottery or something?'

'Not far off it. Maybe get some shut eye for now, yeah? Fishing can be hard work. You're gonna be stiff by the end of the day—and not in a good way.'

'I feel stiff now,' he humours, stretching out his aching limbs. 'Thanks for this, Daz. You're a true friend.'

'Try to relax and clear your mind,' I say. 'That's the whole point of this trip today… to switch off.'

'That's easier said than done, isn't it?' Tom continues to stare out his window. 'I wonder what Rosie's up to now. Do you reckon she's missing me?'

'Of course, she is. How about we buy Rosie a present in Whitby, so that you can give her something nice when you next see her,' I say optimistically, though in truth I'm mulling over when their next encounter will be. After all,

Alice is a woman of her word and rarely goes back on decisions she makes. 'There's a nice fudge shop down by the harbour. Rosie has a sweet tooth, doesn't she?'

'Just like her dad,' he sighs. 'I miss her so much, mate. It's killing me, is this.'

'You'll see her again soon. Keep telling yourself that, pal.'

I turn the radio up and roll down my window. The car's starting to smell of stale tobacco from Tom, but he's a mate — my best mate — and I'm more than happy to accommodate him. This plan of mine better work. I've got to remove Tom from his present environment, where he's surrounded by painful reminders of Alice and Rosie's absence and the temptation alcohol has to offer.

Ultimately, though, I've got to change his venomous mindset — this constant state of anxiety and depression he's trapped in. It won't be easy, but I'm determined — desperate even — to see this through. Tom needs to know that someone does care about him, and that he can overcome his problems. Together, Tom and I will break through these bad habits of his, and hopefully work out what the triggers are to his anxious/depressive thoughts. I'm ready for the challenge, but is Tom? This isn't going to be easy.

Breaking the Habit

Held in the Depths

Thinking back to my childhood days is another coping strategy I use, likely because there are fewer negative emotions attached to them. I was so innocent and naïve, so full of hope and joy, unlike now. Back then, all I had to worry about was when I'd be getting my next chocolate fix and finding rare Pokémon cards. They were far simpler times; they were better times.

One of my earliest memories was when Gran and Grandad took me on holiday to Whitby, just before my sister was born. Daz is taking me there now, and I'm not sure how I really feel about it. I'm a little apprehensive, seeing as I've never been on a fishing boat before, and given the high chance that I'm going to experience another anxiety attack at some point today, but there's not much surprise there. I've got to stay positive. I've got to be like Daz.

The drive to Whitby is nothing short of horrendous. As we pass through Middlesbrough, with its endless sea of chemical factories and traffic jams, a knotting sensation in my stomach becomes more agonising by the second. Just as I start to think the worst is over, we reach the North Yorkshire Moors, where a series of dips in the road add strength to my nausea and self-inflicted migraine. With that being said, the natural scenery is stunning, and I welcome the cleaner air like an old friend.

'We're here!' Daz exclaims on parking his car in front of Aunt Edith's cottage. 'How's your head? I thought you were going to be sick a couple of times back there.'

'It's pounding,' I say, clenching onto my stomach and then at my face. 'I've only got blame myself to blame, haven't I? I'll be fine.'

'Are you sure? We can always give the fishing trip a miss...'

The offer is tempting, but Daz has gone out of his way to bring me here. It wouldn't be fair on him, would it?

'No,' I say. 'Like you said, the sea air might help me feel better.'

Daz removes his seatbelt and then jumps out the car. A gust of cold, salty air instantly hits me, sending a shockwave across my tremoring arms. 'It's a lot cooler by the sea, isn't it?' he adds, taking in a huge draw from the passing ocean mist. 'Here's our digs for the night. Home, sweet, home.'

'Home, sweet, hovel... more like. Is this where we're staying?' I ask, rubbing at my throbbing temples. 'It's a bit on the small side, don't you think?'

'It might not be the Ritz, but it'll do for us.' Daz examines the cottage, then does the same with me. 'All we need is a roof over our heads for the night. What happened to staying positive?'

'I know...'

With my legs akin to a new-born fawn's, I struggle to stand on leaving the car. Most of the roads in Whitby are cobbled, which makes balancing my semi-inebriated self even more a challenge. I shouldn't moan, and I am trying not to. Daz puts up with enough of my moping, and certainly more than others would.

'For an old cottage, it does look pretty nice,' I comment, indiscreetly sniffing at my armpits. 'Does it have a shower? I could do with one.'

'There's no time for a shower—not even a quick one,' he scoffs. 'The boat's setting off soon. Anyway, you'll get a free shower off the sea waves when they hit you square in the face. That'll sober you up.'

'Great. I suppose it'll be something else to look forward to.'

Daz unlocks the cottage's front door with a large, rusty key, and the inside of Aunt Edith's cottage looks just as ancient. I feel as if I've stepped back in time to the 1930's, half-expecting to find a tin bath in the corner of the living room. Funnily enough, I'm not disappointed.

'Please tell me that I don't need to bathe using that thing,' I say, pointing to the dilapidated, human-sized tin can. 'I'll never fit my burly arse into that.'

'The tin bath's just for show,' he assures me. 'Aunt Edith rents her cottage out to other holidaymakers, and they all seem to lap up this antique crap.' He then guides me towards a steep and narrow staircase nearby. 'Our bedroom's upstairs and so's the only toilet. There's an outhouse in the garden, you know, if you're desperate.'

'I'll pass on that offer as well. No offence, mate.'

'None taken. Beggars can't be choosers, though.' Daz looks across to a pendulum clock that's hung above the fireplace, and his eyes immediately widen. 'We need to go. The boat's setting off in ten minutes.'

'The harbour's not that far from here,' I say, trying to sound somewhat reassuring. 'What's the rush?'

Why did I open my big mouth?

I hadn't taken into consideration Whitby's uneven, meandering streets. Navigating them in this hungover state of mine is like trying to tie your shoelaces under anaesthetic. Daz practically carries me as we powerwalk towards the harbour, seeing as my balance is still shot. We pass by several pubs along the way, half of which are open for business, and the temptation to slink off into one becomes ever more appealing.

'There'll be plenty of time for a few pints after the boating trip,' he says, pulling at me, preventing my pathetic and desperate attempts to enter the nearest public house. 'You're gonna love being out on the open sea, mate. It's a whole new experience for you.'

'I'd rather get some fresh air in a beer garden than to be stuck in some old boat,' I whine. 'It's bloody freezing out here.'

'You'll love it, and we're almost there.'

As we reach the harbour a strong scent of fish and diesel attack the fine hairs in my nostrils. Making matters worse, the concrete stairway that leads down to the boat is steep and laden with slipper seaweed, increasing my anxiety tenfold. All I envision is me falling down these worn-down steps into the murky waters below, where I'll sink to the bottom of the harbour only to be nibbled on by crabs. Did I mention to Daz that I'm not a good swimmer?

A haggard-looking pensioner, who himself looks remarkably like Captain Birdseye from the old TV commercials, greets us at the boat. With a wave of his pipe, the man happily winks to Daz but glowers at me. We're off to a great start.

'Who's this?' the man asks Darren, looking somewhat bemused. 'You didn't say you were bringing any pals along.'

'This is Tom, Colin. He's a good friend of mine, and it'll be his first time out at sea,' Daz explains as he gently nudges me down the steps, then onto the rocking vessel. 'Is that alright? I've got the money for him.'

'More the merrier! Come aboard!' Colin grants us a smile, revealing a line of gnarly, nicotine-stained teeth behind it. 'He'll soon find his sea legs. We're about to set sail, boys, seeing as the tide's gone out. I reckon we'll have a good catch on our hands today.'

I nod politely at Colin and then sit down upon a nearby bench, clinging to its metal railings with all my strength. I need to ground myself, to control my breaths. Floating two miles out into the North Sea isn't doing many wonders for my anxiety, it must be said.

'Are you nervous?' Daz asks me, showing some genuine concern within his smirk. 'There's no need to be, mate. Colin's an experienced Skipper. We're in safe hands.'

'I shouldn't have had those vodka shots,' I say, fighting against a new urge to spew up the contents of last night's endeavours. 'It's something different, I suppose. And I'll do my best to stay positive.' I can barely convince myself, but Daz seems to be. I do appreciate that he's trying to help me, to solve my problems, though I'd be much happier for him just to listen—a feat that could have been managed back at home, on dry land. I'll need to talk about my true feelings first, however, which isn't one of my strongest points.

'There's no better feeling than being out on the open sea, away from society and all our troubles,' Daz says, sighing with contentment. 'This is the life, Tom-boy.'

He suddenly swoons, then throws himself down beside me and pulls out his blood monitoring kit.

'What's up?' I ask, steadying him as best I can.

'Diabetes… it's a bitch,' he states. 'I bet I'm well into the twenties.' Daz proceeds to prick one of his fingertips with a small needle, allowing for a droplet of blood to fall onto the machine's sensor thereafter. The device beeps, we both look on in anticipation, then he gives me a knowing smile. 'Twenty-eight — I knew it!' He swiftly retrieves his insulin pen, which is then plunged into his upper leg. 'Don't you worry about me. I'm used to this. It's just a part of life for me now.'

'I thought you had your diabetes under control?'

'There are good days and bad days. I'm not going to let anything ruin our fishing trip, though. No way,' he insists, righting himself now. 'Nothing will put a damper on this chillout session of ours.'

How can he be so relaxed? I'd be on constant edge if I were in Daz's position, never knowing when the next sugar low or high could strike. He has every reason to worry, but I don't.

'Are you boys alright back there?' Colin yells to us as he fires up the boat's engine. 'I don't do refunds, you know.'

'Aye-aye, Captain! All's well!' Daz replies, turning to me again. 'Have you used a rod before?'

'No. I've never been fishing, have I?'

'It's a piece of cake. You'll soon get the hang of it.'

Daz retrieves a couple of fishing rods that are leaning against the boat's railings opposite, handing one over to me. It seems simple enough to use but, knowing me, I'll still likely make some sort of cock-up. I examine the rod's length, its line and reel, looking around occasionally at the other men that are accompanying us. They all look like they know what they're doing, unlike me. I'm not cut out for this. My breaths are becoming more laboured, and I can feel the usual wave of anxiety cramps sweeping through my limbs. If it wasn't for Daz, I'd gladly jump overboard without a second thought, should it mean putting an end to this ordeal.

I cast my line into the dark depths below, praying for it to remain motionless. I can barely control my own movements, let alone those of a floundering fish that's fighting for its life. Daz follows suit, casting his own line out. The urge to light up a cigarette then rises, so I lock the rod between my legs and pull out my packet of cigarettes, catching Daz's attention.

'You smoke too much,' he says to me bluntly. 'What happened to making the most of the fresh sea air? You may as well stick your lips around an exhaust pipe.'

'I know it's bad for my health, but smoking calms the nerves,' I say. Colin's puffing away on his pipe, so I can't see it being a problem with me lighting up. 'I've tried stopping—'

'It's not easy. I understand, mate. Still, you take minutes off your life or every time you smoke one of those things,' he says. 'There's over one-thousand harmful chemicals in just one cigarette, and not forgetting the link to several cancers.'

'So? If I have a choice between living a hundred years in perpetual boredom — where I'll end up being looked after in some god-forsaken care home, eating pureed meals, forgetting who I am, and sitting in my own piss for most of the day — or living a shorter life that's more bearable, well, I know which option I'd prefer.'

Daz sighs and then concentrates on the glimmering waves ahead of us again. It's not been ten minutes, but I've already broken my promise to stay positive. I take in a draw from my cigarette, ensuring to cast its poisonous smoke away from my best friend's position. I couldn't care less what I do to my body, but I don't want Daz to suffer because of my nicotine addiction.

'We'll soon get a bite,' he assures me. 'You've got to be patient, like with most things in life. It's always worth the wait.'

Half an hour passes by and I'm yet to feel a tug on my rod. I must admit that I'm starting to feel a little more relaxed now, with the gentle waves rocking our boat from side to side and the cool breeze coursing over my shaven scalp. I could get used to this, and I am beginning to see the appeal in fishing, though I do feel some guilt about possibly killing an innocent creature — that is — if I do manage to catch a fish today.

While I absorb these new sensations, I remember that Daz had something important to say last night but failed to do so.

'What was it you were going to tell me?' I ask him.

'Hmm?' Daz looks back at me with a confused expression, breaking away from his pleasant daydream. 'What are you going on about now?'

'You know, the big secret you were going to share with me and the other lads…apart from Mikey.'

'Oh, that? Well, it's why I don't want you to worry about spending any money today.'

'Right, so what's the big deal? The suspense is killing me, man.'

Daz leans in closer and whispers, 'You know that my grandma died a few weeks ago.'

'Yeah.'

'Well, she only went and left me twenty-grand in her will.'

'TWENTY-GRAND!' I screech, nearly losing my rod in the process.

'Shhh! Bloody hell, mate. Just tell the whole world, why don't you?'

'Twenty-grand?' I whisper.

'It's mad, isn't it? I didn't believe Gran's solicitor when they first told me, but the money was transferred into my bank account a few days ago — it's real, alright.' I notice how Daz keeps looking at the other blokes with a cautious side-glance; he's never this paranoid. 'I'm gonna put it to good use, starting with this trip of ours.'

'Twenty-grand,' I say, utterly confounded. 'What I'd do for twenty-thousand pounds. It's a life-changing amount.'

'I can imagine what you'd do with that amount of cash,' he jokes. 'I'd like to think you wouldn't spend it all down the boozer, and I wouldn't say that it's exactly life-changing.'

I can't help but consider what I'd do with that kind of money: a new car; a bigger home; a nose job; a crate of the finest scotch whiskey; possibly take Alice on the honeymoon I ruined. But I'm selfish and materialistic, unlike my best friend here. Daz will likely donate most of his inheritance to a good cause or put it into some savings for Nathan i.e. something sensible. He's not selfish. He's nothing like me.

'I'd give it all back if it meant spending just one more day with Gran,' he laments, allowing me a brief glimpse into a side of him I rarely see. 'She fought against her cancer for as long as she could, I'll give her that. Life's not always fair, is it? At least Gran's not suffering now.'

'How's your grandad taking things?'

'He's clueless, mate, with his Alzheimer's and that. You know, Grandad didn't even realise he was at Gran's funeral. He thought we'd turned up at someone's wedding, which we just played along with, you know, so it didn't upset him. They can send rockets to the moon but can't cure Alzheimer's disease — that's what's unreal, not me coming into all that money.'

Daz goes quiet — too quiet for him. He never gets down, and I think that I'm partly to blame. I pat a hand on his shoulder and rub at his back; any kind of comfort I can offer is better than nothing. I should know. I can relate to him, in a certain kind of way, and there's nothing worse than not being able to reach out to someone when you're feeling low. I make a swift decision to change the subject, being that Daz's apparent melancholy is increasing my own.

'This fishing malarkey isn't all that bad,' I say, forcing myself into the same professional stance as the others on our boat are in. 'I reckon we'll catch a shark.'

'A shark — in the North Sea?' he chuckles. I'm not really that stupid. But if making a dumb comment will help cheer him up, then it's worth it. 'You'll be lucky to catch a mackerel in these waters. *A shark…*'

Something pulls at Daz's line, so we both stare at the hypnotising waves in search of whatever it is.

'Whoa! It's big—' he pants, flexing his muscular arms. Mine look like joints of ham in comparison. 'It's a big one, lads!'

'Reel it in!' I say, now fully immersed in this ancient blood sport. 'Come on, Daz! Pull—PULL!'

I'm surprised at how no smoke is coming off Daz's reel as he aggressively turns the handle to draw in his catch. I soon lose interest, however, and return to my own more disappointing and sedentary position. Daz continues to fight against his foe, tugging at his rod with all the strength he can muster. In the meantime, I fall back into a serene, anxiety-free daze, staring out at the open sea and basking in the warm sunlight. Suddenly, the back of my head is struck by something wet and slippery, and a boisterous wave of laughter then leaves from Daz and the other men standing around us.

'Sorry, mate!' he cackles. 'I'm not doing it on purpose.'

'What the hell, man?'

Three fish thrash and scrape themselves across my shaven scalp, leaving a gelatinous substance to then trail down my forehead. I wipe away the disgusting slime only to find that my fingertips are now covered in blood. How is this meant to be relaxing?

'They're little beauties!' says Colin, grinning to Daz. 'You've got two mackerel and a codling there. Well done, my boy.'

'Sorry, Tom. I really am sorry, mate.' Daz bursts into another fit of laughter, followed again by everyone else onboard. 'I didn't mean to hit you with them.'

'Charming. You didn't mention that this could happen.'

As Daz lowers the fish into a nearby container, I begin to sympathise with the little blighters. There they were, minding their own business, getting up to whatever fish get up to, and then we come along and trick the poor things into being tossed into some manky box, where they'll throw themselves around for another ten minutes or so before finally coming to standstill. The appeal of fishing has completely gone now, as has the nicotine in my system. I light up another cigarette but only after discarding my rod, and for good this time. I'm finished with this cruel game. I feel guilty enough to start with. The more inviting thought of sitting in a beer garden re-enters my conscience, turning my arisen anxiety into an animalistic urge to satiate my alcohol withdrawal. That's my kind of sport: drinking until I blackout. At least there's less violence involved, that is, depending on which pub you frequent.

'Are you giving up so soon?' says Daz, as he sits back down beside me. 'You were doing well, mate.'

'I didn't realise how fish bleed like we do. I wasn't expecting that…'

'Oh,' he says, losing his smile. 'It does take some getting used to, dealing with the blood and guts. I should've given you a heads up, mate. Sorry.'

'It just seems like such a waste. What happens to all the fish we catch?'

'Colin sells them off in the harbour, then they're made into crab bait. The fish we catch don't go to waste,' he insists, grimacing slightly. 'They don't die for nothing.'

'I guess it's not so bad then. But, still…' The box is just under my legs, and the fish keep splashing water across the

114

back of them. I've got to stay positive. It's bloody hard work, though. 'I'm sorry. You've gone through all this effort—'

'It's fine, Tom. The whole idea of bringing you along today was for you to wind down and relax. Are you?'

'Yeah. I could do with a pint of strong ale now, mind.'

'We'll visit a pub or two once back on dry land. Shouldn't be long now.'

We spend the next half hour staring out over the horizon in silence. It's been so long since I've felt so at ease and don't want it to end, but I know it will. It always does. I can't stop thinking about Alice and Rosie—especially Rosie. I've never been separated from them before. I soon feel nauseous again and it's not from the hangover. A new problem rears its head: my IBS. That's what the knots in my stomach are. Of all the places for it to play up as well. There's no way I'm hanging my backside over the edge of this boat. Sod that for a laugh. I'll never live it down.

'You know what your problem is, Tom?' says Daz, blissfully unaware of my current predicament.

'What?' I ask, holding onto my bloating stomach.

'You need a decent, hard-earned break. Alice wouldn't leave you for nothing. Maybe, and this is my own opinion, she meant for you to take a break so that you could finally sort out your issues—your anxiety and depression.'

'I've been depressed since I was ten years old,' I say, lulling my head back into my hands. I don't want to talk about this. I don't want to talk whatsoever. All I want is to feed my body with more alcohol, to numb my senses and enter a more welcomed and sedated state...and to find the nearest toilet. I highly doubt Colin has any whisky stored on this knackered old boat of his. He should do, though, for emergencies. I know I would.

'You haven't exactly had the best of help, to be fair. The doctors only threw tablets at you, and you've never been one for opening up about how you really feel.' Daz leans into me again, resting a hand upon mine. 'You know you can talk to me about anything.'

'But I don't want to put you on a downer.'

'It's better to get things off your mind, otherwise they'll only get worse. Talk to me, mate. I want to help.'

In my mind, at least, I'm well beyond any help. The medication I'm currently on has made a huge difference, but not enough. Most days I don't feel anything at all; I'm neither sad nor happy, just floating through life as an empty vessel in some vacuum like a lonely asteroid in space. The counselling sessions did work to some extent, by identifying what some of my anxiety's triggers are. In fairness, I only went to the first one, so shouldn't grumble. I'm still waiting for a miracle cure to happen. Newcastle Brown Ale does the trick in the meantime.

'You've got enough going on in your own life, Daz, with Nathan starting comprehensive school soon and that. I don't want to burden you with my boring shit.'

'You're not a burden, and it's not boring shit.' Daz steadies my hand as I go to light another cigarette, despite his obvious reluctance to assist in shortening my lifespan. 'You're a good bloke and deserve a second chance—everyone does.' The boat's engine kicks back into life, jolting Daz and I. 'It looks like we're heading back into harbour now. We've still got a whole day ahead of us.'

'Thank God.'

The midday sun is fast approaching as we make it back to Whitby's harbour. The desire to further damage my liver is being steadily overtaken by the IBS cramps now crippling my stomach, and I'm only just managing to disguise the discomfort they're causing. Daz, on the other hand, seems to be having a whale of a time. He marvels over all the fish caught, and gladly waves at all the passers-by who are standing along the quay. There's so many of them. Where did all these people come from, and why are they all dressed like the Addams family? This is all I need.

New Acquaintances

How could I have forgotten that it's Whitby's "Goth Weekend"? There are visitors from far and wide all over the place; you can barely move, and Tom hates crowds due to his anxiety. This is a disaster. However, I can tell he's more concerned with his IBS than his social anxiety at this present moment.

We quickly head over to the nearest public convenience, although I can't see Tom having much luck in getting through the mile-long queue outside of it. I've got to stay positive—one of us needs to.

'You've got to be kidding me!' he says, holding onto his gut as if about to give birth. 'It's no good. I can't hold it in for much longer, and I don't fancy soiling myself in public.'

'Deep breaths, mate. Stay calm,' I say, pretending to be at ease myself. 'The queue's not that long.'

'Of all the days for my IBS to play up.'

'Just don't think about it, mate.'

Tom's despair deepens. 'Mind over matter isn't gonna work in this case, Daz. Why are there so many people here?'

'I kind of forgot about it being Whitby's Goth Weekend.'

'You don't say...'

The main reason why Tom doesn't like being in crowds is due to the off chance he'll stand out, that is, according to him. I need to conceive another cunning plan, it seems. A clothing stall nearby provides a solution to this problem; however, it might not be one my friend will particularly accept, not without some gentle encouragement.

'You'll be better off going back to the cottage, to use the toilet there,' I suggest. 'I'll meet you in The Buck Inn pub, say, in thirty minutes? How does that sound?'

'I haven't got a choice,' he gasps, snatching the cottage's key from me. 'I won't make it. I shouldn't have had those vodka shots...'

'You'll be fine,' I say, goading him to move. 'I'll wait for you in the pub. Take as long as you need.'

I hang about until Tom disappears into the crowd before shifting over to the clothes stall like a sly fox. The vendor is a stocky man that looks a little like Hagrid from the Harry Potter movies: tall, bearded, imposing, though also a little friendly. He's selling a variety of gothic clothes, walking sticks, hats and makeup — the perfect solution I'm after.

I purchase a couple of gothic shirts and a pallet of black and white foundation. Tom and I are sure to fit in with these. No sweat. But will he be willing to try something new? Tom doesn't cope well with change.

'That'll be fifty-quid,' the stall vendor informs me. I take out my wallet and then swipe my bank card over his scanner, satisfied by this brash purchase of mine. It's money well spent, even if Tom disagrees with me. 'Thank you. Have a nice day.'

It occurs to me that I hadn't considered Tom's need to journey back through the bustling crowds, and what impact that will have on his anxiety. Perhaps I should go back to the cottage and check on him, otherwise he'll just sneak into the nearest pub. He's a loyal friend, is Tom, but—especially where alcohol's concerned—his weaknesses can overrule such a strong devotion as our close friendship.

I find the front door to my aunt's cottage is unlocked, so gather that Tom must be still inside. I walk into the living room only to be met with an eyewatering smell, which soon confirms my friend's present whereabouts. So, after looking over my purchases again, I make my way upstairs in search of the foul odour's source—Tom.

'Who's there?' he cries out. 'Daz?'

'Yeah, it's only me. What have you killed in there? If this cottage is haunted, I doubt it'll be now. Lord have mercy…'

'It's those vodka shots. They're playing hell with my digestion.'

'I've bought you a little present,' I say auspiciously.

'A present?'

The bathroom door slowly creeps open, revealing my friend. He looks to me first, then to the large paper bag held in my right hand. My senses are instantly hit with a wave of Jasmine-scented air freshener, something far worse than the previous smell.

'Phwoar, Tom. How much spray have you used?'

'Never mind that. What've you bought?' he asks.

'Well, seeing as it's Goth Weekend, and because I know how much you sometimes struggle to fit in, I've bought us these.' I hold up the frilly shirts and persevere with my positive attitude, despite Tom's scowl. 'They're black, like the t-shirts you normally wear. Should fit okay too.'

Tom's face scrunches up as if he's sucked on an out-of-date lemon. 'Where'd you get these from — an antique shop? They look Victorian.'

'That's the idea. We can dress up as Goths to fit in with the crowds. I even bought us some makeup.'

'No way am I putting that muck on,' he scoffs, trying not to laugh. 'I like the music, just not the dress code.'

'It'll be fun,' I insist, dabbing some of the white foundation onto my cheeks. 'Dressing up can't do us any harm, can it?'

Tom begrudgingly slides off his shirt and replaces it with the one I bought for him. 'I look like Uncle Fester,' he says. 'I look like a total prick — is that the look you're after?'

'I think it suits you. Now, are we hitting the pubs or not?'

'Too right, we are. This shirt's proper itchy.'

'Are you not putting any makeup on?' I ask, adding more foundation to my face. 'Do you not want to give it a try?'

'Nah, I'll definitely look like Uncle Fester then.' Tom adjusts his shirt and — no matter how much he tries to deny it — I gather that he does enjoy wearing it. 'It's a snug fit.'

'It's meant to be tight. Are we going out or what?' After getting myself dressed, I lead Tom downstairs to the front door before he has a chance to reconsider. 'I'll get the first round of drinks in.'

'Are you sure?' he says with a look of confliction. 'You've spent a fair whack on me already.'

'How many times, mate? Don't you worry about forking any cash out. This is my treat, so make the most of it.'

We head back onto the bustling streets to mingle among our fellow Goths, some of which seem just as overwhelmed as Tom does. I keep a watchful eye over how he is coping, and he seems to be doing just fine. The atmosphere is electric; everyone passing by smiles at us and there's not any sign of trouble. As far as I can see it, we're fitting in perfectly. But that's me, not Tom. He'll be alright once he gets a few ales down him, even if I wish that wasn't the case.

I take it upon myself to remind Tom that alcohol is a depressant, that it'll only put him on more of a downer. But he still sees booze as being medicinal, his ideal tool in his fight against anxiety and depression. Sadly, he's not the only person who thinks that way. It's such a shame.

'I don't drink that much,' he whines.

'One or two pints isn't bad, but—'

'I know what I'm doing, Daz. Please, don't worry about me.'

We slink into The Buck Inn pub via its alleyway door. It's busy, but not too bad. I hand a ten-pound note over to a young girl serving behind the bar, ordering a fresh glass of orange juice for myself and a pint of mild bitter for Tom. He doesn't seem amused.

'This pint tastes off,' he comments, slamming the glass down on the bar in disappointment. However, Tom then forms an apologetic scowl, hinting that he's somewhat ashamed by this show of ungratefulness. I don't see why, though, seeing as I was expecting such a response. 'Is this Smooth? I asked for the 9% one: Thunder of Thor.'

'Yeah, but you'll be better off drinking the weaker beers, that is, if we're going to see out the rest of the night. You need to pace yourself, not piss yourself. That's what'll happen if you drink super-strength ales over what's left of this day.' He sighs at me, but then nods in agreement. 'I'm only thinking in your best interests, mate. It'll be me that'll need to carry you home, come last orders.'

'Fair point.' Tom raises his glass to me, and I clink mine against his in return. 'Cheers, Daz. I didn't know you cared so much.'

'Of course, I do. Plus, I'm also thinking of my dodgy back.' I briefly inspect the beer pump Tom had held his keen interest on. 'Thunder of Thor? Going off the devastation you left in my aunt's bathroom, I'd say that's the last thing you need flowing through your system.'

'Give it a rest,' he says under his breath. 'It's not my fault that I have IBS, and I'm not *that* bad.'

A man and woman dressed in some expensive-looking steampunk attire come and sit beside us at the bar. Tom hugs into his pint glass, like an eerie re-enactment of Gollum protecting his precious ring in Tolkien's book *The Hobbit*. He never used to be so shy, especially during our band days. Tom often tried to steal the show by running into the audience with his guitar, much to the disapproval of our lead singer, Carrie, who herself wanted to be the centre of attention. He can barely walk through a small crowd of strangers now without becoming a nervous wreck.

'Y'alright?' I ask, nodding to the unsuspecting couple. 'Nice costumes…look expensive.'

'Thanks,' the man says defensively. 'They are.'

'Thank you,' says the woman accompanying him in a politer manner. 'This is our first Goth Weekend. Have you been before?'

'No, we're new to this as well. I'm Darren and this is Tom.'

'Hi,' she says to Tom in a seductive voice, catching him off-guard. 'I like your shirt. It's so thin and frilly. You can see everything.' She twizzles her fingers through the frills on Tom's shirt, then winks at him out of sight from her husband. 'You really suit it, darling.'

Tom looks at her in sheer panic and then consumes his entire pint within seconds. I gently nudge an elbow into him, hinting that he should have the decency to answer back.

'Thanks,' he says apprehensively. 'I don't always dress like this, to be fair. It's a one-off.'

'Why not? What's wrong with how your dressed?' the man asks, seemingly offended. 'We dress this way most of the time, apart from when we're at work, of course. Who gives a toss how you dress? Wear what you want, I say.'

'Here, here!' I say. 'You shouldn't hide who you really are, not for anyone.'

The man grins and raises his bottle of beer to me. Tom, however, still hasn't snapped out of his catatonic stare. 'My mate here's just a little shy,' I explain to our new associates. 'Tom's a good laugh, once you get to know him. Aren't you, mate?'

'He's a right barrel of laughs,' the man sneers. 'I'm Bill. This is my wife, Charlotte.'

'It's nice to meet you both—'

'Call me Lottie,' she insists, coursing a hand through her raven-black hair. 'It's a pleasure to meet you and your friend here.'

'I need the toilet again,' says Tom, scurrying off towards the alleyway door. 'I'll be right back.'

'Doesn't say much your friend, does he?' says Bill.

'Tom suffers with anxiety and depression. He can't help it,' I whisper to him. Perhaps it isn't right of me to share this

information about Tom with total strangers, but I don't think
he should feel ashamed of what he's going through. As Bill
duly pointed out with his statement on wearing what you
want without being ashamed, I believe Tom shouldn't feel
any embarrassment with what he needs to endure daily. I do
feel some guilt, though, but I don't want my best pal coming
across as some ignorant arsehole — particularly when I know
he isn't one. Bill and Lottie's composure noticeably change,
both appearing more sympathetic now.

'Bill has depression,' says Lottie, hugging into him. 'He
doesn't like talking about his illness because he thinks it
makes him weak — typical bloke,' she laughs. I can't see
what's funny about it, though. 'You're all the same, you
fellas, afraid to show your true feelings.'

'Behave yourself, Lottie.' Bill scowls at her and then
mimics Tom by downing his entire drink in one sitting. 'It's
not the side of me I want people to see or know about. And I
don't appreciate you going around telling strangers about
it.'

'You behave. There's nothing to be ashamed of,' she snaps,
landing a hard fist against his closest arm. 'You're not the
only person with depression; it's widespread nowadays.'

'That's the problem with our modern society,' I say. 'Men
like yourself and Tom are wrongfully stigmatised for
something you have little to no control over. It's not right.
And it's about time people started talking about their
illnesses openly, in my opinion.' I'm not sure how well my
comment is being received so far, though Bill seems engaged
and not angry — as I feared he might be. 'Tom thinks that
others don't want to know about his issues, which is half his
trouble. He's the most selfless, funny and sweetest guy

you'll ever meet, but he's just too worn down to show that side of him.'

'I get it,' says Bill. 'Lottie and I often get abuse for how we dress. And there are days where I think: is it worth it? Is it worth all the verbal abuse and getting spat at for how we dress, for listening to the music we prefer? Then I think: why the hell not? Life's too short to worry about what others think of you, ain't it? Fuck the haters.'

'Exactly. It'd be a boring world if we all liked the same things,' I say, briefly looking away from Bill in search of my elusive friend. Where has Tom gone? 'Do you fancy another drink?' I ask, trying to remain civil with these new friends of mine. 'It's on me.'

'That'd be great.' Bill holds onto Lottie's left hand, gently stroking a finger over her wedding ring. 'I could do with another drink after that little chat.' He then looks at the alley way door. 'I think your mate's done a runner on you, by the way.'

'Tom wouldn't do that. He'd never do that to me,' I say, though this thought has also crept into my mind. 'I'll just go and have a look for him and then get the drinks in. I'll be right back.'

'Good luck.' Bill rolls his eyes and then returns to his empty pint glass. 'I'll keep you and your pal's seats while you look for him. He can't have strayed off too far.'

'Tom's not like that. He wouldn't just run off…'

It's not long before I discover my best friend's hiding place, and it's hardly comfortable. Tom's squatting behind a dumpster in the alley, partially knelt in a pool of stale beer and urine. His arms are tremoring and eyes wide open with fright now. He's also holding onto a spent cigarette in one hand and his empty pint glass in the other. The poor guy looks completely lost and paralysed with fear.

I slowly make my approach as not to startle him. 'What's up, mate? I thought you'd done a runner.'

'I couldn't handle it in there, mate. And I'm sure that Lottie's trying to hit on me.'

'They're alright, are Bill and Lottie. I think she's just being sociable with you,' I say with the straightest face possible. 'Bill has anxiety and depression too. You should maybe talk to him about them?'

'Really? I didn't get the impression he seemed anxious or depressed.' Tom seems to snap out of his trance, enticed by the notion that someone else on this planet knows what he's going through. 'Bill seemed pretty chilled out to me. Anyway, blokes talk about things like football, sex, and — at least in our case — music. Blokes don't talk about mental health problems, do they?'

'Not enough as they should do, but everyone's different. Perhaps Bill's anxiety isn't as bad as yours, or he's also good at putting on a false mask?'

Tom shakes his head in disagreement. 'He's certainly better at putting on a mask than me. Lucky him.' His face then quickly reddens with anger. 'Why do you put up with all my shit, Daz? I'm such a miserable, self-loathing sod. You could have brought Amar, Mikey or John…why me?'

'I could have invited the other lads, but I wanted you to come,' I say. 'Come back inside and I'll get you a pint of that Thunder stuff you fancied.'

'No, I'll stick to the Smooth.' A faint smile lifts on Tom's face as he discards his used cigarette into a nearby ash bin.

'I'm gonna pace myself, take things steady, like you suggested.'

'One small step at a time is best the way to do it. Bill and Lottie have kept our seats for us —'

'I don't want to feel like this for the rest of my life,' he adds solemnly. 'I want to meet new people and make new friends. I want to stop being so down all the time. I want to change. On second thoughts, I might have just one pint of that Thunder of Thor, but only if you don't mind.'

'Sure. Why not? I can't see one pint of that gut-rot going to your head,' I say, albeit with some hesitation. 'You and Bill have a lot in common. Who knows, he might be a Stone Roses fan as well?'

Tom doesn't seem convinced, however, and on heading back inside he says, 'How do you manage to stay so upbeat all the time? I'd give anything to be like that.'

'It's a case of balancing out the good and bad parts of life,' I say, ridiculing myself over how cheesy it sounds and the fact I'm one to talk. We all have our own little secrets, don't we? 'Nothing's ever simple, mate. But you'll beat your anxiety and depression… one day.'

'You never know.' Tom manages to force a smile at me and then to Bill. 'Alright, mate?'

'Yeah. I'll get a drink in for you and your friend here,' says Bill, ushering the barmaid over. 'What're you fellas having?'

'A double shot of bourbon,' says Tom, looking anywhere but at me now. 'Just the one…'

Flashback: June 6th, 1998

I'm my ten-year-old self again, sat cross-legged in front of my PlayStation One, playing on Tomb Raider 2, without a single care in the world. I'm content. I'm relaxed. But something isn't right.

Mum calls out from the bathroom, asking for me to come and see her. She sounds concerned, more so than usual. I pause my game, stand, then enter the bathroom with my head held down. I'm young but not naïve. I'm very aware of the arguments she and Dad have been having over the last few weeks, even if they think I'm not. I know what's coming and dreading it. My "perfect" family. But nothing's ever perfect, is it?

'Tom, sweetheart,' says Mum with a nervous stutter. She's been lying in that bath for over an hour now, so the water must be freezing cold. Something is wrong. I take a step closer towards her, ensuring to keep my head held in its present position. For some reason, I just can't look her in the eyes. I know I'm not going to be scolded for anything, but still. 'Catherine's still downstairs, isn't she?'

'Yes, Mum.' I say, also stuttering. My younger sister, Catherine, is only six years old. Her ears must be too innocent to listen in, I surmise. 'What's wrong?'

'We're going to live with Grandma and Grandad for a little while, that is, until we find a new home.'

'Why do we need a new home?' I ask, though I don't want to know the answer. 'I like the house we're in now. I don't want to move.'

'Oh, Son.' Mum holds onto her crucifix necklace with both hands, kisses it twice, then looks at me again. This isn't my mum. My mum is always happy, not sad or scared. 'What it is Tom…' She pauses momentarily before continuing. 'I can't put up with your dad and his tantrums anymore. We're —'

'Getting a divorce,' I say, clearly causing some shock, and mum jumps out of the bath in response. She starts shivering, but I know it's not from the cold water — it's anxiety. Even at such an innocent age, I'm beginning to understand what anxiety feels and looks like. 'I thought we were a happy family,' I say, trying hard not to cry. I've got to be strong. 'I thought you were happy, Mum.'

'You and your sister make me happy, Tom. But there's no such thing as a perfect family, sweetheart. I'm sorry.' Mum says this with an ice-cold precision, her hatred for my father overpowering her usual and more sympathetic demeanour. 'This is the last thing I want, but I haven't got a choice. You'll understand when you're older.'

'But —'

This is it. This is the first time I felt my heart palpate; my brow-line succumb to a cold wave of sweat; my hands and feet go into an uncontrollable bout of numbing cramps, and the feeling of a cannonball being shot straight into my

130

stomach at point-blank range. This is the first time I had a real panic attack, and it wouldn't be the last.

'Tom?!' Mum latches onto my flailing body. The room we're standing in starts to spin, and a shroud of darkness closes in over me. I feel like I'm dying — I'm sure I am. 'Speak to me, Tom! Oh, God! I'm so sorry, Son.'

'Mum!' I cry, a compulsive reaction from the fear that's now penetrating my body and mind. 'I'm scared. I can't breathe…'

She tightens her arms around me, saturating my pyjamas in cold water and soap suds. Mum's maternal touch subdues my anxiety, but not as much as she and I would desire.

'I promise we'll be alright,' she whispers softly to me. 'Everything will be okay. It's not your fault, Son. It's not your fault. Don't ever blame yourself.'

It must have been my fault, though. I should have done more to stop Mum and Dad separating. I should have been stronger for her and Catherine during the heartache that followed. I should have done more to keep them happy. It is my fault. I'm such a coward.

A Vicious Circle

Tom's on his seventh pint of super-strength ale, despite my best efforts to buy him some alcohol-free beer on the sly. One good thing is that he's starting to lighten up a little, but at the cost of his health and ability to hold a meaningful conversation. This is not how I planned for this day to end.

Bill and Lottie were insistent that we tag along with them on their pub crawl around Whitby, something Tom held no hesitation over whatsoever. It's an offer that, in hindsight, I wish we refused. Tom can barely walk let alone manage another drink, and that's if he'll even get served in the next pub. I'm hoping he doesn't.

'It's been fun, hasn't it? But it's home-time now,' I suggest, trying to hint to our new friends and Tom that he's basked in enough merriment for one evening. 'We've got an early start in the morning —'

'Nonsense,' says Bill, who's currently being held upright by Lottie. Like Tom, he can scarcely manage to place one foot in front of the other. 'The night's just getting started! One more drink!'

'Yeah,' says Tom, latching onto Bill like a leech. 'Just one more drink. I'm in the mood for partying.'

'It's getting late, and I need to get back early tomorrow for Nathan's soccer practice,' I lie, but I'm fresh out of excuses. 'We need to go.'

'Just one more drink, Daz.' Tom inadvertently loosens his grip upon Bill's shoulder, almost falling flat on his face upon the cobbled road. 'Only the one…'

'Fine. But make it water,' I say, sounding more like a father-figure than a best friend to him. 'You're off your head, mate. What happened to pacing yourself?'

'I am,' he says in-between a series of hiccups and belches. 'I'm that not drunk, if that's what you're implying.'

'We've had a long day—a good day.' Tom looks at me pitifully, and I'm too soft to resist. 'If not water, then how about a pint of mild beer?'

'So long as it's booze,' he says, swaggering from side-to-side. 'Another Thunder of Thor isn't going to hurt. What's the worst that could happen?'

A cold shudder runs down my spine in response. If only he could see himself from where I'm standing. If only he could see how addicted he has become to alcohol, in destroying his body and mind with that godforsaken substance. There's no point in lecturing Tom, though, because that'll only make him feel more guilty and remorseful, which always leads to him drinking more. It's a vicious cycle, make no doubt about it.

The next pub's barkeepers don't seem too impressed by Tom and Bill's dilapidated appearances, I can't help but notice. Lottie and I guide our drunken associates towards a table in the farthest corner, out of sight and earshot from the vigilant bartenders. It'll be a miracle if we get served, and I pray we don't.

Lottie and I make our way over to the bar, where another inebriated patron wastes no time in trying his luck with her. The man looks like he's in his late sixties; his greasy, grey hair is combed over to one side, and he has an amicable smile. I imagine that, without the influence of alcohol, he'd be quite a pleasant chap under usual circumstances. However, he's giving off some creepy, sex-pest vibes right now.

'Y'alright, flower?' says the stranger to Lottie, as he wipes a line of frothy stout from his handlebar moustache. 'Would you like me to walk you home? There are some dodgy men lurking about these streets, especially at this time of night.'

Lottie turns to me, hesitant to reply. 'Erm...'

I interject to save her from any further distress. 'She's with me, pal. I'll get her home safe.'

The man looks me up and down, scowling at my frilly shirt and gothic makeup. 'You're having a laugh, lad? You don't look much of a bodyguard to me.'

'She's my sister. Thanks for the offer — it's very kind of you — but we don't need your protection.'

The guy just doesn't take the hint. 'Is your sister single?'

'She's happily married,' I say. 'It's not worth the effort, mate, and she's not interested in any extra company.'

'So what? I can still show her a good time.'

I tap at Lottie's arm, pushing her behind me. This is what I detest about alcohol most: it can turn the nicest of people into utter arseholes and/or perverts.

'She's just not interested, mate. Get back to your drink and leave her alone,' I implore, still trying to come across as being calm and friendly. A confrontation is the last thing I want, but you just can't reason with pissheads. Tom's taught me that lesson plenty of times. 'We don't want any trouble.'

'Oh, is that what you're after?' The man's eyes flare like a wild animal's when on heat. I gauge that he's in no position to fight, and I'm not in the mood for taking out someone who's in such a vulnerable position—even if they are extremely annoying. 'I couldn't give a toss if you're her brother!'

'Look, there's no need to go on like that,' I say less subtly now. 'There's no need to get angry, mate.'

'I'm not your frickin' mate! Do you know who I am?' he asks, snarling at me. 'Do you? I could kill you with just two fingers. I'm a blackbelt in Karate.'

There's always one, isn't there?

At this point, Tom's stumbles over.

'What's going on, Daz?' he says, his hands trembling with anxiety again. 'Is this bloke bothering you?'

'No. I'm just getting our drinks in.' I notice how the bartenders have all backed away from me. Perhaps I have taken on more than I can chew with this bloke?

'I'm buying the lass a drink and you can't stop me,' the man declares, before pressing his forehead against mine. I glance across to Bill—held in the assumption that he'll come over to protect his wife—but he's fast asleep or passed out. 'Get out of the way, boy!'

'Oi!' Tom roars, clenching his fists. 'Leave them alone!'

With open palms, I raise my hands to both the stranger and Tom, desperate to keep them apart and put an end to any possible fight. I'm a firm believer that violence doesn't solve anything. Mind, saying that, there's always a first time. Resorting to violence is what my dad would do, and I never want to be anything like him.

Lottie screeches over to Bill, 'Are you just gonna sit there, with your thumb up your arse, while this pervert's hounding me?'

'You think you're big and hard, do you?' says the stranger, glowering at Tom. 'Come on then, fatty, if you think you can take me down!'

'That's enough!' I plead, now resting my hands firmly upon both adversaries. 'I've got this, Tom. Go and sit back down before you get hurt.'

'No!' he cries, his entire body tremoring with rage. 'I'm not having some scruffy old git start on you!'

Finally, and thankfully, one of the bar staff intervene. 'Out! The lot of you—OUT! Leave now or we'll call the police.'

I wrap an arm around Tom and then we leave just as Lottie delivers her judgement upon Bill, regardless of the obvious fact he's completely unaware of the retribution he's about to face. The stranger returns to his bar stool, unphased by the events, and starts sipping on his warm pint of stout again. You couldn't make it up.

Once outside I stand myself in front Tom, his complexion growing paler by the second.

'What the hell's gotten into you?' I ask, doing my best to hold him steady. 'It's not like you to go picking fights like that.'

'I don't know.' He squats down and starts rocking back and forth, clasping onto his forehead with both hands. 'I thought that fella was gonna hurt you. I don't know what came over me.'

'I can handle myself, unlike you with your drink.'

'I want to stop it, Daz.'

'Stop what?'

'I want to stop drinking so much. I want a day where I'm not constantly scared or smoking myself to death. That's why Alice left me—I know it is.'

I lower myself to Tom's level, so that he can't hide from me.

'Alice hasn't left you for good, mate. You've got to believe in yourself—that's the first step on your road to recovery. You'll never beat your addictions with the mindset you currently have.'

'How can I believe in myself?' he says. 'I've tried to cut down on booze and cigarettes before—nothing works.'

'If cutting down doesn't work, then you need to completely stop. It'll take a lot of willpower, but you'll manage it.' I go to hug him, but Tom retracts his body like a spider skulking back into its lair. 'There will come a day when you can put your addictions behind you. But you've got to forgive yourself; it's the only way you'll be able to move on.'

Tom makes a whimpering sound as if he's about to cry, though no tears are showing now. I assist him to his feet, which is by no means an easy task, then begin our short journey back to Aunt Edith's cottage. On nearing the cottage, a young woman walks by us who quickly catches Tom's attention.

'Alice!' he screams, reaching his arms out to her. 'Alice! Talk to me!'

'Piss off!' she replies, hastening her steps.

'She isn't Alice,' I say to him. I knew Tom was under the influence, but not to the extent of hallucinating. 'I'll make you a strong coffee when we get in. That'll put you right.'

'Alice!' Tom's cries become more pained and filled with sorrow. 'Why won't you talk to me? Don't go!'

'Leave me alone, weirdo!' The woman starts to jog now, and I do everything I can to hold Tom back from pursuing her. 'Get stuffed!'

'You're imagining things. She looks a little like Alice, but it's not her.'

'Why did you leave me? Why?!' Tom collapses against the cottage door, panting and visibly drained. 'I'm not a bad man. I'm not a bad —'

'No, you're not. You're not bad.' I unlock the door, allowing for him to crawl inside into the warmth and away from the poor woman he still has his eyes set on. 'I'm going to give you the help you need. We're going to beat this terrible affliction of yours.'

Tom sits down in my aunt's armchair, his eyes locked on the ticking grandfather clock situated opposite. 'She hasn't replied to any of my texts, Daz. Alice hates me. I bet Rosie does too.'

'Have you tried phoning her?' I ask. 'I know it's difficult, but you've got to give Alice some breathing space.'

'I can't live without her.' Tom spots on old bottle of sherry sitting upon my aunt's bookshelf. 'Do me a favour…'

'No. I'm not getting you another drink.' This is the first time I've put my foot down with Tom, something I should've done much sooner. 'You're a different person when you're drunk, and it's not pretty. Not at all.'

He lulls his head from side to side, laughing intermittently. 'I need it, though. I haven't got my meds. You don't know what it's like going cold turkey.'

'Aren't those the same tablets you're meant to take *without* alcohol?' I ask softly, as not to further ignite Tom's frustration. 'You've got it in you to give up the drink and cigarettes. And there may even come a day when you won't need to rely on your medication.'

'I doubt it.' The expression on Tom's face is gut-wrenching. The man sitting before me isn't the carefree guy I played alongside with in our band. Not at all. He's the epitome of depression, of hopelessness, though there's still a spark in him that I want to rekindle — for his sake as well as Alice and Rosie's. My grandfather used to say: "There is always a light in the darkness". I repeat those words of wisdom to Tom, but he just frowns back at me. 'That's easier said than done,' he says. 'Especially when all I can see is darkness.'

'That feeling won't last forever.' I don't know what possesses me, but I pull a picture of Aunt Edith and Uncle Gilroy off the wall and then throw it onto Tom's lap. 'My uncle suffered with depression. That's him,' I say, pointing to the proud-looking man in the black and white photograph. 'He was a fisherman…and suffered with seasickness.'

'Not the best of career choices then?' Tom scoffs.

'Maybe? But Uncle Gilroy did that job for forty years before retiring. He did it because he wanted to keep Aunt Edith happy. She was his light in the darkness — the one thing in his life that kept him going, like Alice and Rose with you.'

'I've never thought of it like that before. All I want is for Alice and Rosie to be content, but I've only achieved the opposite. As for my job, I hate teaching and do it just to keep a roof over my family's head.'

'You don't *really* hate teaching, though, do you?'

Tom grumbles and clasps his hands together. They must be cramping again, as they do when his anxiety's kicking in.

'No, not exactly. It's all the red tape that goes with it, and this promotion I'm being offered. I'm not sure if I'm ready to take on so much responsibility. It's a lot of pressure to deal with.'

'You can worry about that after the holidays, can't you? Try to make the most of your free time.' I head into the kitchen to make us some coffee, checking briefly to ensure he doesn't sneak a mouthful of sherry in. 'You told me that you became a teacher because you wanted to help kids — which you do. You focus too much on the negatives, mate. You're a great teacher, from what Amar's told me.'

'I do try to focus on the positives. But whenever something goes right, I'm just waiting for the bad to come, which it always does. It's like being told you've got a winning lottery ticket, so you make lots of plans on how you're going to spend your winnings, just for it to turn out fake.'

I hand Tom his coffee and then sit opposite him on the sofa, so that I'm just in his peripheral view. Tom doesn't need to see me; he just needs to listen.

'There must be parts of your job you do enjoy?' I ask, trying to lighten the mood. 'It can't be all doom and gloom.'

Tom scratches at his head and takes two, painstaking minutes to respond. 'It's great watching the kids develop.'

He pauses to take a few sips of coffee, burning his mouth in the process. 'I had a young lad who was being bullied confide in me once. He said a few weeks afterwards that I'd helped him get through it. I don't know how, like, given all I said to him was that no one is perfect or better than anyone else.'

'See?' I raise my mug to Tom, but he just shakes his head at me. 'Whether you think it or not, you do make a difference to those kids' lives. You should be proud of yourself. I couldn't do your job.'

Tom bundles himself up like a startled armadillo within the armchair, clenching his lips together as to withhold any response. I understand that it's difficult for him to talk, to accept that not everything is dismal in life. But he's taking those important first steps, and I for one believe he's making some good progress.

'Can we watch a movie or something?' he asks amid yawning. 'Do you have any horrors?' Tom then eyes up Aunt Edith's dusty DVD player and TV set. 'You can choose. My head's banging.'

'That'll be the ale,' I say. 'I'm not too sure what movies we have here. I can't imagine Aunt Edith wanting to watch The Conjuring or Scream.'

'You should never judge a book by its cover,' he adds, smirking slightly. 'What's that one over there?' He asks, pointing to a large boxset. 'It's not Game of Thrones, is it?'

'The Best of Catherine Cookson,' I say, not daring to look at his disappointed reaction. 'There's a Family Guy boxset —'

'*See*? What did I say about not judging a book?' he iterates. 'Your aunt's a right dark horse.'

'Bloody hell. I wonder what else Aunt Edith's got hiding in here?'

After I put the DVD in and go to put the box back in its rightful place, I accidently fall against my aunt's antique bookshelf. A photo album falls off as a result, almost landing on my head.

'That was a close shave,' Tom comments, just holding back his laughter. He goes to stand, to possibly check on me, but immediately slumps back down in the chair. 'What's that?'

'It's a photo album,' I say, brushing off a layer of dust from it. 'I've never noticed this before.'

On opening the album, I find a few damaged photographs of my aunt and uncle and then some that include my nearest family members. There's a picture of me at the age of seven, when I dressed up in Mum's Sunday dress and high-heel shoes. I remember having a lot of fun doing that, dressing up as someone else, but Dad's bitter reaction swiftly shattered that moment's joy.

'No son of mine is dressing up like a girl,' said Dad, moments before he struck me three times across my bare buttocks with his leather belt. Mum just sat and watched the event take place, showing no emotion whatsoever. She was too scared to intervene, I guess. If she did, in fairness to her, Mum would have likely received the same treatment as me. 'No son of mine is going to dress up as a girl or turn out to be some pansy. You hear, Son?!' Dad then struck at me again with his belt, and twice as hard in comparison to the last wave. 'Are you listening? No son of mine is going to turn into some poofter.'

Rubbing at my sore backside, I muttered, 'Yes, Dad. Sorry, Dad.' I wasn't sorry, though. I was angry. And I was too young to understand what the derogative term "poofter" meant, or why Dad felt so threatened by it. I still don't, if truth be told. I never dressed up like that again and continue to keep such desires hidden. We all have our own little secrets, elements of our lives that we strive to keep hidden away from others.

Tom skulks over to inspect my aunt's photo album.

'Is that you?' he asks, placing a finger over my youthful face on the photograph. 'You haven't changed much.'

'Yep, that's me. The angelic-looking one.'

'What's with the bowl-cut hair?' he sniggers. 'That's a corker! Just wait until the other lads see it.' Tom retrieves his phone and goes to take a photo, but then succumbs to a bout of sombre silence again.

'What's up now?' I say to him.

'Rosie.' A tear falls from his face, straight onto the phone's screen. 'My little girl. I'll never see her again, Daz.'

I move my head across to look at Tom's phone, finding that the background image has him, Alice and Rose on it. They're sitting on their sofa at home, hugging into one another. It's Tom's favourite photo and obviously invokes some powerful emotions in him.

'You'll see her again,' I say, taking a moment to look at the photograph myself. 'This break of yours won't last.'

'I want to phone Alice, to hear her and Rosie's voices again. This is torture, mate. But I brought it on myself.' Tom flops back into the chair, clasping onto his phone for dear life. 'What am I going to do?'

'Get some sleep. We'll buy Alice and Rosie a present from the market tomorrow, yeah? It'll be a conversation-starter for when you next see them.'

'I don't think Alice wants to be anywhere near me, let alone accept any presents I might have to offer.' Tom scrunches his fingers into the palms of his hands. I'd dread to think what those anxiety tremors and cramps feel like. They must be agonising. 'I'll maybe call her in the morning.'

'I'll be here, by your side, backing your corner all the way,' I implore. 'Tomorrow's a fresh start. You and Alice will be back together soon enough. I'll make sure of it, mate.'

'Don't make promises you can't keep, mate. Take it from someone who's broken plenty of them. I wonder how Alice is feeling. Do you think she's just as down as I am about this break?'

'I'd reckon so. You've been together for a long time, haven't you? We'll work this out, mate. Get some rest.'

I turn the TV volume down and roll over on the sofa. The light from Tom's phone carries on illuminating the room for another hour or so before going off. Amid Tom's snoring, I can hear the odd sob or two. Trying to lift him out of this depressive bout is like trying to deadlift an elephant, but I've got to persevere. The Alice I know wouldn't cast aside him like this and so easily. But who am I to judge? No marriage is perfect.

Under A Cloudy Veil

The scent of bacon and lard frying would normally be enough to snap Tom out of his hungover state. But these were not normal circumstances, and this was no common hangover. Along with his skull-crushing migraine, dry mouth, and short-term memory lapse, Tom awoke to a new set of anxious tremors and nauseous feeling—withdrawal symptoms from not taking his Mirtazapine, he reasons. It had been two days since his last dose, but it feels more like a lifetime.

Darren, on the other hand, had risen early with the sun to visit a local shop nearby for supplies. He had high hopes for the day ahead, unaware of Tom's present dilemma. Once back at the cottage, Darren momentarily left the frying pan and its sizzling contents to venture outside, to gaze upon the stunning, harbour landscape—its pristine-white cliff faces and sapphire sea waves. The night before was but a small glitch in his eyes, and one that could soon be rectified. Darren was certain that his positivity would soon wear off on Tom, but also accepted that this would take a great deal of time and plenty of patience. He has both, along with a fiery determination to "cure" his best friend.

'What are you cremating in there, Daz?' Tom asks on being met with a wave of thick, black smoke from the kitchen. 'Where are you? I can't see a thing!' He then walks blindly into the kitchen, to where he assumes Darren is. 'Are you there, mate?'

A frantic cry comes from Darren in response. 'Shit—the bacon!'

He speeds back inside to inspect the charred remains of his and Tom's breakfast, just making out Tom's bulging stomach and scarlet red boxer shorts through the dense plumes. 'Come outside into the fresh air, mate. I'll sort this disaster out.'

In Tom's mind he'd already expended enough energy by walking into the kitchen. So, against Darren's wishes, he sits down at the kitchen table instead, under the billowing smoke, with a lit cigarette in hand.

'*Burn, baby, burn,*' Tom sings before taking in a lengthy draw, exhaling his own smoke thereafter into the darkened mass above him. 'It's a good job that I like my bacon crispy.'

'You can't light up in here! Aunt Edith has a nose like a friggin' bloodhound,' says Darren. 'One whiff of tobacco and she'll be on my arse quicker than you can imagine. She's someone I wouldn't mess with, even if she is ninety-two.'

'Won't Aunt Edith be more bothered by the fact you've almost burnt down her Victorian cottage?' Tom humours. He holds a great respect for Darren, however, so begrudgingly discards his cigarette into the garden. 'It's the thought that counts, mate. To be honest, I'm not feeling that hungry.'

'Neither am I now,' says Darren, wafting away some of the smoke from between himself and Tom. 'I do know what will get our appetites going: a long, hard, morning run along the beach. What do you say?'

'Running? Sod that. Do I look like a runner to you? I'll have a heart attack just walking down to the beach, man.'

'Exercise is great for the body and mind. Besides, it'll help you sweat off that hangover of yours.'

Tom shrugs back undecidedly. 'I'm not too keen on the idea. Stepping outside is like preparing yourself for a bungee jump to me—terrifying. I know it sounds dumb, but…'

'I know, but still give it a try. I'll treat us to some ice cream afterwards.' Darren places a hand upon Tom's shoulder now, his usual way of reassuring him. 'There's a café in Sandsend village, at the other end of the beach, where we can get a decent bite to eat. It's only a mile or so from the harbour—'

'*A mile?*' Tom splutters in dismay. 'I don't know.' He looks down at his scrawny calf muscles and sighs. 'I don't reckon my legs can make it that far.'

'It's better to try than not. I've got some spare shorts upstairs,' says Darren with an enthusiastic smirk. 'I'll go and get them for you.'

'But—'

'Exercise is a great medicine, a natural serotonin booster— just what you need! Running helps me to unwind, anyway.' Darren disappears up the stairs and then returns shortly afterwards with a small pair of bright yellow swimming trunks. 'There you go. They look about your size.'

'Really? They're not my colour, mate.'

'What's the colour got to do with anything? Get them on.'

After an arduous struggle, Tom manages to slip on the tight-fitting shorts.

'They look alright…certainly highlight your best bits.'

'They're crushing my bits,' says Tom, adding some curse words under his breath. 'I hope you know how to do CPR, because you'll need to resuscitate me on that beach after ten minutes or so. I haven't run since secondary school. This body of mine isn't designed for exercise, and my anxiety's always worse when I'm outdoors.'

'Running has a lot of benefits, both physically and mentally. Just jog at a slow and steady pace. You'll be fine.' Darren implores. 'The winds are calm and the sun's not too hot today. It's a perfect morning for a little jog along the beach.'

'*A little jog*? This wasn't what I had in mind when you said we were going to have a relaxing weekend.'

'Were you under the impression we'd be spending it all in a beer garden?'

'Yeah,' says Tom, clearly disappointed. 'That's my idea of chilling out.'

'The pubs won't be open for a few more hours. Anyway, you won't be in the mood for booze after your run.'

'No, I'll be needing a defibrillator.'

'Stay positive, mate. It'll be a laugh.'

'Oh yeah, it's just what I need after a night out on the town.'

Getting to the beach is a simple enough task, given that it's all downhill from Aunt Edith's cottage. But still, Tom's lacking enthusiasm grows with each yard gained. In contrast, and despite his friend's negative outlook, Darren starts performing some warm-up moves, insistent that Tom should also join in.

'That's it, mate. Stretch your hamstrings and glutes,' says Darren to Tom. 'Work those legs. Feel the burn!'

'I'm sweating already,' says Tom, pulling out a painful wedgie. The small village of Sandsend lies before them now, but to Tom it looks several miles away. 'How far did you say it is to Sandsend?'

'We'll be sitting in a café, supping on a nice cup of espresso and eating a greasy fry-up in no time. It's not far. Don't give up before we've even started.' Darren eagerly poises himself like an Olympic sprinter at their starters point, keeping a watchful eye on his friend all the while. 'Are you ready?'

'No.'

'On your marks! Ready! Steady! Oh, there's one more thing…'

'What?'

'The loser has to go skinny-dipping in the sea. GO!'

'Hold on, that's not fair! You got a head start!' Within a hundred yards, Tom stops to light up another cigarette. This run is rapidly depleting his energy levels, and — more importantly — his nicotine reserves. 'How's this good for my health? I'm aching all over.'

Watching Darren grow smaller in the distance somewhat snaps Tom back into action. 'Some athlete I'm turning out to be. I mean, who smokes a tab while they're running?'

'The sea looks pretty cold, Tom-boy!' Darren shouts to him. 'I wouldn't fancy a naked dip in it!'

'I'm not stripping off!'

'If you don't beat me, you'll have to!'

'You're hilarious, mate, very funny…'

The cool, sea haze helps to replenish Tom as he presses on ahead, thankfully. He shakes off the pain in his neglected muscles, and even manages to enjoy the adrenaline rush this exercise brings. He's no longer unwilling to participate; if anything, he's revelling in this new challenge.

Halfway to Sandsend, the two friends halt in their tracks for some necessary respite. Darren initiates the break, seeing as Tom is struggling to keep up with him.

'Thank God for that!' says Tom as he falls to his knees, holding out his arms towards the sky. 'I'm absolutely knackered.'

'You're doing great,' says Darren, barely out of breath. 'A little further and we'll be home dry. How are you feeling, mate?'

With a puzzled expression, Tom looks up to his friend. '*How am I feeling?* I'm ready for a lie down, I know that much.'

'I don't mean physically.' Darren guides a pointed finger across Tom's arms and fingers. 'You're not tremoring like usual. Haven't you noticed?'

Darren is correct. Tom's anxiety tremors have all but stopped, a pleasant surprise for them both.

'I don't get it,' says Tom. 'The cramp pains aren't as bad either.'

'You've used up all your adrenaline from running — that's what it is. Like I said, exercise is great for both the body and mind.'

'I'm sure my lungs are about to explode,' Tom utters, still gasping for breath. 'I can't win, can I? As soon as something feels good, something bad comes along to ruin it. It's the story of my life.

'No pain, no gain. Keep your chin up, pal.' After a quick tap on Tom's shoulder, Darren sets off again. 'Think of all the calories you'll burn!'

'Not enough.' Tom examines the fat rolls around his stomach, lamenting over all the nights of binge eating and drinking he has come to enjoy so much. 'I'd rather go through liposuction than this.'

'The quickest option isn't always the best,' are Darren's parting words as he speeds off into the distance again.

Once the friends reach Sandsend, Darren slows his pace to allow for Tom to catch up, making their run a draw.

'I won!' Tom rejoices in a raspy, exacerbated voice. 'Can we get some grub now? I'm famished.'

'Just a sec,' says Darren, holding up a hand. 'It was a draw, which means we both have to strip off and go swimming.'

'No way. There's a bacon sandwich with my name on it waiting for me.' Tom bears his sight on the small café ahead that happens to be named "Wits End". 'Talk about irony! I'm at my wits end with all this running. Anyhow, people will think a whale's washed ashore if I take my kit off. I don't want to scar anyone for life.'

'Stop putting yourself down all the time. You're not fat; maybe a little big-boned.'

'Make no mistake of it, my friend. This here is a beer belly,' says Tom, pinching at his stomach and chin. 'I get plenty of reminders from others that I'm overweight. There's no need to sugar-coat it.'

'You worry far too much about what other people say and think. If you're happy, then that's all that should matter.'

'You're tall, slim and ripped — you don't know what it's like to be judged by others on your appearance,' says Tom, looking to his miniscule biceps. 'Who knows, though, if I do keep up this running business I might get as toned as you are one day?'

'I didn't get this body overnight. It takes time and patience, like I keep saying.' Darren leads the way into the café. 'You could go a step further and buy some fresh fruit instead of a greasy bacon bap for your breakfast?'

Tom licks at his lips, the sensation of some grease coating them being his primary thought. 'That would be the sensible thing to do, yeah, but I need some fried meat…and maybe an inhaler.'

'Trust you.' Darren humours, but only to hide his dismay. 'I'll get us the grub; you go and find us a decent table.'

The table where Tom and Darren sit for their breakfast overlooks the gentle sea waves and golden beach. The image before them looks like something straight out of a meditation video: picturesque, otherworldly, and mesmerising. Over the next ten minutes, Tom's anxiety tremors remain unseen and unfelt. Therefore, Darren utilises this moment to full effect — to press on with more urgent matters, namely Tom's failing marriage.

'Our bacon butties shouldn't be long,' he says. 'The server said they'd bring them over to us, mate. Give it a few more minutes.'

'Nice one.'

'So,' Darren hesitates, 'has she been in touch yet? Have you heard anything from Alice?'

'What?' says Tom, slowly stirring a spoon through his coffee. 'What are you talking about?'

'Alice. Has she sent any texts or tried to call you?'

'No, and I doubt she will.' Tom instantly comes under attack from an electrical surge that courses throughout his spine; and a heavy, invisible force presses hard against his chest. He'd left his phone back at the cottage. What is to say he could have missed a call or text from Alice? 'I haven't got my phone on me. What's if she's tried getting in touch while we've been out running? That'd be just typical.'

'What's been going on between the two of you lately?' Darren asks reservedly. Tom's tremors now increase to their fullest and most painful extent, rendering his rational thoughts. 'It's better to talk about these things, to get them off your chest. I'm not here to judge you; I'm here to listen.'

'I know, but—'

'Alice loves you—'

'You keep saying that, thinking it'll make me feel better, but I know Alice hates me. If she does still care, then why did she leave?'

'She doesn't hate you, mate…'

'Alice is probably sat in her mother's house right now, not giving two thoughts about me. She took Rosie. She's torn me and my little girl apart. She can't care about me, Daz.' Tom's anxiety boils into anger—a festering rage that is being

153

steadily aimed more against himself than at Alice or Darren. 'I don't know what I've done wrong. I haven't cheated on her or anything. After all the things I've done—'

'You did nearly blow up your house with that tin of soup,' Darren comments. 'But I think it's more than that. Alice—'

'What would you know? You don't know her like I do, and your life's going great. You're in a job that pays well, your wife and son worship you, and you don't suffer from anxiety and depression.' Tom pushes his chair away from the table, stands up, then makes for the café exit. After a few seconds, however, he heads back over to Darren with his head held low in remorse. 'Sorry, mate. It's a lot to take in. I'm not used to being alone…not having Rosie around. I'm her dad. I should be with her, shouldn't I?'

'In an ideal world, yes, and you're right: I don't know what it's like for you,' says Darren, his words spoken with compassion and sympathy. He offers Tom's seat back to him, making it clear that he hasn't been offended in any way. 'Michelle and I have never had a single argument, and I don't get anxiety tremors like you do. Some would say that I'm lucky, and I'd agree with them. But there's no reason why you can't work things out. You've got to put in the effort, mate.'

The sea waves no longer bring any calm to Tom's nerves, despite him incessantly staring at them, and his hunger has all but gone. He sees the waves more as a personification of his predicament now—an endless horizon strewn with emptiness, filled with hidden threats. He imagines himself sinking into the murky depths of some ocean, into the unknown, never to see any light again—all the while strangely considering this to be the "good option".

'I can't see her coming back to me, Daz. I mean, what's the attraction? I've lost all interest in things I used to enjoy, which also means not showing Alice the affection she deserves.'

'You're caring, funny, smart—what's not to like?' Darren pauses, considering his next move. He has so much to say in response, in praise of Tom, though his words aren't seeming to have any effect. He quickly reasons that a change in tactics is required. A little more honesty, perhaps? 'Yeah, you have some flaws, but don't we all? I can't control my diabetes, for one thing. If it wasn't for Michelle, I'd have been in a diabetic coma years ago. You and Alice were destined to be together, and you will be.'

'I wish I could tread through life like you do, mate. If destiny wanted me and Alice to be together, it's got a funny way of showing it. I need a moment to think.'

Tom leaves the café, and Darren takes his own advice by allowing the space his friend obviously requires. There is little else to say; little else to dwell on.

As if sleepwalking, Tom saunters back along the beach to Whitby, held deep in contemplation.

'Destined to be together, what a crock of shit.' The wind strikes hard at Tom's face, blistering his skin with the sand particles adjoining it, thus forcing him to retreat inside a small cave along the cliff face. 'Fate hasn't exactly been kind to me, has it? I shouldn't have taken it out on Daz, though. He's only trying to help, and he's the only one who gives a damn about me. I don't see why.'

'Room for one more in there?' a deep voice asks from behind, though the strong winds make it indistinguishable at first. 'Can I come in, mate?'

155

'Daz?' Tom waves him over. 'I didn't mean to take it out on you like that.'

Darren approaches as if Tom were a cornered animal, offers him his bacon sandwich from the café, then kneels before him. Tom goes to apologise again, but Darren stops him with a swift raise of his hands.

'Don't. You've got nothing to be sorry for, Tom. I was out of order. It's too soon to be asking you questions about Alice.'

'No. I need to talk about her. I want to talk about her.' Tom casts aside the sandwich and lulls his head into his hands, rubbing at the coarse sand within them. The friction brings about a mild pain, and pain is a useful distraction that he uses on a frequent basis to cope with his depression, though is something he would never openly admit. 'I'm such a selfish tosspot. I'm a no-good husband and lousy dad. It's as simple as that. It shouldn't be a surprise that Alice left me.'

'You've got some major issues, but there are always solutions to them. You need to change your mindset and stop blaming yourself,' Darren implores. 'Let's start by getting Alice and Rosie some presents, yeah? There's a nice candy stall by the harbour that springs to mind. We can buy Rosie a big bag of fudge and something even sweeter for Alice. What does Alice like?'

'I bought her some flowers for her birthday that seemed to go down well.'

'There's a start. What type?'

'Yellow roses.'

Darren assists Tom to his feet, then directs them both out of the damp and musky cave into the warm and more inviting sunlight.

'I know a place that might sell yellow roses,' Darren adds. 'Like us walking out this cave, you need to draw yourself out of the darkness in your life. Find what motivates you, what keeps you going, and use it to fight your depression.'

'You sound like a cheesy cat poster. Cheers, anyway.' Tom's voice almost breaks, and tears form in his eyes. He had low expectations of how this weekend away would play out. But now, and with Darren's aid, he can now envision a new path forging ahead of him. 'I need to purge all the bad things surrounding me. I know this, but I'm not sure how to manage it.'

'It won't be a walk in the park,' says Darren. 'Look, if you and Alice don't get back together by the end of summer, then… I'll give you that signed picture of Jenna Coleman I have, the one you're always drooling over.'

'The one you paid two-hundred quid for at that charity auction?'

'Yep. It'll be yours to keep.'

'Really? It's a deal!'

The two friends shake hands and make their way back into Whitby's town centre. Tom purchases s a large bag of strawberry fudge for Rosie and a bunch of freshly picked yellow roses for Alice. Darren does the same for Michelle and Nathan, though swaps the yellow Roses for his own personal preference: a bunch of white Lilies.

'Thanks for coming along with me, even if you were a little reluctant at first, mate. Have you had a good time?'

'Apart from the epic run, I have. I'm sorry if I put a downer on your fishing weekend.'

'You haven't. This trip was for you, Tom, to get you to start talking more about your problems. I'll always be there for you, to listen. That's what friends are for.'

'Thanks, mate. It means a lot, having someone who wants to listen…'

Flashback: July 21st, 2004

Grandad insisted that we should go out for a walk alone, leaving Catherine and Grandma to their own devices in our holiday cottage, and kept his reason for doing so secret. He's never this forlorn, and I've got a sneaky suspicion that he's about to break some bad news to me. I can just tell, and my gut instincts are rarely wrong.

After a brief look around town, we make it to the bottom of Whitby's West Cliff. There's an arduous set of sandstone stairs that lead up to Captain Cook's monument at the bottom of the cliff face—a trek we've managed many times before. But now, given how bad his arthritis is, I'm doubtful Grandad can manage it.

'I think we should head back,' I suggest, but he places a foot upon the first step anyway. 'We can always get the bus up?'

'No, I'll manage them. I'm not ready for the scrapyard yet, my lad.' Grandad clasps onto the stairwell's railings with his crippled fingers, then drags himself up them slowly and painfully. I support him as best I can, though he's adamant that he'll reach the top without any assistance. 'I'll be okay, Son. You go on ahead. You're quicker than me nowadays.'

I don't budge. I can't leave him to struggle, to likely fall over. I'd never forgive myself.

'I'm not going anywhere. I'm staying with you, Grandad.'

'There's a good boy,' he says, placing a hand upon my shoulders to balance himself. 'We'll get there, slowly but surely.'

On reaching the stairwell's summit, Grandad directs us to a nearby bench, the same one we always sit on each time we holiday here. 'Let's have a little breather, Tom. I need to catch my breath.'

'Why didn't you want Catherine and Grandma to come with us?' I ask him. 'What's wrong, Grandad? I know something's up.'

'It's a lovely view from up here, isn't it?

'Yeah. Whitby's never changed…'

'But life does, Tom. Life moves on. I'm afraid that this will be the last time you and I will ever sit here, staring out over this beautiful view.'

'What do you mean?'

'It's only right for me to be honest with you, and you deserve to know the truth. I've been diagnosed with a terminal illness,' he says with a heavy gulp. 'I've been given

159

six months, if I'm lucky. Your grandmother is still coming to terms with it, which is why I wanted to tell you here—out of her earshot. Catherine's too young; it'd be unfair to tell her.'

'You can't die,' I whimper. 'You can't. You're not that old.'

'Death comes to us all, no matter the age you are. I've been lucky enough to see your mother grow, and to spend time with my wonderful grandchildren. I'm content with the blessings I've had. I'm not afraid. And don't you be afraid, because life is too short to worry about things which we have no control over.'

'But I don't want you to go. It's not fair!' I cry.

'Nothing ever is, Son. You've got to take the good with the bad. Concentrate on all the happy memories we've made together, because that's what life is all about; to cherish each precious moment you're given.'

I don't want Grandad to die, but there's nothing I can do to stop it. I have no control. I'm powerless. But I've got to stay strong for Mum and Catherine, to be there for them when he dies—that's what Grandad would want. I've got to put on a brave face. I can't show anyone how I feel. It's time I learned how to fake a smile and pretend that everything's okay. I don't want to be a burden. I've got to pretend I'm strong. I've got to pretend that I'm alright. That's what I'll do. That's how I'll take back control.

Flushing Down the Hypo

I hadn't anticipated how difficult it would be in dropping Tom off at home, to leave him there in that empty and lonesome house of his. He seemed content enough, but I know beneath that forced smile of his there's a resentful demon growing. I've got to help him, and I'd like to think he'd do the same for me.

As Michelle and Nathan welcome me back from my trip to Whitby, I dwell on just how lucky I am, in being with my them — unlike Tom, who only has himself for company. There's no doubt that he'll be halfway through a pack of super-strength lager cans or bottle of whisky at this point. I wish he could see how his dependence on alcohol is slowly destroying him, like the rest of us do.

'How did your fishing trip go?' Michelle asks me, hugging into the flowers I bought for her. 'We've missed you.'

'It's only been one night. I missed you guys too. It was great,' I say, smiling to Nathan. He doesn't share the same interest in fishing as I do, sadly. 'We caught a few Mackerel, nothing majorly exciting.' There's an elephant in the room (conversation wise) and, going off her raised eyebrows, I know Michelle's waiting for me to mention Tom. 'We behaved ourselves—no drunken shenanigans.'

'You can't drink, Mr. Type 1 Diabetes,' she states. God, that joke never gets old. 'So, Tom actually agreed to go fishing with you? There's something,' she adds, trying to act surprised.

'Yeah, and he was pretty good at it. I think Tom enjoyed himself.'

Michelle's expression becomes more serious now. 'How is he doing? How's Tom coping with things?'

'It's not good. He's in a bad way. Alice has left him, so it shouldn't come as any surprise that Tom's feeling so low. Anyone would, in the same circumstance.'

'I thought she was just threatening to,' Michelle whispers to herself. 'I can't believe Alice went ahead with it.'

Nathan takes the hint and leaves the kitchen.

'You knew?' I ask, struggling to digest what Michelle has just revealed. 'Alice was already thinking about leaving Tom?'

'Yeah. She sent me a text a few days ago, saying that she was thinking about breaking up with him. It's so out of character for her. I can't believe it.'

'Neither can Tom,' I say. 'He's in a terrible state. But he's starting to talk about his problems and feelings more now, which is one good thing. He wants to make things right.'

'Did he mention to you why Alice left him? Can he think of any particular reason?'

'Tom's a complex guy and a nightmare to get information out of. Who knows what the real reasons are?' I place

Michelle's flowers into the sink and run some water over them. They're already starting to wilt. 'He's like a zombie, wandering around without a clue. I want to do something about it. I've got to get him out of this rut.'

'You're no psychologist, Darren,' she says with a discouraging frown. 'Even Tom's doctor can't fix him. What makes you think that you can make a difference? It'll be like pissing into a hurricane.'

'If I can't show Tom that there's still some hope, then what chance does he have? Other than Alice, I've known him for the longest. Tom's more open with me about things. I'm the one person who can help him destroy the vicious cycle he's in.'

'It'll be hard, don't you think? Even worse if he's at the bottom of a whisky bottle.' Michelle is also versed in Tom's ways. 'Did Tom say anything to you about what's going on regarding him and Rose? It must be breaking his heart, being separated from her.'

'It's killing him — literally. Tom's under the impression he'll never see her again. Do you think Alice would be that cold?'

'No. But we don't know for certain what's happened behind closed doors, do we?'

'Tom wouldn't —'

Nathan comes back into the kitchen and soon notices the bag of fudge I've bought for him.

'Are they for me, Dad?' he asks, licking at his lips.

'They sure are,' I say as he snatches the bag from my hand. 'There weren't any of the mint chocolate ones you like, I'm afraid.'

'It's okay, Dad. Thanks.'

163

'Have you both been up to much?' I ask Michelle. 'Have you two been behaving, dare I ask?'

'Your mum and dad came over.' Michelle's showing some anxiety herself now. I know where this is going, and it isn't good. I prompt Nathan to go back into our living room, then ready myself for more bad news. 'Your dad has booked that holiday for us. He's *really* excited about it.'

'Where at and for how long?' I ask reluctantly.

'It's at some campsite in Berwick…for seven days,' she replies, and with as much reluctance as me. 'What excuse are you planning to use this time to get out of going? Your dad's not stupid, you know.'

'I can't go. I can't stand being around him,' I say with disdain. 'I've never gotten along with Dad. The thought of spending seven days cooped up in some dingy caravan with him won't change anything between us, either.'

'He's a lot calmer now, well, according to him,' she whispers, looking over her shoulder in case our son has re-emerged. Nathan idolises my father. God knows why. Dad's a homophobic, racist, narcissistic monster—and that's being polite. 'What should I tell your mum? She'll be so disappointed with you not coming.'

'Just say that I'm on a business trip or something—anything to put her off interrogating me. Anyway, Mum knows where Dad and I stand. There's no love lost.'

'What will you do while we're away? You get bored so easily.'

I've thoroughly thought this out, make no mistake. I'm not sure how Michelle will take it, however, given how most of my plans fall flat on their face.

'I want to take Tom on a holiday of our own, just the two of us. He needs to be taken out of his current environment, to put his mindset right. He needs to be somewhere new; somewhere he can identify the triggers to his anxiety and learn to combat them without any distractions, and with someone who genuinely cares about him — me. That's my master plan.'

'You're wasting your time, Darren. Tom's too stubborn to change. If Alice has left him, she'd have done so for a good reason. It's between them. You shouldn't get involved.'

'I know —'

'You're not a miracle worker. Let Tom work this out for himself.' She strokes at my face, and then we kiss. It's Michelle's way of showing support for my cause, I assume. 'I don't want you getting your hopes up, that's all. Tom's not an easy guy to work with.'

'Yeah, but I know what needs to be done. I'm his best friend. I can't let him down.'

Michelle pushes at me playfully and then ushers us into the living room. 'We can worry about all that later. I've bought you a present, by the way.'

'What is it?' I ask, rubbing my hands together eagerly.

'Come and see for yourself,' she says, tugging at my shirt. 'It's an early Christmas present for you.'

We make our way into the living room only to find that Nathan has ruined Michelle's surprise.

'Can we watch *Iron Man* first, Dad?' he says, holding up a new Marvel boxset to me. 'Can we?'

'You've never gone and bought me the whole movie collection, have you?' I say to Michelle, my jaw dropping in both shock and joy. 'You shouldn't have...'

'Why not?' she says with a cheeky smile. 'I like treating you every now and then. You're always treating me and Nathan.'

'It must have cost a fortune?'

'You've got twenty-grand in the bank, don't you?'

'Thereabouts.'

'Why shouldn't we treat ourselves? You work so hard, and it's not often we spend money on luxuries.'

I'm not complaining. I love entering these fantasy worlds that Hollywood has to offer; they're a welcome form of escape from life's turmoil. I place myself between Michelle and Nathan on our sofa, and then Tyson jumps onto my lap to join in with this family gathering of ours. This is perfect. But I can't stop thinking about Tom in his solitary confinement. The poor guy.

An hour into the movie, I start to feel all cold and nauseous; there's sweat lashing off my brow, and my eyes are beginning to blur. Is this going to be a hypo or hyper? It's getting harder to tell the difference. Where did I leave my BM kit? I think it's in my suitcase, which I haven't had any chance to unpack yet. I've got to stay calm. It's not like I haven't been through this before.

'Are you okay, babe?' Michelle asks me with a worrisome look. 'Not again. When did you last check your sugar levels?'

'Before I set off from Whitby,' I say, barely able to control my racing breaths. 'My BM kit's in the car—in my suitcase.'

'Go and get it, Nathan,' she orders him. 'Now!'

'Okay, Mum. Are you…alright Dad?' he asks, the dread in his eyes heart-breaking.

'I'll be fine,' I say. 'Don't you worry about me, Son.'

'Get your dad's BM kit—NOW!' screams Michelle as she wraps herself around me. 'Hurry, Nathan.' She then glares at me. 'This is getting ridiculous, Darren. You need to see your doctor as soon as possible. What if this happened when you were driving, or if we weren't here?'

'I'm fine—'

'No, you're not. You're anything but fine.'

Nathan vanishes from sight as mine starts to blur even more. An influx of anger, fear and paranoia steadily enter my thoughts. This is definitely a hypo, going off these unusual emotions.

'Sugar. I need sugar, Michelle.' To me I'm shouting these words, but they merely come out as a pitiful whimper. 'Sugar!'

Michelle leaves my side and then returns with a glass of cola. 'Drink this,' she insists, just as Nathan appears with my BM device. 'You're having a hypo, aren't you?'

'Sugar. I need...sugar.'

I take the risk and consume half of the syrupy beverage in one sitting. Nathan hands me a pricking needle, which Michelle swiftly stabs into the middle finger on my right hand. A blurred line of crimson liquid then trickles along the blurry image of my BM machine. I then hear Michelle say: 'Two-point-four.' Jesus wept, that *is* low. Shit. I need more sugar and fast.

'You'll be alright, sweetheart,' she says to me, with tears welling up in her eyes. 'Drink the rest of it. Drink it all.'

I snatch the glass of cola and down it all out of pure desperation. It's a fickle game, is dealing with diabetes. I can go from being in a hypo to a hyper in a snap, just like Tom with his fluctuating moods. The cola seems to do the trick;

my vision returns to normal, and the stream of sweat pouring down my brow comes to a complete standstill. Michelle, Nathan, and even Tyson are staring at me now like I'm some failed medical experiment. I give them the thumbs up, proving without saying a word to them that their care has worked to full effect.

'You need to see a doctor,' she iterates, kissing at my hands. 'These hypos and hypers are happening far too often. Promise me you'll make an appointment in the morning.'

'I'll go first thing,' I say, nodding my head to her. 'There's no need to stress, babe. I'm fine.'

'You're anything but. Never mind worrying about Tom, you need to get yourself sorted out first.'

'I just need my insulin regime re-adjusting, that's all. There's no comparison between myself and Tom, with what he's going through,' I say. 'Can we watch the rest of this movie now… act like everything's normal?'

Michelle and Nathan fall back into their previous positions beside me, and both go eerily quiet. Nathan has a bowl of popcorn that I try to infiltrate, but Michelle quickly slaps at my wandering hand to repel it.

'Think of your sugar levels,' she snaps, like a teacher scorning an unruly pupil. 'Popcorn's full of carbs and covered in syrup—a diabetic nightmare.'

'And it tastes soooo good,' I say in humour, to a disappointed look from her. Access is denied, and Michelle isn't impressed. Great. 'What else have we got that I can snack on? And don't say carrot sticks.'

'There are some diabetic-friendly chocolates in the fridge,' she says. 'You love those, don't you?

'No, they go straight through me.'

'Well, how about some of those gluten-free crisps I bought for you the other day?'

'They taste and feel like cardboard…'

The more I complain, the more Michelle's patience with me seems to be waning. 'Then go without,' she groans. 'The last thing I need is for you to have another episode. You ended up in hospital last time. Remember?'

Nathan has his say too. 'We don't want you getting worse, Dad.'

'Fine,' I say, accepting defeat. 'I'll go without. I'll just watch you two tan all the popcorn in front of me, yeah?'

'We're not poorly like you are,' says Michelle. She has an intricate knack of making me feel guilty, albeit in a subtle sense. 'You need to watch your sugar levels. We don't.'

'I'm aware of that, but what I'd give just to have one slice of chocolate fudge cake that's been drowned in double-fat cream.'

'It'd kill you,' she says. 'We're only getting on your case because we care. You've got to think of your health and the impact it has on us, too, you know.'

'I know —'

'Then do something about it.'

'I will — alright? Can you see where I'm coming from now, regarding Tom?'

'What do you mean?'

'I've got you and Nath to kick me into gear, but who's Tom got? I've got to be his driving force, to help steer him out of this horrendous situation.'

'Diabetes and depression are different illnesses and can't be cured in the same way. You're talking daft, Darren.'

'But they can be as equally devasting,' I add. 'Tom doesn't have a special medicine to magically draw him out of his panic attacks, like I've got my insulin to pull me out of my hyper episodes. He's stuck in his old ways and needs someone to help him overcome them. That's what I want to do. It's what I've got to do.'

Michelle holds onto my hands and strokes at them. 'You're a good friend to him, you are. But I still think you're wasting your time. Tom will never change. What's the point in trying?'

'Everyone deserves a second chance. I won't give up on him. The red flags are already starting to show, and they'll only get worse if he's left alone to rot in that house of his. I'd never forgive myself, if something bad were to happen…'

'Just don't get too involved, that's all I'm saying.'

'I can't just sit here and let Tom isolate himself. I'd dread to think what might happen…'

Isolation

Down the Hatch

I've never liked Mondays, because they signal the start to an uphill battle that lasts until I can get my weekly fix of hard alcohol on a Friday night, and the wait for that is absolutely torturous. But I can't go without my medication. I've got to head into town, so that I can collect my beautiful tablets, whether I like or not, no matter how much I put the short trek off. I can't survive without my tablets. There's no argument. I can do this. I've got to.

A large queue leads into the pharmacy, and my hangover is getting worse by the second. I need my fix, though. I need my Mirtazapine. I've become reliant on it to nullify my depressive thoughts, to restrain these anxious tremors of mine. It's not as fast-acting as whisky is, but it makes the first half of each day go over a little more pleasantly. Deep breaths, Tom-boy, deep breaths. Breathe. Ground yourself.

The pharmacist looks busy, overworked, and probably nowhere near serving me in the time that I'd desire. I can wait a few more minutes to be served, surely? Patience is key, according to Daz. I've gone almost three days without my tablets, so ten minutes more shouldn't hurt too much. I'd rather superglue my scrotum to a barbeque grill than go through this, being surrounded by strangers in such a cramped environment. Hurry up, Mr. Pharmacist. Come on, I can't last much longer.

'Good morning,' he says to me, a stout chap with a man bun. Alice wanted me to grow my hair like his, but I don't do change. 'How can I help you?'

'You'll be here all day if I went into what help I needed, mate,' I humour, but he just stares back at me. 'Sorry. I'm here to collect my medication. The name's Thomas Grey, and my address is 328 Priestman Road.'

'Thank you. I'll call you over when your medication is ready to collect, Mr. Grey.'

He makes his way across towards a wall of white paper bags. My meds are in there, somewhere, amongst all those goodies. I wait another five minutes, which feel more like five days, before pacing around the room to show my displeasure. For some reason, my thoughts are becoming more paranoid than anxious now – yet another side effect of my deteriorating mental health, it seems. I'm paranoid that the elderly woman standing behind me is laughing at my expense, though it turns out she just has a crackly cough; and I'm paranoid that the pharmacist is judging me, that I'm wasting valuable NHS resources. The sooner I get these tablets, the better.

I try to make small talk with the elderly woman, possibly out of guilt.

'That's a bad cough you have,' I say to her. 'It'll be one of those summer colds that's doing the rounds, no doubt.'

'It's none of your business,' she snaps at me, downgrading my faith in humanity even more. 'Have you been served yet?'

'Yeah. Don't worry, you won't be waiting for much longer.'

'It's ridiculous, this is. You should've let me go first!'

'I'm sorry — okay?'

The pharmacist returns with a worrisome expression on his face.

'Mr. Grey?'

'Yes?' I'm tempted to snatch the bag from him, given that my patience is all but spent. 'What's the matter?'

'I'm afraid I can only give you a two-week supply,' he says apologetically. 'We're suffering from severe shortages. I can order the remainder of your prescription today, and you should be able to collect what's outstanding tomorrow.'

'No worries, so long as I've got something to take now.'

'It's all down to Brexit,' the woman interjects, and I roll my eyes out of view from her — at her. 'These shortages are all down to our government dilly-dallying!'

A few people in the queue applaud the woman's statement; whereas, I stay silent, concentrating solely on the tablets being held out before me.

'What do you think, sonny?' she asks me, poking an arthritic finger into my arm.

Well, it'd be rude not to reply.

'I really don't care,' I state. 'The government don't care about us, do they? We're just a bunch of statistics to them. I've managed to get half my meds, which is better than nothing. There are people in this world that can't even access paracetamol, let alone other more vital medicines. We've no right to moan, have we?'

The woman tuts back, as do the others stood in our queue. I take the hint, along with my half-empty box of Mirtazapine, and leave. I've not thought this through very well. I've got my pills but no drink to take them with. I made the mistake of trying to swallow my tablets dry once, and almost choked myself to death in the process. Anxiety tightens my throat muscles as if it were an invisible noose being fed around them. I can't think, but I need to if I'm going to resolve this latest problem.

As fate would have it, an act of divine intervention comes into play.

There's a pub just over the road, and it looks open for business. Thank the Lord. I can go in there, get a glass of water, then finally take my tablets. That's what I'll do. No booze, mind. It's only eleven o'clock. I'm not that desperate for a beer, am I?

'Alright, boss?' a disenfranchised-looking girl from behind the bar asks me, and I nod back politely to her. Talking requires energy, a luxury that anxiety and depression won't allow me to enjoy. 'What are you having?'

I go to ask for some water, but a blackboard situated behind the barmaid that reads: Happy Hour — 11 'til 1pm stops me from doing so. I've always been one to give into temptation. Water's what I need, and the instructions on my medication box clearly state: NO ALCOHOL. But it's easier to give in, to take the easy road, especially when you're feeling so drained.

'I'll have a bottle of Brown Ale,' I say, tapping my fingers upon the bar, mulling over the shame I'm now experiencing.

'That'll be four-fifty,' she replies, her expression devoid of any emotion. I hand over a ten-pound note, the same I planned on buying some more cigarettes with, then hang my head in remorse.

There are a few patrons sitting around me, each differing in age and appearance. Some look just as miserable as me, while others seem a tad-too happy to be sat in this miserable squalor. I wonder what issues they have, and if any are like mine. Nevertheless, the beautiful sound of my Brown Ale's bottle being cracked open immediately disperses these negative thoughts.

'Thanks,' I say with my well-rehearsed smile, hoping that I can bring some joy into the barmaid's sorrowful existence. Who am I kidding? I'm probably adding to it.

'Would you like a drink for yourself?' I say to her, to see if the "old charm" still works. If looks could kill, though, the look I'm getting in response certainly would. 'It doesn't matter — forget it.'

'Whatever. There's your drink.'

I savour the beer's sweet and hoppy aroma, and at the same time inspect my box of Mirtazapine. There's little effort wasted in removing the protective seal; in popping out a single tablet into my hands; in drooling slightly as I place the small pill onto my tongue; in swilling a mouthful of ale to then swallow my medication whole. God, it's the best relief in the whole world. The effects aren't instantaneous, as I wish they were, but it's better than going without. My emotions, like my beer, are swilling around inside, more alike to a cocktail of sickness than happiness. My head feels as if it's going to explode at any moment. Another bottle of

Brown Ale will put a sharp stop to this purgatory — there's no questioning that.

It takes half an hour for the soothing effects from my Mirtazapine and beer to kick in. I know I shouldn't consume both at once, but I still do anyway. I'm beyond caring. I make the most of this subdued state to check my phone, to see if Alice has tried to contact me. She hasn't, but my little sister, Catherine, has in the form of an instant message:

Hi, Tom. I'll be over yours for around 1pm with Harry. He wants to see you – Cath xx

After some deliberation, I message back.

No probs. See you soon – Tom xx

I best sup down this second bottle I've ordered. Catherine has a short temper, unlike me, and with every right. She's got some mysterious illness that her doctors and hospital consultants are struggling to identify; she can barely walk and is in constant pain, so it's rare for her to visit me nowadays. I should visit her more often, but it's not that simple. It never is.

My anxiety cramps return, compelling me to buy a whisky chaser before I go — anything to stop these bad nerves of mine.

'That'll be three-fifty,' says the barmaid, shaking an open palm at me. Even she's had enough of my company, by the looks of it. 'Today would be nice.'

'There.' I hand over the last five-pound note in my wallet, making it visibly clear that I take pleasure joy in doing so.

The thing is, I see this whisky shot as being another form of medication, which I know sounds ridiculous. Catherine's so ill, though, and it's getting harder to watch her deterioration. She says that by spending time with me it's a form of therapy for her, but that makes no sense whatsoever in my book. This is my therapy — drinking — regardless of what damage it creates. It's worth the risk, or so I've come to convince myself.

I happen upon Karam and his dog on my journey home, who both seem overjoyed to see me.

'Hello, my friend,' says Karam, gleefully waving at me. 'How are you, Tom? Enjoying your time off?'

'All's well, my mate,' I lie, handing one of my few-remaining cigarettes and a lighter over to him. 'How are you?'

'Cold,' he says, his body shivering despite the summer sun. 'England is so very cold.'

'Even we moan about the weather,' I jest. 'Any luck with your housing request yet?'

'No. I am still an illegal alien…unwanted.'

'An alien?' I ask, scrunching my face. 'You're getting your words mixed up again. You're not an alien, Karam.'

'I am an alien, and I am not mistaken. I have faith that Allah will provide me with a new home soon enough. It is a good job that I am patient,' he laughs. 'Patience is a virtue —'

'Shared by few, and certainly not me.'

'Life is not all that bad, my friend. The good times will return.'

For a guy with virtually nothing, Karam appears — at least on the outside — to be so carefree and jovial. I envy him in a way. Still, where's the dignity in sleeping inside a tent that's

178

situated next to the town's sewage line? I wish there was a better I could help him, but I can't even help myself.

'You take care, pal,' I say to him, walking away.

'I will. I have Charlie by my side,' he says. 'May Allah bless you, Tom. You are a good man—a good man.'

'You wouldn't be saying that if you knew the real me,' I simper.

'I can read people well, and you are not bad. Take care, my friend.'

Back in my lonesome household the clock strikes 1pm, then 2pm, and there's still no sign of Catherine. I hope she's okay. Maybe I should call her? But I hate phoning people. The wonderous sedative effects from my dangerous cocktail are starting to wear off, so the temptation to top up my whisky reserves gains strength. That wouldn't be such a good idea, however, seeing as Catherine and my five-year-old nephew could walk in at any given second.

There's a gentle knock at my kitchen door, which turns out to be Catherine and Harry. I check my breath, finding that it's foul but there aren't too many alcohol fumes being let off. I might just avoid another one of Catherine's lectures that involve the dangers associated with drinking while being on medication.

'You took your sweet time to answer the door,' she says, ushering herself and Harry inside. 'It's freezing out there! I can't feel my feet.'

'Come on in,' I say with a wearisome sigh. On closer inspection, I notice that Catherine's wearing several layers of thermal jumpers, thus hiding her emaciated body from view. I feel so bad over my lack of empathy now. Of course, she's freezing. I've got a beer belly to help keep me warm, haven't I? 'Why the sudden visit, Cath?'

'Alice phoned me this morning, saying she'd left you.'

'Oh…'

'Yeah,' she snarls. 'What have you done this time?'

'Nothing! You tell me,' I say, shrugging my shoulders, trying to act all innocent. 'I don't know why Alice left. Has she said anything to you?'

'Not much,' Catherine's voice falters, and I know she's hiding more details from me. 'Just something along the lines of her wanting a break to clear her head — who could blame her?'

Harry lunges forth, wrapping his arms around my waist.

'Hi, Uncle Tom!' he exclaims.

'Hello, Harry. Have you been a good boy for your mummy?'

'Yes! Yes, Uncle Tom,' he says, bouncing up and down on the spot. 'Mummy's seen the doctor today.'

'Has she?' I turn to Catherine, dreading what she's going to say next. She grimaces, insinuating that my nephew has let out some ultra-secret information. 'What've they said? Have they changed your meds again?'

She turns away, clenching her fists. 'Uncle Tom doesn't need to know about Mummy visiting the doctor, Harry.'

'What did they say?' I ask staunchly. 'I'm your brother, Cath. You can tell me anything.'

'I don't want to talk about it.' She relaxes her fingers, then moves over towards my kettle. 'Can I make a cup of tea?'

'Sure. Help yourself.'

'Thanks.'

'Have they worked out what's wrong with you yet? It's only been two years.' Catherine nods in confirmation, slowly, and with some evident anguish. 'Don't I have a right to know? You've been having tests for months –'

'It's called Ehlers-Danlos syndrome,' she says, gritting her teeth. 'It's something I was born with, and there's no cure.'

'Shit,' I whisper, mindful of my nephew's proximity. 'I've never heard of that before. What's Ehlers-Danlos syndrome?'

'I don't want to talk about it.'

'Come and have a sit down on the sofa,' I suggest. 'You don't look very comfortable, standing up.'

'I can't sit down, not without hurting myself. My knees won't bend properly anymore, and my tendons are tense as hell.'

'Are the doctors absolutely sure that's the illness you've got?'

'Yeah. I don't know much about it, either, other than I can barely walk and need to use the toilet every fifteen minutes.'

'Bloody hell, Cath.' I try to think of a better response, anything to reassure my little sister. But that would involve lying to her, wouldn't it? Besides, she knows me too well. I don't do positive thinking. 'Have the doctors not given you any stronger pain relief? You can't be still on just paracetamol and codeine?'

'They've put me on some buprenorphine patches, but they're barely touching the sides. Nothing works. I feel like just giving up.'

'What else have the consultants said?' I ask, in truth unwilling to learn the answers. Catherine's twenty-seven years old. She doesn't deserve to live like this, especially

181

when there are arseholes out there — the dregs of society i.e. drug dealers, murderers and rapists — living life to its fullest.

'There's a list a mile long. I'm so sick of living like this, Tom. I wish I wasn't here…'

'Don't say that —'

'But it's the truth! What have I got to look forward to now?'

'You've got Harry to think of…'

'Don't you think I know that? He's all I'm thinking about at the minute.'

My sympathy towards Catherine is swiftly replaced by guilt and self-disdain. I'd never cope with the physical ailments she has, let alone what mental health issues coincide with them. I've got nothing to complain about, but I do. I've got no right to feel sorry for myself, have I?

'If you need a hand with anything at all, let me know,' I emphasise, gently stroking at her forearms. 'I don't want you to struggle, Sis.'

'I'll manage. I don't need help from anyone. Anyway, you've got your own problems to deal with, haven't you?'

She then turns to Harry, who is presently immersing himself with some of Rosie's toys. I haven't been able to put them away yet, held in the pathetic belief that she'll be playing with them again anytime soon. It helps me to cope by thinking this way: unrealistically.

'You need to behave for Mummy,' I say to him in my father's voice, stern and resolute. 'Mummy isn't very well. You need to help look after her.'

'Okay, Uncle Tom. I'll be good,' he says.

Harry carries on playing with Rosie's toys, clearly unaware of the pain Catherine is going through. He's too young to understand, and too young to bear such a responsibility. I should be telling him to have fun, to make the most of his childhood. Innocence is bliss, they say.

'Have you been in touch with Alice yet?' says Catherine. 'You've really screwed up this time, Bro.'

'I know – I know!' I resent reacting in such a harsh manner, but – without the calming effects from my medication/alcohol intake – it's difficult not to. 'I'm just as clueless as you are. I honestly don't know why Alice left.'

'I'll do my best to see if I can change her mind,' she says, showing some sympathy in her eyes now. 'But I can't promise anything. You've got to be the one who sorts out this mess of yours. Still, I'll try and work my magic.'

'No. You've got enough to think about.' I look across my sister's bony knuckles, protruding veins, and defeated demeanour. I can tell she agrees with me, but she's just too selfless not to act. 'You need to prioritise yourself. Don't worry about me and Alice –'

'What about Rose?'

'What about her? Alice will be taking good care of Rosie. Mothers know best, they say.'

'Rosie adores you, Tom. It's not healthy for either of you to be apart. Don't give up on her so easily.' Catherine suddenly clasps at her stomach. 'I need to use your bathroom. Can you keep an eye on Harry for me?'

'Of course.'

Catherine's knees stiffen as she moves away, making her appear as if she's walking on stilts. Without saying a word to me, I can tell that every step is utter agony for my little sister. I smile to Harry and he smiles back, each of us pretending that there's nothing wrong. He offers me one of

Rosie's dolls and then initiates a conversation between mine and his.

'Mummy's sick,' he says, using the doll as a medium.

'Your mummy loves you lots and lots,' I say with my doll. 'You need to be a good boy and do as your told.'

'I do. Mummy shouts at me…'

'She doesn't mean to shout at you,' I implore. 'Are you a happy boy, Harry?'

'Yes,' he says, bouncing the doll in his hands around enthusiastically. 'I'm happy when Mummy's happy.'

I cast my doll aside and look directly into his eyes, finding relief that there are no tears in them, like there are in mine. 'You *are* a good boy, and Mummy's very proud of you.'

He immediately lowers his sight from me. Even at his young age, my nephew is showing the tell-tale signs of depression, of forging a mask to hide his true emotions from others. I know what it's like, and don't ever want him to feel the same way.

Catherine returns after ten minutes, drained and pale in complexion.

'What have you boys been up to?'

'We're playing with Rosie's dolls,' I say, showing her mine. 'I've been saying to Harry what a good boy he is. You *are* a good boy, aren't you, Harry?'

'Yes, Uncle Tom.' His smile widens, contrasting Catherine's look of utter despair. 'I love you, Mummy.'

'I love you.' Tears steadily form again in Catherine's eyes, so I take her into the kitchen.

'Please talk to me, Cath.' I try to make myself sound like Daz: calm and reassuring. 'What's really going on?'

'I'll be lucky if I make it to forty years old, and my heart can give in at any second,' she sobs. 'That's what the doctor said.'

'They can't know that for certain—'

'You don't understand. You can't possibly understand. I've been told there's a strong likelihood that I'll never see my son reach adulthood. Put yourself in my shoes, Tom.'

I begin to stutter, unable to form a cohesive response. 'Well, erm, the thing is…'

'Harry looks up to you. You're the closest person he has to a father-figure.' Catherine gives me our mother's scornful stare; a look that pierces right through your heart and soul. 'Please spend more time with him. I'm only trying to plan ahead.'

I know what she's saying, and she's wrong. I'm an alcoholic; a teacher that hates teaching; a failure of a husband; an unreliable father—hardly a decent role model or guardian. I am deeply humbled by my sister's suggestion, but also deeply reserved. Harry deserves better than me, as do Alice and Rosie.

'Uncle Tom,' Harry whispers auspiciously. 'Can I call you Daddy?'

'No, mate.' The lad misses nothing, and obviously has better hearing than Catherine and I had presumed. 'It doesn't work like that.'

'Why?'

'I'm your uncle.'

'Why?'

'I'm your mummy's brother, which makes me your uncle. I can't be your daddy. I can't be both.'

'Why? Why, Uncle Tom?'

My thoughts turn again to the bottle of single-malt whisky that's hidden in a cupboard nearby. Within a wave of guilt, I suggest to Catherine that it might do her some good to go home and get a power nap, in secret wishing for some solitude myself—to drown these new woes of mine with copious helpings of alcohol. Alice was right about me, I am selfish.

'It's been lovely seeing you both,' I say to them, holding out a hand towards the kitchen door. 'I've had a hectic weekend. So, if you don't mind—'

'I can take a hint. We'll go,' says Catherine, snapping her fingers to Harry. 'Come on, Son. Uncle Tom needs his rest.'

'Why?' he asks, stamping his feet in frustration. 'I want to play dollies with Uncle Tom.'

Before I have a chance to react, Catherine wraps Harry up in his coat and then makes for the door. Before leaving, she turns to me, scowls, and says: 'I'll text you sometime this week. It'd be nice to see more of you. We only live around the corner, you know.'

'I know. See you soon, yeah?' I hug into Catherine and Harry, consumed with more guilt, giving rise to more anxiety tremors. 'Love you.'

'Love you, Uncle Tom!' Harry grants me a wave, then clasps onto his mother's hand as they vanish off into the distance.

'I'll stay in touch!' I exclaim, wishing to assure my sister that I do care about her. Why am I so self-centred? It should come as no surprise that I've lost so many friends and alienated other family members over the years. After all, who in their right mind would want to be associated with me?

I soon embrace my bottle of whisky, my bastion of good will that holds no ill-judgement over me. But I know where this is going. I know this will only lead to a debilitating hangover, come tomorrow morning. Nevertheless, it'll be worth it. There are a few memories from today that I'd prefer to forget, which excessive drinking always takes care of. Isolation isn't such a bad thing, is it?

I don't want to be around anyone else. I don't want to be a burden.

Thicker than Water

The aftermath of his separation from Alice and Rose is beginning to show more in Tom now. He's taking longer to answer my texts, and he's made several excuses not to catch up with me and the boys. That's not him. That's not the Tom I know. I don't expect for him to be on top form, walking around with a happy-go-lucky smile on his face — that would be ridiculous. But he's not eating or sleeping properly, and certainly not getting out the house enough. You can tell by the dark bags under his eyes and paler complexion of his skin. It's an awful thing to witness, seeing someone you care about slowly fade away before your eyes. But I'm not giving up on my best friend. I'm determined to offer him the help he needs.

I've somehow managed to convince Tom to come down the pub tonight, and I'm hoping it will help lift his spirits. It was no easy feat, however. Regardless, Tom and I have made it to the Tin Donkey, but only after an hour of me trying to coax him out of his front door. He'd usually be brimming with excitement, but he's not. Tom looks terrified, anxious, frustrated — clearly wishing to be somewhere else. This isn't the Tom I know.

'What cologne are you wearing?' I ask him, attempting to lighten the mood. 'It's a bit on the strong side, mate. Who are you trying to impress?'

'It's one Alice bought for my birthday,' he says. 'I don't like it, either, but it reminds me of her. Anyway, it's not *that* strong.' He then takes out a cigarette and struggles to light it with his trembling fingers. I knew Tom's anxiety was bad, but this is on a whole new level. 'I've got time for a quick smoke before we go in, don't I?'

'Sure, and you keep an eye out for the other lads. Amar shouldn't be too far behind us.'

'What's on tonight? There better not be another quiz.'

'Bazza's holding a Karaoke competition. God help us, that's all I can say. We should have maybe brought some earplugs along, do you reckon?'

Tom steps back and finally manages to light up his cigarette. He takes in a deep draw and tilts his head back as he exhales, savouring the moment.

'At least it's not another quiz. Are you getting up to sing?' he asks me.

'I might do. I'll see what the competition is like first. Are you gonna get up? You've got a great voice.'

'No,' says Tom. 'I can't be arsed, mate. I'm happy enough just to watch others make fools of themselves.' He takes in a longer draw, the tremors in hands now noticeably worse. 'I haven't got the guts to get up and perform anymore. Those days are long gone. A few quiet drinks and a chillout session, that's all I want.'

A few quiet drinks to Tom means getting absolutely hammered. I make an expression that suggests to him that I know what he's implying, which Tom just shrugs at, and then make my way inside.

'I was hoping a decent singer would turn up tonight,' says Bazza the Landlord, and I can't tell if he's being sarcastic or not. 'What're you having, Daz? The usual?'

'Yes, please, but make it a mild beer for Tom. How's your pooch doing?'

'Percy's fine. He's pretty much back to his usual self. Tomboy won't be too happy with that choice of yours,' he states, knowing all too well that Tom's usual preference is aimed towards the super-strength ales. 'How's he coping, with his wife leaving him and that?'

Word spreads fast on this town, doesn't it?

'Tom's doing alright, given the circumstances. I'm keeping a close eye on his drinking.' I check to see if Tom's still outside, then lean across the bar and whisper, 'I need you to do me a favour, Baz.'

'What?' he asks, wincing at me. 'What is it, dare I ask?'

'Can you try to put Tom off buying that super-strength gut-rot you sell? Maybe offer him one of the weaker ales instead, if he asks?'

'Gut-rot?!' he scoffs. 'I can't promise anything, Daz-lad. Your pal's as stubborn as they come, especially when it comes to his drink.' Bazza nods to the doorway, highlighting Tom's arrival. 'I'm here to sell booze, not to act as a bloody social worker for people.'

'Getting drunk doesn't help Tom's anxiety, like he says it does.' I give Bazza an imploring look, an expression of pure desperation. 'Please, mate. You'd be really helping him out. I'll take any backlash.'

Bazza rests a hand over the mild bitter pump as Tom makes his approach. 'Too right you will,' he says. 'If drinking's so bad for Tom, then why bring him here? There's too much temptation for the poor lad.'

'He needs to socialise and coming out with us is part of Tom's routine.' I'm attempting to justify this choice to myself as well as Bazza. 'He needs to be around his mates, instead of isolating himself.'

Bazza hands me the pint of mild beer, shaking his head in uncertainty. 'The things I do to keep you customers satisfied. I don't know. I deserve a bloody medal, I do.'

'Nice one, Baz.'

I acknowledge Tom and hand him his beer. He takes a sip, and I wait for his reaction in dread. The beer seems to go down well, though, thankfully.

'Cheers for the drink,' says Tom, licking the froth away from his lips. 'It's not a bad drop. What's the strength?'

'Go easy, Tom-boy,' says Bazza. 'It's as strong as they come, is that ale. You're meant to sip at it, slow and steady, or you'll be on your arse in no time.'

'Stronger the better,' he mutters, before downing the remnants of his drink. 'Same again, mate.'

'Coming right up.' Bazza winks at me as he pulls another pint of the mild beer for Tom. 'There you go, Tom-boy. Go steady with it.'

'Tonight's going to be epic, Daz,' he says, grinning at me. 'I can feel it in my bones!'

I'm amazed at how a single drop of alcohol can turn Tom into a completely different person. It starts off great, but then he always sinks into a self-loathing bout of depression after three or four pints. This is no life for him. It's not the life I want for him, anyway.

'Take it steady, like Bazza said,' I implore.

'I don't need babysitting. I can handle my booze…'

John and Ryan now join us. Ryan's puffing away on a vape pen he bought earlier this week — a new attempt to stem his cigarette addiction, so he claims. I can't get used to the sight of these mobile haze machines. Still, Ryan swears by it. John walks up to me and Tom, rubbing his hands together with a nod of his head towards the pub's stage.

'Evening, boys,' he says. 'Who's ready to sing? I've got a few songs lined up — some right belters!'

'Not *Wonderwall*, I hope,' Tom says to him. 'If I hear that song one more time…'

'No. I've got a new repertoire up my sleeve,' John keenly informs us. 'It'll blow your socks off.'

'I bet it will,' says Tom, waving Bazza over again. 'A pint of cider for Ryan and a Guinness for John, please.'

While Bazza carries out his duties, I make some effort to satisfy John's excitement over this new repertoire of his. John is also prone to depression, though manages to keep it at bay more successfully than Tom. John works in a care home and does twelve-hour shifts, so performing on stage is something that helps him unwind. The other lads mock him for his determination, but I'd rather encourage it.

'What songs have you got lined up for us, John?' I ask him. 'Any we'll know?'

'I reckon so,' he says, brimming with pride. 'Some Iggy Pop, Red Hot Chilli Peppers, Seal — I might even give that new Lewis Capaldi song a go.'

'Now you're talking,' says Tom, surprising me with his enthusiasm. 'I'm starting to get into his music now. Alice really likes him.'

'You can be my backup singer, if you like?' says John to a look of instant dismay from Tom. 'You've got a good set of pipes on you, Tom-boy, and I could do with some extra harmonies.'

'I'd ask Amar to do a duet with you, mate. I'm not in the mood for making a tit of myself in public,' Tom simpers, scouring the pub in search of our elusive comrade. 'Where is Amar? And where's Mikey? Both said they'd be here by eight.'

'Mikey's lost a fortune on horse racing this week, so I doubt he'll turn up tonight,' says John, granting me a knowing look. We had both warned Mikey about how dangerous his 100/1 bet was, but the daft sod still went and put one-thousand pounds on it. I'll never see that two-hundred quid I lent him again. 'Amar messaged me earlier,' John adds. 'He's gonna be a little late, but he's still coming.'

'I hope he's alright,' I say, looking to my empty message app. 'I haven't heard from him. That's strange.'

'I'll sign him up to do a duet with me in the meantime,' says John. 'Amar's not the best singer going, but he'll have to do.'

An hour passes by and there's still no sign of our wayward friend. I message Amar, asking how long he will be, but he doesn't respond. Another ten minutes pass after that before Amar shows up, and he looks just as down as Tom does.

'Hello, boys. Sorry for being late,' he says, raising his hands into the air apologetically. 'I had a slight falling out with Naaz. We're cool now, though. No sweat.'

'Did you forget to lower the toilet seat again?' Ryan humours.

'No, nothing that serious.' With a grave expression, Amar sits himself on a stool beside Tom. 'I received a letter from Sharon, our headteacher,' he explains. 'I'm to appear before the school governors and herself in September. They want to discuss the incident that happened between me and that pupil. It's not looking good, fellas.'

'You acted in self-defence!' Tom seethes, slamming a fist against the bar. 'What's to explain? The lad assaulted you, so you restrained him. You were the victim, Amar. If I were in your shoes, I'd take it all the way.'

'What would be the point in doing that?' Judging by Amar's withdrawn response, I gather there's more to this than he's letting on. 'I was in the wrong. I've got to deal with the consequences.'

'Don't worry too much about it,' I say. 'We'll have a good session tonight. Try to switch off, mate. I reckon your headteacher will understand.'

'She might, but the governors—' Amar cuts his sentence short, intensifying the fearful look on his face. 'I can worry about it all later. Are any of you taking part in this karaoke competition?' He immediately looks to John. 'No Oasis, I hope.'

'What is it with you lot?' John despairs. 'I won't bother getting up, if that's the case.'

'Don't take any notice of them,' I say, patting John firmly on the back. 'It's only because we're jealous of you. Play whatever you want.'

'Thanks, Daz. At least someone has faith in me.' John takes Ryan over to Bazza's dilapidated dartboard, leaving Amar with Tom and me.

'I understand that there needs to be an investigation, but it's disgraceful how you're being treated,' says Tom, his whole body shaking with rage. 'I bet Sharon would have done the same if it was her being assaulted.'

'It doesn't matter, Tom. Leave it out.' Amar shuffles awkwardly on his stool, and I hint to Tom that it would be a good idea to give this subject a rest. 'Have you boys been up to much since I last saw you?'

'Tom and I went fishing last weekend,' I say. Like Amar, I'm also keen to change the conversation. 'Tom did well, bearing in mind that he hasn't done it before.'

'Tom… on a boat?' says Amar, fighting hard not to laugh. 'No way, man. You're pulling my leg, Darren.'

'Yes,' says Tom, attempting to come across as being offended. 'I'm just grateful we didn't drown. The boat we were on must've been at least forty years old. It was a miracle we made it out of the harbour.'

'It wasn't that bad,' I argue, gently nudging into my pessimistic friend. 'We even made some new pals. It was a great weekend.'

'Oh, yeah?' Amar looks to Tom, aware — like others within our close circle — that talking to strangers isn't a task he enjoys. 'How'd that go down?'

'It was a married couple we got talking to. They were pleasant enough… from what I can remember,' says Tom, scratching at his head. 'Daz completely forgot it was Whitby's "Goth Weekend". We were surrounded by people dressed up like Victorians and Roman Gladiators. It was interesting, to say the least.'

'Sounds it.' Amar turns back to me. 'Did you lads get dressed up as well?'

'We sure did, and Tom looked well-smart in his frilly outfit.'

'Leave it out,' Tom snarls.

'Any pictures?' Amar asks, somewhat enjoying Tom's embarrassment. 'It sounds like you guys had a memorable time.'

'We did —' Tom's voice almost breaks as he responds. I can't gather why he looks so startled, that is, until he points me into the direction of the pub's entranceway. 'Don't look now, but isn't that your dad and his mates?'

My positive mood immediately sinks as I follow Tom's line of sight.

'Yeah, but Dad goes through Darlington on a Friday night.' I rub at my eyes, praying that they're mistaken. 'What the hell is he doing here?'

Amar looks even more nervous than me and Tom, and he has every right to be. Dad proudly admits that he's a homophobic, a racist, a womaniser, a Holocaust denier, a Neo-Nazi sympathiser, a wolf hidden in sheep's clothing — and all without any remorse. He's a stain on my life that I'm constantly ashamed to have any association with. You can choose your friends but not your family, they say. Blood's thicker than water. But there's not a cliché phrase around that can duly sum up my father and how wicked he is. What is he doing here? And why of all nights did he have to show up? This isn't going to do Tom's anxiety any favours.

'Shit,' says Amar as he hides behind me, using my larger frame to shield himself from Dad's unwanted attention. 'Your dad threatened to knock me out when I last saw him.'

'He wouldn't dare touch you,' I state, though without much confidence. 'Why should you need to hide from him? Be proud of who you are. Idiots like him need to realise that there are other people in this world who don't look like them, and who don't think like them. Thank God he's in a minority. Never say that to him, mind, otherwise he might try to beat himself up,' I say in jest, but it barely raises a smile between us. 'Just don't look him in the eye, lads.'

To my further dismay, Dad soon spots me and wastes no time in coming over to offer his usual tirade of abuse. He's wearing his favourite Doc Martin boots, bright-blue jeans that are held up with red suspenders, and pristine-white shirt. I can't remember a time when I haven't seen Dad look this way, apart from his spells in prison.

'No one told me this was a gay bar!' Dad cackles, amid a wave of gurgling phlegm from all the counterfeit cigarettes he smokes. 'Alright, Darren?' He never calls me "Son". That's probably because it would be too much effort for him, and we've never been that close. I form half a smile in response to him, then he turns to Tom. 'Alright, Tom-boy? I heard your missus left you?' Tom nods back silently. 'Not in the mood for talking, hey? You're better off without all that shite—marriage. You don't want to be straddled to some miserable slag for the rest of your life, take it from me. There's plenty of fish—plenty of fires to poke.' Tom's face reddens with anger, but he manages to hold back from challenging Dad. He's not that stupid. 'Bunch of poofs. Have you all lost the ability to fuckin' speak or what? Are you trying to piss me off?'

'No, Dad. We weren't expecting to see you.' I tap on Amar's shoulder, hinting he should get out of view before being spotted. 'We're just out for a few drinks. John is getting up to sing on Bazza's Karaoke soon.'

'Oh, yeah? I'd better go and see if he knows any decent songs.'

I feel bad in a way, seeing as Dad's attention is now being drawn towards John and Ryan, but I've got to make some space between him and Amar. John and Ryan react in the same way when Dad approaches them: utterly terrified. I can see John giving Dad a thumbs up, meaning he's fortunate enough to know one song that's being requested. How did I end up with a monster like him for a father? Still, tonight's about us friends having a good laugh. The last thing I want is for Tom and Amar to get more depressed.

Bazza invites the first act to come on stage — a young girl, no older than twenty, and from the first note sung her voice sends shivers down my spine. She's performing Eva Cassidy's version of *Songbird*. Sadly, however, it doesn't go down well with my dad and his mates.

'Boring! Get off the stage, you little whore!' my dad and his friends proclaim in a unified, drunken chorus. Bazza goes to intervene but swiftly slips back behind the bar. Even he knows that it's not a good idea to entice my father's displeasure. 'Take your shirt off! Show us your goods!'

I'll give the girl her dues; she ignores my dad's taunts and finishes the song to a rapturous applause from myself and other (more decent-minded) patrons. Fair play to her. She's got more guts than me.

John walks onstage next, looking everywhere but at my dad and his pals.

'Evening, folks,' he says, stumbling at first, but soon recovers to show some confidence in his voice. 'I'm a little rusty —'

'Get on with it!' says Dad. 'Sing a song we know!'

'Okay…' John rests his forehead upon the microphone, his breaths now slow and laboured. He sees Tom and I waving over, which seemingly gives him the courage to carry on. 'I'm gonna sing *Hurt* — the Johnny Cash version — for you all.'

'Slit-your-wrist music! Shite!' says Dad, followed by some jeering noises from his associates. 'Get off! Bring that bonnie lass back on!'

Amar whispers to me nervously, 'I'm just visiting the gents, Daz. Your dad has done a number on my stomach.'

'No worries, mate.' I focus on John again, though keep drawing my eyes sideways to watch over Amar. He walks by Dad with his head held low, trying his best to keep a low profile. I give it a few more seconds before returning my full interest to John's heartfelt performance.

'I hate to admit it, but John's pretty good,' says Tom. He's sneakily ordered a double-whisky chaser while my attention was turned away from him, going by the looks of it. 'I'm only having the one,' he insists, raising his shot glass to me. 'Don't give me that look. Given the fact your dad's here, I bet you wish you could drink something harder than lemonade as well.'

'The smell of your whisky alone is enough to knock me off my feet,' I joke, but then a wave of dread sweeps over me. Amar's still nowhere to be seen and neither's Dad. 'Won't be a sec, Tom. I'm gonna go check on Amar.'

'Amar's a big boy,' he says, waving a hand at me dismissively. 'He doesn't need you to wipe his backside.'

'Something's up. I'm gonna go check on him.'

As I reach the toilets a series of screams and curse words echo around me. I find Amar lying on the urine-soaked floor, where he is surrounded by my dad and his friends that are all spitting and raising their fists at him. Dad goes to kick Amar in the stomach, lining himself up like a footballer about to take a penalty shot. But then he spots me, freezes, and the look of hatred on his face intensifies.

'This pub fuckin' stinks of curry now because of you!' he roars, shaking a fist at Amar. 'Your lot aren't welcome in here!'

'Leave me alone!' Amar cries, wrapping himself up into a protective ball. 'Stop it! I don't want to fight you!'

'You wouldn't fuckin' dare lay a finger on me,' Dad sneers, laughing to his mates. 'You'd never walk again, my boy. That's a promise.'

I stand myself between Dad and Amar, just as he's about to land the final blow. 'What are you doing?' I ask with an anxious gulp. Dad's anger turns on me now (which is nothing new). And before I know it, he's placed a rigid finger against my windpipe, digging it in. 'Amar isn't hurting anyone. There's no need to go on like this, Dad.'

'Oh! You're taking his side, are you?' Dad clenches a fist around the top of my shirt, tearing off two buttons. I remain still, resolute, barely holding back the urge to headbutt him.

I'd never result to physical violence, though. I'm nothing like my father. 'You're defending him, Darren? He's nought but a dirty Pak—'

'Don't. Don't say it,' I implore, to which Dad backs off slightly with his mouth open aghast. I rarely stand up to him, but—especially where my closest friends are concerned—I'm willing to take a punch. 'Are you really going to hit me? You're going to beat your own son up?'

Dad looks to each his friends, who shake their heads at him, then turns from me. 'No, Darren. You hit me first. *You* throw the first punch.'

'Why?' I ask, genuinely confused. 'I don't understand.'

'Go on! Fuckin' HIT ME!' he taunts, sending a barrage of lager-laden saliva across my face. 'You won't, though, will you? You're just like your mother: soft, pathetic, a waste of oxygen, a fuckin' disgrace,' he whispers into my ear. 'How are you my son?' The feeling is mutual, if truth be told. 'How did I end up with a useless wanker like you for a child? You're no son of mine.'

And he wonders why I make excuses not to go on holidays with him. I casually ignore Dad's threats, instead holding out a hand for Amar to steady himself with.

'Are you alright, mate?' I ask Amar, trying hard to not reveal the fear inside.

'Yeah,' he replies, sighing with relief. 'I didn't say anything to your dad, or even look him in the eye,' he whimpers. 'He just…. went for me.'

'Who, in the fuck, do you think you are, turning your back on me?' Dad seethes, pointing a finger towards Amar and then at myself. 'We'll settle this like proper men. Outside. Car park—NOW!'

As if things couldn't get any worse, Tom walks in at this moment, and — judging by how he's staggering — the whisky chaser has evidently gone to his head. No doubt he's enjoyed two or three more in my absence. He makes his way over to the urinal, whistling to himself, and then unwittingly catches his foot on a raised tile, which results in him falling into one of Dad's friends, Billy, who then flies head-first into the stream of fresh urine. Tom shrugs his shoulders and goes to relieve himself in response, which doesn't go down well with Dad.

'Sorry,' Tom says to Billy, half-heartedly. 'I didn't see you.'

'*Didn't see me*? Are you blind or something, lad?'

'Don't you fret over this dickhead, Bill,' says Dad with a sadistic smirk. 'I'll deal with this knobhead. I'll deal with little Tommy-boy.' He walks up to Tom, smacking his fists together. 'Should I slam your head into a trough full of piss? Should I humiliate you in front of your mates — see how you like it?'

'It was an accident,' says Tom, somehow ignoring the threat now looming over him a.k.a. my father by proceeding to urinate in the same spot Billy had lain in seconds earlier. 'I didn't mean to knock into him. It's just one of those things.'

This is becoming a disaster and can go two ways with Tom: he'll either turn into a gibbering wreck, or — and this is what worries me most, on account of his whisky consumption — he'll become violent due to all the adrenaline and alcohol flowing through him.

'You're a cheeky bastard, aren't you?' says Dad. He then leans into Tom's face, looks down, and laughs. 'On second thought, I won't do you in. I don't hit girls, you see.'

'That's enough!' I plead. 'You've made your point, Dad. You've made yourself look big and hard in front of your friends. Can we not have a nice evening out without any drama for once?'

'It was you dozy twats that started it!' Dad grabs Tom by the scuff of his jacket and I close my eyes, expecting the worse. 'I think you need to be taught some manners, Tom-boy. A good smack or two around the chops should do the trick.'

Tom suddenly slips off his jacket, inadvertently causing my drunken father to lose balance, which results in Dad slipping into the flowing stream of urine. Without any hesitation, me and my friends take this opportunity to make our exit. John and Ryan will understand us not hanging around, I'm sure as much. I'll explain to them why we left without saying goodbye the next time I see them. They'll understand. They'll just have to. We've certainly overstayed our welcome.

Amar unlocks his car frantically and gestures for me and Tom to get in, a mere two minutes after our confrontation with Dad. We sit for a moment, each attempting to contemplate what's just happened. I turn my head to see if Dad and his mates are following us, but they're nowhere to be seen, and I'll no doubt reap the repercussions come Sunday — that's when Mum and Dad will be coming over to share in my family's weekly roast dinner. I can always cross that bridge when I get to it, can't I? Anyway, I've got bigger things to worry about i.e. Tom and his anxiety.

'That was close,' Tom gasps, stretching out his cramped fingers. 'I'm sorry about what happened back there. Honestly, it was a genuine mistake.'

'Why are you apologising?' says Amar, laughing. 'Darren's dad just tried to kick seven shades of shit out of me. You did me a favour.'

'I'm still sorry.' Tom looks across to me with a solemn frown. 'You're gonna get so much grief off your dad now... because of me.'

'I can handle him,' I say. Tom's tremors are getting worse, so I signal to Amar for us to speed up. 'Try to focus on your breathing, mate. That usually works, doesn't it? Focus on your breaths. We're safe now.'

Tom nods back appreciatively, but this technique doesn't seem to be having any desired effect. Amar pulls onto Tom's driveway and we sit again in silence for a few minutes more, that is, until Tom is calm enough to move his aching limbs. He's told me before how his tremors cause painful cramps, which in turn drain his energy and ability to move. He can't keep going on like this.

'I still can't breathe,' he says, his eyes widening with panic.

'Try to imagine this,' I suggest. 'Imagine that all your bad feelings and thoughts have been put into some bricks, which are making a huge wall before you. Breathe in deep and then out slowly. Take control, mate. Now make some cracks appear in those bricks.'

'Where are you going with this?' he asks in perplexment.

This technique — even if it may seem peculiar — works for me, and I'm determined to make it work for Tom. 'If you're struggling, hit those bricks with a sledgehammer. Keep on hitting them until some cracks start to appear — you can do it, mate. It's your imagination, Tom. You're in control.'

'I get it...' Tom takes in a deep breath, exhales, and gradually smiles. 'I've managed to make a few cracks.'

'Now, focus on what makes you happy in life—'

'Rosie,' he says without hesitation. 'My little Rosie.'

'She's behind that wall, Tom. You've got to break it down. It's the only way you'll be able to see her again, to feel the love and warmth you associate with her. Break it down until there's nothing but dust left. And when there's nothing but dust, imagine that it's all blown away by a gentle breeze. Do whatever you can to make that wall vanish.'

He clenches his eyelids together, takes in another deep breath, then gives out a long sigh.

'I did it!' he exclaims. 'I broke through the wall—it's gone!'

'How are you feeling now?' I ask him.

'Much better,' he says, his breathing now notably more relaxed. 'Thanks, Daz. I'll have to remember that technique. It actually worked.'

'Same again next week, boys?' says Amar, hinting at some sarcasm in his tone. 'I think a change in venue might be a good idea, but.'

'I want to go home,' says Tom, retching. He then whispers to me, 'That's the last time I'll ever go out. I can't hack it anymore. I can't handle being around other people.'

'It's not often Dad visits the Tin Donkey, mate. And— especially after that debacle—I doubt he'll be back again anytime soon. Just forget that tonight ever happened.'

Tom doesn't seem convinced, his expression rapidly turning sour.

'I wish it was that simple to forget. These tremors and cramps of mine—they'll be the death of me, they will.'

Amar goes rigid, unsure as what to say. I wink to him and then assist Tom out of the car, into his home.

'I'll be in touch with you during the week,' I say, making it clear to Tom that he won't, in fact, be alone. 'Try and take things easy.'

'I will,' he murmurs as I assist him to the sofa. 'I've ruined a good night out again, haven't I?'

'No, you haven't. Get some sleep. I'll lock the door and post your keys through the letterbox, okay? You'll be fine.'

'I'm nothing but a burden—'

'You're not.'

'I am. All I ever do is let people down.'

'That's not true.'

'It is. Just go home, Daz, and forget about me.'

'That ain't gonna happen, pal. I'll be checking on you.'

'Why? I'm better off alone. I can't hurt anyone that way.'

'That's the alcohol talking. I'll call you tomorrow, and you better answer.'

'Go home, mate. I don't need any help. I want to be left alone. I need to be left alone…'

Melancholic Alcoholic

You don't know what you've got 'til it's gone. I hate phrases like that; they're so cheesy and overused. But I'm finding this one to be true, and through the hard way. It's all my fault. Everything is my fault.

I've managed to wake up, to pull myself together in some fashion; to get off the sofa and walk into the kitchen, where my tablets are waiting for me. But the silence and emptiness now festering within my home makes me think: what is the point? Why don't I just go back to sleep and dream of happier times, of when Alice and Rosie were still here with me? What exactly do I have to live for now? Nothing. I want to be happy, but that just seems impossible. I hate feeling like this. I hate being so miserable…I never used to be.

I'm down to my last cigarette and there's nothing left in my cupboards to eat (not that I'm hungry, anyway). Regardless of how much I want to put it off, I'll need to step outside at some point today for more supplies. The thought of doing that alone brings on my usual tremors, which always lead into a bout of agonising cramps in my fingers and toes. I'm no longer in the same old routine, the same old comfort zone—which I had come to detest, funnily enough—and I'm not sure whether I like this change or if I'm even ready for it.

After some deliberation, I slip on my shoes and then force myself out the front door. The fresh air hits me like a brutal wall of ice, almost forcing me back inside. I don't turn back, though. I forge on ahead, along my route to work, towards the nearest corner shop. I'm all out of whisky and beer, too, so there's no question at all in me needing to leave my home, but it's still such a struggle. The thought of going without some alcohol and nicotine in my system simply isn't worth comprehending. No way, man. I can't let that happen.

I've decided to give my last cigarette to Karam, seeing as I'll be passing by him on the way to the shop. It's not much as gifts go, but I like to think that I'm helping others out in some way, particularly those less fortunate. It's the smallest gestures that matter most in life, after all. However, a rancid scent of burning plastic and meat offend my senses on approaching Karam's current place of residence. I shrug this strange occurrence off, convinced that it's just my overzealous imagination working overtime, but soon come to realise that it's not make-believe. God knows, I wish it was.

I find Karam knelt on the wet grass verge, sobbing into his hands, praying in his own language, slowly lifting his head up towards the charred remains of his tent. It must have only happened a few hours ago, due to how the smoke is still billowing out. Poor Karam. Still, at least he wasn't inside of it.

I walk up to Karam cautiously, as not to cause him any further distress, and kneel beside him. To be fair, there's not much I can do or say that will improve this situation. All I can do is show some sympathy — to prove that there are people in this world who do care about him.

'Are you alright, mate?' I ask him, all the while ridiculing myself over how stupid this question is — of course he's not alright. Karam's freezing, though I suspect him shivering is more to do with the anguish of losing his home than the cold winds. 'What happened?'

'Why?' he whimpers, his eyes locked ahead in a catatonic stare. 'Why has Allah punished me? Why has Allah taken Charlie from me? Have I not suffered enough loss?' he wails.

That's when the harsh truth hits me: Charlie was inside the tent when it burnt down.

'How did this happen? Was it an accident?'

He shakes his head to me, wiping the tears from his ash-laden face. 'I went to relieve myself in those bushes,' he explains, pointing to a nearby garden. 'I then heard some drunken men approach, so I stayed put and out of sight. I've been beaten up before,' he says under his breath bitterly. 'I heard one of the men pour something on my tent — it was petrol, I think. They all started laughing, and then I saw another throw a lit cigarette onto it. They burned my Charlie!' he screams, shaking his fists into the air. 'Why, Tom? Charlie was all I had. I can hear his dying yelps even now.'

'That's awful...evil.' Like Karam, my own sadness now turns into anger. 'Could you make out any features of the men, like what they were wearing?' I pat at his back gently, desperate to offer him some much-needed solace. 'The police might be able to do something. You never know?'

'The man with the cigarette was bald and wore strange clothes—like a beastly troll, he was. He had two belts pulling his trousers up. That's all I could make out of him in the darkness.' Karam blows a kiss towards the tent, his grief for Charlie overriding his rage now. 'My little companion is no more. The police won't care about me. I shouldn't even be here, according to them. I am a public nuisance, so I've been told. But that does not justify what has happened to my Charlie.'

No. It couldn't have been Darren's dad and his mates? Oh yes, it could. They're cruel and heartless enough to do something this malicious. I wouldn't put it past them for one second.

'I'm so sorry, mate. You don't deserve this, and you're not a nuisance,' I implore. 'You've done nothing wrong.'

'I was a doctor. I was highly respected,' he laments. 'Look at me now. What do I have to live for? I have nothing! May I have a cigarette?' he asks, holding out a hand to me. Karam's words echo in my thoughts, plaguing them. I said the exact same phrase, about having nothing to live for, but he has far more right to feel that way than I do. 'It will help calm my nerves. I need a smoke.'

'Of course.' I light up the cigarette in my own mouth and then hand it over to Karam, reeling from the irony that it was a cigarette which brought down his whole world, and now I'm offering the same method of destruction to him. 'That's my last one. I'm just on my way to the shop to get some more. I'll get you a packet, if you like?'

'That won't be necessary,' he sniffles. 'I will be okay. I am still alive, and for that I should be thankful to Allah. I will miss my Charlie, my lovely boy. He helped keep me warm at night.'

My heart sinks further with each step taken away from Karam and his smouldering tent. I'm desperate to tell Daz, for him to enact justice upon his monstrous father, but that won't bring Karam's tent or Charlie back. Anyway, I caused enough damage to their fractured relationship last night. I don't want to add more salt to the wounds.

After purchasing my vital supplies, I take an alternative route home as to avoid that harrowing scene of destruction. I know it sounds selfish—which it is—but I can't face Karam again today, not with how bad my own anxiety and depression already are. I need to dilute them. I'm desperate to remove that image of Karam's burnt tent and smell of Charlie's cremated corpse from my memories. Now, with some strong alcohol at hand, I have the means to. I've got the rest of this day planned out to the minutest detail: I'll go home, open this whisky bottle, down it as fast I can, find my old Super Nintendo console, play on some retro video games until the sun sets, and then dwell in self-pity until my eyelids finally shut. This is my wonderful existence now. Hallelujah! Happy days! What a crock…

When back at home, I open the bottle of whisky and pour a large helping of it into my mouth. The alcohol hit burns at my throat and gullet, though I soon get over the pain; and the after-effect of being devoid of any emotion makes it all worthwhile. I then head into the living room, where I set up my Super Nintendo console after fighting to unravel its wires for almost forty minutes. Again, the effort is worthwhile. Along with the urge to be subdued, I need to be reminded of more innocent times — my childhood, to be precise. This is my latest coping method: to linger in the past.

Playing these old video games of mine brings back fond memories of when me and Uncle Steven would do the same, back when he was still alive. We'd spend many a night playing on Super Mario or Donkey Kong Country, laughing and being happy in one another's company. It makes a pleasant change from all the flashbacks I've been encountering recently, the ones which only focus on negative experiences that are filled with pain, guilt and misery.

This day is how the next seven proceed, sadly, where I'm left alone to mull over all my wrongdoings and failures. Daz, the other lads, and my closest family members have each sent me messages during this time, most of which ask how I'm coping and if they can help in any way. I gave them all the same response, the same lie: I'm okay, there's no need to worry about me, and please don't feel the need to come and visit. They accepted this as being the truth, thankfully. I'm a master of deception, both to them and myself.

Like Alice, I require some time to think — solitude is the simplest answer to that — but not for the same reasons as her. It's nowhere close. Alice wants to evaluate our relationship; whereas, all I want to do is dwell on the past and shorten my life through excessive drinking. I don't want to be a burden on my loved ones anymore, to cut the story short. Nevertheless, Daz doesn't give up on me as easily as the others do. He's sent me numerous links to self-help websites, each aiming to overcome anxiety and depression through remote chat sessions and discussions. But I've visited them all before, and I'm not in the mood to change my ways. I'll maybe visit them tomorrow, just as I do with everything else that seems to be too laborious.

Come the second week, I'm starting to notice how much weight I've lost; my trousers keep slipping down and I can see the outline of my cheekbones for the first time in years. Perhaps living on instant noodles and whisky isn't such a good idea, like Alice has stated countless times before. This weight loss isn't doing any wonders for my complexion, either. But I couldn't care less. I couldn't give a toss. I'm surviving — right? Within this self-inflicted isolation, I'm no longer a problem for those I care about to consider, and that's a good thing — an honourable act, is it not?

I have made several attempts to contact Alice, though I chickened out on each one. She and Rosie don't need me. They can start afresh, find a new partner and father-figure, and live out the rest of their days free from my cancerous presence. I don't want that, though. Christ, I don't know what I want. I wish I could be brave enough to pick up the phone, to call Alice and tell her that I'm sorry. But that's never going to happen. I'm anything but brave; I'm a complete and utter coward.

Now fully immersed within the depths of my anxious despair, I imagine that wall again — the same wall Daz told me to focus on. I reach out my hands and aim them at the bricks, desperate to create some cracks in them, but the wall doesn't budge a single inch; in fact, it only seems to become stronger. Despite my best efforts, this wall then grows to tower over me and then moves in closer. I've got nowhere to run or hide — it's crushing me! I've been beaten. I'm rapidly heading into a panic attack and running out of techniques to combat it. I was wrong to believe I could cope alone. I need my friends and family, but I don't want to suffocate them with my depressing influence. Why did I push them away? I was being so stupid, thinking that I could tackle this by myself.

So, this is it. This is the path I've chosen in life. I'm to spend the rest of my days as a hermit, an alcoholic, consumed with melancholy and self-hatred. This isn't living. This isn't living at all. At least I've got my video games and whisky to keep me occupied — that's something positive. What I would give to enjoy just one day where I'm normal, free from the devil's drink. But what exactly is "normal"? I doubt even Daz knows the answer to that.

My idea of being normal is to live without constantly feeling scared, depressed, resentful, and having to rely on chemicals to survive. But there are so many people in this world who are in the same boat as me. So, therefore, doesn't that make us — we fellow sufferers — normal in some way? And isn't being addicted to gambling; to social media; to falling into debt as a way of satisfying materialistic urges; to overconsuming junk food; to become obsessed with cosmetic surgery; to working too many hours in a job that gives you no self-worth or satisfaction; to choosing technical devices over loved ones — aren't they just as harmful as my dependency on alcohol and mental illnesses? I'm overthinking things again, aren't I? Alice was right. Alice was right about me. I'm not normal and never will be. I'm so much better off alone.

Flashback: November 20th, 2009

I've only been in this godforsaken job for two weeks, this last resort I turned to in order to keep the goblins at the Jobcentre off my back. Working as a salesperson in a discount fabric shop isn't exactly the career I aspired to, but I don't want to lose it either. If I'm fired today that will mean returning to the weekly humiliation of having to visit the dole office, to sign what fragments of dignity and self-respect I have left over to some pen-pushing, emotionless advisors — people who are more interested in cutting off my benefit paycheques to improve the government's social welfare statistics than to guide me along the correct path. No matter how often my so-called advisor tells me they care, I get a slight inkling they don't.

I'm not a statistic. I'm not some "waster" or "sponger" as many would call me. I am a human being. I am an individual who wants to find purpose in life, just like anyone else. But I'm being made to feel the total opposite, and for a crime I had no inclination of committing: selling some of the most expensive material to a customer yesterday at the wrong price — at the cheapest, by all accounts — which my fellow colleagues inform me is an act worthy of gross dismissal.

So, I wait. I wait for Sheila, my manager, to call me into her office — which she does, and with a forced and misleading smile on her face. I try to justify her grave expression by reasoning that she must be nervous — that this is her own way of coping — like how I've learned to feign a smile to avoid such awkward scenarios. But Sheila isn't like me. All

Sheila is interested in is profit margins, not preventing the likes of myself from being cast back onto the dole queue. Can a person not make a genuine mistake? I do despise this job, yes, but I've still worked my arse off to make a good impression. Doesn't that count for anything?

'Come in,' Sheila says to me, fleeting her eyes anywhere but against mine. 'Don't sit down, Tom.'

'What have I done?' I ask myself, though it comes out anyway in an anxious stutter.

'Must I really explain it to you?' Her eyes now meet against mine, and they're filled with anger and disappointment. 'Morgan told me about the silk you sold yesterday, and at what price. Do you realise how much money you lost me? I'm not surprised that the customer purchased so much.' She turns away from me, tilting her head sharply. 'When I hired you, and despite my doubts, I didn't realise just how stupid you are.'

I somehow respond, matching Sheila's anger with my own. 'You can't say that! I'm not stupid. How was I meant to know it was at a different price? There weren't any labels to say it was, for a start.'

'It was a big mistake hiring you. I can see that now,' she adds with little sympathy. Sheila then hands me a thin, brown envelope. 'That's your final pay. I've deducted the cost from the silk which you mis-sold yesterday. I think it's only fair.'

I tear open the envelope, just holding back my dismay. 'There's only forty quid here. Where's the rest?'

'You need to leave now,' she informs me, pointing to the door. 'I'll need to escort you off the premises, Tom. If you're lucky, you might catch your bus home.'

No apologies? No: *Sorry for landing you back into poverty over an honest mistake, Tom*? To be fair, I'm not astounded by her response. I lost my faith in people a long time ago.

'You don't need to escort me off the premises,' I say amid a nervous burst of laughter. 'It's not like I'm going to grab a handful of your tacky fabrics on the way out —'

'Leave — NOW!' she snaps. 'And don't come back.'

In a strange sense, I'm relieved by the sound of Sheila slamming the shop doors behind me, and I'm not even bothered by the heavy downpour outside. Despite this meaning I'm back on the dole, there does appear to be some light within this dark moment i.e. a billboard at the bus stop opposite is advertising some teaching courses at a local university, of which I have the necessary qualifications to apply.

When one door closes, another one opens.

Sod Sheila and her crappy fabric store. I'm on my way up. I'm more than ready to make a better life for me and Alice, where we'll be financially secure and have some meaningful purpose in life. Being sacked is still like being hit with a hot bag of shit, though, and it's something I don't ever want to experience again. It's so humiliating, demoralising, and makes me feel even more worthless (which is how I feel most days, anyway). I've got to stay positive. The last thing I want is to sink back into depression, like I did when my parents split up. I've got to stay positive. I can't go through all that again.

Tearing the Cocoon

It took some perseverance and a great deal of nagging, but I've convinced Amar and John that we should visit Tom today. They both seem apprehensive about the unexpected check-up, though nowhere near as anxious as our elusive friend will be. I understand why, however. Tom has shut himself away over the last two weeks, blatantly ignoring any effort we've made to contact him. Amar and John are under the impression that he just needs some space to himself, to get over his separation from Alice. But I know Tom, and I know — more so than others — how dangerous isolating yourself can be.

There's a collective sigh from myself and the lads as I pull my car onto Tom's driveway, each of us held in uncertainty. But we've gone over this during the journey over, that we're here to listen; that we're here to share our own experiences; that we're visiting our vulnerable friend to show him that we do care about him, and that he's not alone or a burden. No matter what reservations we three might have, we've got to show Tom that he does matter. That's what true friends are for, after all.

'Does he even know that we're coming to see him?' John asks, slowly rubbing at his temples. 'Tom hates surprises, and I don't think he'll be in the mood for visitors. This isn't going to end well, Darren. Did you warn him about our visit?'

'No. Tom hasn't got a clue,' I say, hinting at some guilt in the tone of my voice. 'If we had given him a heads up, he'd just fob us off with the usual excuses. It is a risk we're taking, but a necessary one.'

'The poor lad just needs some time to himself,' says Amar, repeating his earlier thoughts. 'Us turning up out of the blue might make his anxiety worse. I'm only saying...'

'Maybe? But I doubt Tom can sink any lower than where he's at,' I say. 'Let's see how things go. Trust me, lads. I know him better than anyone. He needs his pals around him.'

'We're talking about Tom here — "Mr. Unpredictable",' John sneers. 'And the Tom I know won't appreciate us three turning up at his door without any heads up. I've got a bad feeling about this.'

'The Tom I know will be over the moon to see his closest friends, even if it doesn't come across that way at first,' I argue.

'Not everyone is as optimistic as you are,' says Amar. 'Tom doesn't like surprises — he's said that plenty of times.'

'Remember why we're here, lads, and what we discussed last night down the pub. Be honest with him. Don't hold back. Tom needs to hear the truth,' I beseech.

'I don't know,' says John in confliction. 'It's gonna be hard work.'

I take the lead, practically dragging Amar and John towards Tom's home. I'm tempted to knock at his door but reason that will be a wasted effort, seeing as he'll likely ignore the disturbance. Then I recall how Tom leaves a spare key under one of his flowerpots, for when he's too drunk to search through his pockets. In a stroke of good luck, I find the spare key and proceed to unlock the front door. An awkward moment ensues as me and the lads contemplate our next move. There's a tense atmosphere before even stepping foot inside, and I can tell that Amar and John are becoming more reluctant by the second.

'I'm not happy about this,' John whispers to me. 'I don't like to think about my own issues, let alone openly discussing them. I had a few pints last night before agreeing to this, didn't I?'

'You can do this,' I say to him. 'Tom needs his friends around him, and for us to make it clear that talking helps.'

Amar finds a sudden burst of energy, barging past myself and John to enter the living room.

'Tom?' he shouts out, slowly poking his head around the door. 'Are you there, mate?'

We're met with some initial silence, though Tom's familiar, timid voice soon speaks up.

'Amar?' he asks. 'I'm in here.' Without even seeing him, it becomes obvious to us how weak Tom is now. 'Come in and make yourself at home, boys.'

John and I join Amar at the doorway, the three of us peering into the living room — to the sofa where Tom is lying, wearing the same clothes I last saw him in — where we're hit by a truly disturbing vision, a scene of utter devastation. The whole house stinks of tobacco and beer, and there are empty lagers cans strewn all over the place; the curtains are still closed, despite it being midday, and all the family photographs have been placed face-down upon the floor. This is worse than I thought it'd be.

'Jesus wept,' says John, turning to me. 'I didn't realise it was this serious.'

A groan leaves from Tom as he sits himself up. Under his breath, he then asks, 'How the hell did you lot get in? I'm sure I locked the door last night.' To a roll of his eyes, I hold out the spare key. 'That's meant for emergencies, and it's supposed to be a secret.'

I open my arms, aiming them at the chaotic mess surrounding us.

'I'd say this is an emergency, wouldn't you? And you can't keep any secrets from me – your best mate. You should know that by now, Tom. Plus, I've had to use this key a few times after our nights down the pub, so it's hardly a secret.'

He chunters something to himself and then stands. I immediately notice how Tom's lost some considerable weight and the joyful spark in his eyes. He can't even stand up straight anymore.

'What are you doing here?' he asks, scowling at us. 'Don't you lads have something better to do on a Saturday afternoon?'

'We've come to check on you,' says Amar. 'We're getting a little bit worried…'

'About me – why?' Tom lowers his head as if it were being weighed down by an immense force. 'What makes me so special?'

'Because we care, ya daft sod,' says John. 'You're not answering our messages, leaving the house, or coming down the pub anymore. Something's very wrong, and don't say it isn't.'

'I'm not in the mood to socialise,' says Tom. 'I'm fine, lads. Honestly. You can go now.'

I nudge into John's back, edging him forwards. 'Tell him. Tell him what you said to me and Amar down the pub last night.'

John freezes, but then steadily regains his composure. 'I get that it's not the manliest subject to talk about,' he murmurs, 'but it's okay to discuss things —'

'Like what?' says Tom, taken aback.

'You know, to talk about your anxiety and depression. There's no harm in being open about them.'

'I can't be arsed. No offence.'

'It'll do you some good to talk,' John adds, now starting to lose his patience. 'You're not the only person with mental health problems, you know.'

'You wouldn't understand. I'm all for chatting about rock bands and politics — like we normally do — but not my anxiety and depression. No one really wants to know about things like that, do they? No one gives a shit about how others feel.'

'I've got depression…had it for about four years now.'

Tom looks to John through his fingertips, evidently shocked.

'You've never said —'

'No. Only the wife knew, that is, until I opened up to Amar and John about my problems last night. We got talking about your situation, about your mental health issues —'

'You don't need to have an in-depth discussion,' I interject. 'We're here to listen, mate. Tell us what's on your mind.'

'You know what's up with me,' says Tom, looking to us solemnly. 'Unless you've got a magic wand that can repair my marriage and bring Rosie back into my life, then there's nothing to discuss.' He looks to John again. 'How do you hide it so well, your depression?'

'I manage it, that's all. I learnt what the triggers are and how to combat them,' he says. 'The fact I take some Sertraline every morning helps as well.'

'You're on meds too? But you've never said —'

'And neither have you, at least not to me. There's nothing to be ashamed of, you know. Don't suffer on your own,' says John, before pointing a thumb to Amar. 'Aren't you gonna speak up?'

'Erm…' Amar hesitates, though after a subtle nod from myself he steps forth. 'Look, I haven't got depression, or anxiety as bad as you have, but I do know what it's like to feel scared. That's how I felt each time I left the house in London, always on edge, waiting to be attacked for the way I looked and for being a Sikh. But I came to realise that not everyone is bad. You shouldn't hide your true self.'

'I've got nothing to hide,' says Tom. 'I appreciate what you lads are trying to do, but all I want is to be left alone.'

'To do what?' I ask. 'To rot away in this cold house of yours, getting drunk every day? That's no life, mate. You must be able to see that?'

'I can, and I don't care. Getting drunk helps keep me sane.'

John leans across to me. 'I said this was a bad idea. He doesn't want our help, Darren. We should go.'

'No,' I state. 'We've come here to show that we do care. You're not a failure, Tom, and certainly not a burden.' I notice that he's got his old Super Nintendo console out, a physical example of his greatest holdback: the inability to let go. 'You dwell too much on the past, on what's gone and can't be changed. It's about time you looked to the future, to what new horizons lie in wait.'

'Without Alice and Rosie, I don't have any new horizons to look forward to,' he says, staring at me with a blank expression. 'I don't deserve friends like you. Just… leave me alone.'

'Locking yourself away from the world and your problems won't solve anything,' I say. 'You'll only dig a deeper hole. And the deeper it gets, the harder it will be for you to rise from it.'

Tom shuffles along the floor in silence to pick up one of the photographs, which he briefly examines before handing it over to me. The photo is of him, Alice and Rosie that they had taken on holiday last year.

'I want my family back. Tell me what to do, lads. Tell me how to put things right,' he pleads. 'Tell me how to cure my anxiety and depression, because I haven't got the foggiest idea and I'm starting to give up on any hope.'

'There's no miracle cure. It's a nice thought, but that will never happen,' says John, clearly speaking from his own experiences. 'I was in the same boat as you, once over. All I wanted to do was lie in bed all day, where I could feel safe and not be bothered by other people and their problems. But that made my depression worse, and it almost drove Hannah away from me. I nearly lost Lucy and Sophia, my little girls. I know what it's like to touch into the grief you're now going through, Tom. Let us help you.'

Tom's body contorts, his fingers deforming from the anxiety coursing through them. 'Why do you want to hear about my issues?' he asks, clenching his teeth together. 'Why go through the bother?'

I reach into my back pocket and pull out four cinema tickets, which I then show to him. 'It's not much, but it's a start. I've bought us some tickets to see *Child's Play*. You love horror movies, don't you?'

Tom glances at the tickets and laughs, 'A horror movie? That'll do my nerves the world of good.'

'The idea is to get you out of this house, this stagnant and choking atmosphere,' I add. 'Take the plunge. Fight against those negative impulses and come with us. Please, mate.'

Tom looks over the tickets, scraping a hand across his face. 'I wanted to take Alice to see that movie. I guess it won't hurt to go…'

'That's the spirit. But we'll need to set off now if we're going to make it in time for the showing.'

'Now?' he says, his eyes littered with panic. 'Really?'

Without further ado, Amar and John assist Tom to his feet and then out of the house to my car. It's like drawing some magnets apart in trying to remove him from the front door's pedestal, but we manage — each of us united by a shared determination to make Tom change his current mindset. During the short drive to Darlington, Tom sits in my passenger's seat as if held under some hypnotising spell. He doesn't say a word, merely looking out of the window as if he were some unsuspecting hostage: consumed by fear and lost.

'We're here,' I say, pulling into the cinema's underground carpark. 'Look, Tom, if you don't want to see the movie—'

'I do,' he implores. 'I need to do this. I've got to, Daz.'

'Don't worry,' says John. 'At this time of day, the cinema shouldn't be too packed. It'll be nice and quiet.'

Tom performs his usual fake smile and saunters behind us as we enter the cinema's main complex. 'This isn't so bad,' he comments. 'I feel fine. I don't feel anxious at all.'

'It was this or paintballing,' jokes Amar. 'You're doing well, Tom-boy. Keep it up.'

'I'm trying to,' he chuckles back. 'This is for my own good. I can do this…'

On making our way towards the screening room I pull Tom aside. There's an urgent matter to be discussed, and it's something I can't hide from him anymore. However, a group of rowdy teenagers walk by that immediately send his anxiety into overdrive. His breaths become faint and rapid; his eyes lock ahead in sheer fright, and the colour completely drains from him.

'What's the matter?' I ask him.

'I can't do this—I can't!'

John moves in closer, clasping Tom by his shoulders to turn him around. 'Would you like to try one of my coping techniques, seeing as your breathing exercises aren't exactly working?'

Tom begins to tear and punch at his arms and legs. He's heading into a panic attack, and I'm completely powerless to stop it.

'Do something,' I say to John in desperation. 'You know what it's like, mate.'

'This is a bad attack, isn't it?' John asks him. 'I can tell, and we'll get through this together.'

'I can't breathe,' Tom gasps. 'I can't stop it!'

'You've got ride this out — that's how I cope.' John wraps his fingers around Tom's arms now, centring his balance. 'Your body is being overrun with adrenaline. It's like riding a high-speed rollercoaster, and that's what you need to imagine right now. You're strapped into a rollercoaster's cart, helpless, and held at the mercy of this terrifying ordeal.'

'How is *this* helping?' says Amar, shaking his head in disbelief.

Nevertheless, John continues. 'It's fright or flight, Tom, your most basic instinct — your primal urge to protect yourself. But the thing is, you've got no option to run away. You've got no choice but to see this through. Ride the wave of anxiety — don't resist it. Turn that fear into an urge to survive, to overcome this obstacle and fight back. Feel the terror and accept that it's there. Take control. You must take control. Tell yourself that you're not helpless or weak. Breathe in deep as the cart reaches the summit of an immense drop, then slowly exhale as it falls. You're safe. You've fallen, but you've beaten that sense of dread that something awful will occur, because it hasn't. Breathe. Concentrate on riding the wave and let go of that fear. Let the tension flowing through your fingertips disperse into the air around you, as your cart pulls back into the station safely. You're okay. You're in control. You've survived.'

'I think this is dangerous,' Amar warns me. 'John is telling him to run headfirst into a panic attack.'

'Just wait and see,' I reply. 'John's not daft. He knows what he's doing...'

'Feel the tension rise and fall like the waves on a stormy ocean,' says John, relinquishing his grip from Tom now. 'Reign in the fear. You, alone, have faced the threat and won.'

To mine and Amar's astonishment, it seems that John's technique is working. Tom stretches out his fingers, looks to them, and smiles. His breathing and complexion have also returned to normal, and his tremors are subsiding. Who'd have thought it? John's alternative technique has actually helped.

'I don't know what triggered the attack,' says Tom. 'They usually come after one of my flashbacks, but I didn't have any.'

'Triggers can sometimes be something held deep inside your subconscious,' says John. 'It could be the smallest, dumbest thing that can set off your anxiety. But what you've got to do is focus on riding through the storm — on taking back control — not on what created those awful sensations. You've got to ground yourself in the present. When an attack kicks in, empty your mind of any thoughts relating to the past and future — concentrate on what is going on in the moment. That's what I do. That's how I manage to live with my depression.'

'What if the present is just as shitty as your past?' says Tom. 'Won't it just make matters worse?'

'Regardless of how bad a situation may feel, there's always something positive lying within it.'

I place a hand firmly upon Tom's shoulder, and nod at the people around us. 'There's probably, say, sixty or seventy people in this room. Do you reckon each person here is one-hundred percent happy and content all the time?'

'No,' he says, making every effort not to look at the strangers walking by. 'That'd be impossible.'

'That's my point. You can't be happy all the time, and the same goes for feeling down. Look at where we are, and who you are with, then tell me one good thing about this present moment.'

'I'm with my best mates,' he says assuredly, folding his arms to prove otherwise. 'We're going to see a movie I've been looking forward to for ages, and I managed to stop another panic attack...'

'Right. Now tell me what is bad about this moment.'

'I don't like the look of those kids over there,' he says, directing his sight towards a group of teenagers nearby. 'They look like trouble.'

'Why?' I ask. 'Is it because they're dressed in hoodie tracksuits?'

'Yeah.'

'What happened to *never judge a book by its cover*?'

'They're shifty-looking. I teach kids like them for a living. I can tell the signs. I bet they're carrying knives—'

'They might be thinking the same about us, mate. Who knows?'

'Oh yeah,' he sniggers. 'We look like a right set of thugs.'

Fate intervenes on our behalf, thankfully. Two of the teenagers take it upon themselves to move aside for an elderly couple, thus forfeiting their place in the queue to buy tickets.

'See? Those kids are alright. There's no need to be so paranoid,' says Amar.

'I feel like a right idiot now,' Tom humours. 'But I can't help being the way I am—'

'You can change, though,' I insist, pulling him away from the others. I've got another surprise lined up for Tom, and I'm hoping it will be the push he needs to get out of this debilitating rut. 'You know how we've always gone on about wanting a lads-only trip someday.'

'Yeah.' Tom smirks inquisitively, which then turns into confusion. 'But we're married and have full-time jobs now. When are we gonna get a chance to go on holiday?'

'You're not back at work until September, and I've just so happened to get the next two weeks off. I've got it all planned out, mate, and down to the finest detail.'

'You've got what planned out? You haven't gone and booked us a holiday, have you?'

'Yes, and it's gonna be epic.'

'I don't do surprises.'

'You'll love this one. I'm putting that inheritance money to good use, and don't want to hear a single complaint from you—you hear?'

'But—'

'The movie's about to start,' Amar whines at us. 'We've missed the advertisements—come on, lads!'

'I'll fill you in with more of the details later,' I say to Tom, barely containing my excitement. 'Our seats are on the front row; they were all that was left.'

It's a struggle to find our seats in the dark, though we manage to just as the curtains fully open.

'I've been dying to see *Child's Play* since the first trailer came out,' Tom says to me. 'I can't wait.'

'Neither can I, Tom-boy. You should be proud of yourself for coming out… it can't have been easy.'

'I wish Alice was here.'

'You can always bring her to see it once you've both made things up. Just enjoy this moment in time, sitting here with your mates.'

It was worth the gamble, to tear apart the diseased cocoon Tom's made around himself, to get him out of his house and to spend time with his friends. However, I happen to now notice that there's a substantial number of children sitting around us, and the opening scene to this movie only adds to my disbelief.

'Hold on, this isn't Child's Play!' John bleats. 'This is the bloody Lion King!'

A succession of muffled laughter echo from behind — from parents amused at our mishap, no doubt — which doesn't amuse John and Amar in the slightest.

'Daz, you utter knob. You've took us into the wrong screening room,' Amar moans.

'The movie's started now,' I say. 'We can see always *Child's Play* some other time, can't we?'

A more familiar burst of laughter emerges, and to my relief it's coming from Tom.

'Trust you, mate,' he cackles. 'Anyway, I don't see why John's so upset — he loves watching Disney movies. Tinkerbell's his favourite character, from what I've heard.'

'Shut it,' John snaps to him. 'I've already seen this with the girls last week. I can't believe this.'

With a wearisome sigh, Tom then says to me, 'I wanted to take Rosie to see *The Lion King*. That's never going to happen…'

'Yes, it will. Stop thinking so negatively,' I say. 'This road trip I've got planned should help with that.'

'You've got a road trip planned for us?' he gawks. 'You are full of surprises, Daz.'

'You don't know the half of it, mate. Trust me, it'll be the holiday of a lifetime…'

On the Road

Onwards and Upwards

Today's the big day. Tom and I are setting off on our road trip, which I've been meticulously planning over the last two weeks. I want this venture to help Tom relax, to unwind, and to get him to open up more about his problems. Nevertheless, I'm not too sure how effective this latest plan of mine will be. Tom's a complicated guy, and not the easiest person to read or please.

Tom was reluctant to come at first, when I woke him up an hour ago, but I know he'll love what surprises lie ahead. He hasn't got a clue — not a single inkling. I've even gone through the effort of sneaking his passport into my suitcase, which I only just got away with during his epically long shower. This plan cannot fail. It can't.

I've been sitting in my car now for almost thirty minutes. Tom finally appears and wastes no time in throwing his suitcase onto the backseat, gets himself in, then plants a cigarette between his lips. The tremors are there but won't be for long. We're going to put a stop to them — I'm certain of it.

'I'm absolutely knackered,' he says, aiming a lighter nervously beneath his cigarette. 'Do you mind if I have a quick smoke?'

'If you must. Roll the window down though, mate. I want to set off before the traffic gets worse.'

'So, where is our first destination?' he asks, blowing out a toxic wave of smoke. 'And what's with all the secrecy?'

'Our first stop is at Durham,' I say, before running a finger over my lips. 'I'll give you that much, but I'm keeping the next destination hush-hush. You're so impatient.'

Despite my enthusiasm, Tom hints at some disappointment in his response. 'Durham?' What's so special about Durham? It's only a thirty-minute bus ride away.'

'It's where we went to college—happier times,' I say, hoping he takes the hint. 'We had some good laughs there, didn't we?'

'Yeah, fifteen years ago.' He squirms in his seat, blinking with astonishment. 'Fifteen years? God, it only feels like yesterday.'

'They were great times. My initial plan was to have a look around some of our old haunts, and that includes the pubs,' I add, keen to hold his interest. 'It's gonna be a belter of a holiday.'

'Now you're talking! We'll make it just in time for Wetherspoons' Happy Hour. It's only £2.00 a pint between eleven and one—'

'You don't need to get drunk to enjoy yourself, mate. Seriously.'

'Life's more fun when there's a wee tipple involved, though.'

This is the last thing I wanted: to come across like some old nag. So, after holding back the urge to lecture him more, I point Tom into the direction of my CD collection. 'Put what you like on. And don't take the piss out of my music taste.'

'I won't!' he says, holding his hands up defensively. 'Hold on a sec…Michael Bublé? Come on, Daz—really?'

'That's Michelle's CD,' I say, somewhat unconvincingly. 'It's not mine. I swear down—'

'I bet. You don't need to be ashamed. I won't judge you,' he sniggers. 'We all have our own little secrets. I like *Crazy Horses* by The Osmonds. You can't get any worse than that.'

'I like *Crazy Horses*. Donny Osmond's a good singer.'

'And the hole you've made has just gotten slightly deeper, mate. You'll be telling me that you like Miley Cyrus next.'

'What's wrong with Miley Cyrus?'

'Bloody hell, Daz. You're making it hard for me *not* to take the piss.'

The start of our journey hasn't gone as I had planned, namely my embarrassing obsession with cheesy pop music being unearthed. But Tom seems happy, and that's what matters most. Anyway, the sun is out, and the traffic isn't too bad—so far, so good. Tom and I point out how much the scenery has changed along the A167, our old bus route to college, as we travel into Durham City. I love reminiscing like this, but Tom gives off the impression that he detests doing such.

'I miss those bus rides to college,' I say, glancing across to check on him. 'Can you remember when a wheel fell off the bus that one time? That was something—'

'I'd rather not think about.' Tom lowers his head and clenches his fists. 'I get flashbacks that trigger my anxiety.

Even when I don't think about certain things, they just spring up and there's absolutely nothing I can do about it. I was a nervous wreck that day, when the bus nearly crashed. We were right at the front as well.'

'Flashbacks?' I pull into a layby to gather my thoughts. It appears we've already made a breakthrough. 'If you know what your triggers are, then is there not a way of trying to stop them? Maybe it will prevent your panic attacks before they start?'

'I've had two counsellors who've tried to help me solve this conundrum, mate.' Tom looks out of his window, lost in thought. 'They taught me some of the breathing techniques I use, but it's still hard. There's no fool-proof solution.'

'Surely, when you get those flashbacks, there must be a way of thinking about something else—more pleasant memories?' I suggest. 'You know, to nip them in the bud.'

'It's easier said than done. We're talking about subconscious thoughts that suddenly come to a head. It's like falling into a daydream, only the images you see and feelings you encounter aren't pleasant.'

'There's always an answer, and you'll work out how to beat those flashbacks soon enough.'

'Booze works, in the most part—'

'That's not the perfect solution, mate, and never will be.'

On that note we set off again. I attempt to counter the current mood by rolling down Tom's window.

'It's not that hot, Daz.'

'You can have another smoke, if you want. Just don't let your cigarette fall into the back of my car like you did a few weeks ago.'

'No, I'll be alright. I do feel a little better for talking about things. I've tried explaining my flashbacks to Alice before, but she struggled to comprehend the impact they have. It's bound to be difficult, to understand, unless you've got anxiety and depression yourself.'

'You don't need a degree in psychology to be empathetic, do you?' Anyhow, you've got me to talk to about things. And don't hold back anything. I'm here to listen.' I indicate to turn into Durham City and Tom's mood instantly lightens. He looks up at Durham's cathedral with a joyful smile, his breathing now slower and tremors less noticeable. I never took him for being religious, so investigate. 'You're the last person I'd take as being religious.'

'I'm not,' he says. 'Uncle Steven was, though. He loved visiting that cathedral. I used to be religious, but…'

'Your Uncle Steven?' I ask, dreading where this conversation may lead. 'Your uncle who had the motorcycle accident?'

'Yeah.' Tom lowers his head again. 'He used to take me and Catherine there a lot, especially during the festive periods, you know, for the choir services and that.' He clenches his fists again. 'I can't believe he's gone. It'll be ten years in February.'

'It wasn't your uncle's fault that he died.' Again, the conversation is heading in the wrong direction. This is a subject I'm keen to move away from, but curiosity simply got the better of me. 'You shared in a lot of good times together. That's what counts.'

'It wasn't an accident,' he snaps. 'Uncle Steven was murdered. We could have made more happy memories together, if it wasn't for that drink-driver mowing him down

238

like a sack of shit. Uncle Steven was always careful on his motorcycle — it can't have been his fault.'

I pull into the carpark of the hotel where I've booked for us to stay this evening. Me and my big mouth. So much for making this a pleasant and relaxed holiday.

'Try to not think about it,' I implore. 'Your uncle wouldn't want you to get upset, would he? Anyway, these are our digs for the night.'

Tom's bitter anger turns to confusion. 'What are we doing here?'

'This is where we're staying. It might look rough on the outside, but it's lush when you get in. Appearances can be deceiving.'

He unbuckles his seatbelt and jumps out of the car, somewhat enthusiastically. 'There's a pub just around the corner from here,' he gleams. 'That is, if I remember rightly...'

On getting out of the car myself I try to direct his attention back on the cathedral, away from temptation.

'How about we have a look there first? We can always go on a pub crawl later.'

Tom stares at the gothic monolith for a few seconds before answering. 'Yeah. Why not? I can light a candle in Uncle Steven's memory. I think he'd like that.'

I'm relieved that Tom's anger and frustration has now turned to something more positive. It's a case of strengthening those good emotions, even though I accept this won't be a simple feat.

'That's a great idea,' I say to him. 'I'll book us into the hotel first. Don't forget your suitcase.'

Tom has another cigarette outside while I pay for our room and take our suitcases up to it. Thereafter, we trudge up a winding set of stone steps that lead into Durham's centre, to where the cathedral is situated. Tom's mood changes again, this time into resentment with some new tremors to match.

'On second thought, can we give the cathedral a miss?' he says, holding out his cramping fingers. 'It wouldn't be right, seeing as I'm not religious.'

'How does that matter? You can still show your respects by lighting a candle for your uncle,' I say, but he just shrugs back at me. Tom's eager to shift our direction, moving us closer towards a pub centred near Durham's town hall. 'Are you that desperate for a drink?'

'It'll settle my nerves and ease these cramps. Just one pint,' he says. 'You don't need to pay —'

'I promised that this trip is on me,' I insist. 'If you want to have a drink first, then that's fine. But take it steady. We don't want a repeat of Whitby, do we now?'

'What happened in Whitby, like?'

The temptation to remind Tom of his near-miss i.e. how he almost ended up in a fight with a total stranger does cross my mind, but it would go against the sole purpose of this trip. So, with some hesitation, I mimic Tom by shrugging my shoulders and nod towards the pub. 'Forget it. Let's get that drink in, yeah?'

Tom enters the pub like a kid running into a candy store; he eyes up the available goods, brimming with excitement.

'I wouldn't mind trying that ale,' he says, pointing out a beer called "The Chilton Chastiser". 'I'm up for one of those.'

I call a barmaid over to us and order Tom the pint he's after, albeit against my better judgement.

'Is that all you're after?' the barmaid enquires, as she hands Tom his murky-looking drink. 'Would you like anything else?'

'I fancy a whisky chaser,' he says, sweeping his eyes over some single malt bottles that are located behind the bar. 'Is that okay with you, Daz?'

I calm my thoughts and remind myself of this trip's purpose, when all I want to do is drag him out of this place. Tom needs to come off alcohol but there's just too much temptation, and I haven't exactly helped by bringing him here.

'Sure,' I say. 'One whisky chaser and then that's it. Promise?'

'I promise,' he says, winking to me. 'Cheers, Daz. I knew you'd understand.'

Tom downs the whisky shot and pint in an instant. Soon enough, one pint turns into two and then three and then four. I want to intervene, but don't want this plan of mine to fail. At least he's not isolating himself anymore.

'It's getting late,' I say, sometime after Tom's fifth ale. 'We'd better visit the cathedral now, before it closes.'

'There's plenty of time for that,' he says, followed by a loud belch and a few hiccups. 'It's only twenty-to-four.'

'It's twenty-past-eight, actually. I think we've missed our chance, mate. And you wanted to light a candle —'

'I'll do that some other time. I'm alright staying in here. This is my church.'

Unbeknown to us — especially Tom in his inebriated state — two ladies from a bachelorette party silently make their approach from behind, one of which then runs a finger down Tom's back. He jolts up in surprise, but quickly returns to his pint.

'What are you boys up to?' asks one of the ladies, who is dressed like a deformed bunny. 'Are you handsome fellas here by yourselves?'

'We're out for a quiet drink,' I state, noting Tom's worsening tremors. I manage to remain civil and polite, despite the urge to tell these ladies to do one. 'Who's getting married?' I ask, praying that this may deter them from persevering with their unwanted attention. 'Who's the lucky lady?'

'Neither of us,' says the other woman. She appears to be just as drunk as Tom, given how much she's swaying about. 'We're single, darlin'. Would you boys like to keep us company? Can you buy us a drink?'

Tom clenches his fists together and pushes them hard against his stomach, then turns his head to me with a look of sheer terror.

'It's my IBS,' he whispers, as a line of sweat begins to emerge on his forehead.

'What did you say?' I ask, leaning in closer to him. 'I didn't catch what you said.'

'Your friend is a miserable git, isn't he?' the bunny girl remarks, scowling at Tom. 'He doesn't say much.'

'My IBS!' he cries out. 'I can't hold it in!'

A thick plume of sulphuric gas steadily rises between me and Tom, then hits the ladies standing behind us like an out-of-control juggernaut. The women nip at their nostrils, their eyes now watering, and a burst of cruel laughter leaves from them.

'You dirty animal!' they scream in unison.

Tom responds by cowering into a foetal position upon his stool, placing both hands firmly against his chest.

'That's disgusting!' says the bunny girl, as she and her friend make a hasty retreat. However, they are soon replaced by a group of football fans nearby who have seemingly noticed Tom's anxious state.

One of the men asks: 'What's wrong with him?' The genuine concern that first came across through his voice immediately turns into a sadistic cackle. 'Phwoar! You smell of pig shit, lad!'

Before I have chance to intervene, Tom bravely replies. 'I can't help it. It's not my fault.'

'No, it's not. Focus on your breathing,' I say to him, but the damage has been done. Tom slips from his stool and onto his knees, his face reddening by the second. 'Focus on your breaths, mate. Slow them down.'

'I can't!' he shrieks. 'I can't breathe!'

'Ignore those idiots. They're strangers who mean nothing to you,' I say, though Tom's attack only seems to be getting more intense. 'We've got to get you out of here. Follow me.'

Against the malicious taunts from the other pubgoers, I manage to lift Tom onto his feet and then escort him from the premises. We stand in the marketplace for a few minutes, where he starts to take some hold over his anxiety attack. I hug into him, praying that this attack will stop, and couldn't care less what anyone else thinks.

'That was a bad one,' he pants. 'It's getting harder to control these attacks. They're getting worse and worse.'

'Do you want to try another pub or just go back to our hotel?'

'The hotel sounds good. At least I can't embarrass myself there.'

On reaching the hotel, I notice that there's an Open Mic night taking place in its bar area. Tom also notices this, but just carries on towards the elevator. That panic attack has certainly taken it out of him.

'When was the last time you played your guitar?' I say to him. Tom doesn't respond initially, so I ask again. 'When was the last time you picked it up and played? You always say how much music helps you to cope with things.'

'It'll be years. The last time I played was when we made those YouTube videos together. I lost my musical spark a long time ago.' He rubs at his reddened eyes and presses the elevator's call button. 'My head feels like it's going to burst.'

'How about I get you some water at the bar, then maybe chillout to some music. There might be some decent acts on?'

'Okay,' he says. 'I don't want to end our night on a downer.'

'I'll get the drinks in. While I'm doing that, you go and find us a good spot near the stage.'

As Tom searches for a table, I call over one of the bartenders and say to them, 'Good evening.'

The bar tender looks around at the packed room with a satisfied smirk. 'That it is. Open Mic nights are always popular. We get all kinds of people wanting to perform here: students, pensioners, and even the odd celebrity. Jimmy Nail sang here a few months back.'

'Nice. I'd like two pints of water and a glass of diet lemonade, please.' Then comes my next and most important request. 'Can anyone get up and perform?'

'Sure. If you want to get up and play just put your name down on this list.' He hands the list over to me and I write Tom's name on it, along with his favourite song that he loved to perform in our band: *Livin' On A Prayer* by Bon Jovi. 'There are a few more acts on before you, though it shouldn't be too long a wait.'

'Cheers, pal.'

I make my way back to Tom with our drinks, and he glances down at the pint of water as if I'd offered him a glass of stale urine.

'It'll clear your head,' I say. 'It's a shame about you not wanting to get up and perform. You always came out of your shell onstage.'

'That was a long, long time ago,' he snorts, before downing his first glass of water. 'I'd probably get stage-fright now, knowing my luck.'

'You'll never know, not unless you give it a try.'

'I'd best not,' he states. 'I've already made an arse out of myself tonight. It's been too long…'

'You've got a great voice, and you're one hell of a guitarist. I'd love to see you get up and play again.'

Tom gives me a cold stare, almost bordering on anger. 'Don't kid yourself, Daz. I'm not the same guy I was back then. That part of me is dead and gone.'

'No, it's not. Once a muso, always a muso.'

'Give it a rest, mate. My musician days are just a long-gone memory now.'

Tom and I watch the next three performers go through their individual repertoires in silence—and it's not an awkward or tense silence, more out of a mutual respect for these fellow musicians. We know what it's like to get up

245

onstage, to play your heart out, to reveal your soul to complete strangers. It's a unique kind of buzz of that I greatly miss, and one which Tom has sadly replaced with alcohol.

'Next up is a Mr. Thomas Grey, who will be performing Bon Jovi's *Livin' On A Prayer*,' says the compere. 'Let's welcome him up, folks! Give him a warm welcome!'

A vibrant cheer reverberates around the bar. However, Tom looks petrified and somewhat infuriated.

'You signed me up, didn't you?' he snarls. 'I don't want to perform. I can't.'

'Get up and show this crowd what your made of. I'm rooting for you,' I say, gently nudging him from his chair into the direction of the stage. 'I know you can do this, mate. You've still got it in you.'

Tom approaches the stage with his head held down and his fists clenching again; a total contrast to how he used to make his way onstage. He picks up another performer's acoustic guitar, nervously slips out a plectrum that's nestled between its strings, stands himself before the microphone, and then stares out at the audience for what feels like forever.

'Go on, Tom-boy!' I shout, willing for him to slip out of his anxious trance. 'You can do this, mate!'

Tom rests his mouth against his microphone and glares through the crowd to me, sighing into it. This latest plan of mine is going drastically wrong, it seems. But, to my pleasant surprise, it then somehow seems as if Tom's found that old spark again — that eager performer who he claims died years ago. He looks confident now, bold and resolute;

or it could be just him trying to ward off his anxiety? What possessed me to think this would be a good idea?

'Hi,' he says, stuttering through the mic. 'I want to play a different song.' Tom's met with a sea of perplexed faces and whispers of complaint. I sit myself upright, ensuring that his focus lies solely on me. 'I'm going to perform *The Reason* by Hoobastank instead, because I can relate to the lyrics so much. It's been a while since I last played. Please, go easy on me.'

There are a few noticeable chunters among the crowd, people already casting judgement over Tom before he's even played a single chord. But I know he can do this, to reignite that passionate flame lying dormant inside. Besides, we've played before tougher crowds than this. It should be a walk in the park for him.

Once Tom begins to play it becomes obvious that he hasn't lost his golden touch; he plays each chord perfectly and sings each word on cue and in pitch—just like he used to. I can see an excitement light up in his eyes that's been lost for too long now. I'm so proud of him. If only he could feel the same way about himself. I know he will in time.

Tom is met with a standing ovation on ending his heartfelt performance. With hands still trembling, he rests the guitar back onto its stand, high-fives a few fans of his performance on the short walk back from the stage, and then plonks himself down beside me with a sigh of relief.

'That wasn't as bad as I thought it'd be,' he says, chuckling to himself. 'It was like being back in our band again. I got such a buzz from playing...'

'I told you there was nothing to worry about. We should make a new band, I reckon, once this trip of ours is over. Are you up for it?'

'Really? Do you not think we're a bit too old to be playing in a rock band again?'

'The Rolling Stones are still selling out arenas, and they're well into retirement age. We're only in our thirties, Tom. Life's just getting started.'

'I don't know. It's not a bad idea, in all fairness. It felt great being back onstage, playing a guitar again.'

'It showed. The Tom I watched performing just now is the real Tom,' I emphasise. 'This is what you need to beat your anxiety and depression—something to work towards. In just one hour I've seen a huge change in you.'

'Only because of your help,' he says, sipping at his water. 'The only problem we'd have is finding a decent drummer and rhythm guitarist. That'll be a right headache.'

'I've been teaching our Nathan how to play bass. I could always teach him some chords on the guitar, you know, to prep him for joining our band. Give him a few more years and he'll be ready.'

'It's something else to look forward to, isn't it?' Tom fixates on the stage, its bright lights and atmosphere, his demeanour now fully relaxed. 'It'd be just like old times.'

'We'll do it then, that is, once our holiday's over. We'll get straight onto it.'

'I can't wait. We'll need to think up a name for our new band.'

'I'll leave that to you, pal. The future's not set in stone, and it's not always bleak.'

We leave the bar and retire to our room. I check on my blood sugars again, once Tom's fallen asleep. The BM reading isn't too bad, but it's still nowhere near being where I want it to be. I don't know what I'm doing wrong, in trying to get a grip over my diabetes. It does, however, help me empathise with Tom's inner struggle, though his is mental and mine is physical. We all have our crosses to bear, don't we?

I check to make sure Tom's asleep and then pull out my phone. There's a text message and it isn't from Michelle, as I assumed it might be. The message is from a guy I met online a few weeks ago, a Turkish barber called Shaq. He's something else that I'm hiding from those closest to me. It's not easy putting on a mask and to keep it up, not by any means; it eventually wears you down. I'm determined to shatter Tom's mask, to prevent him from feeling the same way I do. Nobody should be forced into hiding their true self. I do know how Tom feels, and I'm certain that he can overcome his obstacles. Mine will simply have to wait…

Flashback: May 9th, 2003

I should be revising for my exams, but instead I'm sat in some wildflower field, with some mates of mine from school and Alice. Each of us are drained, exhausted from being repeatedly told how important our GCSE results will be, come next year, in determining our futures. The pressure is intense, but Alice is taking things in her stride, which she always does, unlike me and my pals. Daniel — a lad from my tutor group, who has only just joined our little clan this evening — has promised a special treat for us all tonight, a way to help us unwind from the toils of teenage life. Whatever it is, he's got it well-hidden beneath his coat.

'What's that you're hiding?' I ask him.

'Shhh, it's a secret.' Daniel scours the field like a meerkat on high alert, then slowly unzips his coat. 'I persuaded my big brother to buy this.' He reveals a three-litre bottle of white cider — the kind that could easily be mistaken for battery acid or horse piss. 'There should be enough to go around.'

Alice isn't impressed. 'Alcohol? That's why you've brought us out here? That's your big secret?'

'Yeah, is there a problem?'

'No… but I won't be having any. It'll rot your stomach away, that cheap and nasty cider. Disgusting stuff.'

'Chicken. What about you, Tom? I'm gonna give it a go, and so are the other lads.'

I hesitate, ashamed by my failure to stick up for Alice, my beloved girlfriend, and for the temptation that's now rising inside. I hate alcohol; it often turned my dad into a nightmare drunkard and was a contributing factor to his and Mum's divorce. But there's a part of me that wants to give it a try, to see what all the fuss is about, to gain whether it can help put to rest my awkward social anxiety.

'Don't do it,' Alice says to me. 'Please, don't be forced into trying some.'

'She's got you wrapped around her little finger, Tom-boy,' Daniel says to me. 'You only live once, Tom-boy. A few mouthfuls of cider won't kill you. Don't be a wuss.' He opens the bottle and offers it to me. I immediately wretch from the strong alcohol fumes, but curiosity soon takes hold. 'Just one mouthful, mate. I dare ya!'

'Don't do it, Tom. Don't give into the peer pressure — you're better than that,' says Alice, clenching onto my hands. Then she mutters into my ear, 'Remember what alcohol did to your dad, and all the hurt it caused your mum.'

'Chicken! Chicken!' my so-called friends sing in unison.

'Just the one, Alice. I'll be fine,' I say to her. She responds with a piercing stare and removes her hands from mine. 'You've got to try everything once, haven't you?'

'That's the spirit! Go on, Tom-boy.' Daniel thrusts the bottle up to my mouth, which opens willingly, and I taste my first drop of the devil's drink.

'I can't believe you did that,' says Alice, shuffling further away from my side. 'You're so stupid. Are you really that desperate to fit in?'

'It's not that. I just wanted to try something new,' I explain, in truth lying to her. 'What's the harm?'

'What's the harm? I'm going home.' Alice storms off into the distance. I follow her like a lost puppy, torn between the adoration I have for her and my newfound affection towards

251

alcohol. 'If you want to sit here and get drunk—suit yourself!'

'Don't go,' I say to her. 'It's only a mouthful of booze, Alice.'

'Let her go,' says Daniel, offering the bottle to me again. 'You've got to play hard-to-get. She'll come running back to you. Have another drink. You'll still have a laugh with me and the others.'

'I can't let her walk home alone—'

'She'll be fine. Don't you worry, Tom. You're always worrying over daft things. A small tipple will do you the world of good.'

I'm just like my dad, aren't I? I've chosen a toxic substance over the true love in my life. Why did I do it? Why did I choose alcohol over Alice? Why did I let anxiety get the better of me?

Stepping Back

Daz seems far too content, given the huge traffic jam we're stuck in. It amazes me how he can stay so calm and collective, never once uttering any word of complaint. If it were me sat behind the wheel, I'd be spouting off every curse word under the sun. I'd never admit it to him, but I'm actually jealous of Daz. I would give anything to live just one day in his pristine, anxiety-free shoes.

'How's your head this morning?' he asks me.

'Not too bad,' I say, rubbing at it. 'I should end nights out with a few glasses of water more often. I'm barely hungover.'

'Don't get drunk — full stop,' he states. 'Last night could have been fate giving you a subtle hint, a nod in the right direction — the kick up the arse you need to quit drinking?'

'If it wasn't for those two lasses, I'd have been completely fine. They're what set my IBS off.'

'Are you sure it wasn't all that super-strength ale you downed?'

'No, it wasn't that. Booze doesn't set my IBS off.'

'I think you'll find it can and does,' he says with a smug smirk. 'You can be bloody hard work at times, Tom. Alcohol isn't healthy; it's a poison. And don't give me that spiel about it being good for the blood again.'

'But it is…in small quantities.'

'Your idea of a small quantity greatly differs from mine. I'll give you ten quid if you manage to go through today without touching a single drop of alcohol. How about that?'

'I'll try, but I can't promise anything.'

'Just…give it a go, mate.'

'I'll do my best.'

We drive past the Angel of the North sculpture, through Gateshead, across the Tyne bridge, and then arrive in Newcastle's city centre—places I've not visited since being an undergraduate student. I'm waiting for one of my usual flashbacks to kick in, to no doubt render me into an anxious wreck, but only happier memories come into fruition. I forgot how much fun I had here, back then in this amazing city, when I was still keen to learn and become someone better. They were the good old days. That was the good old me.

Daz pulls into a carpark near the university and jumps out before I have chance to comment.

'What's it like to be back in "The Toon"?' he asks, holding his arms up in awe of the university's Edwardian grandeur. 'I can't believe you studied here—it's so posh!'

'Are you trying to say I'm some sort of scruff?' I joke. 'Yeah, I studied here. The work was hard, but I made up for it in the student union bar.'

'That sounds about right,' he says under his breath. 'I always wanted to go to university, but it just wasn't meant to be.'

'I wouldn't lose sleep over it, mate. Getting a degree isn't the big deal it's made out to be.'

'You needed a degree to teach, though.'

'Fair point, but still…'

Daz quickly ushers me towards the university's entranceway — himself bustling with enthusiasm, and me the total opposite. 'Does it feel good being back?'

'A little. I'm not all that sure, to be honest.'

He wraps an arm around me, drawing my body against his.

'That's why I brought you here, Tom. When you're feeling low, the best thing you can do is go somewhere that reminds you of better times. That's what I do, anyway. Should we have a little look around? It'll be interesting to see how much the place has changed.'

I'm somewhat reluctant to retrace my steps here at first, but then remember that the student bar is only a two-minute walk away.

'Sure,' I say eagerly. 'Follow me. I know every inch of this campus.'

'We'd best make it a quick look around,' he adds. 'I don't fancy getting caught by one of the security guards.'

I enlighten Daz with some stories from my student days, most of which involve drunken parties and the best takeaway venues to frequent after a good skinful. He pretends to be interested, and I get the impression he knows I'm up to something less innocent than a guided tour.

'This is a brief walk-around you're giving me,' he says, raising an eyebrow. 'Where are you taking us?'

'You'll see. There's just one more corridor to go down.'

'You've got that sly look on your face—'

'Trust me, Daz, I know where we're going.'

There it is in all its glory: the student union bar—and the beer's still dirt-cheap! Happy days. This is my kind of reminiscence.

'Going without booze didn't last long, did it? Fine. I'll treat us to one drink—only the one, mind.'

'For old time's sake.'

Daz keeps to his word and buys us some drinks. He may as well have bought me water, however, going off how flat my lager is.

'I don't remember the beer tasting this crap,' I say, taking a sip from the disappointing beverage. 'It's rank!'

'Beer's always watered down in bars like this. Don't act so surprised.' Daz scours the students around us, noting the obvious age gap between ourselves and them. 'Do you ever get the inkling that you're out of place?'

'I was twenty-one years old when I last drank in here,' I say, looking over the youthful faces myself. 'These kids are making me feel ancient. I may as well be back at work.'

'You couldn't pay me to drink in here,' he chunters. 'Don't get me wrong, I mean, it's a nice bar but not really my scene. Do you fancy a walk around town instead?'

I look over the youngsters again, and there's just something about their joyful expressions that frustrates me.

'They're all happy now,' I say, hinting at some resentment. 'But just wait until reality hits them… like it did with me.'

'You mean, when they have to repay their student loans? Not this again,' says Daz, rolling his eyes to me. 'It's the government's fault for upping the tuition fees. You should be pissed off with the greedy politicians, not these kids.'

'I'm not pissed off with these students,' I simper. 'But how can they all be so happy? I don't get it.'

'They're probably looking forward to a brighter future, that's all. You should be proud of what you've achieved,' says Daz, patting at my shoulders. 'I've always wanted a degree. Me and Dad are the only members of our family that haven't got one.' He breaks into laughter. 'It's the one thing we do have in common.'

'You'll never be like your dad...'

Daz goes quiet, moves away from myself and the bar, then makes his way over to the exit. 'Are we having a look into town?'

'What's the rush? I've still got half-a-pint to sup.'

'It's for me to know and for you to find out,' he says, tapping a finger against the tip of his nose. 'I'm saving the best treat for last.'

'I don't know how many more of these surprises I can cope with,' I humour, but I'm also being truthful. 'You're not doing my nerves any favours.'

'It's nothing to stress about — why would it be?'

'I'm not a fan of surprises, like you're not a fan of sitting in pubs.'

'Look, I promise you won't be disappointed.'

After leaving the university campus, we head into Newcastle's restaurant district. We're spoilt for choice on where to eat but Daz settles on a McDonald's, which is a shock given how health-conscious he is.

'I'm paying for our meals. No ifs or buts,' he insists.

'But you've spent a fortune on me —'

'Because I want to and can.' Daz collects our burgers and nods across to a table nearby. 'Stop your whinging and get this grub down you. We're on a tight schedule today — no time for mucking about.'

'Please tell me what you've got planned,' I say, clasping my hands together. 'The suspense is getting tedious now.'

'Nope. You've got to be patient, my friend. Patience is a virtue.'

'I'm anything but patient. You should know that by now.'

On finishing our meals, I suggest that we walk towards Newcastle's Central Station, seeing as it will take us by all my old haunts (namely a bar or two). What I didn't anticipate, however, was the presence of two protesting groups that we're now walking right into the centre of. Adding to the horror, we're then surrounded by horse-mounted police and some of the local media. We're in the thick of it, and it's too late to escape. Absolutely marvellous.

'Is there a footy match on today?' Daz asks me, as we try to slither our way through the adrenaline-fuelled crowd. 'We chose a good day to visit Newcastle, didn't we?'

'Bloody hell,' I gasp, wrapping a hand around my tightening throat. 'This is bad, man.'

The all too familiar sensation of an anxiety attack sweeps in. I fall onto my knees, which — given the amount of people pushing against one another around us — doesn't help in the slightest. I manage to decipher what some of these protesters are shouting about; it's something along the lines of climate change, though a few are also crying about remaining in the

EU, which are then countered with screams of "Free Tibet". It's utter chaos. It's an anxiety sufferer's worst nightmare.

All the sounds, the claustrophobic environment, the sweat coursing down my back, the shooting pains in my hands and chest—it's all too much! The urge to vomit makes itself known, along with a strengthening need to pass out. I'm well out of my comfort zone, and I doubt my usual coping techniques will work.

'You'll be alright, Tom. Breathe.' Daz assists me to my feet, keenly aware of my intensifying attack. 'We'll get out of this mess. Focus on your breaths and my voice. You'll be okay.'

'No. This is bad—really bad!'

'Like John said, ride through the storm. Tell yourself that you're in control, and that nothing bad will happen.'

'I can't. There's too much going on!'

Daz's time spent in the gym certainly pays off: he barges through the crowd with little exertion shown, all the while dragging my sorry carcass along with him.

'This way!' he cries, desperate to lift his voice over the deafening roars from the protesters. 'In here, Tom!' We're forced into a Waterstones bookstore, the one place seemingly free from any mayhem. 'We should be alright now, mate. Breathe. Focus. Ground yourself. You're safe in here.'

I take in a deep breath and imagine that I'm in some far-off place of natural beauty, but then get side-tracked by the sound of a young woman whimpering from behind. Darren and I cautiously approach her—a woman in her early twenties who is mimicking my actions from a few moments earlier: the shallow breaths, the tremoring hands, the eyes littered with dread—all tell-tale signs of a panic attack. I recognise the symptoms, and I know how devastating they can be. We've got to help her somehow.

A sales assistant approaches the poor girl, who then makes a half-hearted attempt to assist her.

'Pull yourself together, love. You're making a scene,' they say, and with little thought of how condescending their words are. 'Stop being silly. You're making a scene.'

'Let me talk to her,' I say, gently moving the sales assistant aside. 'I know what's wrong with her. Let me help.' I kneel before the girl, ensuring to keep my eyes held against the ground. I hate being stared at when I'm in the middle of an attack, which is why I do this. 'Hi, my name's Tom. I know how your feeling.' She recoils at first, but gradually lifts her eyes to meet with mine. 'I have anxiety as well. Can I do some breathing exercises with you, to help relieve the symptoms?' She nods back, albeit apprehensively, so I press on. 'Close your eyes, like me. Breathe in through your nostrils for four or five seconds and then exhale for the same amount of time through your mouth. Keep doing this. Now, imagine that you're in a place where you feel completely safe and at ease. For me it's a wildflower meadow in the middle of nowhere, and the sun is setting over the horizon with a golden hue. There aren't any sounds or other people about. You're completely alone, and out of harm's way.'

'What?' the girl says with a puzzled look.

'Trust me,' I implore. 'Concentrate on your breaths. Slow them down and take control. As the sun begins to set, force all your negative emotions to vanish along with it. The darkness of night will come, but it is soon lit up with millions of stars; and each of those stars are your happiest memories. Choose one, reach out and touch it, then focus on the warmth that memory brings to you.'

'I've found one,' she whispers.

'Good. Now, imagine that your being surrounded by this star's brilliant, white light. Let the light remove all those awful feelings and thoughts — don't resist it. Repeat to yourself that you'll be okay, and that there's nothing to feel threatened by. You're at peace. Anxiety is a normal part of life and has been since the dawn of time, but you mustn't let it control you. You are in control. You are calm and there's nothing to worry about.'

As if in perfect unison, the girl and I both start to relax; our tense bodies loosen, and our eyes meet again. Surprisingly, I'm helping myself as well as her.

'Thank you,' she says, wiping at her eyes. 'I haven't had an attack like that for months.'

'Did you get caught up in the protest as well?' I ask, feigning a smile. 'It's mad out there, isn't it?'

'Yeah,' she says, sweeping back her hair. 'I was one of those protesters, but I didn't realise how crazy things would get.'

'We live in crazy times,' I add. Daz then kneels beside us. 'Me and my pal here only came to do some sightseeing. We didn't expect this mayhem, either.'

'Thanks. I'm sorry.' The girl stands up and then runs out of the bookstore, back into the warring crowds.

'You did well there, mate. You really helped her,' says Daz. 'Not many people would have done the same thing, to help like you did.'

'I only went through one of my coping techniques with her—nothing special,' I say, waving a hand back at him dismissively.

'You showed her some compassion when she needed it most. That takes some guts.'

'It's a pity I didn't give Alice the same care and attention,' I say. 'She might not have left me, if I had.'

'It's the smallest gestures we make that can have the biggest impact. And you're not the heartless monster you make yourself out to be, Tom.' Daz makes his way over to the door and opens it for us. 'Are you ready for another run? You'll need to be faster than what you were in Whitby.'

'If it means avoiding this protest, then—yeah.'

My senses are instantly overwhelmed on stepping foot outside again. There are more protesters and riot police now, and the tense atmosphere has worsened dramatically. After an exhausting sprint, we finally reach Newcastle's main train station. I had attempted to enter a few bars along the way, but Daz was insistent that we carry on. All I can guess is that he's preparing me for another one of his surprises.

'Just in the nick of time,' he says, checking his watch. 'We almost missed our transport.'

'Transport? What's wrong with your car?'

'Nothing. We've timed it perfectly.'

'We've timed "what" perfectly? I've had enough shocks for one day.'

Mikey suddenly shows up out of nowhere, and somehow has our suitcases in his possession. 'Y'alreet, boys?' he says, winking to Daz.

'What are you doing here?' I ask, then notice Mikey's Newcastle United t-shirt. 'If you've come to watch a footy match, then why have you got our suitcases? What's going on?'

'Aye, ah've been to a match, and divn't talk aboot it,' he says. 'Ah'm in on Darren's little secret, Tom-boy.' Mikey winks to him again, and Daz does the same back. 'He gave me a spare key to his car last week. Didn't ye, Darren? Ah'd come along with you'se, but ah'm workin' tomorrow, ya see. Ah've gotta pay off me gambling debts somehow. Sorry to disappoint.'

Daz seems anything but disappointed, and I'm just left even more confused. Mikey can be hard to understand at the best of times, in all fairness.

'Cheers, Mikey. I appreciate you doing this for us,' says Daz. He then retrieves our suitcases and hands mine over before I can ask any more questions. 'How did the footy match go?'

'Durn't mention it, lad! It's a touchy subject, put it that way. Ah've lost a fair whack of dosh at the bookies today. Anyhow, ah'm off for a few drinks to droon me sorrows. Ye two have fun on yer little excursion…'

I turn to Daz, unaware that Mikey has now left our company to join his drunken comrades further up the street. 'What's this *excursion* Mikey mentioned?'

With a proud smile, he says, 'Questions, questions, questions. Look, Tom, we've been promising one another for years that we'd go on an epic holiday somewhere, haven't we?'

'Yeah, but we haven't had the time to go on an "epic" holiday.'

'Well, I'm keeping that promise and seeing it through.' Daz licks at his lips, barely controlling his excitement. 'I've booked us a ferry over to Amsterdam. I know how much you want to go there.'

'Amsterdam?' I gasp. 'But I haven't brought my passport.'

'I sneaked it into my suitcase when you were having a shower,' he says, tapping at his temples. 'I've thought it all through, mate. The tickets and accommodation have been paid for, and I forged your signature on the travel documents. I knew you wouldn't have minded—'

'Amsterdam?' My jaw drops and I can barely speak. 'You're a right dark horse, you are. Does Michelle know?'

'Michelle was more than happy. She also thinks it'll do you some good to get away.' Daz's joyful expression suddenly falls foul. 'Mum and Dad are taking her and Nathan on a caravanning holiday. I've made my excuses not to go, and Michelle's fine with it—she understands.' He then pulls at my arm, directing me towards a double-decker bus that's pulling up opposite us. 'That's our bus to the ferry terminal. There's no turning back now.'

'This is all happening so fast,' I say, held in disbelief. Daz then runs across the road, waving for me to follow him. 'Wait up! I'm not as fit as you!'

'Come on, Tom! This is the holiday we've always dreamed of!'

Daz and I hand our suitcases over to the bus driver, who swiftly guides us to our seats. None of this seems real.

'Why didn't you mention anything to me?' I ask, as my fingers begin to tremble again.

'Because it wouldn't have been much of a surprise—that's why. I've been planning this for weeks, mate. It's going to be a trip to remember, and it's just what you need to help put a stop to your anxiety and depression.'

'You shouldn't have. You really shouldn't have, Daz.'

The last time I tried to go abroad didn't end so well, that's the thing. What if the same happens again? What if I have a panic attack on the ferry? What if Alice tries to phone or message me when I'm abroad?

'There's nothing to fret about,' he says while randomly pulling out a packet of spearmint gum from one of his pockets. 'I can tell you're starting to get anxious again. You'll be fine, though. Try one of these.' He hands me a stick of gum, placing two in his own mouth. 'I don't know what it is about spearmint, but it chills me out somehow.'

'I'll give it a shot.' I'm desperate for anything to work. I can't let Daz down…like I did with Alice. 'I was just thinking about my honeymoon, and how it all went horribly wrong.'

'That won't happen this time,' he says, rubbing at his face. 'You're not getting on a plane, for one thing. It's an overnight ferry to the Netherlands, and then a short bus journey —"

'I ruined it. All those months of planning and saving up, just for me to have a panic attack in the airport lounge. Alice was so looking forward to our honeymoon in Reykjavik. I've never even attempted to make it up to her.'

'You've done a lot for Alice and Rose,' he insists. 'Besides, I've organised everything down to the minutest detail. Chew your gum and stop stressing, mate.'

'Telling me not to stress is like asking a two-year-old to be silent in a library. It won't work.'

'You know what I mean.' Daz offers another stick of gum to me, which I take, but I'd much rather it be a cigarette. 'I'll sort out any issues, should they arise. This'll be a great opportunity for you to wind down and think things through.'

I'll be screwed if I have a panic attack abroad, though. But I've got to be positive. I've got to take a leaf out of Daz's book.

'Amsterdam?' I say, forcing myself to smile. 'I can't believe we're actually going.'

'We'll soon be out of England, away from all our stresses and woes,' Darren says, chuckling to himself. 'This is just what the doctor ordered, Tom-boy. This will be a week to remember…'

Across the Distance

Aboard the ferry to Amsterdam, Tom stares out of a small porthole in his and Darren's cabin, immersed by the setting sun's tranquil rays that are being cast upon the North Sea. He's conflicted by Darren's generous gift—this unexpected holiday of theirs—feeling that he does not deserve such charity. He is also in the throes of a claustrophobia-induced anxiety attack, trying all within in his power to conceal it.

'We should reach the Netherlands by sunrise,' says Darren, taking a selfie on his phone. 'It's a short bus journey from the docks into Amsterdam. We'll be there in no time, pal.'

'Great! More travelling,' says Tom, muttering to himself. 'This is all happening so fast—fast.'

'Are you whinging again?' Darren asks, leaning his head over the bunkbed rails. 'You've gone all quiet and broody. What's up?'

'You didn't need to book this holiday. It's not that I don't appreciate the offer, so please don't take what I'm saying the wrong way…' Tom watches on as England's coastline vanishes over the horizon, separating him from Alice and Rose even more. 'It feels like I'm sponging off you—'

'You're not. We've been bleating on about Amsterdam for years. And, now that I've got the money, why shouldn't we treat ourselves to a holiday abroad?' Darren slinks off the bed to land before Tom. 'I fancy a mosey around the ship. We can't stay cooped up in this cabin all night, can we?'

'I thought you'd never ask.'

Darren and Tom leave their cabin and make for the main deck. They are amazed by the sheer size of the ferry, which itself could be classed as a small town. The friends then head into the nearest restaurant, both filled with curiosity and hunger, only to find that it's closed for another three hours.

'Brilliant,' Darren humours. 'There's bound to be another restaurant somewhere around here. Do you reckon there's a salad bar?'

'I hope not.' Tom scrunches his face in disgust. 'There better be a Burger King or Subway, more like. Let's try up this way,' he suggests, pointing into the direction of the ferry's rear deck. 'I could do with some fresh air, never mind some overpriced food. All this rocking back and forth is playing havoc with my guts.'

'I told you those spicy fajitas were a bad idea. But will you ever listen to me? No.'

'I do listen, just not all the time.'

Darren leads the way. Once outside he gestures for Tom to join him at the ship's back rails, where he mimics the scene from James Cameron's *Titanic*, the moment when Jack opens his arms out wide to portray his newfound freedom.

'We're the kings of this world, Tom-boy! FREE-DOM!'

'Behave yourself, man.' Tom gulps and then side-glances to an elderly couple stood a few yards away. 'People are looking at us. They'll think you've lost the plot.'

'So? I couldn't care less. Come and give it a try.'

Tom peers over the railings, to the distance between where he's now standing and the surging waves below. 'That's a pretty big drop...'

'That's why there are railings, so you don't fall overboard. Am I embarrassing you, Tom?'

'No.'

'I am, aren't I? It's only a bit of fun.'

'I'll look like an idiot, though.'

'No, you won't,' Darren implores. 'Lean against the railings and hold out your arms. You'll get such a rush.'

Tom does just so. He rests his churning stomach against the cold railings and holds out his arms, finding that the cool breeze does bring some comfort to him. However, what Tom isn't revealing to Darren is — as he's lurching back and forth — the strange urge to throw himself overboard, and how strong its precedence is becoming. He's heard about this peculiar sensation before, the "Call of the Void" — an irrational desire to throw yourself into harm's way. Tom steps back from the railings and lowers his arms, no longer joyful but riddled with shame at having considered such a dreadful action.

'What's wrong now?' Darren asks, noting the change in Tom's mannerism. 'You've gone a funny, pasty colour. You're not gonna be sick, are you?'

'Now. Is there any chance of finding a bar now?'

'You're spoilt for choice. There's about five or six bars on this ferry.'

'Visiting one will be enough for me.'

'I thought you were giving up on the drink?'

'One pint won't do any damage.' Tom is met with a silent stare in response. 'Just the one — cross my heart and all that bollocks.'

'Living a healthy lifestyle isn't bollocks. But still, it's your holiday as well as mine. One drink shouldn't hurt.'

'Just one. I give you my word, mate.'

'We'll see.'

Tom walks back along the deck, dragging his feet with each step taken, though Darren stays put where he's leaning against the rails.

'Why do you drink so much?' Darren asks, revealing some concern in his tone. 'From what I've seen, it doesn't make you feel or act any better.'

Unwilling to answer, Tom returns to his friend merely out of politeness. 'What was that you said? I couldn't hear because of the wind.'

'Why do you drink so much? You never used to,' says Darren, showing some evident frustration now. 'Just think of what you're doing to your liver and heart, not to mention your brain cells.'

'I drink to forget — that's why. Anyway, there's nothing wrong with my body, other than the few pounds of fat I could still afford to lose.'

'I'm gonna be frank with you, mate —' Darren does his usual act of wrapping an arm around Tom, but not to comfort him this time; it's to ensure he can't wriggle his way out of this important conversation. 'The best I've seen you over the last few weeks is when you've been sober; or at least, partially sober. Take that night out in Durham for instance, when you fought against your anxiety to get up onstage, in front of all those strangers. You played your heart out, and it was like watching the "old you" perform. You did it without being wasted — that's my point.'

Tom clenches his fingers, sensing a new wave of tremors muster.

'You tricked me into getting up,' he says. 'I didn't exactly do it on a willing basis, did I?'

'Yes, you did. You could have turned around and refused to perform, but you played and sung that night just like you used to — with confidence. Deny it all you want, my lad, but I know you loved every moment of it.'

'That was my stage persona coming out,' says Tom. 'It wasn't the "real" me. If it wasn't for the booze already floating around my system that night, I'd have never had the courage to get up —'

'Bullshit. I know you too well. You can't lie to me, Tom.'

'I'm not lying. I've learned how to put on different masks to suit situations. All you saw that night was just me reacting to stress. It was not the real me.'

'I know that, and I can see right through those masks of yours.'

'You can?'

'Every-single-time.'

Darren and Tom venture back inside, where they soon happen across a vibrant cabaret bar.

'This is more like it, some live music!' Darren cheers, goading Tom in. 'I could have a word with the bar staff, see if me and you can get up to perform a song or two?'

'You're not getting me up onstage again,' says Tom, inspecting the array of tap beers on offer. 'I'll get this round in, and don't tell me not to.'

'If you insist?' Darren sighs. 'I'll have the usual, please.'

As Tom heads to the bar, Darren finds a table that's situated beside a grand piano. He doesn't want to admit it, especially to Tom, but the usual indicators of his sugar levels fluctuating are becoming apparent.

Tom returns with the drinks and some sandwiches, his face drained as white as snow.

'Bloody hell, Tom,' says Darren. 'Are you alright?'

'My bank balance isn't. The drinks were cheap, but these ham sandwiches have set me back ten-quid. The bartenders should wear black and white pinstripe suits—it's daylight robbery in here, man.' Tom hands over the goods, only for Darren to just stare at his humble meal with a blank expression. 'What's up with you? You look like you're about to puke.'

'I haven't found my sea legs yet, that's all. I'll be right as rain once I've had something to drink.' Darren sips at his lemonade, soon realising that Tom has accidently bought him the full-sugar type. He initially panics but carries on drinking it regardless. Somehow, the syrupy beverage seems to alleviate his nausea, or so Darren tells himself. 'I wonder when the acts start?' he says, wishing to divert any attention away from his current predicament.

'According to the bartender, there's a piano session first and then a duo act afterwards.' Tom eyes up the grand piano, nodding to it appreciatively. 'I'd love to have a go on that but, knowing me, I'd only go and break it somehow.'

'Don't be daft—' Darren suddenly heaves and clenches at his stomach as if it's about to burst; his temples pulsate, and his hands begin to tremor like Tom's. It's a hyper episode for sure. 'I won't be a sec. Just gonna check on my sugar levels.'

'Okay,' says Tom, turning back to his drink. 'I won't wander off anywhere.'

While Darren sprints to the nearest bathroom, Tom falls into a daydream as he stares at the grand piano. He imagines himself sitting before it, playing Mozart or Chopin; or (Alice's favourite) some Ludovico Einaudi, and at a virtuoso level of expertise. A slender figure then breaks Tom's trance—a pianist, or to be even more precise, an elderly gentleman who struggles to walk up to the instrument.

Tom becomes instantly entranced as the pianist plays the first notes of Beethoven's Moonlight Sonata in C Sharp Minor. He borders on entering one of his usual flashbacks, his painful reminders of the past, but manages to resist the draw. He reminds himself to be positive, that his past doesn't belong here, and that he must look ahead to a brighter future. Then he wonders why Darren is taking so long to return, and guilt sweeps in.

Darren emerges after twenty minutes, rubbing at his upper right leg as he goes to sit back down.

'I caught it just in the nick of time, Tom-boy. I wasn't far off having another hyper episode.'

Tom's interest is torn between the pianist's serene performance and his best friend's diabetic nightmare. 'What was that you said?'

'It doesn't matter. I was just moaning on about my diabetes—nothing new.' Darren applauds the pianist along with Tom, then leans back in his chair and folds his arms together behind his head. He wants to be relaxed. He needs to be relaxed. Otherwise, the whole purpose of this vacation will be in vain. 'Not a bad start to the night, I reckon. Didn't you have some piano lessons during college?'

'Yeah, but I'll never be *that* good,' says Tom. He then approaches the pianist and utters into their ear, 'Do you know any Ludovico Einaudi songs? *Nightbook* or *Nuvole Bianchi* would be great.'

The pianist nods and smiles, then goes straight into performing Einaudi's *Berlin Song*. Tom lurches back in his chair, allows for his arms to fall limp, closes his eyes, all the while wishing that Alice could be here to share in this beautiful music with him. A sharp pain then strikes at his chest and throat—the start of another anxiety attack—but Tom bravely shrugs it off. Nothing can ruin this poignant moment for him, this connection to Alice that he prays will never end.

'This was the song that Alice had played when she came down the aisle at your wedding, wasn't it?' Darren asks reservedly. 'Listening to music can have a real impact on your mood—for good and bad—can't it?'

'I don't know if this is good or bad, mate. It reminds me so much of Alice, of when she still loved me. That can't be a bad thing, can it?'

'No. Alice still loves you, and don't you ever think any different. Try your best to chillout this week, and then see how things go when we get back in England. I have no doubt whatsoever about Alice making things up with you—'

'It should be me making things up to her, not the other way around.' Tom performs some breathing techniques to combat his tremors, but he still lingers on the brink of a powerful anxiety attack. 'It's all that keeps me going; the thought of being back together with Alice and Rosie. My family...'

'You've got a lot to live for,' Darren implores. 'I wish you could see that. Not everything in life is bad. Make the most of what you have.'

Soon enough the Cabaret bar takes on a different and less private atmosphere, once the pianist ends their routine, and it's not welcomed by Tom. He looks on in dismay as a varied mixture of people enter and then take over the quiet space, which he and Darren had enjoyed to themselves for the last hour-and-a-half.

Glancing down at his Black Sabbath t-shirt, Tom says, 'Talk about being out of place. I didn't realise we needed to wear posh suits in this bar. I mean, look at those lot coming in now.'

'You're not out of place,' says Darren, not once moving his sight away from the stage towards the so-called trespassers. 'I didn't see any sign on the door stating that there was a dress code. You look fine to me. It doesn't matter what others think.'

Tom firmly disagrees, despite wanting to accept Darren's laidback response. 'I'm dressed like I'm going to a concert, where most of these people are dressed like they're at some fancy ceremony.'

'Why are you remotely bothered? You don't know any of them, do you? Just listen to the music and relax.' Darren shrugs and nods to the bar. 'I'll get us another drink in. Same again?'

'Yeah, but something stronger this time.'

'You get what you're given, my mate.' Darren heads to the bar, returning not long after with two bottles of lemonade and a packet of roasted peanuts. 'Don't say I don't spoil you. I've gone all out.'

Tom grimaces at the transparent fluid in his glass. 'What the hell is this — water again?'

'Lemonade, you know, fizzy lemon juice. It's meant to be good for your stomach, and it might do wonders for your dodgy IBS.'

'You could have met me halfway with a pint of shandy or something. Why the soft drink?' Tom asks, shaking his head into his hands. 'I need some booze or else I'll go mad.'

'You don't need booze. Jesus, Tom. Go one night without getting drunk. It'll be a big step forward. Plus, drinking only makes your depression worse.'

'How would you like it, if you had your insulin taken away? I'm being serious.'

'Getting drunk and struggling with diabetes aren't in the same ballpark, mate. I need my insulin to live. Too much alcohol does the complete opposite — and you bloody well know it does.'

'Alcohol keeps me sane,' Tom whimpers. 'So, it's not that far off keeping me alive, is it? Do you get what I mean?'

Darren looks to Tom sympathetically. 'I do understand. I understand that what you think is helping you is the root cause of your problems. You're not that stupid, mate, so don't make yourself out to be.' Tom displays some subtle naivety in his expression, which Darren doesn't buy. 'It's a well-known fact that alcohol is a depressant. You suffer from anxiety and depression. It's like adding petrol to an open flame. I really don't know how else to put it. Do *you* get where I'm coming from?' Tom shakes his head in dismissal. 'Put it this way: ever since you started drinking more, your anxiety tremors and IBS attacks have gotten worse and your mood has sunk even lower. I can see that. Amar, John and Mikey can see that. So, why — in all honesty — can't you? You're killing yourself, and it's like you don't care. But you must do, surely?'

Tom's entire body begins to tremble under a cocktail of anger, shame, fear and disappointment. He knows that Darren is speaking the truth, but its lasting sting only drives him further towards his usual cure: more alcohol.

'I need another drink — a proper one,' he states, pushing himself away from the table. 'I know you're only trying to help, Daz, and I am grateful. And you're totally correct — I couldn't give a damn about what happens to me. I've lost the only things that matter in life, so what's left to fight for? What have I got to look forward to? I hate what I've become. I do want to change, more than anything, but at my own pace. I can't just give up alcohol like you want me to.'

'It's your body,' says Darren, holding his hands up in surrender. 'If you want to keep on poisoning it, then go ahead — feel free. You're my best mate. I care a lot about you, Tom. But I don't want to piss you off or come across as being some nagging pain in the arse, either. If you want a lager, then I won't stop you. It's your choice.'

'You're not a pain, mate.' Tom loiters beside his friend, resentful of his previous words. 'You're right about everything. It's obvious that Alice left me because of my alcohol problem, not matter how much I try to deny it.' A sudden, warm sensation courses through Tom's body that overpowers the tremors. He takes in a deep breath, exhales,

277

and smiles. 'There — I said it! I'm an addict. I've got a problem with alcohol.'

'Good for you,' Darren smiles. 'Accepting that you've got a problem is half the battle.'

'Who knows, if I do stop drinking then maybe Alice will come back to me? What do you reckon, Daz?'

'I haven't got a crystal ball but cutting down on the super-strength ale would certainly be a good start. Look, I'm gonna be honest again, even if you don't want to hear it. You want to see Rosie grow, to finish school and maybe get married someday, don't you?' Darren asks, no longer held back by the need to protect Tom from the harsh truths. 'You don't want Rosie losing her dad because he drank himself to death, do you?'

'NO!' Tom exclaims. 'And I don't want Alice to be a widow. I could never do that to them.'

Darren clasps onto Tom's forearms arms, his eyes filled with passion. 'Then, *please*, stop drinking so much. Stop poisoning your body.'

'I will.' Tom sits back down and takes a sip from his lemonade. 'At least I can look forward to waking up in the morning without a hangover again — that's something positive.'

'That's the way to do it. Anyhow, we're meant to be having fun. I think we've had enough meaningful discussions today, don't you?'

'Yeah.'

'What do you think this next act will perform? The poster for them didn't reveal much.'

'So long as they don't play any freeform jazz or Sinatra, I'll be happy.'

'I think they're coming on now…'

A thunderous reception greets the duo act as they walk onstage, who turn out to be a married couple—a man no older and strikingly similar to Tom in appearance, and a woman who could easily be mistaken for a catwalk model—both of whom give off excitable personas, though Tom's interest soon wavers when they start performing some recent pop hits.

'This is bloody torturous,' says Tom, shielding his ears from the duo's performance. 'Why can't they play decent music, like—'

'The Sex Pistols or Disturbed?' says Darren, cackling. 'Oh yeah, your taste in music would *really* go down well, wouldn't it?'

'You can't talk, Mr. I-secretly-love-Abba,' Tom jokes.

'Touché,' says Darren. 'You're hitting a little below the belt there, mate. There's no need for that.' He then looks to Tom with a crooked smirk. 'I fancy a dance tonight, show off some of the old moves. Would you care to join me?'

'No chance!' he scoffs. 'You can beg me all you like, but you'll never get me up dancing.'

'It's your loss. Dancing is a great way to use up all that adrenaline floating around your system.'

'So is walking, which I might do out of this bar in a minute.'

'You're forgetting that I've seen you dance before—both drunk and sober. You've got some skills. It'd be such a wate of talent for you not—'

'I ain't dancing. Full stop. If you want to prance around like a moron, be my guest, Daz.'

'If you say so?'

Tom spends the next hour sipping at his drink until it goes warm and barely tolerable, while Darren gets up and dances with a stag party from Carlisle. Darren's embarrassing dance moves amuse Tom at first, but then the isolation takes hold of him. In not wanting to dampen Darren's fun or suffer anymore reminders of how socially awkward he is, Tom sneaks out of the bar and back to his cabin for some peace and quiet—to free himself from the company of strangers, more than anything else.

Darren returns to the cabin not long after midnight, his body saturated in sweat, his belt suspiciously unbuckled. He checks his wallet for what cash remains and then stares for a while at Tom's sleeping body, listening to the calm sound of his breaths in contentment.

'I'm sorry,' Darren laments, planting a kiss upon his Tom's brow. 'I hadn't realised you'd left. I got too carried away with those fellas from Carlisle. We all have urges that we're ashamed to admit, to confront, to accept.' He nudges a hand into Tom's side as to ensure he is well and truly asleep, then whispers, 'I take no pleasure in keeping secrets from you, mate. One day, maybe, I'll be honest about how I really feel? I wish Alice could see the side of you that I can...'

Drifting Upon the Wave

Daz hasn't said a word to me all morning, not during breakfast or even on our departure from the ferry. I shouldn't have left him alone in the bar, at least not without explaining the reasons behind why. But he seemed happy enough, especially when he was dancing with those blokes from Carlisle. I just can't handle being around strangers. Daz should understand that. I've never seen him look so down.

'Are you worn out from all that dancing?' I ask him, as our taxi pulls up outside of Amsterdam's train station. 'You're too quiet, mate. Is it your sugar levels again?'

'I'm enjoying the scenery, Tom-boy,' he says. 'We've made it. Amsterdam. It only took ten years.' He laughs half-heartedly, tips our driver, and turns to me with a widened smile. 'I bet you're feeling better today, given how loud your snoring was last night.'

'It took a while to drift off, with how bad the ship was rocking and that. But, yeah, I slept pretty well for once.'

Darren kicks out his legs on leaving the taxi, as do I. 'It feels weird being back on firm ground, doesn't it? My legs are killing me. Maybe I am getting a little too old to be dancing around.'

'I'm sorry for skulking off, mate. It wasn't my scene.'

'There's no need to apologise,' he insists. 'I had such a good laugh with those other lads. You'd have gotten along with them, you know. It's a pity you left.'

'That's good,' I say. 'It doesn't matter where you go, you always end up making new friends. I don't know how you do it.'

Darren doesn't respond. He pulls out his phone instead, swipes onto Google Maps, and then looks at me with a puzzled expression.

'Right. We'd best find our hotel first, drop off these suitcases, then try to familiarise ourselves with some of the streets. Does that sound like a solid plan to you?'

'Our plan seems to be not having one,' I humour, trying to hide my cramping fingers from view. Amsterdam's streets are all narrow and disorientating—not good for my anxiety in the slightest.

'You don't happen to know any Dutch, do you?' he asks.

'No. Have you swatted up on any of the local lingo?'

'Only the odd word and phrase. It'll be interesting when we need to ask for directions…'

'Interesting isn't the word I'd use; terrifying would be more accurate.' This is exactly what I dreaded about holidaying abroad. I knew this would happen. We're in unfamiliar territory, completely lost, and ignorant to the cultural and its language. My throat starts to tighten, along with the usual wave of adrenaline coursing through my veins. This isn't good. I need to ground myself. I need to focus on my breaths. There's so much to take in, though.

'Thank God for Google's translating feature, that's all I can say. Let's have a look up this street.' Daz follows the instructions on his phone, which take us down several small alleyways, over two canals, by a dodgy-looking café, until we come upon a hotel that's situated between a peep show and a sex shop. 'Here we are! Looks alright, doesn't it?'

'We're still in the red-light district,' I say, noting the prominent scarlet windows around us. 'You said the hotel looked fancy — this is fancy?'

'It looked nice online,' he groans. 'What's to say it isn't luxurious on the inside? Let's not jump to conclusions, yeah?'

'I'm too not sure about this, mate.'

'Just let me do the talking. I'll keep us right.' Daz approaches a young girl at the hotel's reception desk, who thankfully speaks some English. 'Good Morning,' he says to her, gleaming with enthusiasm. 'We're here for four nights. The name's Darren Pelaw, and this fine fellow beside me is Thomas Grey.'

'Ah! Yes, I can see your names and the booking confirmation on my computer,' says the girl. 'Your room is up the stairs, first on the left. Please enjoy your stay.'

We turn around to find a narrow, spiralling and very steep staircase. I take the plunge and go first, almost slipping halfway up.

'These steps are pretty tight. Watch yourself, Daz.'

'I haven't got size ten feet like you to worry about,' he laughs, pushing at me gently from behind. 'If you fall, you'll only land on me. Just take your time.'

We enter our room, which isn't exactly "our" room as there are eight beds. My anxiety skyrockets, though I soon turn the fear into anger — another coping mechanism of mine.

'This is a friggin' hostel, Daz!'

'So?' he mutters, unphased by this development. 'What's wrong with it being a hostel? There's plenty of room in here, and we only need somewhere to sleep.'

'We might be sharing this room with muggers or complete psychopaths,' I add, my throat tightening more now. 'We might get stabbed or drugged?'

'Or we could be sharing it with innocent travellers and holidaymakers like ourselves? Relax, Tom. You're on holiday, for God's sake.'

'Relax — *Relax*?!' I throw my suitcase onto the nearest bed, as to childishly vent my dismay. Then, as I pull back the bedsheets, my worries increase tenfold on finding a pair of soiled underwear. 'Aren't they meant to leave a chocolate under your pillow, not some stranger's crusty knickers?'

'I reckon you'd suit a nice pink thong like that,' says Daz, trying not to laugh. 'It looks about your size. Get it put on.

'It's not funny — it's disgusting, is what it is.' I just manage to hold back the urge to hurl, making him laugh more. 'How is that funny?'

'Lighten up, mate.' Daz pulls the sheet back again, shaking his head. 'This bed's obviously taken. Let's try the others. Who knows, we might find you a matching bra to go with your new thong?' He rushes across to the last two beds in the room, pulls away their sheets, then grins at me. 'There you go. This one's free and it's clean.'

I kick my suitcase under the bed, inspect the room again, then look back to the door.

'I don't care what you're gonna say, or how much you lecture me, but I need a stiff drink after that.'

'I've never taken you for being a prude,' he says, raising an eyebrow to me. 'We'd go days without changing our clothes, back when we were in the band, and you were the worst culprit! Your clothes back then would've kept a microbiologist busy for months.'

'That was back then, and those were my own clothes.' I rub my fingers over the sheets, sniff them, and turn to the door again. 'Can we go for that drink now?'

'Are you going to whine on like this all week, or are you actually going to let your hair down for once?' he says, folding his arms in disappointment.

I scrub at my shaven scalp in preparation to make a humorous comeback, but I get what Daz is saying. In all fairness, he has spent a fortune on ferrying us over here to have a great time, not to put up with my whining.

'Shall we go and do some sightseeing, on that note?' I suggest. 'Amsterdam's meant to be very picturesque at this time of year.'

'It's a beautiful city—a perfect place to unwind. Don't let some scabby knickers put you off.'

Daz takes his time in going down the narrow stairs and then waits for me outside.

'Those stairs are lethal!' I bleat.

'God help us when you've had a few drinks. You'll never make it up them in one piece,' Daz sniggers. 'We'll have to get a stairlift installed.'

'I don't plan to get drunk,' I say, somewhat taking him by surprise. 'The beer in Amsterdam's probably too expensive for a proper session, anyway. We'll be skint in no time.'

'And here's me thinking you'd given up on alcohol for the sake of your health and marriage. Where should we go first? There's the Royal Palace…Dam Square?'

'I wouldn't mind a look around the local brewery,' I say, rubbing my hands together. Daz doesn't look impressed. 'Fine. How about we start off in Dam Square? There might be some tour guides knocking about that can show us around?'

'That's not a bad idea, actually. I think Dam Square is down one of these alleyways,' he says, guiding us into the nearest one. 'There's another thing you need to know, while we're walking through the red-light district: stay in the centre of the path and keep your eyes down.'

'Why?' I ask. 'The paths aren't that wide.'

'Trust me, mate. A lad from work gave me this advice, and he strongly emphasised that I should take it.'

I soon and sadly come to realise what Daz's workmate was going on about.

'Are those girls sex workers?' I ask, fleeting my eyes momentarily across the half-naked women standing within each doorway we pass by.

'Yeah. Stay in the middle of the path and keep your head down, mate. It's the politest way to show them that you're not interested in what's on offer, if you get what I mean.'

Daz smiles to the women as we walk by them, and I do as I'm told by keeping my head held down. Some of the sex workers attempt to coax us over, to inspect "their goods", while others just look as miserable as I do. What hits me most is that some look like your typical supermodel, while others look like they've only just left school—each of them vulnerable in some way.

One girl does grab my interest, however, who is the spitting image of Alice at the same age—around eighteen or nineteen years old. I make the naïve mistake of making eye contact with her for more than five seconds. Shit.

'You want fun?' she asks me in a French accent. 'Fifty Euros. Come on, baby.'

Daz holds his hands up to the woman apologetically. 'Sorry. No, thank you.' He walks on ahead faster now, signalling to me that I should be doing the same. Once we exit the alleyway, he turns and claps onto both my shoulders. 'Are you alright, Tom? That girl, she looked like—'

'Alice,' I say with a heavy sigh. 'She was the spitting image of her, mate.'

'I know. But she isn't Alice, and don't kid yourself that she is.' Daz becomes flummoxed, his face flushing red now. 'I'm only going to ask this one more time and then I won't mention it ever again.' He rubs at his face, then looks to me through his fingers. 'Has she been in touch with you at all since you separated? It's been a few weeks—'

'No. No, she hasn't,' I say, scuffing my feet over the cobblestoned path. 'I haven't seen Rosie, either, other than the photos Alice uploaded onto Facebook recently. It's not the same, is it?'

'That girl back there wasn't Alice, and you'll never be able to replace her. But—and it's a big but—you have started making some positive changes in your life, even if you can't see them yourself yet. Use this vacation as way to break from your past, to rectify all those bad habits which trigger your anxiety and depression. I'm here to help you as much as I can.'

I'm lost for words, blinking my eyes as to hold back the tears welling up in them. I wasn't expecting this reaction from Daz, this stark and truthful outburst.

'I am starting to feel better,' I say to him, 'but it's harder and taking longer than I thought it would. I'm getting to know what my triggers are, most of which are flashbacks and alcohol. I don't want to drink any booze this week, or feel down, or go into one of my anxiety attacks.'

'And you won't,' he states. 'We'll cure you, no matter what it takes. In the meantime, let's try and have some fun. Dam Square's not too far away.'

'You shouldn't worry about me as much as you do. It's not fair—'

'But I do, because that's what best mates are for. When you're with me, you don't need to put on a mask. Just be yourself, Tom. You've got nothing to hide.'

We make it into Dam Square, the very heart of Amsterdam's city. I'm hit with a sudden wave of anxious thoughts—of feeling like I'm being submerged into an endless pit with hundreds of strangers, with nowhere to run to or hide, and we're all clawing at one another to find a way out. Daz wraps an arm around me again and pats at my arm, possibly sensing that I'm about to go into a full-blown attack. I attempt to dismiss his concerns, but he can see right through my false façade.

'That looks like a tour to me,' he stays, directing us towards a small group of people nearby. 'I'll handle this, mate. I know how much you hate talking to strangers.'

'Cheers.'

A tall fellow situated within the centre of this group spots us, and immediately proceeds to call me and Daz over. I assume he's the tour guide, given his flamboyant aura and corduroy suit.

'Hello there! Are you English?' the tour guide asks us in a half-Dutch, half-American accent. 'You're very welcome to join our group.'

'Yes,' I say, amazed and curious as to how he can distinguish our nationality.

'I knew it,' he laughs. 'It is how you dress, gentlemen.'

'The cheeky —'

Daz swiftly interjects. 'He's not taking the piss, Tom. You're wearing a Stone Roses t-shirt. The chances are, it's probably just a good guess on his part. Chillout, man.'

'I love Manchester,' the tour guide informs me. 'I adore the Stone Roses, Joy Division, and The Happy Mondays — great bands, great music. My name is Klaus. I will show you the many interesting sights within this beautiful city of ours. Some are beautiful, some shocking, and some…very poignant.'

'I can imagine,' says Daz, taking out his wallet. 'How much do you want?'

'Five euros.' Klaus suddenly holds up his hands and waves them at us. 'Please, you can pay at the end. I don't want to carry cash around with me. It would not be wise to do so.'

I whisper to Daz, 'Klaus is a strange fella, isn't he?'

'You think? He's just being friendly, and probably worried about being mugged.' Daz uses his eyes to direct mine towards several, suspicious-looking characters that are circling our group, each with their eyes held upon Klaus. 'My guess is that Klaus is going off previous experiences. You can't be too careful in a big city like this, can you?'

'They'll have no joy in mugging us,' I quip. 'I've only got half a packet of cigarettes and a melted chocolate bar in my pocket.'

'Still, desperate times make people do desperate things.' Daz continues to monitor the two characters as they move in closer. One of them—a ginger-haired man wearing a torn leather jacket—stands himself less than a few feet away from us, making Daz put on his "macho" stance. I notice how the man has countless injection scars across his emaciated forearms and barely any teeth—evidently a heroin addict. For some strange reason, though, I don't feel threatened by him. Afterall, you shouldn't judge a book by its cover, or so Daz keeps saying. Yet, Daz seems just as nervous as I am in this stranger's presence.

'I don't like the look of him,' he says, placing himself between me and the stranger now. 'I swear, if that blokes comes any closer to us…'

'And you have the nerve to tell me to relax?' I note. 'Anyhow, if that bloke does try anything dodgy, you'd easily wipe the floor with him.'

'I don't want to resort to violence; that's what my dad would do. Shit. I thought we'd be safe here.'

'What's gotten into you, Daz? Why are you stressing and I'm not? Has there been a glitch in the Matrix or something?'

'I brought you here to mellow out, not get mugged. I don't want to let you down.'

'You're not—'

'This isn't what I wanted. I thought we'd be safe…'

Unbeknown to Daz, he's setting off my anxiety again. Regardless, I imagine myself wrapping a lasso around these negative thoughts, tightening it around them, ultimately crushing those debilitating emotions. I'm in control. I-am-in-control. I will not have a panic attack. I will not have a breakdown in the middle of some foreign city.

'Hallo, Klaus,' the stranger says to him in a friendly manner, and with a distinct Scottish accent. 'How are ya doin', pal?'

'I'm good, Tam. Have you eaten yet today?'

'Aye, some Spanish fella bought me a sandwich fer breakfast. Ah'm good, jist trying ta stay oot ay trouble, ya know, keep mah heid doon and polis off mah back.'

'I will be in the usual spot this evening. If you haven't eaten by then, I will make sure that you have a warm meal in your stomach,' says Klaus, shaking his hand. 'Take care, old friend.'

Tam looks at me and then clasps his hands together in thanks towards Klaus. 'There aren't many people like you in this world, Klaus. God bless ya.' He walks away, leaving our tour group in an awkward state of silence.

'Tam is an ex-heroin addict,' Klaus explains. 'He has gone clean recently, which is not a simple task to accomplish. Tam is a lovely fellow, that is, when he hasn't had a hit. People are quick to point fingers and judge, but it is much more satisfying to reach out a hand to help those in need.'

Klaus's words resonate with me. I don't know why, but they do. Daz's body is notably more relaxed now, too, and he is also displaying a sense of sympathy in place of the previous fear.

'How did you meet him,' Daz asks Klaus. 'You know, the guy you were talking to just there?'

'I would often walk by Tam and his friend, Erik, during my tours. There were many times when I thought he was

291

dead, and that horrible image stuck with me. I assisted Tam in finding the help he needed at a local rehabilitation centre, although Erik does not wish for any similar aid. We have been good friends ever since.' Klaus takes off, eagerly gesturing for our group to follow him. 'We shall visit the Royal Palace first, then make our way towards the red-light district…'

Now that Daz and I have gotten over that little blip, we begin to take in the sights and sounds of this unique city. Every now and then I can feel the crippling sensation of my anxiety tremors rise, but I somehow manage to hold them at bay, though only just. I feel so calm here. Coming to Amsterdam was a great call on Daz's part. That feeling of wonderment and serenity soon dwindles, however, once we turn a corner into a more modern-looking district.

'Why are these buildings different to the rest?' I say to Klaus, seeing as how all the other structures bear a more medieval appearance. 'They look so out-of-place—they're ugly.'

Klaus drops his jovial manner and replaces it with a pure and gut-wrenching melancholy.

'They are a result from an ugly period in Amsterdam's history, my friend. This area was once the Jewish Quarter— the *Jodenbuurt*,' he tells me. 'It became a ghetto—a place of utter pain, death and sorrow—during the second world war. Apart from the German tank shells, most of this district was destroyed during the Hunger Winter, not long after the war. Prior to that dreadful conflict, there were approximately 80,000 Jews living and working in Amsterdam, but only 5000 remained thereafter. Let that sink in for a moment.'

I go to speak but can't, and I think Daz is in the same boat as me. Our group falls silent again as we each examine the street, our thoughts likely flowing in unison. The reality of what I've just learned strikes an agonising note within my conscience. How can I be so depressed about my life—my privileged, safe from persecution, free to do whatever I want existence—when faced with this daunting reminder of how horrendous those times were? There's no comparison. There's no comparison to the sadness, humiliation, and fear all those innocent people must have gone through. I have no right to be depressed or anxious, but I am.

'It makes you appreciate life, doesn't it?' Daz says to me.

'Yeah. It's certainly making me appreciate things more. We're very lucky.'

'It's an eye-opener…'

Klaus takes us down another canal street that leads us to the Anne Frank house, where there's a queue of at least one-hundred people lined up outside of it.

'If you wish to visit, I'd suggest you book well in-advance,' says Klaus. 'It is worth the wait. I can assure you of that.'

Daz turns to me, showing a glint of sorrow in his expression. 'I think we've seen enough poignant parts of the city for one day, mate.' He nods over to a small café. 'Should we have a look in there for a bite to eat?'

'I'm not that hungry. But sure, let's have a look.'

We're instantly met with a pungent smell of dog faeces on entering the café, despite it looking immaculate.

'It's a nice café, is this,' Daz says, ever the optimistic.

'What's that pong?' I ask, pulling my shirt up and over the bottom half of my face. 'It reeks in here. Let's find somewhere else that's less manky.'

With a knowing smirk, he replies with: 'That's cannabis you can smell. It's a dope café, Tom-boy. You'll soon relax in here.'

'I can't see the attraction—it stinks of crap!'

'Don't knock it 'til you try it. Cannabis isn't as bad as it's made out to be.'

'Have *you* tried it before?' I enquire, wholly astonished.

'I have the odd spliff now and then, mostly when Michelle and Nathan are out. A lad at work grows the stuff, so I know what I'm getting i.e. the pure deal—100% natural.'

'You smoke cannabis?' I say amid some nervous laughter, but it's only to hide how shocked I am. 'I never took you for being a druggie.'

'It settles the nerves and isn't anywhere near as harmful to your body as alcohol is.' Daz goes to the café's counter, pointing a finger at a blackboard situated behind it. 'It'll do wonders for your anxiety. Give it a try—see what you think. Smoking cannabis is legal over here, you know.'

'I'm not bothered about it being legal or not,' I say, pinching at my nose to protect it from the horrid stench. 'It's just, I've never tried it before. I don't know how I'll react.'

'I'll keep an eye on you.' Daz is handed a couple of pre-rolled spliffs from the server, which he offers to me. 'Can I borrow your lighter, mate?'

'I've read some bad things about cannabis. I'm not sure…'

'It's something new and different. I'd never let anything bad happen to you, would I?' Daz inspects the spliffs, nodding approvingly at them. 'Life's too short. You only get one shot to try new things, and a little spliff isn't going to hurt you.'

I finally give in, though I'm reluctant to try this new "miracle cure" that Daz is offering me. I take in a draw and instantly gag on the sweet yet vile taste. It's a stark contrast to the huge draw Daz takes in, and well within his stride.

'Bloody hell,' I gasp, choking on the thick smoke. 'This is strong.'

'It's pure green, not cut with chemicals like what you get back in England,' he explains, taking in another draw. 'It's good, *really* good.'

I take in another draw and it's like I've drank four pints of super-strength beer, only in half the usual time.

'The taste's not as bad as the smell,' I say, trying hard to hold back some vomit. 'Mind, I don't want to get used to this—'

'Why not?'

'It's illegal back home, for starters. What if this spliff does relieve my anxiety? I can't exactly visit a local corner shop back in England and ask for a carton of spliffs to go with my bread and milk, can I?'

'That's what's wrong with our society: synthetic drugs that are made by multi-millionaire companies, which have God knows how many side-effects, are willingly accepted by our government and citizens as being acceptable; yet cannabis— a totally natural product—is ridiculed and vilified. You've said it yourself countless times that you hate being on tablets because of the side-effects, the weight gain and—'

'My tablets help me, though.' I say, pretending to take in another draw. 'I don't want to rely on anything to cope. I want to be normal. I want to be clean.'

'What is normal? You tell me.' Daz rests himself against the café's bar, swirling his spliff around so that the fumes form a pretty pattern in the air. 'Not one person you'll ever meet is normal. To be normal is to follow what people in higher positions, such as in magazines or on television, deem to be aesthetically pleasing to them. I'd rather be different—unique—someone who stands out from the flock of sheep that follow these stupid rules, which somehow deem what normality is.' He looks across to me with eyes reddening and smiles. 'That's why I respect you so much, Tom. Despite being a teacher—a person who's constantly in the public eye—you do everything you can to be different, to express yourself. Not many teachers would turn up to work in a Blink 182 t-shirt, would they?'

'No, and I've been warned on a few occasions about doing that.'

'But you still go ahead and wear what you want,' he adds, brimming with pride. 'Even if you don't realise it, you rebel against the restrictions set down on us by society. You should be proud of who you are, not ashamed.'

I can't help but laugh. 'So, this is what getting high looks like? I think you should go easy on that spliff, mate. What happened to *you don't need chemicals to live happily*?'

'I'm trying to help you, mate! The sooner you realise just how unique and blessed you are, the sooner you'll be free from your mental illnesses. You've got it in you, man. I'll admit that smoking the odd spliff or two isn't the perfect answer, but it works for me. Everybody's different.'

I reluctantly take in another draw from my spliff, hoping that I will also enter a state of utter relaxation like Daz. It doesn't work, though. All I'm left with is a new type of numbness and desire to correct Daz on his false perception of me, even if it might upset him.

'I'll never be proud of who I am. All that matters now is being back with my family. I want to give up boozing, cigarettes, and — eventually — my Mirtazapine. I know you think me trying some cannabis might help somehow, but it's just another addiction I can do without.'

Daz goes quiet, stubs out his spliff, and loses his content smile.

'You're right, I guess. Take that poor Scottish fella we met today — going clean is what helped him out the most, wasn't it?'

'Exactly. That's what I want — to be clean — to be free from relying on chemicals to make it through each day.'

'It's been a long day,' says Daz, eyeing up the doorway. 'Should we call it an early night?'

I nod in agreement. 'We've still got another three days to explore Amsterdam, and I could do with an early night after that walkaround today.'

'Going to bed at 9pm. What's happened to us,' he laughs. 'Some party animals we are.'

Back in our hostel, Daz falls asleep as soon as his head hits the pillow, whereas, I'm by no means tired. I scour through some photos of Alice and Rosie on my phone, mindful of the strangers lying in the beds around me, sobbing all the while.

Whether it's because of the spliff or not, I develop a strange urge to go out and explore more of Amsterdam's hidden gems. I check on Daz again to see if he is asleep, which he is, then venture out into the unfamiliar streets once more. Nothing bad will happen. I'm in control. I-am-in-control. I'll be fine. So, if that is the case, why do I feel like I'm not?

Dawn Beckons

Tom has been wandering around Amsterdam for several hours now, unsure of what it is he wants — some beer, his usual solace; or some company other than Darren's; or another foul spliff to calm his senses, perhaps? Regardless, the torment from his family's absence only seems to be strengthening with each moment spent in this solitude. But solitude is good, because — in solitude — Tom believes he is less likely to cause further harm or disappointment to those he cares about. So, the vicious cycle of anxiety and depression continues.

'I'd better head back,' he contemplates, checking the time on his phone, which reads: 04:30 am. 'Daz always wakes up early, and all the bars will be closed by now. There's not much else to do, and I don't want Daz to notice I'm gone. There goes my chance to sneak in a sly beer or two.' He saunters into the nearest alleyway where a trail of red lights come to surround him, along with a another, excruciating bout of anxious tremors. 'At least the hostel isn't far away now. I'm okay. Nothing bad will happen...'

Tom thinks back to that startling encounter earlier, when one of the sex workers tried to grab him. He doesn't have Darren to intervene this time, nor does he wish to land himself in a similar predicament, especially if a situation should arise that may involve him upsetting one of the pimps (who are diligently patrolling this alleyway).

'I can't turn back now; it'll look too suspicious. What a daft idea this was, walking around a foreign city all by myself,' he frets. 'Why didn't I just stay in the hostel with Daz? What was I thinking?'

Suddenly, as if being compelled, Tom comes to an abrupt stop. In his peripheral vision he sees the sex workers performing various dance moves and sensual gestures, though these have the opposite effect on him — he's absolutely petrified and not in any way aroused. Tom walks by the girl he met before, the girl who bears an uncanny resemblance to Alice. He can't help but look at her, despite all efforts not to. She reminds him of what he has lost, and her familiar beauty brings some comfort.

The girl moves away from her window, making eye contact with Tom the whole time. He tries to look away but can't, held under the hypnotic presence she now possesses over him.

'Hey, you! Come here!' she commands, waving Tom over seductively. 'You want some fun, big boy?'

'I'm just out for a little walk,' he says, stammering. 'Thanks, anyway.'

'Come here,' she insists, stroking a finger over her underwear. 'You look so lonely. Don't you want this? Don't you want me?'

'Yes – No!' he screams, turning from her. 'I can't…'

'Please, come in. I will make you happy,' she whispers, allowing her breaths to run over his lips. 'There is no need to be shy. I will take care of you.'

With a stark image of Eve accepting the serpent's forbidden fruit, Tom reluctantly enters the girl's domain. He reminds himself that she isn't Alice, that this is a bad idea, and that he's only going to regret anything that may follow. But, as always, temptation overrules rationale. He simply cannot resist.

The room is lit up with a low-level, scarlet hue. There's a grandfather clock situated opposite a leopard-skin bed that is ticking loudly, which adds more weight to Tom's anxious disposition, and there's a strong smell of bleach floating through the air. He clenches his fists against the painful tremors coursing through them, all the while praying that his IBS doesn't play up.

Tom hasn't even done anything yet, but already he feels dirty and filled with shame.

'This isn't right,' he says, as the girl pulls him onto her bed. 'I don't want to.'

'Are you nervous?' she asks, feigning some sympathy. 'There is no need to be. I will be gentle, and I can tell you want me.'

'I don't even know your name,' he says amid some nervous laughter. But in truth, Tom doesn't care what her name is or even where she is from. He's married, albeit unhappily on Alice's part, and shouldn't be here in the first place. 'I have a wife. I can't do this. I'm sorry to waste your time.'

'Most men who come to visit me are married,' she says, yawning. 'My name is Dawn. Does that help?'

'A bit,' Tom lies. 'I don't want to, you know, do it.'

'Then why did you come in? Do you not find me attractive?' she asks, somewhat offended by his last statement. 'I saw you staring at me. I didn't force you to come in!'

'You remind me of my wife…Alice. She left me a few weeks ago.'

Dawn's patience is wearing thin. 'Do you want to fuck me or not? You only get fifteen minutes.'

'I don't want to,' he whimpers. 'I'm sorry.'

With panic in her expression, Dawn looks at the clock and then to a man clad in a full-length leather coat who is now standing at her doorway. 'You need to pay me — or else.'

'I know. I don't want anything bad to happen,' Tom says, also aware of the intimidating figure stood outside. 'Can we just, I don't know — talk?'

'You want to *talk*?' she chuckles. 'I've had some pretty messed up requests before, but —'

'It'd be nice to have a chat with another woman, someone other than my mother and sister,' Tom explains, fighting hard to keep his tremoring hands out of view. 'I'd really appreciate it.'

'What exactly do you want to talk about?'

'You're a girl, right?'

'Yes!' she states, clasping onto her breasts to verify Tom's bizarre question. 'Can't you see that? Do you need to see my passport for verification?'

'No,' he humours. 'Do you have a boyfriend or husband?'

'I have a girlfriend, actually,' she says, flouncing her eyebrows. 'It's a little personal, don't you think? Why ask?'

'I have anxiety and depression, and I think they were why my wife left me,' he says, trying to keep a straight face. 'Would you do the same to your girlfriend, if she was like me?'

'No, I wouldn't. I would support her as much as possible. Did your wife honestly leave you because of that?' Tom scratches at his brow in response. 'If so, then you're better off without her. I doubt that's the only reason…'

'Well, I drink and smoke a lot—too much, if being honest—and I have a habit of embarrassing her in public,' Tom adds. 'I hope you don't mind me babbling on like this. I need a female perspective on things, on what I should do, that's all. Blokes just tell me to move on and find another girl, but I only want to be with Alice. There's just my best friend who has any faith in that happening, though.'

Dawn turns to the clock again. 'We don't have long. Do you want me to pleasure you? Will that make things better?'

'No, but thanks again for the offer,' he says, wiping at his eyes. 'You look so young. I find it hard to think you enjoy doing this job, and it can't be very good for your self-esteem.'

'I don't enjoy a single second of it, but this job pays the bills,' she says. 'How would you like to fuck complete strangers for a living, some of which are double your age?' She squirms awkwardly, as does Tom. 'I'm trying to save some money up for a better life. I want to move to Norway with my girlfriend, so that we can be happier, safe, find real jobs, and maybe even start a family. I'm almost there.'

Tom pulls out his wallet and hands over its entire contents: sixty euros. 'Here, I hope this helps.'

Dawn accepts the cash but with some reluctance. 'I haven't done anything for you. You could have gotten away with giving me twenty euros.'

'You've talked to me and that's all I wanted. If this money will go towards making your dreams come true, then I'm happy and more than satisfied.'

Dawn looks to the clock again. 'Your time is up. It's been interesting,' she laughs. 'I've never had a man come in here before just to talk to me. It is usually my body they are after, not my thoughts and opinions.'

'I'm not your average bloke,' he states, standing to leave. 'Thank you, Dawn, and take care. I do hope your dreams come true.'

As Tom makes his exit the tall figure lurking at Elena's doorway briskly stands right before him, and he doesn't seem amused.

'Hey, you!' he shouts. 'Did you pay the girl?'

Tom slowly exhales, collects his thoughts, and forces himself to speak. 'Yes, I paid her. I don't want any trouble.'

'Timewaster!' the man snaps, grunting like a wild beast. 'Get the fuck out of here before you get hurt, pussy-boy!' He then produces a twelve-inch, blood-stained knife from the belt around his trousers, which he aims at Tom's throat. 'Don't you come back here, because—if you do— I'll cut you up from ear to ear. You understand me, Englander?'

'I understand. I won't be coming back.' Tom breathes a sigh of relief as the blade's tip is moved away. 'I'm sorry, mate. I'll go--'

'I'm not your fucking friend. Get out of here!' The brute sheathes his knife and gestures for Tom to move with a firm nod. 'You're lucky, boy. I'd love to carve you up good.'

Tom makes his way back into the hostel, into his room, where he soon falls to his knees and weeps. He'd been in some tight scrapes before, but never one where he had come face-to-face with a knife-wielding maniac.

'That was close,' he gasps. 'What the hell was I thinking?'

Darren is still asleep, and Tom wants to keep it that way as he creeps into his own bed. Now more than ever, Tom appreciates the fact he can swipe through the photographs of his wife and child on his phone, to breathe, even to be anxious, and more so to be alive. He had come uncomfortably close to death.

As morning breaks, and with little meaningful rest managed, Tom opens his eyes to find Darren getting dressed beside him.

'Did you have a good sleep?' says Darren, stretching out his aching limbs. 'I slept like a log, despite the mattress being lumpy.'

Tom considers telling Darren the truth—that he ventured deep into the red-light district, into the welcoming arms of a sex worker and then a violent thug—but it would go against their ideal vision of him reforming himself. There'd always be another opportunity to reveal the sordid details, he reasons.

'I slept great,' says Tom. 'It's the best sleep I've had in ages.'

'Where did you go? I saw you sneaking out last night, and it was sunrise when you got back in,' says Darren ominously.

Tom pulls the bedsheets up to his face, remorseful of the fact that his closest friend knows that he's lying. 'I went for a walk down the canal. I fancied some fresh air.'

'You took your sweet time,' Darren humours, hinting that he knows more. 'I thought you'd maybe gone for a cigarette or sly pint.'

'Yeah,' says Tom, latching onto the false excuse with all his might. 'I went for a walk and a few cigarettes, that's all.'

'You're lying, mate. You were gone for hours. For somebody who hates exercise, that's some walking you did.'

'Amsterdam's a big city, and I got lost at one point.'

'At least you found your way back here and in one piece. I was starting to get worried about you.'

'We've played gigs in rougher cities, mate. Walking through Amsterdam's far safer than getting lost in Sunderland.'

'Still, don't be going off on your own little adventures without me. I'd hate to think anything bad would happen to you.'

'I'm not completely helpless,' Tom whines. 'I can handle myself.'

'I'm just saying, you've got to be careful.' Darren looks down at his phone, reeling in horror. 'We've missed half a day!'

'What's wrong with that? We're on holiday, aren't we?'

'I didn't spend a small fortune on this vacation just for us to sleep through most of it. That spliff must've been stronger than I thought?'

'How about we go through the rest of this holiday without any booze or cannabis?' Tom's suggestion is met with a look of joyful astonishment from Darren. 'I'd like to see more of Amsterdam's sites, like what you suggested in the first place. I want to remember this trip.'

'Good. I'm well up for that—' Darren then collapses onto his bed, clenching at his stomach. He reaches into his suitcase for his blood monitoring kit and then opens it with shaking hands. 'I need to check my sugar levels before we do anything.'

'When did you last check them?'

'Yesterday. I don't know what I'm doing wrong.' Darren pricks a finger with a disposable needle and winces as the blood droplets seep onto the BM machine's testing strip. 'What a shitty thing to be born with, diabetes. I'm low,' he says, showing Tom the device's display screen. 'Well, isn't that a surprise—not!'

'What are you gonna do? I ate my last chocolate bar yesterday.'

'A late breakfast should do the trick. Are you up for another look out, or are your legs too tired from all that walking you did last night?'

'I'm fine. There's a café around the corner from here we can go to. I noticed it during my little walkaround last night.'

Darren throws his BM machine back into his suitcase and then turns to Tom with a fake smile of his own. 'I haven't got a choice. I need some sugar and carbs—and fast.'

'I'll buy this time,' Tom implores.

'No, I'm paying. This is my treat.'

'Let me buy our breakfast. I insist, mate.'

'Okay, but we need to be quick. My vision's starting to blur.'

Tom escorts Darren to the café, ensuring to keep a watchful eye over him throughout their short journey. Inside, and after finding a relatively quiet place to sit, Tom heads across to the serving counter. There, he calls over a server and directs them towards a shelf that has some small cupcakes on show.

'Can I order two of those little cakes, please? he asks. 'They look delicious.'

'They are. Thank you,' the server says, returning shortly after with the cupcakes. 'That will be twelve euros.'

'Twelve euros?! They better be worth the price.'

'Every cent. I can assure you.'

'Is this your idea of a decent breakfast?' Darren laughs, as Tom hands one of the petite cakes over to him. 'They're a bit on the small side, aren't they? There's barely a mouthful here.'

'Everything's smaller nowadays. They're full of sugar — what you need,' says Tom, taking a bite from his. 'They taste okay, but still not worth six euros each.'

'Six euros? That's a bit pricey,' says Darren, taking a bite himself. 'Out of interest, which shelf did you order these muffins from?'

Unaware of Darren's concern, Tom says, 'The top one. Why?'

'These aren't breakfast muffins, Tom-boy. Didn't the guy serving you say anything?'

'No.' Tom now notices a small piece of paper accompanying the muffins, which reads: WARNING - Do not eat more than half a cake in twenty minutes. If you feel any adverse side-effects, consume a sugary drink immediately and/or seek medical advice. 'Aww…shit.'

In contrast to Tom, Darren is showing little concern.

'Trust you to buy us space cakes,' he says. 'What are you like, Tom?'

'I didn't mean to buy cannabis cakes,' says Tom, his tremors now reaching their pinnacle. 'What's gonna happen? I've eaten half already.'

'You're going to feel more relaxed than you've ever felt in your entire life,' Darren says optimistically. 'You bought one of the stronger brands, going by the looks of it. The weed should start kicking in within the next thirty minutes or so.'

'What have I done?' Tom's next thought is to forcefully regurgitate his spiked breakfast, but there's a part of him that wants to experience this ultimate relaxation; this release Darren is promising; this cure he's been waiting his whole adult life for — to be free from anxiety's cruel hold. 'I've heard some bad stories about wacky-backy cakes.'

'I've eaten cannabis before and nothing bad ever happened to me,' says Darren, taking another bite without any evident dread. 'You'll be fine. Just go with the flow, mate.'

Tom isn't convinced. 'Just because you were alright, it doesn't necessarily mean I'll be the same.' He holds up his cake, inspecting it with both hope and fear. 'I've got such a bad feeling about this, man.'

Seeking New Addictions

What's the harm in Tom trying some weed? A hefty dose of cannabis might do the trick in getting him to be more open about his issues — the whole point of this vacation. That's what I'm aiming for, anyway. In fairness to the lad, he is starting to come out of his shell and acting more like his old, happy self again.

What am I saying? Am I really that naïve and selfish?

Cannabis is just another drug, another foreign substance that Tom could do well without. But smoking the odd spliff or two helps me to unwind, so it can't be all that bad. It's not like I'm plunging some heroin into his system, is it? I'm prepared to take any drastic measure, should it mean getting my dearest friend firmly back on his feet again.

'So, what's the verdict?' I ask him, after taking the last bite from my space cake. 'You can't really taste the weed — that's a sign of a good brand.'

Tom shrugs back undecidedly. 'All I can taste is cheap and nasty chocolate, and I don't feel much different. I certainly don't feel relaxed. We'd have been better off downing a few shots of whisky for the money I wasted on these stupid things.'

It suddenly dawns on me that he's eaten all his cake in the same time I have i.e. way too fast. I wasn't paying attention. I was too busy eyeing up a Tom Hardy lookalike who's sitting opposite us, albeit discreetly as not to raise any suspicion.

'You weren't meant to eat it that quick,' I say, looking to his empty plate. 'You'll be high as kite in no time.'

'You did. You almost ate yours whole!'

'Yeah, but I'm used to the stuff. You're a newbie, mate.'

Tom coughs as if about to choke. 'It's not my fault. If they hadn't made the cake so small, I might've taken more time eating it.'

'Don't worry. Besides, you won't have a choice once the weed kicks in,' I humour. 'Give it ten more minutes.'

Tom's eyes fleet around the café, his breaths quicken, and his hands start twitching. He's on the brink of another attack, though the tremors in his fingertips aren't as bad as usual.

'It looks like the cannabis is already taking effect,' I say with emphasis. 'You seem alright to me.'

'This is so strange,' he murmurs, staring at his hands. 'It's such a weird sensation, like when you suck on some laughing gas.'

'Sit back and enjoy the ride. That's my plan of action, mate.'

'I'm gonna be sick,' he says, his eyes blinking rapidly now. Tom looks at his fingers again, as if they're not his own anymore, and then smiles as their spasms gradually cease.

'That's crazy! Maybe a little weed is the miracle cure I've been searching for all this time?'

'It's not ideal to rely on any kind of drug to solve your problems, but at least you're having some positive effect. I don't see why they won't legalise it back in England. There are always pros and cons with anything. Personally, I don't see the damage.'

'What about the impact on your health it can have, such as inducing paranoia and psychotic episodes? I taught a pupil once that suffered with terrifying hallucinations because of their addiction to weed. I don't fancy any of those on top of my flashbacks.'

'That's never happened to me,' I say, shrugging dismissively. 'Everyone's different, aren't they? It's all down to your metabolism—'

'What about the social impact?' he adds. 'Just look at where we live, Daz. There are impoverished parents prioritising drugs over feeding their kids, and then there's the connection to domestic abuse and surging theft rate. The list is endless.'

'And alcohol doesn't have a similar impact?' I jibe, compelling Tom into silence. 'Doesn't alcohol have a dire impact on your health, on relationships, and on society as a whole? I'd rather spend an evening in the company of a stoner than a violent alcoholic—put it that way.'

'You mean, like your dad?'

'Precisely. It's why I'd love to see you give up on the booze. You're better than that. You're better than him.'

Despite my enthusiastic outlook, the remorse I feel from plying my vulnerable friend with a new drug—something else he'll no doubt get addicted to—becomes overwhelming.

Tom made it clear that he wants to go clean, that he wants to walk down a new and brighter path. But I've willingly allowed for him to consume a mind-altering drug and out of selfish desires only, which makes this betrayal even worse. Desperate times make people do desperate things, though, don't they?

My space cake is well and truly kicking in. I slide down in my chair, lull my head back, taking in the second-hand weed that's floating around as an additional bonus. This is perfect.

'This is the life, Tom-boy. I could get used to this: you and me, chilling out together like old times. It can't get any better —'

'Is it normal for things to move *really* slow?' He asks, gazing around the café, clearly mournful of the fact how no one else seems to be as distressed as him. 'I don't know whether to be happy or scared. I'm getting paranoid, man. This is weird.'

'Life's weird, mate. Going through life is like travelling down a river — it can be smooth and pleasant at times, but then there's always going to be a few obstacles thrown in along the way to screw your journey up. You can either crash head-first into those obstacles or find a way around them, which might not always be the easiest option. Your anxiety is like a concrete pillar that's been thrown into your river…'

'What are you babbling on about?' he asks. 'Is talking crap another side effect from eating weed?'

'Sometimes. What I'm trying to say is, you've started to break down that concrete pillar of yours. Don't stop, not even if it's exhausting you, or you'll never move on.'

'Down this make-believe river of yours?' he sneers.

'Through life.' I think my point hits home with him, seeing as Tom wipes the smirk from his face. 'You're taking hold of your anxiety and depression, and properly now. But if you stop, if you give up and go back to a life of drinking yourself stupid and abusing your body, then you'll never be able to move on. You'll never get Alice back.'

Tom plays with his cupcake paper, twisting and tearing at it, lost within thought. 'So, from what I can make out, my Mirtazapine is like a sledgehammer that can be used to smash apart this pillar, but alcohol just does the total opposite—it makes it stronger. Am I right?'

'In a way…yeah.'

'Cheesy metaphors aside, you're saying that I need to work out what will help and what won't help me get over my mental illnesses, so that I can move on from them?'

'It's not rocket science.' I tilt my head from side-to-side, trying to work out whether he's taking the piss or not. 'In a perfect world you wouldn't need to depend on medications. But if they do help you, by any means, don't stop taking them.'

'Do you not think I've already tried doing that? My doctor said he wants to eventually wean me off the Mirtazapine, but God knows when that will be. I don't think I'm ready to come off it. In fact, I'm not sure if I ever will be. It's these flashbacks—they're relentless. They come and go at random, and I've got no control over them.'

'You'll get there, mate. Keep taking your tablets for as long as you need to. Do what works best for you.'

'Smoking cannabis is how you cope?'

'Only now and then. Like I said, everyone copes differently.'

The cannabis is seriously soaking in now; all previous concerns are falling away from me, including Tom's own issues. I smoke dope to forget about my past, namely the abuse I received at my father's hands, making me no better than Tom and his alcohol dependency. I'm a total hypocrite, aren't I? But who cares? I don't. Cannabis stops me worrying about such trivial things. I can always worry about Tom again once this euphoric hit wears off.

'I've got a funny urge to hug everyone around us,' he says, 'but I hate being around strangers. What the hell is that space cake doing to me?'

'Ride the wave, my friend. There's nothing to stress over,' I suggest and then nod across at a man wearing a tailored suit, then to a guy who's giving off an eco-terrorist vibe. 'I don't think your hugs would go down well with some of the other blokes in here. It goes to show how varied drug users can be, doesn't it?'

'You're right there.' Tom examines the other patrons. 'There are people in here from all walks of life: high-flying business folk, students, a young couple, and —' He gasps on noticing a black-robed fellow sat in the farthest corner, who is reading a copy of John Milton's *Paradise Lost*. 'I'm sure that fella's a priest. There's an eye-opener.'

'Calm down,' I implore, noting how the priest is now staring back at us. 'Make the most of your ride uphill before the munchies kick in — that's the bad part. Once the blind happiness fades away, all you're left with is an insatiable hunger, and — regardless of how much you eat — the hunger pains just get worse and worse. Lucky for us, we're spoilt for choice when it comes to choosing a restaurant around here.'

'Great. That's gonna do wonders for my IBS.'

'You'll be too high to give a damn, mate. Plus, it already stinks of crap in here—no one will bat an eyelid.'

Over the next ten minutes, Tom and I watch a soccer match that's playing on the café's TV set. Neither of us remotely enjoy the sport, given we agreed long ago that soccer players are grossly overpaid for what they do (jealously plays a part as well). But, under the present and serene influence of weed, watching the players running around and kicking the ball somehow captivates us.

'I think I'm tripping,' says Tom, his eyes now notably red and pupils dilated. 'The walls are moving like they're a sheet of paper being blown about in the wind, and I can't feel my teeth...'

'That's normal,' I say with a reassuring smile. 'It's your first-time eating weed, so it's bound to feel a bit strange. You'll be alright. I'll take care of you.'

What I hadn't considered was that Tom had bought the strongest space cakes available—in the whole of Amsterdam it turns out. I'm also succumbing to some unwanted side-effects. It's as if I've had a two-tonne ball of metal placed into my stomach, and that happy-go-lucky sensation is rapidly turning into a state of frantic paranoia. I'm guessing by Tom's expression of sheer dread that he's also going through the same dilemma.

'Daz...'

'Tom...'

My head starts to spin and pound, turning everyone around me into fragmented shadows—and I'm certain that they're all out to get me. This is going drastically wrong. I've had bad trips before but never on this scale, and the answer is always a good dose of sugar. Lots of sugar. That will inevitably force me into a diabetic hyper episode, however, which is the last thing I need. Yet again, another of my well-thought-out plans has backfired on me.

Tom mumbles under his breath, 'I'm gonna be sick,' and then he clenches at his face in agony. 'I think I'm dying.'

'You're not dying. We need something sugary to counteract the weed, that's all.' I clench at my forehead with both hands, trying to remember where the nearest fast food joint is. 'There's a Burger King nearby. We can get some cola—'

'I don't want to die! I don't want to die, Daz!' he howls, gaining the unwanted attention of several café dwellers. 'When will it stop?'

No way am I telling him it can stay in your system for up to seventy-two hours. Like that would help.

'Not long, mate. Just focus on your breaths and calm down. You *are not* going to die.' I hold onto his hands, which he immediately crushes through panic. I try to free myself from Tom's grip, but his adrenaline rush is giving him a strength that not even I can overpower. 'Come with me. Let's get some proper food, yeah?'

I drag Tom from his chair and lead him outside. Matters deteriorate as we attempt to navigate the narrow streets into Dam Square, where a tram starts moving towards us. To me and Tom the tram is travelling at breakneck speed and is heading straight at us, although it's probably topping five miles per hour—if that.

'Daz—WATCH OUT!' Tom rugby-tackles me to the ground, out of the tram's slow-moving path. 'We were almost killed there! My voice is all slow, but everything else is super-fast. I don't like this, mate. I'm scared.'

'We're not far from the Burger King,' I assure him, attempting to hide my own fear. 'I think it's this way. Go, Tom — GO!'

We stagger into the restaurant, nearly falling into an unsuspecting family in the process, and are met with a unified look of sheer disgust from the staff members standing behind the tills, who — given their rolling eyes — have encountered idiots like us before who can't handle Amsterdam's pure-cut weed.

I try ordering two regular colas, but the words just don't come out right. One of the servers returns with two cheeseburgers and a chocolate doughnut, which I pay for, though it's not exactly what Tom or I want.

'Where's the cola?' he whines. 'You must've pronounced it wrong, mate. Why didn't you ask for it in English? We don't know a word of Dutch.'

'I was trying to be polite,' I explain. 'Look, we'll head back to the hostel — we'll be safer there. How about that? We need to sweat this trip off. That's what we've got to do.'

'I want to go home. I want to be with my family!' he exclaims. 'My mind is made up, there's no doubting it. I want to go clean and for good this time. I want to live my life without having to rely on drugs, legal or illegal. I want Alice. I want my Rosie. I can't live without them.' Tears form in Tom's eyes and his hands begin to tremble uncontrollably. 'I'm sick of living like this, always waiting for another anxiety attack to strike. I'll never touch cannabis again...'

Through my blurring vision, I manage to make out the exit and waste no time in dragging Tom towards it. 'Let's get back to the hostel. The only thing we can do now is throw up what's left of those space cakes in our stomachs.' Then I whisper to him, possibly out of remorse, 'I'm so sorry, mate. This wasn't what I had planned. I just wanted for you to relax.'

Tom doesn't say a word to me on our journey back to the hostel, which takes twice as long as it should have due to the disorientating effects from the cannabis still coursing through our systems. Together we crawl up the winding stairwell, into our room, and then towards the communal bathroom.

There's a German couple lying on a bed nearby that are staring at us, but I couldn't give a toss about what they're thinking. Tom is my priority. I position him in front of the toilet bowl, and we both take in a deep breath against the foul stench of lingering urine. Some holiday this has turned out to be. Some friend I am.

'Stick your fingers down your throat,' I say, as Tom kneels before the faeces-coated toilet bowl. 'Make sure you get it all up. I won't leave your side.'

Tom forces two fingers into the back of his mouth and then hurls up the remnants of his space cake into the putrid bowl. With a pitiful whimper, he wipes his mouth and then moves aside for me to perform the same humiliating act.

'You were right,' he says. 'This is the push I needed to change.'

'This is *not* what I had planned for our vacation,' I say, resting two fingers along my tongue. 'I'm glad it's helped you in some way, though. Maybe we'll laugh about this later?'

'I'd prefer to forget about this sorry episode. No offence,' he says. 'I still feel sick and high.'

'It'll go in time. We just need some decent rest.'

Tom and I assist one another back to our beds, where we lie and stare at the ceiling for over an hour before speaking again.

'Does Michelle know you do weed?' he asks in a drawn-out groan. 'Is she okay about it?'

'There's a lot about me that Michelle isn't aware of,' I reply. 'The poor lass. I hope Dad's not stressing her out. I told Michelle not to go on holiday with him and Mum, but she wouldn't listen. Our Nathan always comes back sounding like him — that's the worst part.'

'What? Like your dad?'

'Yeah, and it takes ages to remove his poisonous influence from Nathan.' I'm trying to remain positive, more so for Tom's sake, but it's proving difficult. 'Nath's at such an impressionable age. He doesn't understand what a monster my dad is.'

'But Nathan's always been so close to you,' says Tom, rolling over to face me. 'You and your dad are total opposites. I can't see why Nathan would like him, and to the degree you're making out.'

'He's ten years old and is going through a lot of changes. My dad's a master of deception and manipulation — a snake in the grass. I hate him. I hate the fact my son is now with him, listening to his foul-mouthed rants. The thing is... it doesn't matter. The last thing you need is me moping on.'

'No,' Tom implores. 'Nathan loves you to death, mate. There's no way your dad could turn him against you — that's the vibe I'm getting. Is that what you're worrying about?'

'I never said that...'

'I'm not a moron, Daz. It's a thought that's crossed my mind as well, about Alice and Rosie. I'm worried my little

319

girl will be turned against me.' Tom shuffles across to sit on my bed. 'You've helped me, now let me help you. Don't think about how your dad might influence Nathan, because that'll never happen. At the end of the day, Nathan's a clever lad and will soon understand what an utter prick your dad is. It only took me half an hour or so to realise that, the first time I met him.'

'I wish it was that simple. But the older Nathan gets, the closer he seems to be getting to Dad. I don't know what to do.'

'Just be yourself. You alone have convinced me to stop drinking, and that's a miracle in itself. Stop fretting over things that aren't going to happen. Your dad's a mindless thug, and surely Nathan will see that?'

'Cheers.' I don't give Tom the option to resist as I hug into him, ensuring to make my grip as tight as possible. 'I know you're after Alice's forgiveness, but you've got to forgive yourself first.'

'I'm ready to ask for hers,' he says, smiling at first, but then it turns into a bitter frown. 'I'm ready to change for the better. But forgiving myself, after all the misery I've caused, just ain't gonna happen.'

'You've got to forgive yourself,' I plead, stroking a hand against his face. Tom looks uncomfortable at me doing this, so I quickly remove my hand and place it upon my chest. That was a close call. 'Alice should realise what an amazing husband you are.' Tom shows a great deal of confliction in return. 'Honestly, you're not a bad bloke. Let's sleep off the cannabis and spend the rest of our holiday sightseeing — no booze or cannabis. Agreed?'

'Agreed.' He sits back on his own bed and looks out the window. 'When we go home to England it'll be a fresh start for us all, won't it?'

'Of course. Things can only get better from here on in.'

Tom rolls over and soon releases some deafening snores not long after. I pull out my phone to find two unread messages; one is from Michelle and the other is from Alice. Michelle's message states that she and Nathan have arrived safely at the campsite in Northumberland with Mum and Dad. A renewed urge to vomit arises at the very thought of my dad bonding with Nathan, so I delete the message and move onto Alice's.

Hi, Darren. Michelle mentioned that you and Tom have gone to Amsterdam – I'm so jealous! How is Tom? Has he said anything about me? Speak soon – Alice x

Ever the opportunist, I respond with:

Hi, Alice. Tom hasn't stopped talking about you and Rose. He misses you both so much, and he's genuinely sorry for all the stress you've been put through. Believe me, Tom is a changed man. Please give him another chance. I know it might not be my place, but it's tearing me apart to know you're both suffering because of this separation. Take care and speak soon – Darren x

Alice doesn't reply, leaving me in a limbo of wondering whether I've just made things more complicated between her and Tom or not. What was said in that last message had to be said, though. I won't tell Tom about Alice's message. He needs to make the effort now, which he should have done weeks ago. I only wish he felt the same way about me as he does with Alice. Life always isn't always fair, they say. It's a sad fact that he'll never feel the same way about me.

Flashback: May 4th, 2018

Doctor Kain has kindly invited me into his consultation room, just like he did during my first visit after Mum and Dad divorced. I wonder if he'll say that I'm attention-seeking or suffering from indigestion this time around? That's what he said back then, clearly under the impression I was wasting his valuable time; or will the fact I've had a mini stroke change his opinion of me? Either way, I'm only here because Alice forced me to come, along with the strict advice given to me by my stroke consultants a few days ago.

'Good morning, Mr. Grey,' he says, fleeting his eyes between me and his computer screen. 'How might I help you?'

I don't look at him. I can't look at him. In fact, I'm desperate to be free of his company and the intrusive questions that'll no doubt be lined up. But I can't let Alice down, and I've got to think of Rosie. I need to stop being such a selfish coward.

'I was admitted to Durham University Hospital on Saturday with stroke-like symptoms, Doc. It was pretty bad.'

'I see. Did you feel unwell at all leading up to the suspected attack?'

'I felt a little under the weather, but nothing out of the ordinary.'

He looks back at his computer screen and proceeds to scroll through my medical history. Apart from the odd chest infection, it's all to do with my mental health. What an exciting read.

'Your recent blood test results came back negative, and your blood pressure itself wasn't too high—nothing that would raise concerns...'

'My speech went all funny, and the left side of my face felt like it was being electrocuted,' I mutter with resentment. 'There's no way I could have put it on.'

'I'm not insinuating that,' he says, turning back to me. 'You've been very fortunate, in a sense. What advice have the stroke consultants given you?'

'They told me to come here and get my meds reviewed. They put my TIA down to stress and hinted that I may need to change what antidepressants I'm on, you know, to combat my anxiety and depression more effectively. They mentioned sedatives.'

'Well, you're currently on the highest dose of Citalopram, and—going off your last questionnaire, which placed you at a high risk of suicidal thoughts—putting you on benzodiazepines, such as Lorazepam, is completely out of the question. We could always reconsider trialling beta-blockers with you again, such as Propranolol. It worked pretty well before, according to your notes.'

'Yeah, it worked wonders with my anxiety but did nothing for my depression,' I say, now steadily losing my patience. 'I don't want to be on a load of tablets.'

'Nobody does, Mr. Grey. But if the benefits outweigh the risks—'

'My short-term memory's not been the same since the weekend, either. Is that a normal side-effect from having a mini stroke?'

'It can be, but it's difficult to be certain.' Doctor Kain starts typing on his keyboard, while my throat tightens and heart plummets into an even lower depth. 'We'll keep a close eye on you over the next few months…see how things go.'

'My moods are fluctuating more as well. One minute I'm fine; the next I'm angry for no reason at all,' I add. 'I'm getting worried about how they will affect my marriage. My wife is beside herself at the minute.'

'Maybe keep a diary of your thoughts and feelings? We can look it over at your next appointment to see if there are any patterns that can be established,' he suggests. 'Let's try you with some Mirtazapine, starting off at a 15mgs dose. You'll need to slowly reduce the amount of Citalopram you're on whilst starting this new medication. It may take up to a month, but—if you don't titrate your doses—there could be some nasty complications, should you not follow this advice. I'd offer you further counselling sessions, but you've repeatedly missed the previous ones we offered, and there's a long waiting list.'

'I'll stick with the drugs,' I state bitterly, hoping he takes the hint to hurry up with writing out my prescription. 'Thanks, Doc. See you again soon, yeah?'

'If you have any concerns in the meantime, please don't hesitate to see me again. Please take care, Mr. Grey.'

I accept the prescription from him and leave the surgery as fast as feasibly possible. The last thing I want is to become dependent on drugs, but it's looking that way now. Mirtazapine, my latest addiction. He forgot to mention that I'm not supposed to drink booze on this stuff, which I notice on being handed my meds from the pharmacist. Oh well, ignorance is bliss. I need alcohol to stay sane, and I can't see that changing anytime soon. It'd take something bigger than a mini stroke to curb my alcohol-reliance, that's for sure.

Parting Ways

Darren and Tom sadly spent their remaining days in Amsterdam trying to recover from the skull-crushing migraines and nausea brought on from the cannabis-laden space cakes, instead of sightseeing as they had envisioned. Both loitered around Dam Square like zombies, that is, until the time came when they would depart for the ferry home, back to England, back to reality.

It was an overnight journey across the North Sea to the Port of Tyne, which proved to be completely uneventful, unlike the trip over. Tom had wanted to revisit the piano bar and Darren fancied some more dancing, but they just ended up lying on their bunkbeds, both struggling not to vomit, held at the mercy of the harsh waves crashing against their cabin. Nevertheless, Darren felt that it had been a successful vacation, that Tom had made some meaningful progress. His plan had not been in vain.

'How're you feeling, mate?' Darren asks, looking up to where Tom is lying on the top bunk. 'Are you still feeling queasy?'

'I think I'm still high from those dodgy cakes we ate,' says Tom amid some retching noises. 'That's the last time I touch those things. I don't see the fascination in cannabis — it reeks of dog shit.'

'You haven't drunk much water,' Darren adds, reaching into his suitcase. 'I've got a spare bottle. Here, have some of mine.'

'Cheers,' says Tom, accepting the bottle from Darren. 'My mouth tastes like a badger's arse...'

'Charming. You always have such a way with words,' Darren sniggers. 'You keep it. I've got a few more bottles in my suitcase, anyway.' Everything then goes quiet apart from the crashing waves and howling winds. Darren slowly forces himself to stand, and then to lean over Tom's bedside. 'Apart from the ropey cannabis trip, have you enjoyed yourself? I hope so.'

'Yeah, of course. We've been going on about visiting Amsterdam for ages,' says Tom, grinning to Darren within the darkness of their room. 'How about you?'

'I wanted to visit the Anne Frank house. I guess there'll always be another time for that — same again next year?'

'Maybe? A lot can change in a year, though, can't it? I'll probably be a deputy headteacher by then, with little to no time to spare.'

'What's your possible promotion at work got to do with anything? You'd have more disposable cash, for starters.'

'That's if I get it. And if I do, I'll pay for the next trip over. I'd dread to think how much you've spent on me over the last few weeks. I've got to make it up to you somehow, mate.'

'I don't want your money, Tom, and I don't want you repaying me for this holiday. All I want is to see you get over your anxiety and depression—which you are.'

Tom shakes his head, reluctant to accept what Darren is saying.

'I am better but nowhere near perfect. I've still got to convince Alice that I've changed my ways and given up alcohol.'

'You will,' Darren says with confidence. 'Once she sees how much you've bettered yourself, you'll be back in her arms in no time.' He grabs Tom by the hand. 'Trust me on this. When have I ever let you down?'

'I wish I could have just an ounce of your optimism,' says Tom, chuckling faintly. 'We'll have to wait and see, won't we? I'll need to contact Alice first—that's the main problem. If I were her, I wouldn't want to speak to me.'

Darren returns to his bed, now feeling his own familiar tremors emerge. He reaches through the darkness for his BM kit, pricks a finger, then waits for the light-up screen to reveal if he should be concerned or not.

'My sugars are low again. It's a good job you bought those chocolate bars earlier. Can I borrow one?'

'Sure. Help yourself,' says Tom. 'Take a couple, never mind borrowing one. Anyway, how would that work out?'

'I'll be able to hand it back to you come this time tomorrow. It might not look the same, though.'

Tom gags, clenching at his mouth to prevent any laughter from leaving it. 'Keep them. That's rank,' he laughs.

Darren consumes the sickly chocolate as if it were the first meal in weeks. His tremors gradually dwindle and the line of fresh sweat on his brow begins to cool. It was yet another close call, Darren tells himself.

'That's done the trick,' he says. 'Goodnight, Tom.'

'Goodnight, mate. Thanks again for the holiday.'

'Don't mention it, pal.'

The lads make it back into Newcastle's city centre by Midday. Now on land they have thankfully lost their seasickness, and the unwanted aftereffects of cannabis are also wearing off.

Tom rubs at his gurgling stomach, then looks to a nearby Wetherspoons pub.

'I'm starving,' he says. 'Do you fancy a bite to eat before we set off home?'

Darren questions himself as to whether this would be a good idea, given how well Tom had been doing without alcohol over the last three days, though soon gives in. 'Just food, yeah? No booze.'

'I don't want to go on a session, believe it or not. All I'm after is a nice, greasy breakfast and some extra-strong coffee.'

'Are you sure? You're not going to sneak in a sly whisky chaser when I'm not looking?'

'Positive.'

'Promise?'

'I Promise.'

'I'll hold you to that, mate.'

The pub is practically vacant, making it easy for Darren and Tom to find a seat and then get served. Darren orders a naked steak and Tom does the same.

'Honestly, I'll have the same as you,' Tom insists. 'It's healthy living from now on—no more junk food.'

'What happened to wanting a greasy fry-up?' Darren asks with a look of bewilderment. 'Are you feeling alright, Tom-boy? Do you need a lie down?'

'I want to make some drastic changes, and that means eating healthier.' Tom grabs at the small bulge of fat resting along his belt buckle. 'I've been meaning to get rid of this "Dad-Bod" for a while now. There's nothing wrong with eating steak and salad, instead of steak with some lovely, golden, greasy chips.' He licks at his lips and slaps at his face. 'I can do this. I can do this!'

'Now I come to think of it, I actually fancy a couscous wrap.' Tom's jaw drops in response, which then forms into a disappointed frown. 'I promised myself that I'd try out the Vegan Diet once we got back. Why not start now?'

'You want to go Vegan?' Tom asks, somewhat in shock. 'But you like eating bacon and chicken and steaks? It'll be a nightmare for you, won't it?'

'You liked drinking yourself into oblivion. But you've put a stop to that now, haven't you? Me going Vegan is my way of trying to support you, mate. If you are going to go without, then why shouldn't I? We can encourage each other to stick at it.'

'I feel well guilty now, robbing you of your bacon baps,' says Tom, smiling half-heartedly. 'You don't have to give up meat for me, you know.'

'It's better for the environment, apparently. I'd like to think I'm doing my bit to make Nathan's future more secure. The thought of him living in a world that's dying faster, because of our generation not doing anything about it, is starting to keep me up at night.'

'It's not just our generation,' Tom scoffs, 'and don't you use swine insulin to treat your diabetes?'

Darren rubs at his face in despair. 'I never thought of that. Still, I can cross that bridge when I visit my doctor next week, can't I?'

'Always looking on the bright side,' Tom quips. He orders two diet lemonades and then clinks his glass against Darren's on receiving them. 'Here's to a better future, Daz. Cheers!'

'Cheers! Here's to being sober!'

'Yeah… cheers,' says Tom, albeit reservedly.

After twenty minutes, one of the bar stewards strolls over with Darren and Tom's meals. Darren looks at his plate hungrily, but Tom looks at his in disgust.

'It smells funny,' says Tom, scrunching his nostrils. 'What the hell is couscous, anyway? It looks like bird seed.'

'Don't knock it 'til you try it,' says Daz, waving his fork around. 'Get it down you, pal. There's a first time for everything—'

'Like those space cakes? Yeah, don't remind me.' Tom collects his fork from the table and then stares in awe at how steady it is in his hands. 'My tremors…'

'They're not as bad as usual,' Darren interjects. 'You see? You're starting to beat your anxiety. All that alcohol won't have done your tremors much good…'

Tom takes a bite of the spicy couscous, allows for it to simmer on his tongue, then gives Darren a thumbs up. 'It's alright—hot as Hell, but not as disgusting as I thought it'd be.'

'You've got to try everything once, that's what I say.' Daz glances down at his phone. There's a message from his secret acquaintance, Shaq, which he merely chooses to ignore. 'When we've finished here, do you want to go straight home or hang around Newcastle for a while?'

'Who's this Shaq fella?' Tom asks, noting the stranger's name that's still on display. 'I can read upside-down.'

'I told you, he's a lad I talk to online.' Darren nervously shuffles the food around on his plate before putting his phone away. 'We chat about sports and stuff, that's all. Nothing interesting.'

'You should invite him down the pub sometime, so he can meet me and the other lads. More the merrier.'

'Pubs aren't really Shaq's scene.' Darren pushes his plate away, his previous hunger now robbed from the twisting knots in his stomach. 'I've only met him a couple of times in person. Shaq's not into drinking or socialising.'

Tom shrugs and returns to his food. 'Don't mind me, mate. I'm just being nosey.'

'When are you not?' Darren turns to nearest door, compelled to leave. 'I need some air. I'll wait for you outside, okay?'

'To be honest, I'm not that hungry anymore,' says Tom, also pushing his plate away. 'I want to get home, to forge a plan of how I'm going to convince Alice to give me another chance.' He gets up to stand by Darren at the doorway. The friends then peer out onto the bustling roads and sea of strangers walking by, seemingly entranced by it all. 'I could never live in a big city, me. There's too much noise and pollution.'

'Neither could I,' says Darren, patting Tom on the back. 'Home is where the heart is, my mate, even if it is Aycliffe.'

'Aycliffe's not that bad. You should never forget where you come from, should you?'

'It'd still be nice to live on a tropical island somewhere, though, wouldn't it?'

'Too right. But when are we ever gonna get the money for that?'

'It's a nice thought, something to work towards,' says Darren with a content smile. 'Life's always full of opportunities, Tom-boy. You've got to work towards something.'

The friends make their way back to the car and a sigh of relief leaves from Darren on reaching it, seeing as he was anticipating a penalty notice to be left on the windscreen.

'That's lucky,' says Darren, wiping at his forehead. 'There was only an hour left on the ticket, and I wasn't too sure about relying on Mikey to pay the full parking fee.'

'You've still got about twenty-thousand in the bank, so a hundred-pound fine should be nothing to you,' Tom jokes. Darren laughs back, but only as to not dampen their joyful mood.

'Do me a favour and put my Linkin Park or Nirvana CD on, please. I need something heavy for this journey home.'

'Linkin Park it is.' Tom carefully places the CD into its slot on the dashboard, mindful of how he almost broke it before. 'Alice and I were lucky enough to see Linkin Park play a gig in Newcastle, back in 2010. It was an amazing night.'

'I'm jealous,' says Darren, his expression now turning forlorn. 'It was a sad day when Chester Bennington died. He had such a great voice. It was such a waste of talent and life.'

'That's what Alice and I said when we found out he committed suicide. His death just goes to prove how devasting mental illnesses can be,' Tom comments, as a new wave of tremors emerge. 'It's always the people you least expect who are the most vulnerable, isn't it?'

Darren nods in agreement and his fingers also start to tremble. 'There's always a light in the darkness, Tom. Please promise me that you'd never do anything like that.'

'Suicide, you mean?'

'I know it's easier said than done, but you've got to find something worth living for and to look forward to.' Darren stutters over his words, his concern for Tom's wellbeing made clear to see. 'For me, my light is Nathan. He and Michelle keep me going.'

'It's Rosie for me,' says Tom. 'I love Alice with all my heart, but it's a different kind of love with Rosie. She's my daughter. It's a much stronger connection — unbreakable.'

'If Rosie's your light, then focus all of your energy into making her as happy as possible. That way, then you'll be happy as well.'

'I guess so, but it's hard when she's not in my life anymore.'

'Focus on her, mate, no matter what. Rosie needs her dad, just as much as you need her. Even if you're apart, that love is still there and always will be,' Darren emphasises.

'But I'm such a failure,' says Tom, stamping a foot in frustration. 'What kind of father-figure am I to her? Alice was right to leave me.'

'Stop saying that!' Darren implores. 'You'd do anything for your little girl — anyone can see how much you love her. No one is perfect; everyone screws up at some point in their lives. The difference is if you're willing to keep fighting through all the bad to preserve the good, and that's the stage you're at now. Life is a balance between joy and sadness, being content and living through uncertainty. Concentrate on the good aspects, Tom. That way, you will overcome your anxiety and depression.'

'It's a nice thought…'

Darren pulls up at Tom's home which still looks so cold and empty from the outside. He turns the volume down and watches Tom as he unbuckles his belt, consumed with many conflicting emotions.

'Home, sweet, home. Happy days,' says Tom, sighing heavily.

'You'll be fine, mate. I'm only a phone call or text message away.'

'I know, and the same goes to you.'

'I'll see you again soon, Tom-boy. Don't be a stranger.'

'See you, Daz. Take care. I'll stay in touch…'

As Tom reaches across to the door handle, Darren suddenly clasps onto his leg. He is reluctant to let go, fearful of what Tom might do once away from his positive influence.

'Remember what I said,' says Darren, his eyes widening with determination. 'I'm always there for you. Always.'

'I know —'

'Be patient. Stay positive. Learn to forgive yourself, and don't dwell on the past. You'll be okay. You'll be alright, Tom.'

'Don't you worry about me. I've changed. I know what I need to do now…' Tom gets out the car, takes in a deep breath, then turns again to face Darren. 'Thanks for everything, mate. I mean it. Thanks for being there for me when I needed you most.'

'You'd do the same for me,' says Darren, suppressing his true concern. 'Get some rest and then make that call to Alice — don't send her a text message, for God's sake. Let her hear your voice, how genuine and desperate you are to change. You've got to prove yourself to her.'

'I will.' Tom slowly backs away, repeating Darren's words in his mind. On reaching the front door, he turns around one more time to see him off. 'So, are we having a look down the Tin Donkey this Friday?'

'Yes, and the lads will be expecting you. You'd better come.'

'I'll be there. I'm not going to lock myself away anymore.'

'Good. See you soon, mate, and send my love to Alice and Rose.'

Darren then drives off, leaving Tom alone to dwell on what steps must now be taken in order to put things right. Tom enters his home, the vacant space and eerie silence immediately hitting him like a thousand needles. He pulls out a packet of cigarettes from his suitcase, places one into his mouth and lights it, then sits on his sofa with his phone held tightly within the palms of his hands. He was excited before, to contact Alice, but his anxiety tremors and depressive thoughts are rapidly returning with more ferocity. A heavy weight begins to press down on his shoulders; his mouth becomes dry; his throat tightens even more, and the desire to subdue his ailments with alcohol gains precedence. Regardless, Darren's words continue to will Tom in the right direction.

'I'm a different person,' he tells himself. 'Alice will take me back — she must. I'm a new man now, aren't I? I've got to do this. I've got to make this call. I've just got to…

A Light in the Darkness

Of Little Comfort

Home, sweet, home. But there's nothing sweet about being back here. Nothing. Zilch. All that's left are reminders of the blessings I once had; of the family I so selfishly tore apart.

The house is in a right state; there are empty lager cans and cigarette cartons all over the place, and the kitchen sink has a funny, rotten egg smell to it. I'll sort them out later. I need to unpack. I need a shower and shave. I need to make that call to Alice before anything else, but I'm afraid of how she'll react. Like most things in life, I'll just put that off as well until tomorrow. Things are always okay, so long as they're to be done tomorrow.

I light up a cigarette and fill the kettle with some fresh water, all the while trying to hold onto the positivity that wore off on me from Daz. But Daz isn't here now, is he? And all those wonderful, positive vibes are quickly wearing off in my best friend's absence. I'm left to my own devices, to sink further into depression, which is never a good aspect of isolation. Everything just reminds me of Alice and Rosie: the furniture, the scented candles, the family photographs

339

hanging up on all the walls, the awful cushions with cartoon kittens on them that Alice bought last year — everything. Wherever I look, all I can see are their disappointed faces. I'll never see their beautiful smiles ever again. It's not fair. This is bullshit!

I inhale a large dose of cigarette smoke and then watch it slowly disperse into the air above me, making the most of its calming effect. I want to quit smoking, too, but that will also have to wait for another, far-off day. It's been hard enough giving up alcohol, and the temptation to crack open a can of super-strength lager is still playing heavily on my mind, especially as I know there's a few tins left in my fridge. I'll make myself a cup of tea instead, though it's hardly a decent substitute. Nevertheless, it'll have to do.

I walk into the living room, sit on the sofa, then watch the sun as it begins to set. Boredom soon sweeps in. I turn on the TV but there's nothing worth watching on, just the usual dross gameshows or repeats of Midsomer Murders. I then flick onto a news channel only to endure thirty tedious minutes of Brexit discussions. I'm depressed enough without having to sit through all the lies and false promises being spouted off by these so-called "caring" politicians of ours. God, they make me sick. I hate hypocrites, but I'm just as bad.

As a last-ditched attempt to find something of interest, I turn onto a music channel that's playing some popular hits from the nineties. I lie back down, close my eyes, and take myself back into childhood. I want to drift off, to be free of this purgatory, but it's just not meant to be. It never is.

There's a knock at the front door. Shit.

With my breaths racing, along with an emergence of crippling anxiety tremors, I roll off the sofa and make my way to see who it is. I can just make out the faint silhouette of a woman with long hair and a smaller figure standing beside her through the bevelled window. Could it be Alice and Rosie? Could it?! It can't be. I'm not that fortunate. Lord have mercy if it's just some cold callers.

On opening the door, I find my sister, nephew, and Mum. This is a surprise. For starters, how did they know I was in?

'What are you lot doing here?' I ask them, likely coming across more abrupt than I had intended to. 'I wasn't expecting a visit.'

'Hi, Tom. Are you not going to invite us in?' Catherine asks, scowling at me. She's wearing a long-haired wig, which is why I thought it was Alice at first, and it doesn't take long for Catherine to notice me staring at her new hairpiece. 'My hair has started falling out. It's another side-effect from my condition, according to the consultants. My body can't absorb nutrients properly anymore. My teeth are in the same state, too, Tom.' Catherine bares her brittle teeth at me, and I can't help but recoil. 'See? They're like chalk now.'

'Bloody hell, Cath,' I gawk, quickly ushering them inside. 'Hi, Mum. Hello, Harry!' I go to hug my nephew, but he just runs past me to take control of the TV remote. 'Charming...'

'You don't spend enough time with him,' says Mum, giving me her tried and tested look of disappointment. She then whispers, 'Your sister is getting more ill by the day, Tom. You need to spend time with Catherine and Harry. They love being around you.'

I know what Mum is saying. She's thinking ahead to the dreaded day when my sister's condition finally reaches its grim climax, which could be anytime. I give Mum an awkward hug in response and then pull out some additional coffee mugs from one of the overhead cupboards. 'Can I make you a cuppa?' I ask, seeing as the conversation is forcing me out of my comfort zone. 'I've got some of that green tea you like, Cath.'

'We're not staying long,' she snaps. 'If it wasn't for me noticing Darren's car, we'd have never known you were in. You haven't visited us for almost three weeks now. Why?'

I scratch at my head, trying to look all innocent and slightly offended. I've got a ton of excuses at hand, but none of them can justify the neglect I've shown my chronically ill sister and vulnerable nephew.

'I've been bad with my nerves,' I say, 'and I've only just gotten back from Amsterdam—'

'Alice told me about your little trip abroad,' says Cath, and Mum gives me a judgmental stare in return. I wasn't aware that Catherine and Alice were still in touch with one another, seeing as they would often clash. Why didn't Cath say anything? 'You'd have known about Alice messaging me if you'd bothered visiting us,' she adds. 'We literally live around the corner from you. It's a five-minute walk.'

'I know, but—'

'But—what? Is it because you can't be bothered to spend some time with your family? Are we that much of a nuisance to you?'

'No. It's not that...' I'm starting to stutter, signalling the onset of an anxiety attack, which swiftly ferments into anger.

'You haven't a clue, not a single idea of what I'm going through.'

Mum makes her thoughts known. 'You're Catherine's big brother, Tom. You should be there for her and Harry, not swanning off down the Tin Donkey or sitting in here playing on old video games.' She points out my Super Nintendo console nearby with a stern frown. 'You should've thrown that decrepit thing out years ago. Always dwelling in the past...'

'I've cut down on the drink,' I state, but I don't think either of them are convinced. Harry even laughs, although that could be just coincidental. 'Honestly, I've cut down on drinking. I want to prove to Alice that I'm a different man. I want to win her back.'

'You'll have your work cut out there,' Catherine sneers. 'Can you blame Alice for leaving you, after all the shit you've put her through?' She immediately winces and looks to me with some remorse. 'I'm sorry, but it's the truth. And it's what you need to hear.'

'You're right,' I say. 'I don't blame Alice at all. It is my fault she left, and my fault alone. I was actually going to call her today, but I'm not sure if that'll be such a good move.'

Mum's scowl turns into pity. 'You've lost so much weight, Tom. What's happening to you?' She starts to cry, though quickly wipes away the tears before Harry notices. 'You're killing yourself, Son. I'm worried sick about you and Catherine and can't bear the thought of losing the both of you.'

I feel guilt, then shame, and then anger again. I'm not perfect, but I'm not wholly responsible for all this misery, am I? People are constantly telling me to be more open about

343

my thoughts and feelings—so I will, but with a great deal of reluctance.

'You've got a bad heart, Cath, but you still drink tons of coffee and energy drinks,' I say to her as gently as possible. 'You're not exactly helping yourself, are you?' Catherine is taken back by my outburst, understandably. But, like she said, the truth must be heard. I'm sick of people pointing fingers at me, telling me that I need to change and let go of my anxiety and depression. I'm so sick of holding back how I really feel, and in being made out to be the bad guy all the time. Enough is enough.

'What's any of that got to do with you?' Catherine asks me, her eyes flaring with rage. 'I can eat and drink whatever I want, and you're hardly in the position to lecture anyone about healthy living.'

Despite my reservations, in knowing that there could be some serious repercussions, I can't hold myself back for some reason.

'You've been told time and time again by your consultants that you could go into cardiac arrest at any moment, but you still don't help yourself. You eat and drink all the wrong things, knowing fine well that they will only make your condition worse. You give off the impression that I'm the one who's making Mum miserable, when you're just as much to blame.'

With a loud gasp, Mum pushes me away with a look of pure disgust. 'Stop it, Tom! Catherine's going through enough as it is. It's not her fault—'

'She's not helping herself, though,' I argue. 'I'll tell you the truth, shall I? I'd love to spend more time with Cath and Harry, to be a positive influence on the poor lad and help my little sister out. But all Cath ever does is nag at me about how bad I've treated Alice. I know that I've been a terrible husband and father, but I'm trying hard to change that. None of you believe me, though, do you? The only person who has given a damn about me is Daz — and he's not even family!'

'This isn't all about you,' Catherine simpers, picking Harry up into her arms. 'If that's how you feel, then don't bother with us at all. Suit yourself. If you want to be alone, then we'll leave you alone.'

'I'm only being honest, like everyone keeps telling me to be.'

'I can take a hint. Suit yourself, Tom.'

Catherine storms off and is closely followed by Mum. My heart instantly sinks, and my depression reaches a new low. What have I done? Why did I say those awful things? I love my little sister. Why did I say those terrible things?

'Wait!' I plead as Mum takes Catherine and Harry outside. 'I'm sorry. I didn't mean what I said — I didn't mean to upset you!'

'Oh, Tom.' Mum shakes her head solemnly, then opens the gate to leave. 'I'll come around tomorrow afternoon. We need to have a good chat, I think.'

'Please wait.' I lean against the door and pull out a cigarette, my one bit of solace within this disastrous situation. 'I'm so sorry. Please don't leave me…'

It's too late — they've gone. Like Alice and Rosie, they've left because of my selfish actions. I'm so pig-headed. They deserve better than to be associated with me.

I light the cigarette and return inside, riddled with even more guilt and self-hatred than ten minutes ago, which I thought would be impossible. I'm a master at pushing those closest to me away, regardless of how much I try not to. I should be there for Catherine and Harry, but I can't even look after myself. How can I possibly be of any benefit to them? It's just a ridiculous fantasy of Mum's, that's all. Perhaps it's her way of coping, to escape from the harsh reality of life—her own mask? I should be there for them more often.

Harry's turned on a children's TV channel, yet another sordid reminder of not having Rosie by my side. I choose to ignore my mother's advice and plug in my old Super Nintendo console and then place the Donkey Kong Country 2 cartridge into its socket. I make it to the game's opening titles, where the 16-bit music reminds me of when Uncle Steven and I would play this game, long before he was murdered.

After an hour, I turn off the console and look for something else to occupy my mind. In a peculiar sense, I'm missing those space cakes I tried in Amsterdam. At least they numbed me to how boring life is, well, the life I'm presently leading. I could do something productive, such as play on my guitar, like Daz suggested—to rekindle that old spark in me—but it's been so long, and I've lost all interest in things that used to bring me such joy. Besides, I'd only get frustrated at how crap I'd play. It's not worth the risk or energy.

More of Daz's advice enters my thoughts, namely, to contact Alice and to put right all the wrongs I've made. My phone is resting on the edge of the sofa, just inches away. I pick it up, unlock its screen, then stare at until my cigarette burns out. I can do this. I can make the call. Alice will answer — I just know she will. All this anxious dread can't be for nothing. I bet she feels just as down as I do about this separation of ours. Jesus wept, man! This is so hard.

As I click onto Alice's contact details, where the green phone light comes on to signal that a call has been initiated, I frantically swipe it off. I then try again but my nerves still get the better of me. All the worst-case scenarios course through my mind: she'll just ignore the call; or she'll answer it and start shouting at me; or — even worse — Alice will inform me that she's met a new partner. I'll probably just bottle it and sit on the other end in silence, either way. I wish Daz was here. He'd know what to do. He'd know how to charm Alice back.

I go into the kitchen for another cigarette, compelled now more than ever to open one of my lager cans. The cigarette carton's empty, I find, so I search through the cupboards for my emergency supply; it's there I happen upon a bottle of whisky, one I'd somehow forgotten about. I tell myself: No! Don't do it, Tom-boy. You're a changed man. Alcohol is not the answer. Alcohol always makes things worse. But it is the easy solution I'm after, and it's never failed me before. I simply cannot resist the urge.

My hands are trembling like mad, and my fingers are going into their usual, agonising cramps. I can't bear another panic attack. I can't stand this miserable existence for a moment longer. One small shot of whisky won't hurt, will it? Just the one. I might even just put a drop on my tongue, to savour the taste and not get drunk. That'll be alright, won't it? Yeah, that's what I'll do.

Within minutes I've drained half of the whisky bottle, and I steadily become more desperate for some nicotine and companionship. The alcohol coursing through my system makes me feel like I'm being submerged into a warm and soothing bath, numbing the pain and emptiness inside. My tremors ease off, but they're soon replaced by depressing flashbacks and impulses. Not this again. Please, God. Not this again. Not another flashback.

I stumble back into my living room and start playing on my old video games again. I imagine Uncle Steven sitting beside me, telling me how to get onto the next level like he used to, then I hear his infectious laughter. This is how I want to spend my evening: living in the past. Contacting Alice will just have to wait until tomorrow. I mean, it's not like she's going anywhere, is it? She'll be fine without me bothering her for one more night.

Old habits die hard, they say. Well, drinking myself into a pleasant and incapacitated state certainly fits the bill. The whisky bottle is all but dry now, and I've smoked all my emergency cigarettes. If someone was to walk in at this moment, it'd be like watching a guest come through the smoke-filled doors on *Stars in their Eyes*. I've plummeted to a new depth. Any chance to think positive has gone, including all those wonderful feelings of nostalgia, hope, and freedom I recently felt. All I'm left with is an empty void in both my heart and soul. I can't stop thinking about Alice; about Rosie; about Uncle Steven; about my promotion; about where my life is heading, and I want it to stop. I'd do anything to stop it.

I pick up my phone and then, after several failed attempts to call Alice, smash it off the nearest wall. Daz said something along the lines of: *When you reach your lowest point in life, you're more willing to make significant changes.* Well, I am at my lowest point, and I can't see anyway way out of it. All I ever seem to do is screw things up. So, on that dire note, where do I go from here? How did I end up in this mess? When did I turn into such a pathetic wretch?

Another of Daz's wise phrases comes into thought, to *look for the light in the darkness*. My Rosie. My beautiful, sweet, little girl. Rosie's my light in the darkness, but she's gone, and she probably hates me now. I'm such a terrible person. All I ever do is let people down, and they would all be better off without me. If I were to stop existing, the world would keep on spinning around and not a single soul would care. That's how I see it, anyway. Happy days and all that.

On scouring the bare living room, I notice that Alice has accidently left one of Rosie's comfort blankets behind, which I retrieve from beside the sofa in an instant. I'm no knelt in the centre of this room, this room where all the walls seem to be closing in on me, with Rosie's blanket nestled up against my face. The blanket still has some of her scent on it, which smells a little like strawberries. I inhale the lulling aroma and it initially consoles me, but then all it does is remind me of her absence again. This is unbearable…excruciating. What am I going to do? What have I got to look forward to now?

A heavy weight then forms in the back of my throat, and an agonising surge of anxiety shoots through my body as if I were strapped into an electric chair. I can barely breathe and think. This isn't living; this is just existing. To exist only to exist isn't worth existing at all. I go into autopilot, where all my senses and rationale are robbed from me, then fall into a lifeless state — an empty vessel devoid of any emotion or conscience. I want this feeling to end.

I now find myself staring at a picture of Uncle Steven, during his youth, that's hung up on the wall opposite. I wish he was here, but he's not. It's not right that he's dead and I'm alive. Like Daz, he always looked on the brighter side of life, never once letting anything get him down. If Uncle Steven were in my position, he'd have phoned Alice by now and begged for her to come back—not even that—he wouldn't have taken her for granted in the first place... like I did.

So, I remove the belt from around my waist, wrap it around my throat, tighten it, but then quickly release its hold from me. The belt has cut into the flabby flesh under my chin, which I deem to be hardly a comfortable end. I deserve better than that, surely? A part of me tries to break through this desperate act, though I grab Rosie's blanket and wrap it around the belt instead, before frantically repositioning it around my throat. I make good this time, ensuring to cut off my air supply.

The living room starts to fade into darkness, into the darkest of colours I've ever witnessed. It's then that I begin to hear voices in my head; of Rosie giggling; of Alice saying that she loves me; of my parents and Catherine asking "Why?"; of Daz pleading for me to stop, and then of Uncle Steven telling me that I'm a complete and utter selfish twat.

People often say that your life flashes before you as death kicks in. I'd half-expected all the worst memories to come flooding back, like how I've brought nothing but misery to others, but all I can see are the faces of those whom I love. I don't want those images to fade and disappear. If I do die, I'll never see them again. I really didn't think this through, and alcohol had a huge part to play in that—which I see now, but only at the end.

Thankfully, self-preservation kicks in before it's too late.

I struggle to unbuckle the belt with my oxygen-deprived fingertips, compelled to do so by the lasting vision of Rosie in my mind, and manage to release its grip from me before the darkness completely takes over. Thereafter, I lie in a foetal position upon the hard floor, sobbing like a baby, staring ahead at Uncle Steven's photograph, held deep in shock over what I had just contemplated. When did suicide become a viable option? I hadn't even left a note to say goodbye.

I understand what Daz meant now—how when you reach your lowest point, you'll be more willing to change. I reached that moment, and I beat it. I beat it. I didn't really want to die. I wanted to kill a part of me that I hate, yes, but there's still so much more in life that I need and want to do. I'll sleep off my drunken state, wake up early with the birds and risen sun, call Alice and Catherine to apologise for everything—that's what I'll do! I will amend my wrongdoings. Tomorrow will be a fresh start. There is a light in the darkness. I know there is. There must be…

A Tragic Love Triangle

The coast is clear, unlike my conscience. I've secured the front door, lined the stairs with scented candles and roses, got some romantic music playing — it's perfect — and I knew Shaq would appreciate all the effort I've made for him. But this is a big risk we're taking, a very big risk. However, seeing as Michelle and Nathan aren't due back until tomorrow, we've got a whole night of fun ahead of us. You only live once. Life's too short not to take such risks.

  Shaq's lying on mine and Michelle's bed, wearing only skin-tight boxer shorts, with a red rose planted between his teeth. I can't stop staring at him, at his huge muscles and entrancing smile. My heart's pounding, but my mind is being consumed with fear and guilt. What if someone does see us? But no one knows that he's here, and all the curtains are closed. I'm the one who invited Shaq over. I'm the one who will need to deal with the consequences, should any arise.

'Are you coming to bed, or do I need to drag you in?' says Shaq, stroking a hand over the bedsheets.

I laugh back nervously and then hop in beside him without any further hesitation. So much for making this a romantic evening. I'm dripping with sweat already and we've not even kissed yet. Anyway, I'm ready for a taste of some forbidden fruit — some real action. It's been too long. This is the real me.

'Why so nervous?' he asks. 'You said we'd be alone.'

'Yeah, but you never know.' I quickly check Michelle's recent messages on my phone. There's nothing to suggest that she and Nathan will be back before tomorrow evening, apart from Dad having an argument with the campsite's security team, so I start to relax and hug into Shaq. Our pheromones immediately override any previous anxiety, and it's not long before we're kissing and exploring one another's bodies. I've waited years for this, to be my actual self.

Nevertheless, it's not long before I reach over for my phone again.

Shaq gives me a look of pure exacerbation. 'What's wrong now?'

'I've got a strange feeling that something bad is going to happen. I don't know what it is, but I'm sure of it.' A maelstrom of possibilities course through my mind, mostly of me being caught out and stressing over Tom's vulnerable mental state. 'I'm worried about my best friend. He's made a lot of progress with his depression, but—'

'Your friend will be fine,' Shaq implores, rubbing a hand up my inner thigh. 'Relax, Darren. Have a little fun and think of yourself for once.'

'I can always check on Tom tomorrow, I guess.' Shaq pulls at my forearms, placing them upon his chest. 'I've still got a bad feeling.'

'It's just you and me. We'll be okay. Let's have some fun.'

The bedroom door suddenly flings open, catching both Shaq and I off-guard, and just as we were starting to kiss again. To my horror, I find Michelle stood at the doorway with two suitcases — hers and Nathan's. Her mouth opens aghast, and her eyes fill with shock and tears, as do mine. She's caught me red-handed. My biggest lie has been unearthed.

Michelle screams, 'What the fuck is going on here, Darren?' She then glares across to Shaq. 'Who the fuck is he, and why are you both naked? Talk to me, Darren!'

Panic sets in, rendering me almost speechless. 'I can explain. Please, let me explain…'

Matters dramatically deteriorate when my mum steps out from behind Michelle. She proceeds to look at me and Shaq, faints, and then lands like a deadweight upon the floor. Just as I think things can't get any worse, Dad pokes his head around the corner next. He's certainly not afraid to make his thoughts known.

'You dirty, filthy, BASTARD!' Dad roars, lunging with clenched fists towards Shaq. 'My poor son! What are you doing to him?'

I try to gather my composure, to respond, but it only comes out as a strained whisper. 'He hasn't forced me to do anything, Dad. Shaq is a friend of mine.'

'A *friend*?!' By this point Dad has got his fingers wrapped around Shaq's throat, to which I try forcing myself between them. He looks confused at first by my actions, though his

354

expression is quickly replaced with one of sheer revilement and shame.

'No, Darren. Y-You can't be? You're a fuckin' poofter?' Dad starts pacing the room, shaking his head in dismay and retching as if about to vomit. I try to speak, to defend myself and Shaq, but I can't. I don't know what to say or do. I've never concocted a plan to deal with this scenario.

Shaq moves into a fighting position, aiming his fists against my dad.

'No!' I beg, desperately trying to pry them apart. 'Just go, Shaq. Go!'

'You heard him!' Dad snarls, looking to Shaq as if he were a piece of steaming dog faeces that he's just stood in. 'Get out of here, unless you want me to ruin that pretty face of yours?'

'Oh, you want to fight me?' Shaq throws an impressive right hook against my dad's face but misses by less than an inch. Dad reacts with a counterpunch, sadly hitting his target with perfect precision. 'Darren! Do something! Help me!'

I leap into action by dragging my father — who is now completely consumed with bloodlust — from my secret lover. The adrenaline rush blurs my ability to think, but I manage to somehow keep Dad at bay.

'Get off him, Dad! I plead. 'I don't want anyone to get hurt.'

To my further surprise, Dad then backs away. He looks across to Michelle, who is still stood at the doorway crying, and his face distorts to reveal the true monster lurking inside.

'You've caused enough hurt, Son.' He spits on the floor, just missing my toes. 'Son?' he laughs. 'How can I call you that now? You're a disgrace. You make me sick!' He grabs me by the chin, digs his nails into my flesh, then stares with his cold eyes directly into mine. 'I'll never forgive you for this. You're an embarrassment to our family — to Michelle and Nathan!' He glances back to my distraught wife. Michelle merely lowers her head, as not to look at the grim scene taking place, and I couldn't blame her. 'Look at her – your wife! How can you live with yourself, Darren?' Dad proceeds to spit on my face. I recoil from the sensation of my father's phlegm sliding down my lips, and not just because of the foul act, but because of how foul the stale smell of tobacco is from it. That's one reason why I've been put off letting Tom know how I really feel about him — because I find smoking to be such a turnoff.

Shaq uses this opportunity to make a swift exit, just as I use it to confront my abusive father. Michelle moves aside, sobbing heavily into her hands. What have I done? I can't believe this is happening.

My despair swiftly turns into rage.

'You'll never forgive me?' I cry, pushing Dad away. I've never confronted him before, purely out of fear and in wanting to preserve what relationship we have left, but — if there's ever going to be time — now seems to be the right moment. 'It should be *you* asking for my forgiveness! All those years of having to live in your shadow, never being perfect enough for you… always the disappointment. Yeah, I've lied to you, to my family, and to my friends. But I've also lied to myself. I've become someone I never wanted to be, and it's all because of you!' Dad swipes at my face,

356

catching the tip of my nose with his knuckles. The physical pain only lasts a few seconds, but the mental torture I'm now under doesn't seem like it will ever end. 'You're the disgrace, Dad. And I will never let you harm Nathan... like you did with me. I might have been six years old, but I can still remember what you did — everything,' I whisper into his ear. 'We've all got dark secrets, haven't we?'

Dad takes a few more steps back, seemingly shocked by my defiance (not to mention unearthing his own sins), but then goes to punch at me again. I don't let him close enough this time, however. I manage to avoid his right hook and perform my own uppercut, sending him straight into Michelle's floor mirror to shatter it on impact. Dad collapses to the ground like a slab of dead meat, covered in his own blood, showing no signs of consciousness.

Despite my bitter anger, and rising sense of remorse, I go to check on him but are prevented from doing so by Michelle. She positions herself between us, trembling in shock, with a look of dismay and sheer bewilderment.

'Why, Darren?' she asks. 'Why didn't you tell me? Why weren't you honest about being gay?'

'I couldn't,' I say ashamedly, ensuring to keep a watchful eye over Dad's twitching movements. 'I love you, Michelle. I really do. It's not as straightforward as it seems, and you deserve to know the truth — the truth about me. I'm attracted to all kinds of people, regardless of their sexual identity or gender. It's more complicated than just being gay or straight. I've hidden my true self for too long, to the point where I can't fathom out who I am anymore. I never wanted to lie to you... not once.' A release of tension suddenly lifts from me. For thirty-two years I've wanted to tell someone — anyone —

the truth, but I've never had the courage to because of the possible reprisals; out of fear of how my bigoted father would react, more than anything else. 'I'm so sorry. I know that might not mean much, given what's happened, but I am.'

During the skirmish I had failed to notice Nathan, who is currently gawking upon his unconscious grandparents and our blood-soaked carpet at the bedroom door. He looks like he's seen a ghost; his face is as white as a sheet and his whole body is going limp. It can't get any worse than this, surely?

'Who was that man?' he asks me, his voice wavering just like mine. 'What's going on, Dad?'

'He was just a friend,' I say, hoping that he had not overheard my last conversation with Michelle. But I know my boy and he's not stupid. Nathan can see straight through the veil of fog I'm trying to create. 'It's just a big misunderstanding, all this.'

'He was naked, like you are,' Nathan whimpers, examining my sweat-covered body with disgust. 'What have you done, Dad?'

I turn to Michelle for support, but she's too busy staring at the blood that's pouring out from my father's forehead. 'Listen, Nath, I can explain everything to you. Please, just let me explain—'

'Why have you hurt Grandpa?' he screams, pulling at his hair. 'You've killed him!'

'No! No, I haven't!' My frantic response isn't exactly helping to calm the situation. 'Grandpa will be fine. He just had a nasty fall, Son. Please, listen to me. I love you, Nath—'

'I hate you!' he cries, turning to leave. 'I hate you! You're not my dad!'

'Nathan!' I run into the passageway after him, but he's already managed to blockade himself within his bedroom. 'Please let Daddy explain what's happened. I'll tell you the truth. I'll tell you everything.'

Nathan sobs from behind his door, 'I don't want to know. You'll only tell me more lies. I don't want to know you. Go away!'

'He doesn't mean that,' says Michelle, gently resting her head upon my shoulders. 'We'll get through this, Darren. I love you and so does Nathan—'

'No, I don't!' he screams at the top of his voice, booting the door. 'Go away! I never want to see you again!'

'What have I done, Michelle? What-have-I-done?' I repeat this as I sprint back into our bedroom, where I quickly get dressed and then grab my BM kit and phone off the sideboard. Amid my frantic thoughts and emotions, I head downstairs towards the front door, desperate to look back, desperate to rewind time and put things right. But it's too late. The wall I've created has finally been torn down and it's landed right on top of me. There's no escaping this. There's no going back.

Michelle stays put at the top of the stairwell, and with a breaking voice she shouts, 'Please, Darren! Stop! Where are you going?'

I don't know the answer to that myself, if truth be told. My entire world, everything I've come to know and love, has collapsed in the mere space of ten minutes. My lustful desires have well and truly caught up with me. This is all my fault. I want to console Michelle and Nathan, and beg for their forgiveness, but that isn't going to resolve this situation… nothing will. I know it won't.

Despite the compelling urge to turn back, I sprint to my car with what energy remains. Once inside, I put my favourite Joy Division CD on and choose the track *Twenty-Four Hours*, which seems fitting under present circumstances. So, this is permanence. So, this is where my life has led. How can I ever make Nathan love me again after this? I can't. I've lost him.

Before driving off I look through my BM kit, at all the needles and insulin cartridges within it, and soon come to the gravest of conclusions: my light in the darkness has burnt out. My light in the darkness, Nathan, no longer shines down upon me. He'll never forgive me — there's too much of my father in him for that to happen. Michelle will likely say that she will, but I don't deserve her forgiveness. I'll never see that wonderous light again. All I can do now is drive off into the darkness, alone, filled with dread and shame. So, this is what it's like to reach your lowest point…

Without Rumour

Am I dreaming? I'm sure that's Alice's standing over me, but it can't be her. Wait — it is her! But it can't be?

'Alice, is that you?' I ask, wiping the sleep away from my eyes, trying hard to focus on the angelic figure leaning over me. 'Alice?'

She replies in a staccato-like whisper, 'Tom.'

'How did you get in?'

'I've got a key, haven't I?' she says with a wearisome roll her eyes, which I notice are tearing up. 'Why on earth are you sleeping on the living room floor?'

'I don't know,' I say, shrugging back to her indecisively. I wasn't expecting this surprise visit, but I'm not upset — not by any means. If anything, I could leap up with joy straight into Alice's arms. That's what I want to do. That's all I've wanted for the last five weeks. I doubt she'd be as enthusiastic, though. 'What are you doing here, Alice. Have you... come back?'

'It's not that simple,' she says, clenching her eyelids together. 'Where's your phone? I've been trying to call you all morning.'

I hesitate, ashamed by my actions, knowing the truth. 'It's over there. I dropped it yesterday. It's knackered.'

Alice kneels beside me, pulling out her own mobile. 'Jesus. Then that means… did you not see the video Darren posted on Facebook last night? Please tell me you did.'

'No. What video? What's Daz done now?' I laugh, though it's only to mask my rising anxiety. Alice's expression falls graver, solemn even. 'What's this video you're going on about?' She just stares at me as if lost, completely silent, shaking her head in dismay. 'Has Daz posted some more funny TikTok videos? He made a few while we were in Amsterdam—'

'No, Tom,' she snaps, holding her phone out to me. 'You need to go onto Darren's Facebook page. You need to watch the last video he uploaded.'

I'm not that naive. I know something's up. But Daz is the most laidback guy I've ever met, and there's no way something bad has happened to him. It's impossible. It wouldn't be right.

'Seriously. What's up, Alice? Why are you crying?'

'Tom…' She places a hand onto mine, somewhat reservedly. 'Turn the volume up. You need to hear what Darren says in his video.'

This isn't how I planned on being reunited with Alice, but to feel her touch again is rejuvenating and euphoric. However, I can also sense the tension in her fingertips, which only leads me to suspect that something terrible has, indeed, taken place. After a few deep breaths, I swipe onto

Daz's profile page and click on his latest video that's simply titled: Confession. As the video begins, I notice Alice turning her head away from me again. This can't be good.

Daz is sat in his car. It's obviously late evening, given that it's dark and he's barely visible under the neon-blue light from his phone. Despite the darkness, I can see he's been crying – but why? I've never seen him display any negative emotion, be it sadness, anger, frustration… not once. Why does my best friend look so upset, and why didn't he phone me if something was up?

Daz stares directly into the camera, slowly exhales, takes in a shuddering breath, and then begins.

'Hi,' he says in a shallow voice. 'I know it's late, and that most of you will be still in bed, but there are a few things I need to get off my chest; a few things that I believe you guys have a right to know. I've not been honest, and for that…I'm sorry. I truly am.'

'What's all this about?' I ask, trying to hold onto some positivity.

'Watch the video, Tom,' Alice scowls. 'For God's sake, just watch the video.'

Daz scratches at his nose, revealing a reddish substance upon his knuckles. 'You're probably wondering where the blood is from? Well, it's my dad's. In all fairness, some would argue that he deserved what he got. But I don't. Violence doesn't solve anything, does it?'

'Shit,' I say, to a slap on the back of my head from Alice. 'Has he killed his dad? That wouldn't be such a bad thing –'

'For the love of Christ, Tom, watch the video!' she yells. It's hard to watch the screen, though, because I'm struggling to focus my vision, my breaths, and to hold onto any desire to see what else may transpire.

Daz continues, his expression bordering on a terrible state of sorrow.

'I'll start off by saying that I'm sorry, Dad. We've had our differences, but I had no right to assault you. Anyone in your position would've reacted the same way, if they —' Daz cuts himself off mid-sentence and then quickly reaches down for something that's just out of view, which he then slams against his upper-right thigh. 'From being young, I've always tried to look on the brighter side of life, to strive at being the best person I could be. That's how I was raised, to fit in — to be normal — to make something of myself. I tried my best, I really did, but that came at a heavy cost; it meant I had to go through life living a huge lie, and I wouldn't wish it on my worst enemy.' Daz plunges at his upper leg again, winces slightly, then says, 'I know many of you watching this video will be confused, and may even be taken back a little, because I've always been the guy to put a smile on peoples' faces; the guy who never lets anything get him down; the guy with all the answers. Well, I'm sorry to disappoint, but you're all very much mistaken. I did my best to comfort you all because I know what it's like to suffer, to wake up each day feeling like shit, and to believe that you're worthless. I was just good at covering up those horrible feelings and scars, that's all. I couldn't bear to see anyone else feel as down and lonely as I did, which is why I would go out of my way to make you all happy. I hope I achieved that.'

As Daz punches at his upper leg again, I slowly turn to Alice. She still won't look at me, and I'm starting to understand why.

'No. That's not—it can't be?' I gasp, clenching at my mouth. 'Daz would never…'

'It's hard, Tom, but you need to watch this,' she implores, steadying the phone in my hand with hers. 'The video is almost finished.'

Daz looks as if he's in utter torment now. I wish I could jump through the screen to comfort him. God, I'd do anything for that.

'We've had some great times together, haven't we?' he says, forcing a smile to emerge. 'Michelle, I love you more than you could ever possibly imagine. And the same goes for you, too, Nathan. You've always been Daddy's shining star. I've been proud of you from the moment you were born. I just hope you'll be able to forgive me one day.' Now weeping, Daz punches at his leg again, and I start to sob along with him. 'Mum, Dad, I'm sorry that I've let you down. I never did get that university degree you both wanted so much, did I?' He punches at his leg again and for longer this time. 'Amar, don't you worry about work. You'll get through this difficult time, mate. Naaz is an amazing wife, and I know she'll be there to support you no matter what. Mikey, you need to give up on gambling your wages away, pal. Make the most out of life, and don't worry about that two-hundred quid you owe me.' Daz begins to laugh, but his expression quickly turns solemn again. 'John, you keep on writing those books of yours, even if you do get the odd negative review. I still enjoyed reading them… if that matters?' He then moves his head closer towards the camera, looks down, and back up to it again. There's a glimmer in his eyes now, that spark I've always known and adored. 'Tom—'

'No,' I say, swiftly offering Alice her phone back. 'I don't want to watch anymore. I can't.'

'You've got to,' she whimpers. 'You've got to, for Darren's sake…'

My thumb lingers above the play button for a good two minutes before I eventually touch it. I don't like where this is going. Daz is talking about himself as if he's not here anymore. He can't be? He wouldn't?

'My dearest friend, Tom,' he says, smiling fully now. 'We've had some crazy moments over the years—too many to count. There was the band, our escapades down the Tin Donkey, those retro gaming sessions… Amsterdam. You're the best friend I could've ever wished for. I love you, mate.' He plunges a fist against his leg again, then again, then again, and then again. Daz's speech starts to slur now and his eyes gradually close, convincing me that my worst fear is becoming a reality. I'm desperate to tell him that everything will be okay, to hug him, just like he would do for me. But I can't. Daz is all alone in his car, parked in the middle of who-knows-where, pouring his heart out over the internet.

'I can't watch this,' I say to Alice, choking on my words.

'Please watch it, Tom. You need to hear this,' she says, stroking at my arms. 'You need to hear what Darren says.'

'You've made some big improvements over the last few weeks, Tom-boy,' Daz adds with a proud smirk. 'You kept saying that you couldn't do it, but you have. You're finally making a stand against your problems. If you're listening to this, Alice, please give Tom another chance. He *has* changed.

I know he has his flaws, like we all do, but he's turning his life around for the better. It's too late for me now, though. My light… my light has gone.' He punches at his leg one last time before slumping back into the car seat. 'I loved each and every one of you. I'm sorry. I'm so, so sorry.' Daz now looks at peace, showing no pain or sadness in his expression. He goes to take another breath, but it takes some great exertion to do so. He then slowly peels open one eyelid, reaches out a hand towards his phone, and the screen goes completely black thereafter.

Alice embraces me from behind, nestling her head against mine. 'I don't know what to say, Tom.'

Her phone falls away from me, my tremors now making it impossible to hold onto it. All goes silent, still, and not even Alice's sobs can be heard in my mind. It's like we've been sucked straight into a black hole or something. I don't know what to say or how to act. I just feel empty. There aren't any words that can describe this tremendous pain. It just can't be real.

'He's dead, isn't he?' I ask, barely able to speak. 'My best friend is gone.'

'Yes,' says Alice after some hesitation. 'I spoke to Michelle this morning. She saw the video when Darren uploaded it last night, but the police didn't get to him in time. They found him parked up by the big tree near your school. He —'

'Took an overdose,' I say, detesting the very notion. 'That's what Daz was plunging into his legs throughout the video — his insulin. The one thing that was meant to keep him alive.'

'I know it's hard to accept,' she says, rubbing her fingers over mine. I don't know what comes over me, but I go to kiss her, and Alice immediately recoils in response. 'No,

Tom. It wouldn't be right. There's still so much we need to talk about, to sort out.'

I punch at the ground beneath me in anger, out of grief and resentment. 'I've lost everything! I've lost you, Rosie, and now Daz. He's not dead, Alice. He's not dead!' I punch at the floor again, at which point she goes to leave. 'Don't go. Please!'

'I can't stay, Tom.' Alice looks at the empty lager cans that are scattered around us with a heavy sigh. 'It's such a shame. I guess, Darren was wrong…'

The sound of the kitchen door slamming behind Alice reverberates throughout my empty household like thunder, rendering me into a pitiful mass of tears and anxiety tremors upon the living room floor. I want to watch the video again, to somehow convince myself that it isn't real; to convince myself that Daz isn't gone. But, no matter how much I play on my doubts, I know that Alice and Michelle wouldn't lie to me, and certainly not about something so serious. Daz loved his pranks, though I don't think he'd go this far.

Fuelled by rage and grief, I pick up my beloved Nintendo console and proceed to smash it into several pieces off the back wall. Then I kick a wave of empty cans along the floor, cast a fist firmly into my TV, turn over the dining room table, and then — now completely exhausted, and with my adrenaline spent — collapse. This violent outburst has solved nothing. It hasn't brought Alice or Daz back. If anything, I'm worse off than before.

The landline phone rings a few minutes later. I try to calm my breaths and focus on the device, but I'm in no mood to speak. I'm in no mood whatsoever to interact with any other human, other than Daz. The phone continues to blare out its annoying chimes, so I make my way over to it — quite prepared to put it out of its misery — to answer it. Darren's home number comes up on the phone's display screen, granting me some small glimmer of hope.

The phone just keeps ringing and ringing, and the migraine that has arisen worsens and worsens. It can't be Daz, but I'm holding onto the thinnest of chances that it is, and that all of what has just transpired might be just a horrifying nightmare. It must be.

I pick up the phone and answer, though there's only silence on the other end. Could it be Daz calling from beyond the grave? That's just stupid. I really am losing the plot.

'Hello,' I say, praying that it's not some random cold caller.

'Tom?'

It's Michelle. Of all the people she could phone, to be comforted by, why me?

'Hi, Michelle. Are you okay?'

'Have you seen the video?' she asks, and the heavy breaths that follow send a shiver down my spine. 'Have you seen it?'

'Yes.' I pause, afflicted by a sudden, drowning sensation. 'Yeah, I've watched it.'

I imagine Michelle to be thinking the same thoughts I am: Why did Daz do it? What drove him to such desperation? Why didn't he say anything to us? It then hits me that Michelle must know the truth, but it's not my place to ask. Besides, it's far too soon.

'He's dead,' she cries. 'Darren killed himself.'

'No, he hasn't!' I bite at my lower lip, knowing that I could have perhaps handled that response more delicately. But I'm in complete denial, and I bet Michelle is as well.

'He is, Tom. Darren took an insulin overdose. The cops also found an empty bottle of Amitriptyline — I didn't even know he was on the stuff. He must have kept them hidden in his BM kit or something. I honestly didn't know.'

'Aren't they sleeping pills? Neither did I,' I say, genuinely shocked to discover that Daz was also on medications. 'He can't be dead. He's playing some sort of sick prank on us all.'

'He is, and he meant it. I'm sorry, Tom, but Darren clearly meant to take his own life. Even if the cops got to him in time, there would have been little chance they could have done anything to save him.'

Michelle can't see it, but I'm shaking my head vigorously at the phone. He can't have meant it. What happened to holding onto the light in the darkness and staying positive?

'Maybe it was a cry for help gone wrong?' I suggest. 'I don't think he —'

'Whatever he intended; my Darren's gone. He's dead.' Michelle breaks down while I try to think of something meaningful and comforting to say. What would Daz's response be? He'd know exactly what to say. 'There'll need to be a post-mortem, but I've started making some arrangements for the funeral. I don't know where to put myself, and I've still got to tell Nathan. What am I going to say to him, Tom?'

'I don't know, but if there's anything else I can do to help —'

'There is,' she says, her words spoken as if frantically pleading to me. 'You were Darren's closest friend, so it only seems right for you to do a speech at his funeral, and I'd really appreciate it.'

'You'd be better off asking John, you know, with him being a writer,' I say, but what I really mean is: I can't accept that Daz needs a funeral and that I'll need to speak at it. 'I don't want to let you down. I'm not good at speaking in public.'

'I don't want to ask him. You were Darren's best mate.' Michelle's heavy sobs turn back into faint whimpers. I'm also on the verge of breaking down, the necessity of using the word "were" plaguing my thoughts. I *am* his best friend, not *was*. 'I'll understand if you're not comfortable talking at the service, with your anxiety —'

'No,' I say, firmly held in resolve. My anxiety has done enough damage, and I promised Daz that I'd beat it. I need to be there for Michelle and Nathan — my Godson. I've got to be there for them. 'I'm honoured that you're asking for me to do a speech at his service. I just can't believe —'

'I know. None of this seems real, Tom, but it is. He's gone.'

'I'll stay in touch with you, okay?' I try to sound level-headed, to be a pillar of strength for Michelle. God knows what she and Nathan must be going through, and to think that I had contemplated taking my own life on the same night as Daz. I can't help but think what it must have been that drove him towards the same, morbid conclusion. I daren't ask. And, in a sense, I don't want to know. I want to remember Daz for being a beacon of hope and positivity, not the complete opposite.

'Thanks, hun. I'll keep you updated,' she says, before hanging up on me.

My mind goes blank, and an overwhelming urge to vomit takes precedence. I replace the phone into its holster, look at the chaos I've caused through my aggressive outburst, and then go into the kitchen for a glass of cool, refreshing water.

I rest the glass against my lips, stare out of the window at the blaring sun outside, trying to keep myself together as best as possible. I want to cry and feel that I should be, but it seems like all my tears are spent up. This can't be happening. None of this is real. He's not dead. Daz isn't dead. He can't be…

A Bittersweet Reunion

Tom hates and will often avoid attending funerals, seeing as they bring to the forefront how death will also reach him one day; how the same fate will inevitably meet his beloved Rosie who he wants to live forever, to never grow old or experience life's crueller moments. Tom has no choice but to attend a funeral service today, however, for it marks his final farewell to Darren — his closest friend — the one person he never thought would fall into the destructive throes of depression.

It has been two weeks since Darren's death, but the loss still hasn't set in. Even the weather is pleasant, with the forecast stating it will be the hottest day on record. The stage is set; the time has come, and all Tom wants to do is escape from this impending nightmare. But he can't. He must stay strong. He must face this horrendous ordeal, whether he wishes to or not.

'This is bollocks,' comments Mikey, on making his way up to Amar, John, Ryan, and Tom. All are stood outside of

Coundon's Crematorium in their best suits, the same they wore to Darren's wedding. 'Where is everyone – this can't be it? We can't be the only people who've turned up?'

'We're early,' says John. 'There's still twenty minutes for any stragglers to show up. Darren was a popular bloke, so I reckon there'll be a big turnout.'

'Ah never thought ah'd see yee wearing a suit again, Tom,' Mikey snorts to him.

'I couldn't exactly show up in a t-shirt and pair of jeans, could I?' Tom replies, granting Mikey a look of contempt. 'Michelle has asked me to do a speech, you know. I've been working on it all week, but –'

'I hope it's better than the one you did at their wedding,' Amar humours. As with Mikey, Tom scowls back at him in response. 'Sorry, mate. I need to have a laugh. I'd cry, otherwise.'

'Same here,' John adds, scuffing his feet across the road's searing tarmac. 'Don't worry about your speech, Tom-boy. I know you'll do Darren proud. Just speak from the heart, and don't worry about what anyone else is thinking.'

In truth, Tom making out that he's concerned about his speech is nothing but a distraction from what is really eating away at him. He can't and won't accept that today is Darren's funeral, that their friendship has come to such an abrupt and sorrowful end. Tom is quite confident that his speech will do Darren proud, but wishes that there was no need for it in the first place.

'There are some more cars coming in now,' says Amar. 'No hearse yet, though. Darren always said he'd be late to his own funeral, didn't he?'

'Yeah, and he was never one to disappoint,' says John.

Six cars pull in at a slow and steady pace. Tom inspects each individual as they make their way up to the crematorium doors, towards him and his friends, though he only recognises three faces among them.

'They're Michelle's sisters,' he notes, nodding to them.

'I tried to hump that one,' says Mikey with a pig-like grunt, pointing a finger to the youngest-looking sister. 'Darren wouldn't have it, though. The cheeky git said it'd be weird for me to gan oot with Michelle's little sister. Ah couldn't see any issue.'

'Darren probably didn't want you to be a part of his family,' Amar suggests, causing himself and John to cackle. 'To be fair, who in their right mind could blame him? You're hardly a gentleman, Mikey.'

'Remember where we are lads,' Tom whispers, shaking his head to them. 'Show some respect, yeah.'

'Sorry,' says John and then the other lads in unison.

'It's alright. Everyone copes with grief differently, don't they?' Tom rubs at his face and then looks across to the memorial garden nearby. 'It's beautiful here, isn't it? Daz was always a keen gardener.'

'He tried to help me put up a shed once — only took three days,' says John, trying to hold back his laughter. 'It was an absolute nightmare. *Keen gardener,*' he sniggers. 'We got there in the end, eventually, after I hired some professionals to finish the job. Still, Darren tried his best. He was determined to help me.'

'Darren helped me dig oot a pond for me mother-in-law,' Mikey adds. 'He covered up the hole with some tarpaulin but forgot to tell the missus, then left me to pull her oot and take the wrath. I can't exactly moan, but, seeing as he treated

375

her to some fancy chocolates, as a way of making up for the back injury she sustained. It did calm her doon…for a short while.'

'Yep. Darren will be sorely missed,' says John with a lengthy sigh. 'He'd be happy that we're reminiscing over the good times. Darren wouldn't want us moping around, would he?'

'I guess it does help to have a bit of a laugh,' says Tom. 'And he definitely wouldn't want us to feel down. That's the last thing Daz would want.'

Amar steps forward, clearly anxious to share his next thought.

'Do any of you know why Darren took his own life? I don't particularly want to ask Michelle, for obvious reasons.'

'No,' Tom says insistently. 'I think it's best we leave it that way, too. If Michelle wanted us to know, she'd have said something by now. Just let it be, mate. Finding out the truth won't bring him back, anyway, will it?'

Ryan—who hasn't spoken a single word up to now— suddenly slaps Tom on the chest to grab his attention. 'Is that Darren's hearse coming around the corner?'

'Yeah,' he gasps, 'that's him. That's Daz.'

The four companions place themselves before the crematorium doors while a line of at least sixty people form beside them. Tom struggles again to recognise most of the fellow mourners, though it is clear to see that many of them are already in the process of crying, some even howling, as Darren's hearse comes closer into view.

Tom gets a sudden glimpse of Alice, who has come to the service with her mother, presumably for emotional support. He goes to wave at them but resists the innate urge. Instead, his attention returns to Darren's hearse, on the flowers carefully placed alongside his coffin that read: Dad.

'Poor Nathan,' says John. 'To lose your dad at only ten years old. God, it's awful.'

John's comment immediately makes Tom think about Rosie, about how he almost did the same thing to her — to leave her unprotected and fatherless in this cruel world of ours. The very thought tears him apart, but then he reminds himself that he needs to stay strong for Michelle and Nathan. He must.

Darren's hearse pulls up in front of the four companions. A tall, slender woman then steps out from the front of the hearse, introducing herself as the funeral director, then instructs the friends on how to safely carry Darren's coffin. She is met by some silent nods from them in return, and a feigned smile from Tom.

'Are you ready?' she asks them, unlocking the hearse's rear door.

'Ah'll never be ready for this,' Mikey says to Tom. 'Darren cannot be in that little box — it's too small.'

'But he is,' says Tom. 'Let's just get this over with.' He steps forward first while staring at Darren's coffin, imagining that his best friend will pop out of it at any given moment to reveal this to be nothing more than some elaborate and twisted prank. Nevertheless, Tom dismisses this notion as being ridiculous, despite the fact he'd love for it to be true. 'Come on, mate,' he says to the coffin, tenderly. 'We'll take good care of you, Daz.'

Michelle and Nathan finally step out from the car behind Darren's hearse, both hugging into one another, weeping, and riddled with despair. They look at the four friends and smile, then bow their heads solemnly before their fallen loved one.

'Thanks for coming,' says Michelle, trying desperately to hold herself together. 'At least it's not raining…'

'That's one good thing,' says Tom, and then he looks to Nathan. 'How are you doing, wee-man?'

Nathan doesn't respond. Instead, he copies Michelle by keeping his eyes down to the floor—anywhere but on the coffin now.

As Tom tries to think of something else to say, he notices Darren's mother and the fact that there's no sign of his father. 'Where's Nigel? Where's Darren's dad?' he asks Michelle.

'He's not coming!' she snaps, hinting that this is a sore subject. 'Nigel's not welcome, Tom, and I'd appreciate it if you don't mention him again.'

'Sure. He's the last person I want to think about, anyway.'

A priest suddenly appears at the crematorium's doorway—an elderly, portly man, whose expression of sincerity and humility brings some relief to the mourners. After introducing himself to Darren's loved ones, the priest then signals to the funeral directors for proceedings to commence.

'Short-arses to the front,' says Mikey, fleeting his eyes between John and Tom. 'Ah know Darren was always up for a laugh, but ah durn't think he'd want us to drop him at his own funeral.'

Tom smiles, desperately clinging onto this moment of humour, but is soon struck again with a sickening jolt to his stomach on coming face-to-face with the coffin. It's not real, he says to himself. But it is.

Tom and John grab a handle each, then — with a fair bit of assistance from the funeral directors — they carefully slide Darren's coffin out from the hearse, place it onto their shoulders, and — with Ryan and John's help — carry him into the crematorium's service hall. A wave of sobs and sniffling noises follow the friends as they walk on ahead, making it feel like the journey is taking twice as long. They slowly lower Darren onto an oak slab and are then shown to their respective seats by the priest. It still doesn't feel real to anyone present.

The track *Good Riddance* by Green Day is played while the remaining mourners enter. Tom admires the lyrics and how they perfectly match Darren's persona, reminiscing over the times when they would often jam along to such music on their guitars together. They were happier times, moments Tom would do anything to relive, even for just one minute.

As the music comes to an end, the priest places himself before a pulpit and signals for everyone to sit down. The crematorium is packed to its full capacity, meaning that many mourners have no choice but to stand. The impact Darren's death has had on so many people comes to haunt Tom. He had no idea of just how devasting such an event could be, an event he himself had considered only two weeks prior. So many friends and family members have been affected. So much suffering has been wrought. Tom realises that he, too, could have inflicted the same misery — and for what reward? He concludes that whatever it was that drove Darren to such an extreme conclusion, it must have been utterly torturous. He wants to know the truth, but simply cannot face any further heartache.

379

Once the priest finishes their religious verses and a brief history of Darren's life, he invites Michelle up to speak. She kisses Nathan on his brow and then makes her way over to the pulpit, ensuring to keep her head held down low.

'Thank you all for being here, for showing your love and support at such a difficult time,' she says, barely able to speak. 'Darren and I first met when we were twenty years old, at one of his gigs in Middlesbrough. There was something about the twinkle in his eyes and warmth in his smile that attracted me to him straight away. We were only twenty-one when we married…' Tears course down Michelle's face, and she falls silent for a few seconds before continuing. 'Our son, Nathan, meant the world to Darren. I'd often find them both playing on his bass guitar, or on some old video games together. He loved us all so much.' She then looks to Tom with a piercing glare. 'He really did love you. Darren would want us to remember all the good things he did, and there were so many. I don't know where to start.' She turns again to the coffin and finally breaks down, struggling to form her next sombre words. 'You were such a caring husband, father, and friend. You were too good for this world, babe.' She turns her sorrowful frown into a resolute smile, her fingers clasping onto the pulpit. 'Darren believed that things always happened for a reason, so let his untimely death be a lesson to us all; that those who appear to be strong on the outside may, in fact, be struggling the most within. No matter how busy our lives may be, we should always make time to ask those we care about if they're alright, and if they do need help or just someone to listen. Look for the warning signs and act on them. Don't let my husband's death be in vain…'

The priest kindly supports Michelle back to her seat. Then, after a moment of contemplation, he gestures for Tom to stand.

'Darren's closest friend shall now enlighten us with his own fond memories of him,' the priest says. 'Please, Thomas, come up and share your thoughts.'

Tom takes in a deep breath, clenches onto a piece of paper that he's written his speech on, then walks past Michelle and Nathan towards the priest. At the pulpit he looks across the sea of saddened faces, slips the paper back into his jacket, then looks to the only spot in the hall which is empty. He somehow imagines Darren standing there, looking back at him with that reassuring smile of his, and all seems fine again.

'Daz — I mean, Darren — was a friend you could always turn to during a crisis,' he says. 'He was a friend that would go well out of his way to make sure you were okay; a friend that would give you the shirt off his own back just to make sure you didn't go without. He was my best mate, was Darren.' Tom gulps, the word "was" torturing him beyond any measure. He looks again to the empty space ahead, to where he images Darren standing, telling himself that he must get through this; he must stay strong. 'Daz would hate to see us all so upset. That just wasn't him. He taught me recently to always look for the light in the darkness, for what matters most in life, regardless of how impossible that may seem. I'll hold onto those words forever, and I know he would want you all to do the same.' Tom's eyes unwittingly fall upon Alice, who looks back at him with a vacant stare. 'It might sound cliché, but there is always a light in the darkness. When you think of Darren, don't think of today;

think of all the good he has done instead. He will be in our hearts and thoughts, acting as a guiding force to remind us of how precious life is.' Tom then turns to the coffin, still held deep in denial. 'We love you, mate, and we'll see each other again… someday. I know we will.'

Tom returns to his seat and it's as if the whole world has come to a standstill, for the next part of this funeral service is the part he has been apprehensive about more than anything else: The Committal.

Michelle has chosen an acoustic performance of *Stuck in A Moment* by U2 — which Darren and Tom had recorded together for his YouTube channel some years prior, where Darren sang and Tom played guitar — to coincide with the curtains as they are pulled around the coffin, signalling the stark moment when Darren is hidden from ever being seen again. The fond memory of performing this song with his best friend brings some momentary solace to Tom, but the curtains seem to enshroud Darren at a painfully slow rate, imprinting that this is it — that he is well and truly gone.

Tom sinks his face into his hands, his thoughts torn between the pleasant memories from that recording session and the morbid situation he's currently in, and it's only when Amar assists him to his feet that he finds the strength needed to stand, to leave this peaceful crematorium, to face a life without Darren's positive influence.

'That was a beautiful speech,' Amar says to Tom. 'You did really well, mate. Darren would have been very proud of you.'

'I just want this day to end,' says Tom. 'I don't care about anything else. The sooner this day is over, the better.'

'Yeah. You're not wrong there, Tom-boy.'

Back at Darren's home, where his wake is being held, Michelle is stood at the front door to thank each mourner who has been courteous enough to show up, and there are many who haven't. Tom hides himself behind Amar and John, reluctant to step foot inside. He regrets not following Ryan to the pub, in not using the same excuse he did: *wakes are for family members only.* But it wouldn't be right. To Tom, Darren was family — a *brother from another mother*, as they would both say. However, like his own home, Tom knows that he'll only be reminded of what he has lost once he enters, and he's putting it off for as long as possible without coming across as being rude.

Michelle spots Tom loitering around in the garden and calls him over as he goes to light up a cigarette. 'Are you coming in?' she asks him, pleadingly. 'There are some beers in the fridge. Help yourself.'

It's a tempting offer, but that would go against everything Tom and Darren have strived so hard to amend. And, more poignantly, the last time Tom touched alcohol was when he had contemplated taking his own life. What once was his cure, to flood his body with this poison, had now become a strong reminder of his own close encounter with death.

'I'll have a black coffee, if that's alright?' Tom says to her. 'I'm not in the mood for drinking.'

'Sure,' she says with a look of perplexment. 'You're more than welcome to take a few beers home with you, mind. They'll only go to waste, otherwise.' Michelle then pulls on Tom's arms, dragging him inside. 'Thanks again for doing that speech. It was lovely, very heartfelt.'

'Don't mention it...'

The first step into Darren's home is like walking upon hot coals for Tom—he's compelled to move back, to flee, to relinquish the agony. He goes to make a coffee, desperately trying to block out all the loud voices speaking around him, and it proves to be a difficult task. There must be at least forty people crammed into Darren's small living room, which isn't doing Tom's anxiety any favours. He waits for Michelle to disappear into the crowd before venturing back outside, where he lights up another cigarette, savouring this momentary solitude.

A familiar-looking car pulls onto the curb, just outside the garden. Tom examines it and then immediately throws his cigarette into the neighbouring garden, all the while choking on the tobacco fumes. He's sure that it's Alice and her mother. Under the oppression of an oncoming anxiety attack, Tom skulks back into the kitchen and then into the living room to tag alongside Amar and John, who are both situated within the farthest corner. *We're out of sight and mind*, is how Tom sees it.

'What's gotten into you?' Amar asks, as he leans into Tom's personal space. 'You look like you've had a right-old fright.'

'I have, mate. I'll be fine—just don't move.' Tom quickly rights himself in not wanting to draw any further attention, then manages to sneak a tuna sandwich from John's plate.

'Oi!' John protests. 'Get your own grub. The table's only over there.' He points to the dining table a few yards away, but that's too close to the kitchen and Alice for Tom's comfort. 'What's gotten into you, man?'

At that moment, Alice walks in and approaches Michelle. Amar and John nod to one another, both now fully aware of why Tom is acting so strange.

'Oh, I see. You can't hide from her forever,' says Amar. 'She's not going to make a scene. Alice isn't like that, Tom.'

'I know,' he says, feeling somewhat ashamed over his evasive actions. Tom's eyes then briefly meet with Alice's, but that's as much attention as she grants him. 'I know that I'm being daft, but it's just so hard seeing her again.'

'I bet it is,' says John, brushing a hand over Tom's arm sympathetically. 'It's been a shitty day for us all. It'll be over soon, though, and then we can get back to some normality. Won't be long now.'

Amar and John then discuss how moving Darren's funeral service was, that it was a fitting send-off for him, before babbling on about some local sports news. Meanwhile, Tom turns toward the fireplace, to a large canvas of Darren, Michelle and Nathan. They seem so happy in the photograph, so full of joy, contentment and love. Tom's thoughts instantly focus on Nathan, who himself is currently nowhere to be seen.

'I'm just nipping to the toilet,' he says to Amar and John. 'I Won't be long, lads.'

'No worries,' says Amar. 'Don't be doing your disappearing trick, mind.'

'I won't. I've just got to check on something.'

Tom imagines himself to be a ninja from some cheesy 1980's movie, like the ones he and Darren often enjoyed watching together, as he stealthily shuffles through the crowd to reach the kitchen. He makes it past Michelle and Alice without being noticed, thankfully, though it breaks his heart to think just how much Alice must hate him, given how easily she seems to be ignoring his presence.

Tom then makes it to the downstairs bathroom, where he gradually distinguishes the faint sound of guitar strings being plucked from upstairs. Without any reservation, he heads upstairs towards the music's source: Nathan's bedroom.

'Are you okay in there, Nath?' he asks, knocking on the door timidly. 'Can I come in, mate?'

Nathan doesn't respond, however, and the sound of guitar strings being plucked comes to an abrupt halt.

'Would you like to talk?' says Tom, albeit edging further away from the door now. 'It's only me.'

'Yeah,' says Nathan, holding back some sobs, 'you can come in.'

Tom finds Nathan sat on his bed with Darren's bass guitar resting on his lap. It's a difficult battle for Tom to wade off his tears as he stares at the musical instrument, the same bass guitar Darren used when they were in the band together.

'If that guitar could talk,' Tom comments, as he moves in a little closer. 'Your dad was one hell of a bass player. He could learn any riff after just listening to it once, you know.'

'I know,' says Nathan. 'Dad started teaching me how to play a few months ago, but I'm crap at it.'

'I doubt that. Can I sit down?' Nathan shrugs back, then begrudgingly moves across to free up some space on the bed. 'Thanks. I bet you're just as good as your father —'

'I'm not. I'll never be able to play like Dad,' Nathan simpers. 'He only taught me the basics.'

'We all have to start off somewhere,' Tom adds. 'With a good dose of patience and plenty of practise, you'll be able to play just like your old man in no time at all.'

'But I don't have Dad to teach me anymore, do I? And I can't even tune it up.'

'I can help with that. Pass it here.'

Nathan hands the guitar over to Tom, showing some sign of reluctance as it leaves his grasp. 'It might sound dumb, but I feel like Dad's still with me when I'm playing on his guitar. Does that sound dumb to you, Uncle Tom?'

'Not in the slightest,' he implores. 'It makes perfect sense to me.' Tom then rests an ear against the guitar's body, carefully tunes each string, and then hands it back to Nathan. 'This guitar meant a great deal to your dad; he poured his heart and soul into playing it. He loved his music, but he loved you and your mum more than anything else.'

Nathan scowls. 'Then why did he kill himself?'

'We'll never know. But you've got your mum, your family, and your dad's friends — like me — who will help you to get through this. It'll take some time, Nath, but you'll be okay. I promise.'

Nathan looks aside to a photograph of himself with Darren that is situated upon a bedside table nearby, his expression returning to one of sheer torment. 'Everyone's saying the same thing; everyone's telling me that I'll be fine, but I can't see how it will be. Is that the only reason why you came to see me — to say that?'

'No, I came up to see where the cool riff was coming from,' says Tom. 'I did mean every word, though. You were playing *Paranoid* by Black Sabbath, weren't you? I've never taken you for being a fan of heavy metal.'

'Yeah,' laughs Nathan amid some sniffles. 'I'm sick of playing it, though. I want to learn something new, but Dad's not here to teach me.'

'I can,' says Tom, his voice trembling with anticipation. 'I don't mind teaching you some new tunes.'

'You'd teach me?' Nathan gasps. '*Really*?'

'Of course. I'd be a pretty lousy godfather if I didn't, wouldn't I?'

'I'm not sure. Some of the music you listen to is awful — even Dad said so.'

'We're all entitled to our own opinions, even if you and your dad were wrong there,' Tom humours. 'Here, I'll teach you a new riff right now. It's a classic.'

Tom enters a state of pure ecstasy as he performs and then teaches Nathan the bass riff from Ozzy Osbourne's *Crazy Train*. His joy is then ignited further when Nathan comments on how much he likes this new song, and the fact that he's easily picking it up.

'I've got it! Nathan exclaims, raising his fists into the air. 'That was easier than I thought it'd be.'

'Why don't you try playing it through your dad's amplifier? It'll sound loads better.' Tom collects the amplifier's adjoining cable before Nathan can protest. 'I know you can do it, mate. It's in your blood to perform, and music is a great way to express yourself — to vent off all that anger and frustration you're feeling.'

Nathan's cheeks flow red with embarrassment, though Tom's persisting smile convinces him to act. 'Okay. I'll do it!'

'There's a good lad. Don't hold back.' Tom plugs the bass into the amplifier, adjusts the settings, then gives Nathan a thumbs up to begin his performance. 'You can do it, Nath. Play with all your heart...'

With every note played, Nathan senses the loving connection he and his father once shared steadily return. The low-resounding frequencies send a trail of ecstatic shivers down his spine, and he's headbanging alongside Tom within minutes—just like Darren and Tom used to do during their jamming sessions, which Nathan himself would frequently watch. The crippling sensation of sorrow and grief then disperse from both musicians, and—for the first time in over two weeks—Nathan finally forms a genuine smile.

'I did it!' he rejoices. 'Thanks, Uncle Tom.'

'You played it perfectly,' he says, scrubbing a hand over Nathan's hair. 'Your dad would be so proud of you. That was a flawless performance. Top marks.'

A knock at the door suddenly breaks the joyous atmosphere. Michelle enters, her facial expression a mixture of disgust and pleasant surprise.

'Have you lost your mind, Nathan?' she asks. 'I've got a room full of people mourning downstairs, and you're up here blaring out your bass guitar.'

'It's *Dad's* guitar,' he groans, carefully rubbing a hand over the instrument. 'Uncle Tom has taught me a new song. Would you like to hear it, Mum?'

'I heard it perfectly well downstairs,' says Michelle, but then she sees a light in Nathan's eyes that has been missing since Darren's death. With an appreciative nod to Tom, she looks back upon Nathan and the guitar in his hands. 'And what I heard sounded great. I'd love to hear you play it again, Son.'

Nathan performs his encore to a resounding applause from both Tom and Michelle, lifting his spirits even higher. 'Uncle Tom said he'd teach me from now on, since Dad's not here anymore.'

'Did you?' says Michelle, forming a pitiful smile at Tom. 'That's so sweet...'

'I just want to help in any way I can,' he replies, barely able to control his own emotions. 'Nathan's going to be a great bass player, just like Daz.'

'That's so sweet,' she iterates. The door then opens again to reveal Darren's dog, Tyson. To Tom's shock, Michelle scowls at the animal as if it were some annoying pest. 'Back downstairs, Tyson! Naughty dog! Go to your bed!'

Nathan, too, shows some similar disdain towards Tyson, though not as obvious as Michelle. 'Go on, Tyson. Be a good boy and do as your told.'

Tom kneels to stroke the dog, somewhat confused by Michelle and Nathan's brash reactions.

'He is a good boy. Aren't you, Tyson?' The dog jumps straight into Tom's arms, almost knocking him off-balance. 'What have you done to upset your mum and brother?'

'Tyson was Darren's dog,' Michelle snaps. 'He won't listen to me, and all he does is howl at night now. I'm taking him to a dog shelter, first thing tomorrow. Someone else can have him.'

'Really?' Tom can't help but display his astonishment. To him, Tyson should be a pleasant reminder of Darren, not be a burden in his wake. 'Tyson's kind of old, though. The shelter will probably struggle to find some new owners for him.'

'I know that,' says Michelle, almost breaking into tears again. 'But I can't cope with him. Nathan can't either.'

'I'll take Tyson,' says Tom, nestling the dog into his arms. 'I don't mind, especially if it'll help you and Nathan out.'

'You'd honestly do that for us?' she says, confounded. 'That's so kind of you, Tom. At least, I know Tyson will be well-cared for.'

'I'll make sure of it.' Tom hears the familiar ripple of Alice's laughter from downstairs, fuelling him with a renewed desire to leave. 'I've got to go. Call me if you need anything, or if you just want to talk. The same goes to you, Nath.'

'Thanks, Uncle Tom. Thanks for everything.

After a lengthy embrace, Tom moves away from Michelle, gives another thumbs up to Nathan, then makes his way into the kitchen with Tyson by his side. He briefly glances into the living room, noting that Alice's attention has been taken by Amar and John—the coast is clear. Michelle rushes downstairs with Darren's signed photograph of Jenna Coleman, which she eagerly plants into Tom's free hand. Tom thanks Michelle and then wastes no time in leaving, though only after looking at a pair of Darren's prized Converse shoes. It's funny how the smallest things can affect you the most, he says to reflects.

Halfway home, Tom turns a corner to where Karam usually resides. He is relieved to find that a new and more protective-looking tent is now pitched where the burnt-out one previously stood. Karam is sat on the pathway, a few feet outside of his new tent; and — on seeing Tom and Tyson — he waves to him frantically.

'My friend! You look very smart in your suit,' says Karam. 'And who is this marvellous creature?' he asks, clapping his hands to Tyson. 'What a beautiful dog. Is he yours, Tom?'

'He belonged to someone close to me,' he says, goading Tyson forward. The dog immediately pounces on and then licks at Karam, cementing in Tom's mind what needs to be done next. 'His name is Tyson. Do you like him?'

'I love him,' says Karam, tickling the dog behind both ears. 'He reminds me so much of my Charlie. Such a good, little doggy.'

'He's yours,' Tom states. 'He's yours to keep, mate.'

Karam's smile falls, his breath seemingly taken from him. 'What do you mean? What are you saying?'

'Tyson needs someone more special than me to care for him. He can keep you company, and I know that his previous owner would be thrilled for you to take him,' Tom implores. 'He's a bundle of energy, mind.'

'I do not care,' says Karam, shedding several tears of joy. 'I love him already. Thank you. Thank you, my friend.'

Tom reaches into his pocket for a cigarette, which he then hands to Karam. 'You deserve him. I like your new tent, by the way.'

'Ah, yes. Some kind folk from the houses nearby bought me it. There are many bad people in our world, but there are so many good, too, like yourself. You are a good man, Tom — a good man. You have only ever shown kindness to me, while others mostly tend to show disgust. It is… greatly appreciated.'

Tom reflects on Karam's words, yearning to hold onto them, wishing for them to be true. There is always good and bad within life in general, and in-between lies a balance — a perfect harmony — an equilibrium where inner peace is to be discovered. Tom considers that if he can reach this balance, then perhaps he can defeat his anxiety and depression once and for all.

'Are you going home now?' Karam asks, stroking a hand along Tyson's back. 'Will you not stay and chat?'

'I fancy a walk along the nature trail before going home,' Tom says, admiring the tranquil, sunlit stream nearby. 'Today's been hard. I had to say goodbye to my closest friend.'

'Life is filled with difficult challenges,' says Karam in an ominous undertone. 'I was once a respected doctor, caring for all sorts of people — rich and poor. But when the civil war began in Syria, those same people turned against one another — against me. My closest friend from childhood, Nabil, had joined a militant force out of desperation to save his family.' Karam pauses, his rapid breaths flaring the cigarette between his lips. 'It was his group that stormed the hospital I was working in, who held me, my colleagues and our patients, hostage. As he held his pistol to my forehead, I prayed to Allah — not for my salvation, however, but for his. It was Nabil who showed me a safe way out, so that my life could be spared. My family were not shown the same mercy by Nabil's group, though. They were slaughtered like animals while they slept, my wife and children. I still forgave Nabil for his terrible actions, for we are not born evil, and it is never too late to turn back to the light — to salvation.'

'That's awful,' says Tom, struggling to comprehend Karam's horrific ordeal. 'How could you forgive him? I couldn't have.'

'Nabil had been manipulated through fear and anger to take the wrong path. It is down to us to choose which road we take in life, be it for good or bad. I would rather forgive my old friend than to dwell in hatred. I pray each night that my family are at peace, knowing that one day I will join them again in Paradise. That is what keeps me going, my friend—'

'Your light in the darkness,' Tom says to himself. 'I take it you don't believe in fate?'

'I believe in having a destiny, a will of your own to change for better or worse. You must choose the path that lies before you—and wisely. But you are a good man, Tom. I know you will make the correct choices in life. I do not doubt that for a single moment.'

Strolling Through the Meadow

What a day it's been. What a day. Doing that speech at Darren's funeral was worse than I imagined, and to see Alice again only for me to not even say a word to her — that really hurt. But still, the look on Nathan's face when I taught him that new song, and Karam's when I handed Tyson over to him… it wasn't all that bad. There have been some positives to come out of this miserable, horrendous, god-forsaken day. If only there was a miracle drug or superpower to erase certain memories; to micromanage the parts of life you'd prefer to remember or forget. I'm overthinking again, aren't I? I always overthink things.

Drugs aren't the perfect answer, though, supposedly. But they do help numb my emotions to a more tolerable level and distort reality into a less-excruciating mess. There'll come a day when I can come off my Mirtazapine for good, just not yet. I always saw my medication as being something to be ashamed of, but not anymore. It's merely another weapon I can use in my everyday fight against anxiety and depression. At least I'm tackling them with all my might now, which counts for something.

Moving on, I thought taking a stroll along this picturesque nature trail would be relaxing — who wouldn't? I thought it'd be a perfect place to clear my thoughts, but it's only gone and turned into a complete nightmare. I've managed to so far: inadvertently walk through some stinging nettles, unwillingly attract the attention of some cider-guzzling youths, and — to top it all off — get chased by a vicious chihuahua. I cannot wait for this friggin' day to end.

However, on reaching the end of this nature trail, I soon come across a wildflower meadow where me and my childhood friends would often play, which does bring some solace to me. It hasn't changed at all. I can't believe I forgot about it. I made so many happy memories there, ones I'd gladly revisit. I had my first kiss at the ripe-old age of fifteen in that field, along with my first taste of alcohol. I remember thinking, back then, that by the age of thirty I'd be wealthy; that I've have a secure; that I'd be in well-paying job; that I'd be married to my true soulmate with three kids; that I'd be going on frequent holidays abroad; that I'd own the latest sports car; that I'd be able to go out partying every night like a Hollywood celebrity — nothing too far-fetched, of course. It's good to have dreams, to have something you can aim for in life, just so long as they're realistic. I've only come to understand this now, albeit fifteen years too late.

I'm not the only one, however.

Alice thought she'd be a successful accountant. Amar thought he'd be a successful entrepreneur. John thought he'd be a famous author. Mikey thought he'd win big on the lottery, and then spend the rest of his days on a remote island in the middle of nowhere. Now I come to think of it, Daz never revealed what his goals in life were to me, just that he wanted to simply "go with the flow".

That's been my biggest drawback over the years: setting my expectations too high. In greater hindsight, I am content with what I've gained. But I've gone and blown it all because of my mental illnesses and addiction to alcohol. I was rich in every sense, but instead focused solely on the bad aspects — on what dreadful events might lie ahead — instead of the blessings I'd been gifted with. Not anymore. That mindset needs to change. I need to change.

There's little else to do now but go home. Stay positive, Tom-boy, stay positive. You're alive and breathing, not a pile of ashes kept in an urn like some ornament that's to be put out on public display... like Daz will be now. I'm still so torn between grief and anger over his death. I'm so mad at him for what he's done, in leaving Michelle and Nathan to pick up the pieces of their new lives without him. Daz had a secure job, a loving family, and mates who would do anything for him. He had so much to live for. Christ, I'm one to talk. I almost took my own life, and I never considered the lasting consequences. I'm such a hypocrite. Alice was right.

Beside the anger, I'm also devasted that Daz felt there was no other way out, and that he didn't turn to me instead of those medications. I could have talked him round — there's no doubt in that. We never kept secrets from one another. But Daz obviously kept some secrets from me, going off that last video of his. Why didn't he say anything? What made him do it? Why couldn't he take his own advice?

Nevertheless, I want to remember Daz for being the amazing friend he was, not dwell on the horrid nature of his demise. And I will. You can choose what path you're taking in life, like Karam said. I've hit my lowest point and I'm rising from it, slowly but surely. I will win Alice and Rosie back—I know I will. I've changed. I-have-changed. I've just got to prove that to her now, somehow.

Out of the Darkness

Tom returns home after his lengthy walk along the nature trail. His body shivers from the cold, passing breeze; his thoughts still distant and scattered, and they keep on returning to that dreadful image of the curtains closing around Darren's coffin. He will never again see his best friend. He will never again laugh nor share in life's more poignant moments with him. Despite this mournful realisation, Tom is determined to be positive. Otherwise, all the effort he and Darren made recently — to help combat his mental health issues — will be for nothing. He can't let that happen. He won't let that happen.

   Once back inside, Tom takes a moment to admire the signed photograph of Jenna Coleman that Michelle gifted him with. He had spent the last five years hounding Darren for this photograph, almost to the point where they had their first argument. But now, under present circumstances, Tom only feels guilt in possessing it. The photograph is just another, bittersweet reminder of what he has lost.

Tom rests the signed photograph upon Alice's pillow, telling himself that *there's no harm in fantasising*, removes his clothes, and then decides that a hot shower is needed. In a hopeful sense, he believes that by removing the physical dirt it may also remove the painful memories of this day too. But Tom isn't that naïve and knows that today will soon become yet another addition to his frequent, anxiety-inducing flashbacks. Regardless, he keeps repeating Darren's words in his mind, that there is always a light in the darkness. He must stay strong, in memory of his fallen friend, even if it is does seem to be impossible.

On entering the bathroom Tom walks by its wall mirror and immediately removes any eye contact from it. He still can't look at his own reflection, upon the pitiful creature that will inevitably stare back at him. He steps into the shower and allows for the soothing heat from its water to course over his tremor-inflicted body. The cramps in his fingertips and toes gradually ease off, although this relief does not last for long. The hairs on his arms stiffen. Tom knows something isn't right. He tells himself that it's all in his head, that this is just some unexpected reaction to his grief, but that feeling of dread only continues to intensify.

There are some scuffling noises coming from downstairs, proving his paranoid fear to be true. Tom holds onto his breath, praying that he may not be noticed by the apparent intruders, then finds enough courage to step out of the shower as to investigate. He carefully tiptoes down the stairwell with only a towel around his waist, his breaths now rapid and thin. All the while, Tom tries to think of what possible weapon he might use against the would-be burglars, but there's nothing close to hand, that is, other than the small towel he is wearing. This means he'll have to use his bare fists, his hands that are shaking now like a broken washing machine. It's in this moment when he reluctantly accepts that his chances of defeating these intruders will be slim, remote even. However, Tom doesn't consider this to be a bad thing, for what else does he have to live for now? If he is to be injured or killed, it simply doesn't matter anymore.

'Who's there?' he cries out, contemplating whether he'll be given enough opportunity to grab one of his kitchen knives in time. 'Take what you want! I haven't got any money!'

A feminine voice responds to him, 'I know you haven't.'

'No...it can't be?' Tom gasps as if the very air in his lungs has been drawn from them. 'Alice, is that you?' As he creeps into the kitchen, Tom finds two suitcases placed within the centre of it — the same ones Alice took with her on the night she left him. 'Alice?!'

With a heavy sigh, she walks up to him with Rose nestled in her arms. The child is fast asleep, snuggled softly against her mother's bosom. Alice has gone over this reunion in her mind before and during the journey here. But now, on seeing Tom in person, she can barely speak nor think.

'I didn't mean to scare you,' she says, moving closer to him. 'Oh, my God...' Tom's naked body comes as a terrible shock: his protruding ribcage, bony knuckles, malnourished skin, and darkened eyes. It has been so long since Alice last saw the scars from his self-harming days, which cover Tom's entire chest — he was always so careful to keep them out of sight, even from her. 'You've lost so much weight — '

'I needed to,' he replies, nipping at his abdomen. 'Losing a few pounds hasn't done me any harm, and you always said that I needed to lose some weight.'

'Not that much! Have you stopped eating altogether?'

'No…'

Tom's eyes are torn between Alice and Rose. He reasons that this is some strange hallucination, a possible side-effect from alcohol withdrawal perhaps. It's just too good to be true.

'You look amazing,' he mutters, holding out a hand towards Alice. 'Rosie's had a growth spurt, hasn't she?'

'She's constantly asking after you. It's been hard.'

Alice removes the blanket from around Rose to reveal the child's face.

'My beautiful princess. My Rosie,' Tom whimpers, clasping onto his mouth. 'Why have you come here?'

'I've come to talk, something we should've done in the first place,' says Alice, hinting at some resentment.

'What is there talk about?'

'What is there to talk about? Us!' she emphasises. 'Our family. It's been over a month now —'

'Since you left me? Yeah, I know.'

'You didn't exactly try to contact me, did you?'

'No. I didn't know what to say or how you'd react.'

'Look, I haven't come here to start an argument. I want to say… I'm sorry.'

'Don't be. You had every right to leave, and I don't blame you for doing it.'

'I should have explained more why I left — that's what I want to apologise for.'

'Don't be sorry. When you and Rosie needed me most, I wasn't there. I spent most my evenings getting drunk and being alone instead, when I should have been spending them with you. I let my anxiety and depression take over

402

and did little to tackle them, other than become dependent on alcohol. I was a complete dick, Alice.'

'I appreciate you saying that,' she says, placing Rose into Tom's arms now. 'I did understand why you turned to alcohol, because of your anxiety and depression. But that isn't the way to deal with them. You should have talked to me. I was watching you slowly die—I couldn't bear it.'

Tom bundles Rose against his chest and a series of teardrops steadily fall from his face, landing upon his daughter's blanket.

'Nothing can justify the way I treated you,' he says, resting his chin upon Rose's crown. 'I thought getting drunk would help put a stop to my flashbacks, anxiety tremors, and depression. But it didn't. Drinking just made them a hundred times worse, and you bore the brunt of it. It's me who should be sorry, and I am.'

Rose begins to stir, twisting and stretching out her petite body within Tom's arms. She opens her eyes and smiles on seeing her father again, to which he fully breaks down.

'She's missed you,' says Alice, sobbing herself now. 'I have. It's not been easy living with my parents.'

'I can imagine,' Tom sneers. 'Your mother can be a little overbearing at times, can't she?'

'It's not that. It's the fact I've been so used to having you around, I guess. Come next February, we'll have been together for eighteen years.'

'You'd get less for murder,' he humours. 'I've missed you both so much.' Then he whispers to Alice, 'I've changed. I've changed for good this time.'

'But you've said that before, countless times. You've made and broken too many promises to me. But according to your friends — Darren in particular — you have changed. That was the last message I received from Darren, him pleading with me to give you another chance.'

'Daz messaged you?' Tom asks, somewhat aghast. 'When?'

'While you were in Amsterdam. He said that you'd made some real progress, and I know Darren wouldn't lie to me. He had no reason to.'

'I have changed,' Tom beseeches. 'Darren and the other lads helped me to work out my triggers and how to tackle them. But you don't believe what they've said, about me overcoming my issues, do you? And I don't blame you.'

Wiping at her face wearily, Alice says, 'I want to. I want to believe them. But how can I know that you mean it?'

Without saying a word, Tom hands Rose back to Alice and proceeds to crumple his last cigarette carton in front of her, then pour the remaining cans of lager down the kitchen sink, smiling throughout this frantic display.

'Is that proof enough?' he asks, amid some nervous laughter. 'I love you and Rosie more than anything else in this world, and I'll do whatever it takes to make up for all the bad things I've done. Just tell me what to do.'

Initially reeling from the pungent alcohol fumes, Alice blinks her eyes and then lunges at Tom, wrapping him into her embrace thereafter. Rose joins in by nipping at her father's face; herself, like him, unsure as to whether this is real or not.

'I want to give you another chance, Tom. But please, don't ever let me and Rose down again. Don't put us through the same turmoil as before.'

'I won't,' he says, guiding his family into the warmer dining area. 'We all make mistakes, but they shouldn't define us. I've lived for so long dwelling on the past, on what I thought were my failures and misgivings. I've also focused too much on the future, on expectations I'll never be able to fulfil. I know where I've been going wrong.'

'At least you're seeing that now,' Alice says, managing to form half a smile. 'You're not a failure, Tom, and never were to me.'

'I've decided that I won't go for that promotion at work, because all it will do is add more stress, which will just turn me back onto the drink. I realise what matters most. I'm grateful for what I do have, for being blessed with you and Rosie in my life. But I've caused so much hurt. You'd be better off without me. I'm nothing but a burden.'

'No,' she insists, shaking her head to him. 'Darren was right — there is something different about you. I don't know what it is, but it's something I've not seen for a long time.'

'The thing is, I know that I've got a long, hard road ahead of me. I won't cure my anxiety and depression overnight, or even at all. That's the truth, as harsh as it sounds. Why should you need to put up with it? Why should you need to be lumbered with me?'

'Because you're making those important steps,' says Alice. 'You're beginning to face your problems. You're actually tackling your addictions now, which I lost all hope in you doing.'

'Only because of Daz,' Tom laments. 'But he isn't here anymore to put me on the right track. There weren't any warning signs, you know. Not once did I notice that he was struggling. Not once. What kind of friend does that make me?'

'Even Michelle didn't notice.' Alice moves in closer again, preventing Tom from looking upon anything but her and Rose. 'What's happened has happened, and there's nothing that can bring Darren back. You're not blaming yourself for his death, are you? It was nobody's fault.'

Tom shrugs as Alice nestles a hand beneath his chin. In his heart, at least, he is partly to blame. 'I should have recognised the warning signs, like how he was always positive — no one can be that happy all the time, can they? It was just a mask. I do the same myself, put on a brave face when all I want to do is scream and lash out at the world. I should have known!' he wails. 'I should have helped Daz like he helped me, but I didn't! I could have stopped him!'

'It's okay to cry, Tom. There was nothing you could have done. It's not your fault,' says Alice, stroking at his scalp. 'Michelle told me about you and Nathan. He's over the moon with you wanting to teach him how to play bass.'

'I had to take his mind off what was going on. God knows how the poor lad's coping. I'd dread to think.'

'He's got you — his dad's best friend — to be there for him, though, hasn't he?'

'I'm no role model. I'm hardly a decent substitute.'

'You're not a bad person,' Alice implores. 'Despite what you might think, you're not. No one is perfect.'

Tom looks to Rose who, regardless of his sorrowful expression, performs an endearing smile back to him.

'My daddy,' she giggles, reaching out to touch his face again. 'My daddy!'

Tom kisses at her brow and then Alice's. 'Are you really giving me another shot?' he asks pleadingly. 'Are you?'

'I want to. You'll need to prove to me that you have changed, and more than just pouring some booze down the sink. I want you back in our lives, but that will only happen if you keep this promise to me: you've got to promise that you won't fall back into your old habits again.'

Tom replies, eagerly held in resolution, 'I'll book an appointment with Doctor Kain to review my meds and request some more of those counselling sessions I've put off for so long tomorrow, and I won't put it off. I'll start going to that local mental health group, and I won't rely on alcohol anymore to solve my problems—that's for certain. I won't break these promises to you, Alice. I swear…'

'You really mean it?' You're not just saying these things to trick me into giving you another chance?'

'I promise. I'll never hurt you ever again…'

A weight seems to lift from Tom's shoulders, as it does with Alice. The tense atmosphere that had grown between them vanishes, leaving only an air of serenity to endure. Then for the first time in many months, Tom looks up at his reflection in the mirror opposite, no longer ashamed of what he sees—the man smiling back at him, filled with hope and determination. He no longer feels restrained by the destructive emotions that had once ruled over him. In fact, Tom is adamant that he can now fight back against his mental health issues and win, even if it is just one battle at a time. He is fighting a brutal war, an internal struggle that has consumed his life since childhood, but there's a definite turn in the tide now—a renewed and stronger desire to defeat his anxiety and depressive thoughts.

'I will beat this infliction,' he whispers to himself, with tears of joy in his eyes. 'There is always a light in the darkness…'

Thank you for reading my novel.

It would be greatly appreciated if you could leave an honest review on Amazon and/or Goodreads.

With regards,
Andrew John Bell

Acknowledgements

Thank you to my wife, my children, my family, my friends (offline and online), my colleagues, my GP, the stroke consultants at Durham University Hospital who helped me after my mini stroke, the counsellors who helped me identify my anxiety's triggers, the mental health groups who continue to help raise awareness and provide support to those who—like myself—struggle with anxiety and depression, and to you, the reader, for purchasing my novel. Thank you all so much.

Printed in Great Britain
by Amazon